I0817834

ELECTRIC

FIRE

BENJAMIN FRANKLIN'S TIME TRAVEL ADVENTURE

ELECTRIC FIRE

BENJAMIN FRANKLIN'S TIME TRAVEL ADVENTURE

GLENN CHRISTMAS

Electric Fire is a work of fiction. Names, characters, places and incidents are products of the author's imagination or are used fictitiously. Any resemblance to actual events, locales, or persons, living or dead, is coincidental.

Book Cover design by Ebook Launch
Author Photo by Joanna Seaman
Edited by David Aretha

Published in the United States by Glenn Christmas.

First Edition: July 2018

ISBNs: 978-1-7324045-0-2 (ebook), 978-1-7324045-1-9 (hardcover), 978-1-7324045-2-6 (paperback).

Grateful consideration is made to Project Gutenberg for their permission and use of Benjamin Franklin's historical letters documented in the pamphlet "Experiments and Observations on Electricity" and for the use of the images documented within this pamphlet.

Printed in the United States on acid free paper.

In memory of Dad.

For your undying support, thank you to my beautiful wife, Jo.

Dedicated to my mother, Donna, and my three wonderful kids, Robert, Joanna, and Randy.

Tell me and I forget.
Teach me and I remember.
Involve me and I learn.
Benjamin Franklin

ELECTRIC

FIRE

BENJAMIN FRANKLIN'S TIME TRAVEL ADVENTURE

PROLOGUE

SATURDAY, JUNE 10, 1752

THICK, DARK CLOUDS have defeated the morning's sun. Inside the Franklin home, several candles cast a dim yellow glow on the room's distressed timbers. Benjamin sits in an upright wooden chair at the family table and unwraps a white cloth, which attempts to preserve his bread's freshness, and spreads it before him. He tears off a large piece for his breakfast. The crumbling of the hard crust sprinkles brown flakes in a mess across the cloth. His mind drifts far from the simple meal while he stares through the window before him. The tan-colored curtains are swept to the sides and tied back, but they still limit his view.

"*Boom!*" The thunder rumbles and rolls, fading into the distant clouds.

Benjamin stands and scuttles toward the window for the third time this morning. He winces for a brief second from a dull ache in his elbow as he reaches to pull the short, coarse-textured curtains further out of his way to provide a better view. Peering through, he studies the sky's dark clouds. He is concerned the earlier hard rain and the continued light drizzle will make for a difficult, muddy ride to the field, but at the same time he is excited for the opportunity to attempt his newest experiment.

He hears footsteps on the stairs behind him. He turns to find his twenty-one-year-old son, William, making his way down. His five-foot-eight-inch frame is strong and spry, but his lack of sleep has left him a bit lethargic. His shoulder-length brown locks are in desperate need of a comb, but instead he runs the fingers of both hands through them a few times in a weak attempt to make himself presentable. The rumbles of thunder were William's alarm, and clue, that the experiment may occur. Being prepared, he has dressed similar to his father in ankle-high brown boots, long white leggings, and loose-fit brown breeches—that snug just below the knee—and a white button-down long-sleeve shirt. The shirt sleeves are swollen with ample material. He sits at the table.

Benjamin returns and sits across from him. He leans forward, eyebrows raised, and speaks quietly. "William, it is time," he states with a Colonial English accent, which many times tames the *r* in words. "I see you have dressed appropriately. We must load the buggy and make our way to the field. The lightning is near and if we are to fly the kite, we best be on our way. I rented Myrtle and a buggy from Mr. Stevens' stables. She and the buggy are under cover outside. If you will bring Myrtle and the buggy around to the workshop, we can prepare for the experiment."

"Yes, Father," he says with a yawn, trying to shake off his sluggish state. He pulls the white cloth toward him and tears off a chunk of bread for himself. After finishing his meal, the two men grab their brown, weathered great coats—where the length reaches the knees—and their tricorn hats from pegs near the door. As they slip on their coats, Benjamin's wife, Deborah, steps from one of the upstairs bedrooms.

Deborah is a few inches taller than five feet. Her simple, full-figured physique approaches the balcony railing in a light blue Dutch gown, the front partially covered by a long white apron. Two rows of white buttons tightly secure her beige, long-sleeve shirt, while white laced fringe adorns the neckline and sleeves. Her long brown ponytail drapes her back from underneath her white laced bonnet. With one hand she fidgets with the bonnet, while the other grasps the railing. She questions in a concerned tone, "Benjamin, you two are not going out in this rain?"

"Deborah, we have business to attend that cannot wait."

"Benjamin!" Deborah barks with disgust in her voice. "Out in this weather, you and William both will be sicker than a wet cat. Surely, your business can wait for a better day."

"It cannot, Deborah. And a light sprinkle will not harm us," Benjamin declares as he closes the door behind him.

Nine-year-old Sally, wearing a puzzled look, steps onto the balcony with her mother. She swipes at the white apron covering her short, dark beige dress as the bottom of the apron has gotten turned up somehow. The dress covers all but the short-sleeve blue shirt underneath and her white stockings and black shoes. Her shoulder-length, straight, blond hair extends below her white bonnet.

"MEN!" Deborah barks. "They don't know when to stop. Sally, I hope you have more brains than your father and your brother. Going out into the rain, knowing the fever could grab you at any moment, is not worth the risk."

"Mama, they are smart men, but sometimes I think they have the common sense of a mule."

Deborah smirks, amused at her daughter's wittiness. "You are so right, Sally."

Benjamin steps into the clammy shadows of his workshop, where the steady sounds of drips resonate through the room as they dot the puddles of water just outside. "Pew. That putrid smell," he murmurs, cheeks raised high and lips curled, as he waves a hand in front of his nose. He struggles to see in the workshop's scarce light. The thick, dark clouds have smothered the sun's light, which barely penetrates the room's two small, unobstructed windows.

From a tin mounted eye-level near the door, Benjamin pulls a long matchstick, strikes it, and lowers it inside the wall lantern to light the candle. His eyes tighten as he winces at the ache in his elbow. He shifts to another candle on a bench, stepping in a plate-size puddle of water that has formed on the dirt floor. He lights it and steps to another, then another. Now, the wood-lined workshop glows with enough light for him to see the damp, muddy floor, which is creating the distinct musty smell.

Benjamin grasps the cold glass of his Leyden jar, with which so many of his electrical experiments have been conducted. He is careful not to damage its wax phial base or the ring-tipped wire electrode that extends from the outside bottom of the jar and rises parallel to the top of the jar—equal in height with another ring-tipped wire electrode that extends from inside the jar. He lays it on the workbench in the center of the room. He turns to the other side of the room and retrieves the white silk kite he and William made a few days earlier; its knotted tail dangles close to another puddle of water on its short journey between the two benches. The kite's inspiration occurred from the results of a suspended scale experiment he and William conducted a few days before.

William opens the door and steps inside. "Father, I have Myrtle outside, but I have a question. Why do we not fly the kite from here? Why must we go to the field? The lightning will strike here just as it will in the fields. Am I correct?"

"You are correct, William. But I cannot be seen flying a kite in a lightning storm. If my theory is wrong everyone in town would make a fool of me. My electrical work would be for nothing and I would never again be taken seriously. We must go to the fields and perform the experiment alone. If my theory is proven correct, then I will write an article and print it in the weekly circular."

"I understand." William is a bit deflated, because he knows their ride will be very wet. "What shall I load first?"

"We may need some tools. If you could gather a few from the workbench," Benjamin says, pointing. He then lays a metal rod, a wrap of wire, a piece of white ribbon, and a large ball of twine wrapped around a short tree stick on the workbench next to the Leyden jar and the kite.

"These are ready as well."

William carries a few tools out to the wagon.

"Now, where is that iron key?" Benjamin murmurs as he scours over another workbench.

Moments later, William returns. "I placed a couple pieces of timber in the wagon in case the wheels become stuck in the mud."

"Great idea," Benjamin says while still searching for the key. He picks up a dirt-stained, white cloth rag. "Ah, there you are." He picks up the key and sticks it in his pocket. He grabs the kite, the twine, and the metal rod. "If you can carry the ribbon, wire, and the Leyden jar, I believe we will be ready."

With their items loaded, the two men board their wagon.

Benjamin utters a *click, click* sound. "Let's go, Myrtle." He snaps her reins.

Benjamin steers Myrtle into the light rain and through the deserted, muddy streets of Philadelphia. The metal rings securing Myrtle to the wagon clink and clang with every jolt. He paces her on a slow gait to limit the mud spray from her hoofs. It's not long before the wooden buildings of Philadelphia fade into the air's dense moisture.

Benjamin rubs at his elbow again. His eyes twinge. "William, I believe you will find the field a suitable place to conduct the experiment. The field is near two hundred acres, not too far south of town and surrounded by trees. I discovered it two days ago, when scouting for the experiment. At the far side of the field there is an abandoned cabin where we can fly the kite from its porch. My only concern is that a hard rain could make the field muddy and difficult to cross."

"I am excited to see the experiment work."

"It would please me as well."

"Father, I have noticed you rubbing your elbow. Is it hurting?"

"A little, but it is minor. During the last year or more, I have noticed it hurts every now and then. But it was not until recently when I associated it with the occurrence of weather changes. I sometimes wonder if it is attributed to the many shocks I have taken from conducting the electric fire experiments. I will be fine."

Soon, they approach a thick line of brush and trees.

"Father..."

"No worries," Benjamin interrupts, anticipating his concern. "It appears thick and impassable, but I know a passage through and the trees will provide a little protection from the weather, at least until we get to the other side."

They coerce their way through the dense thicket, and soon a sizeable field appears before them. The weather worsens, but they continue. They joggle about the wagon when a sudden gust of wind stings their faces with driving sheets of tiny rain pellets. The thunderstorm's cooling air sends a shiver through both men, forcing them to pull their coats tighter and bury their heads to their chests, letting their tricorns shield most of the onslaught. The raucous pounding of thunder races across the clouds, fading to a low grumble the further away it travels.

William peeks up, wincing and using a hand to secure his hat from the wind while shielding his eyes from another stout burst of tiny pellets. He points beyond the tall, golden-brown prairie grass that's jolting back and forth with stern wind bursts. "Father, that must be the cabin at the far end of the field?"

Raising his head just long enough to see into the distance, he replies, "Yes, it is."

Moments later, as quickly as it started, the wind eases and the rain relaxes to a steady, tolerable light sprinkle. They continue their slow trek across the field. Upon reaching the cabin, the thunderstorm unleashes another sturdy gust of wind along with a vigorous shower.

"Father," William says with his eyebrows cocked and a hesitancy in his voice, "it looks more like a dilapidated old shack than it does a cabin. It is leaning to one side, there is a hole on this side of the cabin," he says pointing, "and this end of the porch appears to be rotting away." He points to the end of the porch nearest them. "Do you believe it to be safe?"

"I have checked it out and it is sturdier than it appears. I believe it to be safe enough for us to conduct our experiment. Let's unload our equipment and place it inside, then we can set up the experiment."

"*Boom, crackle, boom!*" Lightning strikes close by with an explosion of crackling sounds that fill the air. Both men jump.

"William, we had better hurry."

They unload their items, setting them on the cabin's porch. Curious, William pushes the wooden door open and steps inside. He removes his hat with one hand and sweeps the fingers of his other hand through his brown, shoulder-length locks in another weak attempt to straighten them. Three small windows allow William enough light to scrutinize the small empty room and its pitched roof. He steps in further, stepping face first into an unseen cobweb. His fear of spiders causes him to holler, drop his hat, and quickly swipe at his face with both hands to remove the web, hoping a spider was not among the web's fibers.

"Are you okay?" Benjamin questions.

"Yes, just a spider web and you know my fear of spiders."

"Ah."

After a careful check, William believes there are no spiders on him. He bends over to pick up his hat from the dusty wooden floor and notices the dust on the edges of the hat. He swipes the hat against his wet great coat a few times, attempting to knock off the collected dust. He gazes at the brown stone fireplace, charred black from its useful days. He believes this to be the stronghold of the deteriorating structure. Two iron kettle supports remain attached to the stone, though the kettles are long gone. Ashes and a few small pieces of burnt wood in the fireplace are all that remain from the cabin's last occupant. With the creepy feeling of the spider web still lingering on his face and hair, he wipes both again.

Benjamin sets the Leyden jar down on the cabin's porch. He attaches the twine to the kite, then the metal rod to the top in hopes of drawing a lightning strike out of the clouds. Benjamin calls out, "William, if you are finished with the spiders, I could use some help."

William returns to the porch. "I'm sorry, Father. I had to look around." Again, he swipes at his face while his body shudders and grunts. "*Uulgh.*"

"Can you carry the kite out into the field?" he asks, handing the kite to William.

"Yes, Father." William grabs the kite, steps off the porch, and trudges into the tall wet grass.

As Benjamin stands on the porch, both of his hands possess a loose grasp of the stick spun with twine. It spins freely in his hands, and with each step William carries the kite further into the rain.

"That's good," Benjamin yells. "Lift it into the air."

William pulls the twine tight and releases the kite. It climbs higher and higher. William races back to the porch to join his father, where Benjamin regulates the kite's altitude just below the dark, heavy clouds. They watch the kite and its long-knotted tail wave back and forth across the sky as the stern breeze pushes the kite along its restricted course.

"Now, to attach the key. William, can you hold the twine?"

"Yes, sir." William pulls down on the twine to surrender a little slack for his father to tie a knot.

Benjamin attaches the key. "Now the wire from the Leyden jar to the key," he says as he joins the two together. "And last, the ribbon to the key." Now that he has finished his three-way communion, he takes control of the experiment.

"Now we wait."

A few hours pass, and though lightning has been present in the area, it has not struck the kite. Benjamin has a wary feeling that his theory may be wrong. Then, he notices a strange phenomenon. "William, look."

William approaches. "What is it, Father?"

"The strands of the twine. Look at the strands of the twine. They are standing straight up, each separated from another. Could this be the lightning? If so, is the electricity causing the strands to stand apart from each other?"

"Did you see the lightning strike the kite?"

"No, but this is unusual." Benjamin passes his hand near the key. *POW!* A resilient spark lunges to his knuckle. Benjamin jumps in the air as he lets out a shriek and shakes his hand violently as if he were shaking out the pain. "William, I received a spark from the key. Lightning is electricity! It is proven—lightning is electricity!"

"You did it, Father! You did it!"

Both men embrace each other.

ONE

TUESDAY, MAY 7, 2019

BEEP! BEEP! BEEP! the Spiderman alarm clock wakes Zach to another school day. He lies there for a moment wanting to go back to sleep, but instead he pulls the Spiderman covers back and rolls out of bed in a pair of Spiderman boxers. The superhero's posters cling to his bedroom's walls, displaying his affection for the web-spinning acrobat. He strolls to the bathroom and hears his fraternal twin, Zane, moving around in his room.

He stares into the bathroom mirror and pinches at a growing pimple on his chin. He tugs and pushes on his short blond hair to stand it in place, which is wherever it ends up, and he's satisfied with its messy appearance. Zach returns to his bedroom and slides on a pair of blue jeans, a red Polo shirt, and his favorite tennis shoes—orange, red, and yellow Nikes—and makes his way downstairs for breakfast.

Soon after, Zane arrives downstairs wearing blue jeans, a blue Polo shirt, and white and blue Nikes. His short blond hair stands with the same messy style that his brother and the younger crowds don these days.

Both boys are good-looking with green eyes. Though the brothers are not identical, their five-foot-eight-inch, thin, fit frames are similar to their father's, though they hope for one last growing spurt to reach his six-foot-three physique. Both excel well in their education and share a very close bond, like most twins.

Jeremy strolls across the dark wood floors of the modern kitchen, lined in white cabinets. He wears his typical casual-business attire, which today is a light blue long-sleeve shirt, Dockers, and his favorite pair of light brown slip-on loafers, the kind with two tassels. "Good morning. The eggs smell great," he says with an upbeat tone. His trip toward the coffeepot steers him around the large white granite island that's embellished with gold swirls. First, he stops behind his beautiful wife, who cooks breakfast at the island's stainless-steel cooktop. He swipes her straight, shoulder-length, blond hair behind her ear and leans in for a quick kiss.

Sarah turns and kisses him back. "Good morning," she says with a smile and continues to scramble the sizzling eggs in her sky blue capri pants, white, three-quarter length shirt, and black flats. She's not a frufru woman, but she is proud of her diamond earring studs, her heart-shaped diamond pendant necklace, and her Rolex. Her white apron, with a scene of Mama and Papa brown bears and their two cubs playing in the front yard of a cute cottage, protects her clothes from cooking splatter. A play on words is written at the bottom: *"A Beary Nice Family."*

Sarah may be short at five-foot-three inches, but she is a positive, smart-thinking, well-organized, confident woman capable of handling just about any situation. She is a caring mother who only wants the best for her sons and her husband and will do whatever it takes to make sure they have what they need to be successful. She loves her family.

Their two sons sit in the breakfast nook at the round, glass breakfast table. The six reclining chairs are comfortable with their gray and white checkered cushions. Their gray-painted frames are made of flat steel bars, which support the back and arms, and sit atop five black casters. They each respond with a "Good morning" of their own.

Jeremy pours himself a cup and joins the boys at the table. "I love the smell of fresh-brewed coffee in the morning." He takes a sip. "Boys, it looks like another beautiful day." He scratches his head, then pats at the area to make sure his short, brown, parted hair is back in its place.

"It does," Zane replies.

"What's new on the agenda with your CTE classes? Any new electrical projects?" Dad asks in his usual upbeat tone.

The boys are nearing the end of their first year of electrical studies in the Career Technology Education program at Philadelphia's Swenson Arts and Technology High School in the suburbs near the small Northeast Philadelphia Airport.

Zach, the oldest of the sixteen-year-old twins, but only by a few minutes, replies, "Tap Jackson, our electrical instructor, said now that we have finished with our transistor circuits project, our next topic would be capacitors, but first we would discuss the beginning of electricity and Benjamin Franklin's earliest electrical experiments, and what led him to the famous kite experiment."

"That sounds interesting," Dad replies.

The toaster pops up. Sarah turns off the cooktop burner, scoops the eggs onto four separate plates, and lays a piece of toast on each plate. She removes her apron and hangs it on the back of the laundry room door. She picks up two of the plates and sets them in front of the two boys. She returns, grabbing the two remaining plates, and says, "Here's your eggs, honey," and sets them on a placemat for her husband and herself.

"Thanks, dear," he says.

"It's pretty cool," says Zach. "We started with the basics of how electricity works, and now we've progressed toward electrical components and how they work on circuit boards. And you know how jacked I am with electricity and what makes it work. Learning about its beginnings should be very interesting."

"It sounds like fun, especially if you try to see it from Benjamin Franklin's point of view," Dad says. "Remember at that time, nobody understood electricity. Try to imagine yourself in his shoes, trying to figure out how electricity works, especially with it being invisible. What makes it do what it does and how, or even why?"

"His detailed experiments and his meticulous processes are what provided him a glimpse into the most basic forms of electricity. His experiments and discoveries were not just new and interesting; they were groundbreaking. His experiments were by trial and error and had to be performed many times to see how the electricity would respond. He would conduct the same experiment over and over, each time changing a variable or an object and each time logging the results. He would perform that same experiment many more times, the same way each time, and compare the results to see if there were any changes. Then, he would move on to a new experiment and go through the same process. After a while he began to see some patterns."

"You know," Zach says, "when you put it like that I can imagine how whack it must have been. Today, people understand electricity. If you have a question, you can usually find the answer on the internet. But for him, there was no internet, not a person to ask or even a technical book that would explain it. It was new, and he had to figure it out on his own. That had to be interesting, fun, and maddening all at the same time. I know from my own experiments it drives me nuts when I can't figure something out or make it work, but then, when I do, I'm lit."

"Benjamin Franklin's an interesting man, to say the least." Dad persists with more information. "Not only was he a founding father of our country and an influential person in its fundamental development, but he also was an inventor, to which he has many accomplishments to his credit. Of course, his most famous electrical experiment is with the kite, but there's a lot more to learn about him than electricity."

"His inventions and discoveries were always about the improvement of people's everyday lives. Many of those improvements still exist today and most people don't even realize it. And many of his inventions he never patented, which cost him a lot of money. But, money was not his motivator. Life was hard in those days and he wanted everyone to have an easier life."

"For example, did you know that he invented bifocal glasses? And catheters, which are used by millions of people all around the world, were also invented by Benjamin Franklin. He invented the Franklin stove. To us it does not sound like much, but for people in those days the stove allowed more heat to be transferred to the room than other stoves and it allowed the smoke to escape without filling the room. This invention made a huge improvement, because it allowed people to have a stove inside their home to both cook on and keep the house warm during those cold winter days and nights."

"It must have sucked to live in those days," Zane ponders out loud.

"Zane!" Mom barks. "No need for such language."

"Sorry, Mom."

Dad continues. "He invented swim fins, although the ones he invented were for the hands. But that invention allowed him induction into the International Swimming Hall of Fame."

"He improved people's lives in other ways too. He created fire insurance to help protect people when they lost a business or home due to a fire."

Boredom creeps onto the boys' faces, though to them their father's long explanations are not anything new. Even his own mother calls him Jabber-Jaws Jeremy.

"Also, at that time, books were scarce and expensive and were only accessible to the few who could afford them. He met with the members of his JUNTO organization, which consisted of twelve men who shared his same ambitions to learn. They met once a week to discuss the books they had read—morals, politics, and science—and decided that in the best interest of education, they would pool books from their personal collections and allow others to check them out for a simple fee. Therefore, the first library had been created."

"Boring!" Zach teases. "What'd you do, read his autobiography?"

"As a matter of fact, I did. And I read a couple of other books about him as well. His autobiography and the other books are in the study. It wouldn't hurt either one of you to read them. He's a fascinating man. You could learn a great deal about him, his accomplishments, and how they affect your lives today—and in the process, learn a little history about our country. You know, he also invented..."

"Thanks for the history lesson, Dad," Zane interrupts and jumps from the table, "but we'll let the school teach us the real lessons."

"Ha, ha," Dad replies with his own sarcasm as he glances at his watch.

"Zach, you're driving, right?" Zane asks.

"Yes, sir, I have the keys."

"Great, let's go."

They rush out the door and hop into Zach's new silver Ford F-150 Crew Cab pickup and leave for school.

TWO

TUESDAY, MAY 7, 2019

CLASS BELLS RING.

Upon entering the classroom, Mr. Jackson raises his positive voice over the chatter of his aspiring electrical students. "Good morning."

A few "good mornings" are returned as the room begins to quiet down.

Mr. Jackson, a thin five-foot-three black man in his early forties, is a distinguished dresser. Today he wears black slacks, a salmon-colored long-sleeve shirt, and a red and black diamond-patterned pullover sleeveless sweater. The students make fun of him behind his back because of his nerdish style. But at the same time, he is one of the more popular teachers, because his teaching style lets them get involved, which makes the learning fun. He's known throughout school as "Tap Jackson" because of his pointed dress shoes. With each step, they clack on the floor's surface as if he is wearing tap shoes. His dark mustache and thick curly hair give him the resemblance of Mr. Kotter from the popular '70s sitcom *Welcome Back Kotter.*

He slowly paces in front of his desk, his fingers interlocked together at his chest while his thumbs twiddle around each other. "Now that we have finished our transistor circuits project, we will move on to capacitors. But first, our introduction to capacitors begins with an important history lesson with the earliest form of a capacitor—the Leyden jar."

"A simple glass jar became a magnificent tool for Mr. Benjamin Franklin. This tool allowed him the ability to store the electric fire, as they called it back then, allowing him to experiment with the electricity and learn how it would react in different scenarios with an assortment of materials, including people and animals. He detailed his experiments for several years, but most importantly over the course of a three-year span he wrote five separate historic letters, which are now known as, 'Experiments and Observations on Electricity.'"

He grabs a pamphlet from his desk, which details the experiments, and holds it up for the class to see.

"Today, we will perform one of his earliest experiments, as well as another that led him to fly a kite in a lightning storm and then we will discuss the famous kite experiment and how its results led to one of his greatest inventions.

"Today, electricity is the hidden engine of our lives, and even though you are here learning about it, like me, in our daily routines, we usually don't give it a second thought. It's so common to us that we take it for granted, like the air we breathe. We expect it will be there when we need it. We flip a switch and the lights come on. We push a button and our device works. We usually don't think about the electricity that makes our gadgets work. And then, when the electricity is lost, our life becomes disrupted, causing us to become frustrated, annoyed, and most of the time, delayed.

"For Benjamin Franklin, or anyone in that era, they did not have electricity. Light occurred either by sunlight or the glow of a fire. There were no televisions, radios, cell phones, or any type of luxuries that you are so accustomed to today."

"Sounds like a difficult way of life, if you ask me," Zane blurts out.

"Yes, it does," he says, then directs a question to a girl on the front row who is known to always be on her phone. "Allie, how would you survive without SnapChat, Instagram, Twitter, or Facebook?"

"No idea, but life would be boring without 'em," she replies with typical teenage attitude.

"Exactly!" he replies, while steering his eyes back to the rest of the class. "Our world is much different now. The phone has become a tool for us on many different levels. But back in the 1750s, tools were much simpler. There were no power tools like we have today. Projects were completed because of hard work, ingenuity, and muscle. In those days, a job took many more hours to complete than what it takes to accomplish today. So, when we talk about Benjamin Franklin's experiments, imagine yourself as if you were in the 1750s, without any of our modern-day luxuries."

"But before the experiments, how did Benjamin Franklin become interested in electricity?" He paces the floor, placing his left hand is his pants pocket. "Contrary to many, he did not discover electricity." Raising his right hand, he waves his index finger back and forth, gesturing *no*. "Benjamin grew up in Boston, but at the age of seventeen he ran away to Philadelphia and got a job as a printer. Though, in 1743, at the age of thirty-seven, Benjamin decided to travel back home to visit family and friends. It was in Boston where he witnessed his first electric fire show by a gentleman named Archibald Spence."

"Archibald?" mocks one of the students. "You wouldn't survive one day here with a name like Archibald."

Snickers fill the class.

Mr. Jackson ignores him. "After watching the show, he realized that even though Mr. Spence could produce the electricity with his contraption, he did not understand the mechanics of how the electricity worked, or why. His electricity show was nothing more than novelty entertainment and a means to make money. But the electricity show did one thing for Mr. Franklin: it sparked his interest in electricity. And yes, the pun was intended."

"Since that day, he began to perform his own electricity experiments, but little progress was made. About four years later, in 1747, Benjamin received a glass tube from a friend he met in London, named Peter Collinson. The tube is known as the Leyden jar. With it were some instructions for its use and a note indicating that it should be helpful in his electrical experimentation."

Mr. Jackson turns to the chalkboard and writes the dates "1747–1752." He turns back to the class.

"Benjamin Franklin performed many electrical experiments from 1747 through 1752. He received help from his family, friends, and neighbors when conducting the experiments and soon began to see some patterns. Over this period, he summarized his results in five separate letters." He raises his hand with his thumb and fingers spread apart. "Which he sent to his friend in London. He believed that since Mr. Collinson provided him the Leyden jar, he should provide the results of his experiments, so they could be discussed with others in London."

"Benjamin's first letter, dated July 28, 1747, contained eleven different experiments. He detailed each of the experiments, explained their materials and their processes, and shared their results. His most noted observations in these first experiments were 'positive and negative' or 'plus and minus' to describe the states of electricity. Terms he coined then and are still used today. The experiment we are about to perform is one of those experiments."

Mr. Jackson gestures toward a long table beside his desk. On it is a tall wooden A-frame support, which towers five feet above the unusual glass jar, and suspends a large balance scale to the left of the jar. "The Leyden jar is capable of storing static electricity. Its two electrodes allowed Mr. Franklin to conduct his experiments. First, I will explain the parts of the jar, and then we will perform our experiment.

"First, we see two ringed electrodes extending above the jar and resting about four inches apart." He points to each as he explains. "One is attached to the outside bottom of the jar, where it is wrapped in aluminum foil. And the other extends through the top of the jar, through a cork stopper, and down into the water that fills the jar about halfway. To insulate the jar, it rests on top of a wax block. And last, an A-frame stand rises above it. Suspended above the Leyden jar is a single piece of silk thread with a small piece of weighted cork. Attached to the cork are six smaller threads, giving it the resemblance of a spider.

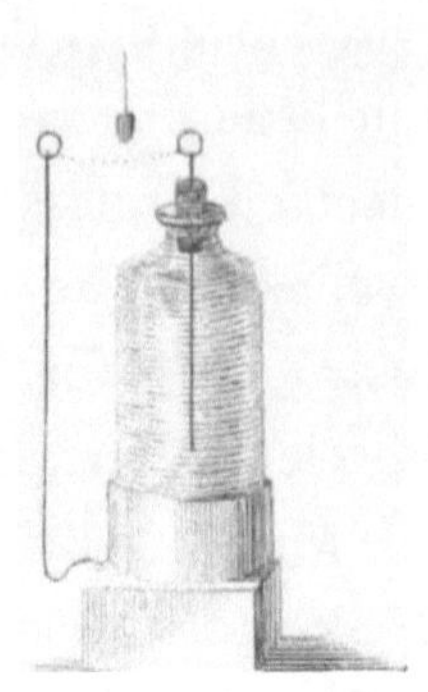

"We will charge the jar with static electricity by rubbing its outside with this silk cloth." He holds up the silk cloth. "Much like if you were to rub your feet on the carpet and shock your best friend. Of course, afterwards, they may no longer be your best friend." He pauses for a laugh, but nothing. "Tough crowd today," he murmurs. "Then, we will lower our imitation spider between these two rings, and the electrical charge in the jar will cause the spider to jump back and forth between the two rings.

"Now, Benjamin believed that all things were charged equal. Through his experiments, he concluded that there must be plus electricities and minus electricities, known today as electrons, which are either positive or negative charges. In previous lessons you have already learned about these positive and negative electrons. But, for the sake of our lesson, we must understand how Mr. Franklin understood the electricity.

"Benjamin explained his thoughts this way: 'In a normal state, the Leyden jar is electrically balanced and cannot provide a spark when the inside of the jar contains twenty positive charges and the outside of the jar contains twenty negative charges.'"

With one hand clutching the wax base, Mr. Jackson vigorously rubs the silk cloth against the glass jar. After multiple rubs, he stops and continues with his explanation. "Benjamin also wrote: 'If we rub the Leyden jar twenty times, hypothetically, with each rub of the jar the number of positive charges inside will increase by one and the number of negative charges outside will decrease by one. This will create an imbalance of positive and negative charges. The ring connected to the inside of the jar will now have forty positive charges and the ring connected to the outside of the jar will have zero negative charges.'

"Let's conduct the experiment. I will lower the imitation spider between the two rings." He unwraps the thread from a small nail in the wood frame and lets the spider slip down between the two electrodes. The spider sinks to the level of the two rings and suddenly springs to life, jumping back and forth between the two rings. "Benjamin noted: 'With each swing, the spider takes one charge from the inside of the jar and passes it to the outside of the jar until the jar again becomes balanced with twenty positive charges inside and twenty negative charges outside.' Now, it may swing back and forth many more times than the twenty, but it will stop once the jar becomes balanced again."

"That's cool," says one of the students.

"How much voltage does each spark create?" asks another.

"That all depends on how much of a charge is given to the jar. It could range between a couple of hundred volts to near four thousand volts. And with the right circumstances, there is potential to reach upwards of thirty-five thousand volts. This is not a toy!" he says, shaking his head. "Although, if you were to touch it, not only would you receive a spark, but because of the electricity in your body, you would dissipate the jar's electricity, restoring its balance and the spider would stop swinging. But I would not recommend touching it, because the spark could be significant.

"And, in case any of you get the idea to do this at home, with a larger jar charged to its maximum potential, it is possible to generate enough current to kill a person." Mr. Jackson reaches for and holds up a C-shaped metal wire tool with a wooden handle protruding from its center section, then continues with a serious tone. "To prevent being shocked we always use a discharge tool to ensure our Leyden jar has been completely discharged. As we have always stressed, and as our banner says above the chalkboard..." He turns around and points toward it. "...ELECTRICITY

MUST BE RESPECTED."

"Before I move on to our next experiment, I recommend that each of you read his letters." Again, he holds up the pamphlet. "There will be questions on your final exam concerning details from each of the letters. Here is a tip: What is Benjamin's common discovery with the experiments of each letter? For example: in the second letter, he discovers that sharp, pointed objects drew off the electric fire much quicker than blunt objects. You can find the letters on the internet at Project Gutenberg." He turns to the chalkboard and writes "Project Gutenberg—Experiments and Observations on Electricity." "They are free and easy to access."

"And now, onto our next experiment that Benjamin documented in his fifth letter, dated July 29, 1750, and titled 'Additional Papers.'" Again, he paces before the class. "Benjamin Franklin learned that sharp, pointed objects drew the electric fire at greater distances than blunt objects. He reaffirmed his thoughts through this next very important and interesting experiment, which I will demonstrate.

"As you can see, I have a large balance scale with two suspended brass plates balancing on a cross arm." He steps to the side of the table, pointing toward the two plates. "Each of the plates are a foot in diameter. I have replaced their supporting chains with light string to ensure there is no connection between the two plates, just as Benjamin had done. I have suspended the entire scale from the A-frame support stand to ensure there is no connection to ground. Benjamin suspended his from the ceiling.

"When Benjamin performed this experiment, he placed his scale about a foot above the ground, but that would make it difficult for everyone here to see. So instead, I mounted two metal brackets onto a long, thin board and connected them to the ground wire of an extension cord and removed the two electrical prongs, so no voltage could be induced. This allows me to plug it into any wall receptacle and connect the brackets directly to the building's grounding system. Electrically, it is the exact same concept as Benjamin's experiment; it's just up on a desk.

"I have placed an iron punch in the first support bracket with its blunt end rising to about a foot below the brass plates." As he describes the contraption, he connects an insulated wire to one of the electrodes of the Leyden jar. He rubs the Leyden jar with his silk cloth, giving it a sufficient charge. "I will spin the scale so that the cord will tighten." He grabs the scale's cross bar and provides a few twists. "The untwisting of the cord will allow the scale to rotate at a slow pace, just as Benjamin had observed." He carefully steadies the scale and its brass plates, so they are motionless and balanced. Then, he releases.

The scale slowly spins. "Now, to apply a charge to the plate. Everyone be quiet and watch closely." He touches the wire to one of the plates. As the charged plate approaches the punch, it dips down. *Zap!* A spark jumps from the plate to the punch and the scale rises and appears to be pushed away.

"Then, he tried it again. But this time, he secured a needle to the end of the iron punch with its sharpened point protruding above the punch." Mr. Jackson tapes a needle to the end of his punch. He charges the jar again and provides a couple of twists to the scale. After steadying the scale, he again releases and applies the charge to the brass plate. "Now watch what happens."

The scale begins to spin. It approaches the punch, but instead of a dip and releasing its spark, it instead rises higher and silently repels away.

"It didn't work. What happened to the spark?" asks one of the students.

"Ah," he says while raising the index finger of his right hand, "but it did work. From previous experiments, Benjamin had already understood that sharp, pointed objects would silently draw away the charge without releasing a spark, as we just saw, and then it rose higher, indicating it was being repelled away.

"But he wanted to try it a third time. Except this time, Benjamin placed the needle on the ground next to the punch with the punch rising several inches above the needle." Mr. Jackson removes the needle from the punch and secures it to the separate support bracket, leaving the needle far below the blunt end of the iron punch. Again, he charges the jar, spins the scale, steadies it, and releases. He charges the brass plate one more time. They all watch closely. The plate approaches the punch and slowly rises again without releasing a spark.

"That's lit," Zach states.

Mr. Jackson explains, "This proved that not only will sharp, pointed objects draw the electric fire at a greater distance than blunt objects, but that they will do so silently and without a spark.

"Remember from earlier lessons, while opposite charges attract, equal or like charges repel. And that's what Benjamin saw. In the first attempt, with the scale charged it dipped to the punch because it was close enough to be attracted, but when the spark occurred the two became of the same charge and suddenly repelled each other. In both experiments with the needle, the scale never dipped, indicating the needle drew off the fire before it came close enough to be attracted, but as it approached the needle it was repelled away, rising higher, indicating that it was of the same charge, even though a spark never occurred."

"That's just lit," Zane replies again.

"Benjamin thought so too. Maybe not lit, but interesting. But the curious question in those days was, 'Is lightning electricity?' Although electricity had been known about for hundreds of years, little was known about how it worked, much less how its use could be beneficial.

"With his scale experiment and another experiment with a ten-foot tube, which produced the same results, he questioned: 'If the electric fire were the same as that of lightning, then on a larger scale and at a greater proportional distance, an electrified cloud of ten thousand acres may discharge its electric fire to the ground, a tree, or a church spire once the clouds become close enough. If this is so, then would not a sharp, pointed rod fixed to the top of a building with a wire connected to the ground allow the electricity to silently discharge out of the cloud before the lightning would explode to the building?'

"He believed it would, but first he had to prove that lightning was electricity, and that would prove to be a difficult task. Then, about two years later, he had another idea.

"If he could fly a kite close enough to the clouds and with the twine wet from the rain, he may be able to extract the electricity from the clouds and capture it in a Leyden jar. And he thought, if he could attract a spark out of the Leyden jar, his theory that 'lightning is electricity' would be proven. But, he also knew that if he were seen flying a kite in a lightning storm he would receive a lot of ridicule if his experiment failed. So, he decided to keep his experiment secret and worked only with his twenty-one-year-old son, William.

"On June 10, 1752, on a stormy day that looked promising for his experiment, he and William traveled into the fields where they came across an old shack that appeared suitable for the experiment. Benjamin and his son set the kite out into the rain. After several hours and no lightning strikes to the kite, they began to believe his theory was wrong. Disappointed, he thought the experiment was a failure. He and William were about ready to give up when he noticed the threads of the twine mysteriously standing, each separated from the next. When Benjamin passed his knuckle near the key he received a strong spark, and with a scream his theory was proven—lightning is electricity.

"This experiment created one of the most important inventions in history. The 'Lightning Rod.' And it has saved countless lives and protected millions of structures from the catastrophic damage that lightning can cause."

Bells ring.

"Okay, that wraps it up for today," Mr. Jackson says. "I will see you tomorrow and everyone have a great day. Don't forget to read his letters online. You have two and a half weeks before finals."

THREE

TUESDAY, MAY 7, 2019

INSPIRED FROM THE day's earlier experiments, Zach searches the study for the books that his father talked about during breakfast. Finding one, he pulls it down. "*Franklin's Autobiography*," he reads to himself. He again scours the bookshelf and pulls down another. "Here's another one: *Experiments and Observations on Electricity*," he blurts out. "Cool, this is the book of Benjamin's letters that Tap Jackson talked about."

Zach carries both books upstairs to his room. He sets the autobiography next to his Spiderman clock. Excited, he props up a red and blue pillow etched in the white lines of a spider's web against the light brown headboard of his bed, sits back, and opens the book of letters. A couple of hours pass and not even halfway through the letters, he is astonished and remarks under his breath, "These experiments are so detailed. It's incredible how meticulous he was with his processes."

The small black Echo Dot speaker on Zach's end table near the bed is activated. "Zach, dinner's ready."

"Okay, I'll be down in a minute."

Zach reluctantly closes the book and trots downstairs to join his family for dinner in the breakfast nook. The day's earlier experiments have energized Zach's enthusiasm. "Dad, you know it's amazing that back in Benjamin Franklin's days, when they didn't understand anything at all about electricity, that he could figure out so much and all he had to work with was a glass jar?"

"Ah, yes. You boys learned about Benjamin Franklin's electrical experiments today. So, what happened?"

"Benjamin Franklin must have been a very inquisitive and detailed man to accomplish what he did," Zach says. "Tap Jackson performed this one experiment where he suspended a fake spider between two charged rings of a Leyden jar and the electricity made the spider jump back and forth between the two rings. That was cool, but then he performed another experiment that was lit. It was Benjamin Franklin's scale experiment that simulates how electricity in the clouds would discharge to the ground and ultimately led to the invention of the lightning rod."

"Interesting," Dad exclaims. "How did it work?"

Zach explains the details over dinner.

"That's interesting. Zane, you haven't said much. Did you not like the lesson?" Dad asks.

"Oh no, I thought it was pretty cool, but you know Zach, that's right up is alley."

"Yes, it is," Zach says. "And Dad, I took your advice. I found the books on Benjamin Franklin you talked about this morning and started to read them. After dinner, I'm going back upstairs to continue."

"That's fantastic!" Mom says. "It sounds like your dad's not so boring after all."

FOUR

WEDNESDAY, JUNE 5, 2019

ZACH AND ZANE are kicked back in the recliners of the media room couch watching the anime program *Naruto*. Zach's white T-shirt sports the flying "VH" of the '80s rock band Van Halen while Zane's black T-shirt features an image of Bruno Mars. Both are wearing khaki shorts and no shoes.

The small black Echo Dot speaker on the counter near the popcorn machine activates. Dad asks, "Zach, Zane, can you boys come downstairs? I need to talk to you."

Zane responds, "We'll be right down."

After the Dot disconnects, they look at each other.

"Uh-oh. What'd you do?" Zane's asks, with an eyebrow raised.

"Nothing that I know of. It must have been you."

"I don't think so, but I guess we'll find out in a minute."

Downstairs in the family room, the boys find their mother and father relaxed in their wide, brown leather chairs. Two lamps and a small planter of orchids are symmetrically spaced on top of the decorative wrought iron glass console table behind the chairs. A small square glass end table, matching the console table and the coffee table, stands between the leather chairs. Mom, in a pair of bright green capris and a bright yellow, short-sleeve blouse and bare feet, is curled up in her comfy chair reading a murder mystery novel.

Dad, still in his work attire, scooches to the edge of his chair and lays the newspaper on the wrought iron glass coffee table. He lounges in his Dockers and bare feet—his brown socks and loafers with the tassels have been cast to the side—and he has rolled up his long-sleeve white dress shirt to the middle of his forearms. His toes scrunch at the red, yellow, and violet colors of the Persian rug that contrasts with the dark stain of the hardwood floors.

The boys sit down on the brown leather couch across from their parents. The white stone fireplace, to the boys' right, is the focal point of the room's contemporary design. The TV is mounted over the dark wood mantel above the gas fireplace insert. Life-sized polished brass dachshunds stare at each other on opposite sides of the fireplace hearth.

"Did we do something wrong?" Zach asks.

"No, but now that school's out for the summer you boys can help out your mother and I around the house."

"Sure, no problem," Zach says.

"Yeah, sure," Zane agrees.

"Do either of you remember the invitation I received a few weeks ago, to attend the Wormhole lecture?"

Both boys snicker.

Zach replies while covering his mouth with his fist, "Oh, how could we forget."

"Yeah, yeah." His eyebrows raise with a slight smirk. "I need you two to do me a favor this Saturday. It's necessary for my research. I need you to bring EMITT down to the park near the lecture. Two colleagues of mine, Sam and Mark, have offered their assistance with an issue in EMITT's software programming."

"Why don't you bring them here to the house?" Zane inquires with one eye partially closed.

"A couple of weeks after I received the lecture invitation I discovered a possible math problem with EMITT and I need their help. But they had already made flight arrangements back to Boston a few hours after the lecture, so their time here will be limited. I thought, if EMITT were near the lecture, then afterwards we could review the problem before they leave for the airport. I would bring her myself, but I'll be in the lecture throughout the morning and I do not want her left unattended. I need you two to stay with her until we arrive. It is imperative that you do not to leave her alone."

"What is so important about this trailer you call EMITT?" Zach asks.

"Yeah, and what does EMITT mean?" Zane asks.

"Well," their father explains, "EMITT means to send forth or discharge, which applies to my research. As you know, EMITT is my laboratory where I have been heavily involved in a project, which involves some complex calculations and a lot of research. But lately, I have questioned my calculations and I need a little help.

"I believe Sam and Mark's mathematical knowledge could be helpful, and they may be able to provide some insight to solving the problem. I have discussed it with both and they have agreed to help."

"Why don't you email the problem to them?" Zach asks, trying to provide a solution.

"It's not that simple. It is a custom program I developed, and they will not have a platform to open the program and view the equations. They have to review the problem within EMITT's computers."

"What's the project about?" Zach asks.

"For now, it's a little premature to discuss. I would rather keep it to myself until I have the issues worked out. Maybe after their visit, I can discuss it a little more, but we must wait and see."

"Okay, so where do we bring EMITT?" Zane asks.

"Independence Park is a block from the hotel. You could bring her there and text me your location."

"I don't have any plans," Zane determines. "What about you, Zach?"

"No, I'm good. What time do we need to be there?"

"The lecture should be over around noon, so sometime before then would be great. But don't be late. If you need to leave a couple hours earlier, then please do so. Time will not be our friend Saturday."

"No problem, Dad," Zach says with confidence. "We will have EMITT there for you in plenty of time. You can count on us."

"Thanks, boys, I do appreciate it," Dad replies, proud that his boys are growing up.

FIVE

THURSDAY, JUNE 6, 2019

IN THE MEDIA room Zach, in a plain dark blue T-shirt and blue jean shorts, flips through a tablet, surfing the internet. Zane, in blue jean shorts and a black T-shirt outlining the angry anime face of the Japanese character "Naruto," plays on his phone. With the volume low, Naruto again plays on the big screen, but neither of the two boys pay it much attention.

"Zane, do you remember those Benjamin Franklin experiments Tap Jackson showed us in class?"

"Yeah, what about 'em?"

"You know, after we read the book of Benjamin's letters and experiments, I thought they were interesting, but they contained nothing about the kite experiment. So, I did some reading and I have an idea. Wouldn't it be cool if we could duplicate his kite experiment?"

"Have you lost your mind?" Zane exclaims, with his eyes wide open. "We could be killed."

"Benjamin Franklin did it and it didn't kill him," Zach points out.

"Yeah, but...uh...but...um..." Zane tries to find a good reason why they should not, but he is intrigued with the idea. "If we could ensure we were isolated from the lightning, like ol' Ben did, then maybe we could. It would be cool, but, Zach, we need to be careful. Flying a kite in a lightning storm is dangerous—borderline stupid."

Zach ignores his comments and continues to press the idea. "You know, Zane, I saw on the internet that thunderstorms are possible for Saturday morning. We could arrive early enough to set up EMITT for Dad and his friends, then, like Benjamin, we could fly the kite from EMITT's porch."

"If we do that, we need to do some research before Saturday so we can be prepared. That gives us today and tomorrow. Do we even have what we need to make a kite?"

"Probably not, but let's give it a shot," Zach says. "I'll go to the garage to see if I can find some kite string, the sticks, and a metal rod for the kite, while you try to find some material to make the kite and maybe an old bed sheet that we can tear apart to make the tail."

"Cool, let's do this."

The two boys go in search of their items.

Soon, Zane has collected his items, then jots to the garage to find Zach. "No luck, I see, since you are still scouring the shelves."

"You already found yours?" Zach questions.

"I did. I found a couple of old silk Halloween costume shirts that were in my closet. I hope you can deal with the bright orange and black material. I also found an old bed sheet in the hallway linen closet. I'm sure Mom won't miss it."

"I found the metal rod," Zach says, "which is nothing more than an old coat hanger, but I can't find any sticks for the kite's frame. I did find some string, but it's not near enough. We need to go to the hobby store where Mom buys her crafts. I know they have balsa wood to build model airplanes. We should be able to find what we need there. But before we go, we need to make a list."

Zach pulls out his phone to start one. Both boys rattle off the items they need, Zach typing as fast as his thumbs will allow.

"We need a large roll of kite string, the sticks, and some thread to sew the kite together," Zach says. "We also need a ribbon. Oh, and a key."

"Wouldn't it be cool if we could find one of those old-fashioned keys," Zane adds. "Maybe add a little nostalgia to the project?"

"That would be cool. Oh, we need some wire and a Leyden jar too."

"Where do we find a Leyden jar?" Zane asks. "I don't think they sell those at the hobby store."

"Good point," Zach agrees. "Then we'll need to make one, which shouldn't be a problem. I'm sure there's lots of ideas on the internet. C'mon, let's go to the store."

Back home from the hobby store, Zach gestures toward the ceiling, holding up their bag of purchased items. "Let's go build a kite."

Zane laughs.

The boys race upstairs to the work room to start their project.

A couple of years ago, their mother and father converted one of the home's five bedrooms into a craft/work room. It became apparent, with their mother's crafting, Zach's experiments, and Zane's computer-building hobby that such a room would be beneficial to the entire family.

Zach lays the materials down on the large square table that sits in the middle of the room. He cuts the dowel rods to size, while Zane trims his Halloween shirts into two separate pieces of square material. Zach lays out two dowel rods in a cross pattern and adds a dowel on each of the four sides to form the diamond frame of the kite.

He binds the rods together with the string, while Zane sews his cut-down shirts into a single piece of material. Once Zach has completed his frame, he tears the sheets into two-inch-wide strips, tying them together with old-fashioned square knots to create the fifteen-foot-long tail.

With the frame and the material completed, Zach says, "Lay the material down and I'll place the frame on top. We can pull the material over the frame's edges and sew it into the material."

"Sounds like a plan, Martha Stewart," Zane mocks with a smile.

"Bite me."

With the sewing complete, the kite takes on its familiar shape. They each tie a piece of string from the four corners, each long enough to meet in the middle to tie a center loop for the main line to attach to the kite.

"I'll attach the metal rod to the top of the kite," Zach informs his brother, "while you attach the tail."

"Sounds good."

Moments later their kite is complete.

"Eat your heart out, Benjamin Franklin," Zach shouts as if he has conquered the world. "Our kite will be stronger, fly higher and..."

"It looks like a pumpkin," Zane interrupts.

"Ha, ha. At least we will be able to spot it close to the clouds," Zach says. "Now, to make a Leyden jar."

"I'm on it," Zane says. He opens his laptop and performs a Google search: "How to make a Leyden jar." Several options appear on the screen. He opens one of the links. "This will be easier than I thought. We need a two-liter plastic Coke bottle, some aluminum foil, two pieces of wire—each about fourteen inches long—a cork, and some water. That's too simple. I will bet we have everything except the cork."

"Nope," Zach says. "Mom has that wine cork holder in the kitchen. I'll take a couple corks from there, if you can find the Coke bottle and aluminum foil."

A few minutes later, both have their items and return to the work room.

"Buuuuuuuuuuurp." Zane lets out a long, loud, deep belch.

Zach's impressed and laughs. "Way to go, Zane!"

"Sorry. I had to down the last of the Coke to empty the bottle."

Zane returns to his laptop and provides the instructions to each of the steps. "Bend each wire at one end to make a ring." He watches Zach perform his instructions.

With pliers from the work room's limited toolbox, Zach bends the wires from a coat hanger as instructed.

"Attach one of the wires to the outside bottom of the bottle."

Zach complies with some tape.

"Wrap aluminum foil around the outside bottom of the bottle, then place the bottle on top of a wooden block."

Zach again complies.

"Now, insert a metal wire through the cork and install it in the bottle's spout, making sure the wire extends three-quarters into the bottle. Then add water."

"There it is. A Leyden jar," Zach marvels. "That's one of the easiest contraptions I've ever built for any experiment."

"Hey, Zach, we can use some of the leftover silk from the costume to rub the bottle."

"Great idea. But first we need to fill the bottle with water, then we can test it."

Zach takes their new device to the bathroom and pulls out the cork. Zane follows behind. He turns on the water in the bathtub and fills the bottle half full. They return to the work room, where Zach inserts the cork and its wire into the top of the bottle.

"Zane, rub the outside of the bottle with the silk cloth," Zach says, excited about their new gadget.

Zane rubs the bottle to charge it.

Zach, so excited, picks up a piece of the leftover coat hanger and touches it to the jar's two electrodes.

POW!

Zach screams. "Holy crap!" He grits his teeth as pain races across his face. He jumps up and down, shaking his hand. "I was so excited I forgot the wire needed to be insulated. That hurt. How much did you rub it?"

Zane's hysterical laughing makes it difficult for him to respond. Once he regains his composure, he says, "Obviously enough to shock the piss out of you. I guess it works, but we may want to insulate that wire. Imagine what the lightning would have done!"

"No kidding. I won't make that mistake again," Zach adamantly states, his hand still throbbing from the effects of the shock. "I'll insulate the wire, so we'll be ready on Saturday. Now, all we need is lightning."

SIX

SATURDAY, JUNE 8, 2019

ZACH AND ZANE rise earlier than normal to take EMITT downtown to Independence Park.

Zach gets dressed in a pair of long jeans and his orange, red, and yellow Nikes in case the weather cools because of the possible rain. He pulls on his favorite black Spiderman T-shirt—Spiderman in the city's darkness swinging high over the lights below, legs spread wide and bent tight at the knees, his right arm extended forward, thumb and pinky spread wide, the remaining fingers pulled tight toward his wrist, preparing to spin off another line fiber.

Zane also thinks about the possibility of rain and slips on a pair of blue jean pants and his blue and white Nikes. He flips through his closet and pulls out his favorite white superhero T-shirt—the green enigma of the Incredible Hulk and his angry face throwing a three-dimensional punch across the T-shirt. His clothes ripped to shreds from his raging growth as he races after his villain.

Their father left for the lecture an hour ago. EMITT sits behind the garage and is only accessible via a pass-through blocked by two oversized garage doors.

Zach's truck is parked under the porte-cochère, which overhangs the front of the three-car garage. Zane puts the Leyden jar, the kite, and the other items they will need in the back seat of Zach's truck along with his backpack. He raises the tall front and back garage doors for Zach to back his truck through and up to EMITT.

With the hitch connected to the truck, he hollers at Zach, "Okay, you're hooked up." Zach inches EMITT through the garage, careful not to damage her.

Zane closes the garage doors and hops into the truck. He stares at Zach with a big smile and says, "Let's go fly a kite."

"Oh yeah, baby," Zach shouts, pumping a fist in the air as he pulls away.

EMITT is an old barbeque trailer that their father bought from a man in Texas who had competed in national barbeque cook-offs. The Texan created a unique rustic look featuring a decal wrap around the entire trailer, which gives it the appearance of an old, wooden cabin. It even includes a stubby, pitched, shingled roof with a fake stone chimney on top, which served as the vent for the pits.

The Texan added two long doors on the passenger side, which span the length of the trailer and open with the push of a button. The top door opens upward, and the bottom door opens down, exposing the cabin's rustic front porch. A four-inch-square metal post on each end of the porch hinges to fold up and provide a false support. The posts also include a decal wrap to make them appear as if they too are wood. The bottom door is covered with wood planks, which serve as the wood floor of the porch.

Jeremy loved the rustic look so much that he wanted to keep its appearance intact, but he also wanted to have the word "EMITT" displayed on the side. To do so, he had a wrap created for the outside portion of these two doors. When opened, a rustic cabin appears, but when closed for travel, the name "EMITT" is prominently displayed in large, white, pointed letters against the dark background of a space scene, with the bright sun in the distance and a few of our solar system's iconic planets scattered among the universe's many stars.

SEVEN

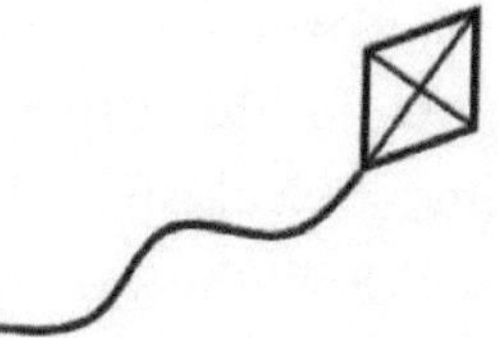

SATURDAY, JUNE 8, 2019

"TIME TRAVEL. THE dream of many, the ultimate challenge of a physicist, and long considered the holy grail of our universe. We all dream of traveling through time, maybe to the medieval times to witness a battlefield of soldiers wielding their swords, hundreds of arrows flying across the battlefield in search of their enemies, or catapults hurling balls of fire at a castle.

"Maybe your agenda is devious with a purpose, and you wish to have Adolf Hitler assassinated before his rise to power and save six million Jews from murder in the Holocaust. Or, maybe you wish to travel forward in time to learn this week's winning lottery numbers and then return to purchase them and claim your millions."

Jeremy, Sam, and Mark listen to the petite Asian presenter in her teal-colored pantsuit. Her confident voice is carried to the auditorium speakers for the fifty or so people in attendance. She sweeps her long, dark, straight hair behind her ear. "Most people don't believe it's possible. What we do know is that it has yet to be accomplished. But that does not mean it's impossible. Some physicists believe it is achievable and that the avenue occurs through wormholes.

"Let's assume for a moment that time travel is possible. Many questions come to mind. Is it life threatening? What happens to our bodies? What will happen if someone sees you appear out of nowhere? What are the ramifications of our travel? Will we change history? We will talk about all of that and more throughout the morning.

"But first let's talk about wormholes." She clicks her pointer. The video screen behind her comes to life, displaying a green grid on a flat, three-dimensional view against a black space background. "If we look at time in a grid presentation, we show the year 1000 AD on one end of the grid and the year 3050 AD on the opposite end. If we were to pick two distinct time periods on the grid—for example, 1500 and 2019—the travel distance between the two time periods is quite long. But, what if we were to bend time?" She presses the pointer's button again. The computer program folds the grid on the screen and aligns the two periods, one directly above the other. The program links the two periods with a grid-shaped tunnel formation. "Now, the two time periods are much closer. The tunnel shown between them is our wormhole."

She continues, "Albert Einstein's Theory of General Relativity suggests that time travel is possible by bending time, as demonstrated here. The travel would be through the wormhole, but first a wormhole must be created. It may be possible to create a wormhole, but to do so may require large quantities of negative energy. But wormholes are complicated—they do not stay open long enough for even a single particle of light to pass through. Just as quickly as they open, they collapse on themselves, leaving them unstable.

"We understand that a vacuum is filled with electromagnetic waves, each fluctuating in size. With time bent, or folded over as we have shown, some of these electromagnetic waves become too large to fit between our two parallel plates of time." She uses the red laser on her pointer to outline the upper and lower plates of time shown on the screen's grid presentation. "This creates a negative energy, also known as Casimir energy, and in large quantities, may be able to hold the wormhole open long enough to send a pulse of light through.

"In the late 1980s, at the California Institute of Technology, physicist Kip Thorne suggested that with the use of Casimir energy, wormholes might be kept open long enough to send messages back and forth.

"In 2014, professor Luke Butcher added, if a wormhole were much longer than it was wide, there may be enough natural Casimir energy within the wormhole to keep it open even longer.

"Recently at CERN in Geneva, Switzerland, physicists discovered a new particle, Z(4430), also known as exotic matter. Exotic matter is thought to provide never-ending energy, continuous perpetual motion. Exotic matter may be powerful enough to keep a wormhole stable and open long enough to send a person through. But, we believe it too will take massive amounts of exotic matter to do so.

"Let's assume for a moment that we have figured out the time travel aspect. What happens? Where would we land? Let's explore this scenario. Assume I was to go outside and get into my car, which happens to be my time machine. I decide to travel back to a time well before Philadelphia. I dial up my travel date and time..." She animates her actions as if operating dials and buttons. "...and off I go through time, back to June 8, 1000 AD. Do I actually move?"

"No," shouts a man from the audience.

"I agree," she says, pointing to the man. "Only time would change. I would be in my car in the exact same place, except now I am in the year 1000 AD. There would be nothing there. I would be in my car in the middle of a grass field. Let's assume I stay there for a week. Of course, I want to see what's there, so I leave my car and explore the area. After a week, I come back to my car and I travel back to today, just a few minutes after my original departure time. Now, let's assume that I discovered something in my first travel and now I want to go back and explore it a little closer. Can I just go there?"

She pauses for a second. "Sure, I can, but it might be a good idea that I park my car in a different parking space from the first time I traveled. I don't want to land on top of it or morph into it, or whatever may happen.

We have no idea what would occur in that situation. So, I park on the other side of the parking lot and travel back to the day after my original arrival date. When I arrive, will I see my car from the first time I traveled?"

A man in the front row raises his hand. She points to him. "What do you think happens?"

"I believe it would be there. Time is relative and it works the same today as it did then. So, once time occurs it will always be there."

"I agree. I will see my first car across the field as well as the car I am sitting in, even though they are the same car! Now, there are two time machines, at least until the week is up and my first self returns and takes that time machine back home. That also means there are two of me as well. It could be a bit awkward if I ran into myself." Imitating a surprise, she opens her mouth with her eyes spread wide and places her hands over her mouth. "But that too would be possible. What happens if I did this several times? Would I not discover multiple cars and multiple versions of myself?

"What happens if the worst scenario occurs? Two people see me arrive in my time machine. They fight it out to steal my machine and one of them dies. What if that person were a famous person in history and they died, but before they became famous? Would history change? Could we prevent it from changing or prevent the person from dying? Time travel could be tricky."

Jeremy's smartphone vibrates. He pulls it from his pocket and reads a text from Zach. "NO PRKNG AT INDPT PK. AT VACANT LOT, SEVERAL BLOCKS AWAY. CALL US AND WE WILL PICK U UP. SORRY, NO CHOICE."

EIGHT

SATURDAY, JUNE 8, 2019

STANDING AT THE back of the truck, Zach returns his cell phone to his pocket. "I'll bet Dad didn't expect us to park this far away."

"I'll bet you're right," Zane says. "I don't know what's happening at Independence Park, but there wasn't a parking space anywhere, much less a place for EMITT."

"Zane, look at how dark the clouds are now," Zach says, nodding toward the sky. "Let's set EMITT up for Dad. Then we can fly the kite."

"Sounds like a plan."

Zane retrieves the tool from EMITT's generator room at the front of the trailer and lowers and stabilizes each of EMITT's four jacks.

Zach lowers the front wheel and unhitches EMITT from the truck. He steps to the front of EMITT, and with a press of a button he opens the side doors, revealing EMITT's rustic front porch appearance.

With EMITT prepared for their father and his guests, they retrieve the kite and other items from the truck. Zach remains outside on the porch to prepare for the experiment. In the front sitting room Zane lays his backpack next to one of the four brown leather chairs that are arranged in a circle around a small, oval, dark wood table that sits on top of a plain red and blue fake oriental rug.

Zane hollers to Zach, "You can tell Mom added her two cents' worth to the decorating of this room. You know it was her idea to add these comfy leather chairs, with the throw rug and the coffee table. Dad would have put four folding chairs and a box in the room."

Zach laughs. "Isn't that the truth."

Zach ties the ribbon onto the key. "C'mon, Zane, let's get this kite in the air before we miss our opportunity."

"Give me a minute."

Zach straps the wire from the Leyden jar to the key and hangs the key on a cleat on the front porch post. He mumbles to himself, "Now to attach the string to the kite and I'll be ready." With his brother still messing around inside, he barks, "Zane, let's go."

"All right, all right! I'm coming. Hold your toes," he hollers back, his forehead tight with a scowl. A moment later he exits EMITT and snatches the kite from Zach's hands and starts toward the empty lot.

"Zach, you ready?"

"I am."

"Let's go, then. It's starting to sprinkle."

Zane steps back to tighten the line, while Zach pulls and lifts the kite into the air. Zane sprints back to the cover of the porch, where they watch it climb high into the sky.

Zach continues to let the string out as their orange kite zig zags higher and higher, its tail waving with the wind. The kite stands out against the background of the dark clouds. With all the line let out, Zach ties the kite's string to the key and holds the ribbon under the cover of the porch to remain isolated from the lightning.

Thunder rumbles in the distance.

"Did you hear that?" Zach asks, with wide eyes.

"I did. Do you think we might be lucky enough to catch some lightning?"

"I don't know, but I hope so."

Again, thunder fills the sky.

Both boys are excited at the possibility of recreating Benjamin Franklin's experiment. They believe it will be uber-cool to catch some lightning in their jar.

Forty-five minutes pass and no lightning has struck the kite. Zane becomes bored and steps inside EMITT, leaving the door open. He starts to rummage around the front room.

Zach calls out, "Why are you inside?"

"I was bored and thought I would look around."

A moment later Zane hollers out, "Hey, Zach, have you ever been inside Dad's laboratory?"

"No. He won't let anyone in there. It's like it's top secret or something."

"I know. But it looks like Dad forgot to lock the door, because it's cracked open a little."

"Stay out. Dad won't be happy if you go in there."

His curiosity tugs at him and he ignores Zach's instructions. He pulls the door open and peers inside. His eyes grow wide. "Holy crap!" Zane cries out.

"What?"

"Zach, you have to see this."

"What is it?"

"Dad's lab. You just have to see it."

"I can't right now. And I told you not to go in there. For God's sake, don't touch anything. Dad won't be happy if you mess anything up. C'mon, you need to get out of there."

Suddenly, lightning strikes nearby. *Boom, boom, boom*! Thunder explodes through the clouds, scaring the crap out of the boys as they both jump.

"Holy mackerel!" Zach yells.

Zane screams, "Did you catch it? Did you catch the lightning?"

"No," Zach hollers, "but it scared the crap out of me. Obviously, electricity is in the air. I can feel my skin crawling. But we'll catch it soon."

Zane steps inside. "Zach, you have to see this room."

"I can't right now. The wind has picked up and I can't let go of the kite."

The rain now beats down on EMITT's shingled roof and porch, making it difficult to hear.

Zane stands in awe of a large, ten-inch round, clear, acrylic tube standing against the back wall. The tube is filled with an intermingling glow of plasma-like colors of yellow, red, green, blue, and violet as they slowly dance amongst each other. The tube forms a perfect circle that reaches from the floor to the ceiling. Multiple wires and thin stainless-steel tubes connect to various points on the acrylic tube. Its beauty hypnotizes him.

An array of electronics lines the wall to his right, and in front of the tube stands a computer desk with two computer screens, both at a slight angle to the other. The desk and the electronics are deliberately arranged to block any access to the tube. An ergonomic office chair sits in front of the desk. The word "EMITT" tumbles between the two monitors in their screen-saver mode. The colors of the tumbling word intermingle with each other like those in the tube. Zane is awestruck by the sight.

Boom, crackle, boom, boom! Another bolt of lightning hits nearby, detaching Zane from his trance. Again, thunder races through the clouds, followed by a chain reaction of grumbling thunder rolling away through the clouds.

"Holy crap!" Zane yells in a frightened state as he jumps. "Did we get that one?"

"No. Just another lightning strike. But that one was closer than the last one. It appeared to hit right behind the buildings."

Zane returns his gaze to the colors in the tube. "I cannot believe its beauty," he utters to himself.

"Zach, you have to see this," Zane yells again.

"I can't right now. The wind has picked up and it's raining even harder now."

Zane steps forward for a closer look at the acrylic tube. He accidently bumps the computer desk. The monitors come to life, exiting their screen saver mode. Zane bounces away and notices a timer on one of the screens counting down from just after three minutes. Right above the countdown timer, the cursor flashes at the "password" field.

The computer speaks in a woman's soft voice, "Please speak or enter a password."

"Uh-oh!" Zane shouts.

"What now?"

"I don't know, but I bumped the computer desk and a timer started counting down and now the computer is asking for a password.

"Way to go, Zane," Zach screams in an irritated tone. "I told you not to mess with any of Dad's stuff. What's the counter for?"

"I don't know. There's a couple of dates on the screen, but that's it. It's just counting down."

"Good Lord," Zach says while shaking his head in disgust. "Let me tie the kite to the pole and I will come in and see what's going on."

Zach pulls the ribbon around the front porch post and cinches it tight, pulling the kite's string tight up against the cleat. As he is about to walk away he notices the strands of the string are standing up, separated evenly apart from each other. "Zaaaaane," he hollers, "I need you out here. NOW! The strands, they're standing up, just like it did for Benjamin Franklin. Oh my God, it's working. Zane, hurry up—get out here."

With Zane in awe of the tube and Zach busy with the kite, it never occurred to either of them to open the laboratory's door. But now, with Zach catching the lightning, Zane flings the door open and glares at Zach. "Touch the key. See if there's any electricity."

Zane hears the woman's voice on the computer: "Password accepted. Time travel sequence initiated." Puzzled at the computer's phrase, Zane looks back inside and sees the colors inside the acrylic tube begin to spin faster and faster.

"Zaaaach," Zane yells nervously, "something's happening!"

"Zane, what in the world is going on?"

They hear loud, crackling noises, like that of static electricity.

"Zane, are you seeing this?"

Electrical arcs surround EMITT. Rounded arcs, many of them, engulf the trailer, as if they are forming a bubble around EMITT. Suddenly, a deafening *POW* and a brilliant flash of light, knocking both boys to the floor, stunning them into a daze of silence.

NINE

FRIDAY, JUNE 9, 1752

LYING ON THE porch, Zach sits up, shakes his head, and rubs his eyes. "What in the world just happened?" he mumbles to himself. His vision is temporarily blinded from the bright flash of light, but it slowly returns.

"Zane, you okay?" he hollers.

"I'm not sure. I can't see."

"I'm the same, but my vision is starting to come back."

"Zach, what happened?"

"I don't know, but that was a bright flash of light," he says as his vision focuses. He peers inside to find Zane still sitting on the floor but leaning against one of the walls with his hands over his eyes.

Zach stumbles inside. "Zane, you okay?"

"Yeah, I think so. My sight is coming back." Zach helps him to his feet.

Both boys look around the room, which appears normal.

Zach sees the acrylic tube for the first time. The colors leisurely intermingle with each other. "What in the world is that?" he screeches.

"I'm not sure, but isn't it beautiful? This is what I've been trying to get you to come in and see. I have no idea what it does or what it's for, but my guess is it has something to do with that countdown timer on the computer and that bright flash of light. And, when everything started to go haywire, the colors were spinning around the tube real fast."

"Zane, I'm not so sure the two are related. You said it asked for a password, and unless you entered a password I don't think the timer had anything to do with it."

Zach glances outside, but something is different. Confused and still a little dazed, he steps outside. "HOLY CRAP! Zane get out here—NOW."

Zane bolts outside. "WHAT THE...WHERE IS EVERYTHING? Where did the buildings go? What happened to the cars, the people? Where are the freaking streets? Zach, what in the world just happened?"

"I don't know. I'm confused."

A warmth comes across Zane's face. He looks up. "The sun's out. What happened to the clouds? Where's the rain? Where's the lightning? Why is the grass dry? Zach, what's going on here?"

"I don't know, but I don't think we're in Philly anymore," Zach states.

"No kidding, Sherlock. Figured that out all on your own, did you? With your sharp eye, you better keep an eye out for the wicked witch and her crazy flying monkeys too."

"Bite me."

Both boys, in their stunned state, stare in disbelief for a few minutes. They stare at a vast open field of tall brown grass, gently swaying in a light breeze. A long tree line in the distance frames the field. "Hey look, there's the kite. It looks broken," Zane says, pointing.

"I'm not too concerned with the kite right now. Zane, we need to figure out what happened. We need to go back over all the events before this occurred. I was flying the kite and you said a countdown timer had started. How much time counted down?"

"It started at a little over three minutes. But the computer asked for a password."

"But you didn't enter one, correct?"

"Correct, but the computer spoke, asking to either type or speak a password."

"What did you say to it?"

"Nothing." Zane pauses for a second. "But, you said the strands were standing up on the twine like Benjamin Franklin's experiment, then everything went crazy."

"What did we say?"

"I'm not sure." He thought for a second. "Wait a minute. The computer did say the password was accepted and something about time travel initiated. That's when I noticed the tube and its colors started to spin real fast."

"Time travel?" Zach shouts. "Are you freaking kidding me? You're telling me that Dad's project is a time machine and he has figured out how to make it work? Then, his two bozo sons take it for a joy ride into the freaking future, without his permission. Are you freaking kidding me? Oh, Zane, we are in deep trouble. I mean we really stepped off into a huge pile of you know what."

Zane grabs Zach by both arms. "Calm down, Zach. We need to figure this out. Also, if we did travel in time, I'm not sure we traveled to the future. I think we may have gone to the past."

"What?" Zach screeches. "You mean you actually believe we traveled through time? Holy crap, Zane!" Zach grabs at his hair while walking in circles.

"Zach, if you think about it, it's a little odd that one minute it's dark clouds and raining with thunder and lightning. Then there's a bright flash of light and the next thing we know the sun is shining, the buildings disappeared, the streets and the cars no longer exist, and we're standing in a field in the middle of nowhere. So, something happened!"

"But what, Zane?"

"Maybe the computer can tell us. Let's check it out."

"Good idea."

Zane sits down at the computer and views the screens icons. He finds one labeled "EMITT."

He double clicks the icon. It opens and asks for a password. "Any ideas for passwords?"

"Got me. Uh, try EMITT."

Zane types the word "EMITT." The computer responds, "Invalid password."

"Try our names."

Zane types in each of their names separately. Each time the computer replies, "Invalid password."

"Try them backwards." Again, each press of the "Enter" button returns the same response.

"Oh man, we have a real problem here. We will be grounded until we graduate," Zach says, sounding defeated.

"Grounded!" Zane replies with a puzzled look on his face. "If we don't figure out where we are or how to get back home, we may be stuck here, forever. Worse than that, I don't even know where 'here' is. Grounded would be a vacation at this point."

Zane tries several more passwords, but no luck. The boys are feeling a little scared now and have no idea what to do. They leave the computer and step outside to look around.

"Oh, man. It's even worse than I thought," Zach cries out.

"Now what?"

"The truck's not even here. How are we supposed to get around?"

"And we thought it couldn't get any worse."

"All right, let's think this through," Zach says. "We need to turn this into a positive somehow. Dad always told us that bad results come with negative attitudes and good results come with positive attitudes. So, what do we have here that is positive?"

"Good idea, Zach. Let's make a list."

Zane retrieves a pencil and paper from the computer desk inside and sits on the front porch. He jots a couple of obvious items down. Zach remains inside and rummages through the lab area, blurting out items as he sees them. After a few minutes, they have a list of items they can work with.

"EMITT for shelter."

"Computer."

"Generator."

"Hammer."

"Screwdrivers."

"Flashlight."

"Lighter."

"Twine."

"Knife."

"Duct tape."

"Leyden jar."

"A kite."

Then, Zach blurts out sarcastically, "Oh yeah, and a FREAKING TIME MACHINE!"

Zane ignores his little outburst. "Okay, we have a few tools to work with, but what do we not have that we may need?"

Zach responds, "We need food and water."

"Wait a minute," Zane says. "I put a few waters and some peanut butter crackers in the backpack."

"What backpack?" Zach asks. "I don't see it."

"I set it beside one of the chairs in the front room."

Zane chases Zach into the front room, where they find the backpack lying beside one of the chairs.

"Fantastic. Zane, you're a lifesaver. Sometimes your planning amazes me."

"Thanks," Zane responds with a smile.

They sit down on the front porch and each open a bottle. "Zach, we should go easy with our food and water. We have no idea how long we will be here or where we can find more. We may want to be smart with what we do have."

"I agree," Zach says as he opens a package of peanut butter crackers.

"Let's split this one."

"Sounds good."

"So again," Zane continues, "we know what we have, but what don't we have?"

"You know, we might need some wood for a fire tonight," Zach responds.

"Wait a minute," Zane says and jumps up. "That's it."

"What's it?"

Zane zips back to the computer; Zach follows. He types in another password: "Touch The Key." The computer comes to life. Information displays on the screen.

PREVIOUS TRAVEL DATE:	JUNE 8, 2019	TIME:	11:12	AM
CURRENT DATE:	JUNE 9, 1752	TIME:	12:17	PM
NEXT TRAVEL DATE:		TIME:		
PASSWORD:				
SET COUNTDOWN TIMER:				

NOTE: COUNTDOWN TIMER ALLOWS VOICE COMMANDS. COUNTDOWN TIMER WILL STOP COUNTING DOWN IN SCREEN SAVER MODE. IT WILL AUTOMATICALLY RESUME WHEN SCREEN SAVER MODE IS EXITED.

Both boys shout at the same time, "1752!"

"Oh man, that's uh...that's uh…" Zach calculates the years in his head. "That's two hundred and...and...and...267 years!" Zach screams. "Zane, we traveled 267 years into the past? That's not possible. How did that happen? Did you tell the computer a date?"

"No, but I do remember now that there was a date on the computer, but I didn't pay any attention to it."

Zach continues, "Dad must have been working on this last night, but he didn't close the program down. The date must have already been entered before we ever stepped foot inside EMITT, and when you bumped the computer desk it still wanted the password. Dad must have clicked on the microphone so he could speak the password, probably because he was busy doing something else at the same time."

"Now that we know how to operate it, let's go home," Zane says. "I assume we enter the date and password and press 'Enter.' That should take us home."

Zane enters the date and time—"June 8, 2019, 11:15 AM"—and the password. "Before I hit enter, close your eyes so the bright flash of light doesn't blind us this time."

Both close their eyes. Zane presses the enter button. They do not hear the woman's voice on the computer. They wait several seconds. They hear no static or crackle noises like the first time, no loud bang or a brilliant flash of light. They open their eyes.

"It didn't work," Zach says. "We did something wrong."

"But what?" Zane asks with a puzzled look on his face. He pauses for a moment. "We need lightning to make it work. We caught the lightning the first time it worked. It must not have worked for Dad either. But when we caught the lightning, it started. The lightning is what makes EMITT work."

"Lightning!" Zach shouts, eyes wide open. "You're telling me we have to fly the kite again, in another lightning storm? No way—once was enough."

"Yes. That's exactly what we need to do, the same way we did it the first time, Leyden jar and all," Zane says. "All we need is lightning."

"I'm reluctant to say this, but I guess we need to fix the kite."

"Wait a minute," Zane says smiling with both eyebrows raised. "EMITT didn't work a minute ago, when we tried it. I'll bet Dad tried it many times and it didn't work for him either. That's why he needs Sam and Mark's help. They were supposed to help him figure out why it doesn't work. He doesn't have a math problem. He needed lightning."

"Dad is going to be pissed when we don't call to pick them up," Zach ponders out loud.

"Oh my God. Zach, that means we are the first people to make EMITT work. We are the first people to ever travel through time. Zach, we just made history."

"Oh great. And now we took Dad's thunder away. He is going to be furious with us."

"Now that we know where we are and how to travel home, we need to check out the kite," Zane says as he stands from the chair and steps outside. "I'll fetch the kite and wind up the twine, if you'll take care of the Leyden jar."

"Sure," Zach says as he steps off the porch. He reaches for the key on the cleat. *POW!* The vicious explosion of electricity throws Zach from EMITT. He lies unconscious in the tall grass.

TEN

FRIDAY, JUNE 9, 1752

"ZACH!" ZANE SCREAMS as he races to him. Down on one knee, he pats Zach's face. "Zach, are you okay? Zach? Zach?" he yells. "Wake up. Oh, God. Zach, wake up." He slaps his face a couple more times.

No response.

Zane puts his ear to Zach's heart to listen for a heartbeat. He hears it beating. He watches his chest rise and fall with each breath. "Thank God he's alive."

"Zach, please wake up." He slaps his face a couple more times.

Zach's eyes flutter, then they open wide.

"Oh my God, you're alive."

Zach coughs. "What happened?" he says as he tries to sit up.

Zane helps him to a sitting position. "Are you okay?"

"I think so. What happened?" he asks again.

"You grabbed the key that was still connected to the Leyden jar. The jar was still charged from the lightning. And when you grabbed the key, the charge knocked you back about seven feet. You have to discharge the jar before you touch it, or anything connected to it. The next time, it may kill you." Zane trembles at the thought of his brother dying right before his eyes. "Stay here and don't move," he says, then jumps up and rushes into EMITT. He returns with one of the bottles of water.

"Here, drink some water."

After a few sips, Zane helps him to his feet. "Are you okay?"

"Yeah. I think so. Wow! I don't want to do that again." Zach brushes himself off. "C'mon, let's fix the kite. I think I'm ready to go home."

"Wait a minute," Zane says. "I want to discharge the jar one more time before we touch it, just to be safe." He scurries inside EMITT and returns with their discharge tool. He attempts to discharge the bottle, but this time there is no spark. He picks it up and hands it to Zach. Zach takes the bottle and places it inside EMITT's front room, while Zane winds up the twine and retrieves the kite.

"Oh, that sucks," Zane hollers.

"What?"

"One of the kite's backbone sticks snapped in half."

"Isn't that just great. We'll fix it later, because I don't think it's going to rain today and we need to find some firewood for tonight. It'll be dark soon and we need to be prepared."

Zane lays the kite on the floor in EMITT's front room. They start their search for firewood. After an hour or so, they have collected several miniature twigs, some sticks, and several nice logs. They even found a log that they have manhandled back for a place to sit near the fire.

"I wonder what time it is?" Zach asks.

Zane reaches into his pocket. "I don't have my phone. I must have left it in your truck."

"The phone," Zach says. "That gives me an idea." He reaches into his pocket for his cell phone. "I'll try to call Dad. Maybe the cell phone will work and we really didn't travel."

"If he answers," Zane says, "we will have a different problem, but at least we can explain and he can help us figure it out. Be prepared, though, because he will be mad."

Zach finds his father's phone number and presses "Send," but immediately the phone gives a busy signal. He notices he has no bars and there is no time displayed.

"Great, no signal," he barks. "Man, did we jack this day up or what? We need to catch the lightning again or we'll be stuck in the past forever."

"I know, but for now we need to make the best of what we have. Let's scout the area and see what we can find. We will need food and water soon. What we have won't last long."

"I agree," Zach says.

They leave EMITT and walk toward a dilapidated old cabin in the distance. "This tall grass is difficult to walk through," Zach comments.

"Yeah, it is. And I'm sure my Nikes will look like crap by the time we're done here."

"Mine too, but I think that is the least of our problems."

"I agree."

As they near the cabin, it appears it has not been lived in for a while. Though it appears vacant, they approach with caution. Zach peers through one of the windows. "Nobody here. This place is vacant. C'mon, let's check it out."

They enter and find nothing but a charred fireplace that appears to be the strongest part of the structure. After a couple of minutes of looking at the old wooden cabin, Zane says, "C'mon, let's go. There is nothing useful here for us."

Soon, they come upon a tree line. They hear a familiar sound in the distance beyond the trees, the faint ring of a bell. They enter the trees and after a few minutes of high-stepping through the brush and ducking under the low limbs, they make their way through. "Oh my God. Zane, look. Is that an old clipper ship?" Zach points to a ship with several of its many masts deployed for the wind to push it upriver.

"Holy crap, Zach. It is. Look." He points through the trees. "There's a couple more anchored further upriver."

At the water's edge, both lean forward to see around the trees. "Zach, we're in Philadelphia, in 1752, and this must be the Delaware River. This is unbelievable."

"Let's make our way upriver," Zach says. "Philadelphia should be that way." He points north.

They climb their way out of the brush and trees to avoid the dense thicket and follow the tree line up the river.

They hike through the tall grass for another forty-five minutes, then through a line of trees. "Zach, look, there's the town." They stop for a minute and stare in amazement. They see the wooden structures of the buildings that make up old Philadelphia. A few men can be seen riding horses between the buildings.

"Zach, we can buy some food and water in town. Let's get a few things to take back to EMITT."

"What? Are you crazy?" Zach states. "We can't just walk into town. We don't belong here. What will they say about your Incredible Hulk shirt or my Spiderman shirt? And we're wearing blue jeans and bright-colored tennis shoes and I'm pretty sure none of this stuff has been invented yet. And what would I say if someone asked me where I bought my tennis shoes? 'Oh, they were on sale at the Nike store'? I'm sure we would get an odd look or two, maybe even locked up. Not only that, we have no money. I'm not even sure our money is the same as theirs and I'm pretty sure they don't accept credit cards. And we can't even explain where we're from. No, I think if we're smart we will stay away from town."

"Okay. Okay. I got it. I didn't think about that. I agree. We should find our way back to EMITT. We need to keep a low profile while we're here."

They start back. After a while in what they believe is the general direction of EMITT, they approach a tree line. They proceed through. Several minutes later they exit into an open field. "Oh yeah, there she is," Zach blurts out.

"It will be dark soon. When we get back we should clear out a place for our fire," Zane suggests.

Back at EMITT, the boys use a hammer, a knife, and their two feet to stomp and clear an area large enough for them to build a fire. Soon they have an area cleared so that they feel comfortable enough it won't catch the entire field on fire.

They use dry grass as their base, a pile of twigs on top of the grass, then several sticks and a couple of logs across the top to build their fire. But they will wait until darkness falls before they start the fire.

"At least we have a lighter," Zane says. "I'm not sure we could start a fire by rubbing two sticks together."

The two boys sit down on EMITT's front porch. "I hope a thunderstorm with lightning happens within the next few days," Zane says. "I don't want to be here long. We need to do exactly what we did the first time. Maybe it would be a good idea if we retraced the events, so we can be prepared. We don't want to miss our opportunity."

"Our luck, they will have a drought this year."

Zane laughs. "God, I hope not. Let's start with flying the kite. How high do you think we flew it?"

"That's easy. I let out all of the string."

Zane writes it down on his notepad.

Zach continues, "It was about forty-five minutes later before we started to hear thunder rumble in the background. That's when the lightning started."

Zane recalls, "After I noticed the electronics and the acrylic tube, I accidentally bumped the computer table. That's when the computer asked for the password and the countdown timer started. That's when you decided to come inside."

"Right," Zach recalls. "I tied the twine to the cleat on the front porch post when I noticed the strands on the twine standing up."

"You attached the twine or the ribbon?" Zane asks.

"Both, because of the way I wrapped it," Zach replies. "That must be how the lightning passed through EMITT. And that's why it worked, because EMITT has to be electrified for the time travel to work."

Zane continues to recall, "Then, I said 'Touch the Key,' which is the password to start the time travel event." Zane makes more notes on his pad. "Okay, I think I have the procedures down." Zane reads his notes out loud.

Let all the string out and attach the key to the twine and the Leyden jar.

Attach the string to the cleat of the trailer.

Once lightning is present, we should see strands stand up on the string.

Start EMITT on the computer.

Set the travel date and make sure the timer has started.

With the strands standing up, speak the password.

Be sure to turn on the microphone so it will accept the password.

Close our eyes.

"I think that's it," Zach says. "I think we have a plan."

"I agree, Zach. Now, all we need is lightning."

"Zane, it's almost dark. Maybe we should start the fire."

"I agree."

Zach jumps up to retrieve the lighter from inside EMITT. He returns and lights the small mound of dry grass they have placed under the twigs. The dry grass burns fast, igniting the small sticks, then the larger sticks, and soon they have a nice roaring fire.

As the fire dances, Zane says with a dumb look on his face, "You know, Zach, we're a couple of boneheads."

"Speak for yourself."

"No, really. We're a couple of boneheads. We could've used a couple of those burning sticks to fix the kite."

Zach glances at Zane with the same dumb look, turns back to the fire, and says, "You're right, we're a couple of boneheads. I guess we will have to find some more sticks in the morning before we can fix the kite."

As the last glimmer of daylight turns to darkness, the two boys gaze into the night sky. "Zach, have you ever seen so many stars? At home, there are too many lights in the city that keep us from seeing this many."

"Look, the Big Dipper," Zach points out.

A few minutes pass. Hypnotized by the yellow and orange dancing flames, they listen to the popping sounds as the fire heats up small pockets of oxygen trapped inside the wood. Each time they explode, they create the crackling noises of the fire. In the background, the familiar chirping sounds of the crickets fill the night's cooling air.

Zane reminisces. "Remember when we were little kids at Christmas, how we would be so excited to see what Santa brought us? We would run downstairs and see a stash of toys in front of the tree. I miss those days."

"Me too," Zach recalls. "Remember those science kits?"

"I do."

"I remember once, when I accidentally broke one of the pieces, Dad would say in his typical insightful voice, 'Don't worry, duct tape is the greatest tool; it fixes almost anything,'" Zach mocks.

"Yeah," Zane jumps in with a chuckle, then speaks in a mocking tone, "and his other favorite: 'Think outside the box; you may surprise yourself.'"

They both laugh. They spend the rest of the evening reminiscing about different memories from their childhood before they decide to lie down for the night.

ELEVEN

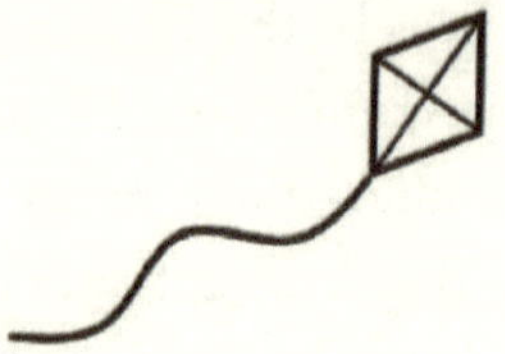

SATURDAY, JUNE 10, 1752

ZACH WAKES TO the sounds of a light thunder rumbling high in the distant sky. He's groggy from his restless sleep, and a minor back pain reminds him that the events of the previous day were very real. He stands and stretches, hoping to relieve the hard floor's infliction, before checking the time on EMITT's computer. He hears Zane stirring in the other room and returns.

"What time is it?" Zane asks.

"Eight-fifteen. I took a quick peak outside and dark clouds have rolled in. Today may be our lucky day. We need to fix the kite before it rains."

Zane springs to his feet and rushes outside. "You're right, it doesn't look good. That's fantastic."

After finding a variety of sticks that will be suitable for the kite's mending, Zane determines, "This should be easy enough to repair. Only one of the kite's two backbone sticks broke."

"That's good. At least we don't have to disassemble the whole kite."

With a little ingenuity and a little duct tape, Zach states, "It's almost as good as new. Let's give it a test flight to make sure it's sturdy enough to handle the wind."

"Good idea."

After a low, short flight, the kite appears to soar with no problems. Satisfied, they retrieve it and store it inside. Even though a steady sprinkle falls, they will wait until the lightning arrives before they put the kite into the air again.

"Zane, I'm hungry. How many packages of crackers did you put in the backpack?"

"There should be three more packages and a couple more bottles of water."

"Let's eat a package each. I'm really hungry."

"Me too," Zane says as he grabs a package of crackers and the bottles of water they rationed from the day before. They return to the porch, where they observe the weather's progress, hoping the steady sprinkle, which has extinguished any remnants of their fire from the night before, turns to a barrage of lightning strikes.

Zach raises his nose to the sky for a sniff. "You can smell the rain in the air."

"Yeah, I smell it too. But I could care less about the rain. I want lightning. I want to go home. I don't think I'm cut out to live in the 1700s."

"Isn't that the truth."

An hour passes.

"Zach, it appears the clouds are a little darker now and maybe even dropped a little lower."

"I noticed the same thing."

Thunder rumbles off in the distance.

"There it is," Zach exclaims. "Maybe we should put the kite in the air."

"I agree."

They retrieve the kite and the Leyden jar. When they step into the wet grass, Zane shouts in a sharp whisper, "Get down!"

They both duck into the tall grass.

"What is it?" Zach questions with a loud whisper. "There's two people in a buggy coming out of the tree line." He points toward their direction. "And it appears they are headed in our direction. We need to lock ourselves inside EMITT. We cannot let them see us."

Staying low in the grass, the boys take the kite and Leyden jar back inside. Zach locks the lab's door. They meet in the front room. Zane peeks through the window's curtains. Zach locks the front door and joins him. They watch as the two men ride in their direction.

The steady sprinkle turns to a vigorous light rain, while a stout gust of wind pushes against the trailer.

Fearful of being discovered, Zane asks, "Zach, what do we do if they stop here?"

"I don't know," he says with a nervous shake in his voice. "We didn't plan for this. We have to play this one by ear."

"Zach, this is more than we bargained for."

"I know, but we need to keep our cool and don't respond to them. Let them think nobody's here and maybe they will go away."

"What if they try to come inside?"

"If there's one thing Dad did well, securing EMITT was one of them."

With both hands on his hips, his head cocked slightly to the side and his forehead wrinkled and his eyes wide opened, Zane says in a condescending manner, "Really, we had no problem."

"You know what I mean. If they try to break in, we will have no choice but to confront them."

"All right," Zane says with some hesitation.

They watch as the men near. They're almost close enough to see their faces. Both are protected with their long brown coats and brown Colonial hats to fend off the rain, which now has turned to an energetic shower.

"Look at that one guy," Zane whispers with a smirk. "He's dressed up like Benjamin Franklin. What a clown!"

They both snicker but continue to watch. Then, a surprised expression of disbelief creeps onto Zach's face. "Wait a minute. You don't think that could be...no way." He answers his own question.

Now, outside of EMITT, one of the men yells with an English accent, "Hello. Is anybody home?"

They stay quiet.

"Hello, anyone home?" the man hollers again.

Again, they stay quiet.

With the rain beating down on top of EMITT's roof, the boys strain to listen to the men's conversation. "Father," the younger man says, "it does not appear anyone's home. Let's conduct the experiment here. I do not believe it advisable to cross this field in such a downpour."

The father stares at the cabin as a confused expression emerges onto his face. With his head cocked a little, his left eye squints and his lips tighten. "William, this is most unusual. I do not remember this cabin when I conducted my search a couple of days earlier. I do not know how I could have missed it." He peers across the field and finds the old dilapidated cabin he visited a couple of days before, confirming he is in the right field. "The other cabin is not in the best of conditions and this one looks mighty fit for the experiment. It will be difficult to traverse this field without becoming stuck in the mud. I agree. The wisest decision is to conduct our experiment here. Let's unload the wagon and place our equipment on the porch, out of the rain."

"Thank you, Father," William replies.

"Holy crap!" Zach whispers with an excited tone. "He called him by his name, 'William.' That's his son's name. It's freaking Benjamin Franklin! I don't believe it. It's freaking Benjamin Franklin! We really are in 1752!"

"Zach, if this is Benjamin Franklin and his son, and they're setting up for an experiment as William said, then that means..."

"OH MY GOD!" Zach interrupts trying to control his excitement in a whisper. "We're going to witness Benjamin Franklin conduct his famous kite experiment. Oh my God, this can't be real. This must be a dream."

"It's not a dream," Zane whispers. "It's our opportunity to go home. We know he captures the lightning. We need to program the computer.

When he sees the strands stand up, you fling open the door and scare them off the porch. I will enter the password and we will be on our way home. And the best part, you don't have to fly the kite."

"Zane, it's not that easy. Benjamin will have the ribbon in his hand when he notices the strands of the twine stand up. But for EMITT to travel through time, the twine needs to be connected to the cleat on the support. Somehow, I need to snatch the ribbon from Benjamin without touching the twine, tie it to the cleat, and scare Benjamin and William off the porch, all at the same time?"

"Good point. This will be a bigger challenge that I thought."

Benjamin and William step onto the cabin's porch. The boys hear the doorknob jiggle, but it's locked and won't open. They hear Benjamin say, "This is an odd cabin. I have not seen a cabin built like such. The door handles, I have never seen anything like them. The windows, they too are different. This is a most unusual cabin that I would like to explore, but we have a purpose here and that is to conduct an experiment. The lightning must be our priority."

Both boys stare at each other in disbelief and want to scream with excitement, but they know they must remain quiet.

"Zane, it is Benjamin and he's here to conduct his kite experiment," Zach whispers. "We need a plan."

The boys quietly run several scenarios past each other, none of which they like. Fifteen minutes pass and they still have no solid ideas.

Zach recalls, "I remember reading about his experiment and he said they waited several hours before he noticed the strands. He began to believe his thoughts were wrong about lightning. But then, he noticed the strands stand up on the twine and that's when he realized the kite had captured the lightning. So, FYI, we may be locked up in here for several hours."

"Whatever it takes," Zane says as he directs the mouse and watches the computer screen come to life. He enters the date "June 8, 2019," changes the time to "11:45 AM," and enters the password "Touch the

Key." "When we're ready, all I have to do is press 'Enter.'"

What he did not notice is that the clock for their arrival time continued to keep time from the moment the new time was entered, an unrealized flaw in their father's system. Just prior to the computer screen switching to screen saver mode, their arrival time changes to "11:46 AM."

PREVIOUS TRAVEL DATE:	JUNE 8, 2019	TIME:	11:12	AM
CURRENT DATE:	JUNE 10, 1752	TIME:	10:32	AM
NEXT TRAVEL DATE:	JUNE 8, 2019	TIME:	11:46	AM
PASSWORD:	TOUCH THE KEY			
SET COUNTDOWN TIMER:	MINUTES			

NOTE: COUNTDOWN TIMER ALLOWS VOICE COMMANDS. COUNTDOWN TIMER WILL STOP COUNTING DOWN IN SCREEN SAVER MODE. IT WILL AUTOMATICALLY RESUME WHEN SCREEN SAVER MODE IS EXITED.

A couple of long, tense hours pass. The rain periodically beats down on the roof, with an occasional rumble in the distance, but nothing to get excited about. They try to listen to the menial conversations between the two men outside.

With all the empty time to fill, Zach filters many scenarios through his head of how that dreaded first conversation with his father will go. He is so concerned with the conversation's outcome that his thoughts find their way out of his mouth. He whispers, "How are we going to explain this to Dad? Will he ever trust us again? He will be so mad when we walk in the house."

"Zach, relax. He won't even know we've been gone. Remember, we have a time machine and we can return whenever we want. I programmed EMITT, so we will arrive soon after we left. He won't even know we were gone."

Another rumble in the sky.

"Zane, that's a fantastic plan. And once back, we can explain our events to Dad when we're ready." This relieves Zach's mind and allows him to become focused again. "I don't like any of our ideas to attach the key to the cleat. I will try to scare them off the porch and somehow steal the ribbon from Benjamin and wrap it around the cleat."

"I agree," Zane says. "I don't know how you would plan for somebody's reaction to being scared, because it could go several different ways. Let's do this: Before you open the door, I will shake the mouse to take it out of screen saver mode. You do your thing on the porch and when you're ready, holler at me and I will press 'Enter.' If we have the lightning, the events will start and we will be back home in time to pick up Dad and his two friends and nobody will be the wiser."

"It's not much of a plan, but that's all we have," Zach states. "All we need to do now is be quiet, listen to what they say, and be ready."

A few more minutes pass. "Zach, this was a pretty cool idea to recreate Benjamin Franklin's kite experiment. Not only did we perform the experiment, but now we get to watch Benjamin Franklin perform it as well. How many people can say that?"

"It is pretty cool, isn't it?"

"I'm glad you talked me into it."

Another hour ticks along. Zach whispers, "It's pretty quiet out there. You don't think they left, do you?"

"No. I think they're waiting for the lightning, just like us."

Boom, boom! Thunder bursts, sharp and quick, from a nearby lightning strike. Rumbling trails across the sky.

"William, the lightning is much closer," Benjamin says.

"I wish it would hurry. My body is shivering from the cold."

Boom, crackle, crackle, boom! Both men jump. Thunder erupts in the clouds from a bolt of lightning they spot exploding onto a nearby tree. A puff of smoke billows up from the flames of the sturdy branch that now dangles. The rain quickly extinguishes the trees flames. Another series of rumbles ramble across the heavy, swollen clouds.

"My goodness," Benjamin shouts. "That one was close."

Rumbles growl through the dark and angry cumulonimbus. But still no signs of a lightning strike to the kite.

Boom! Another lightning strike farther away.

"William, many lightning strikes have occurred around us, but none has struck the kite. I am beginning to believe my theory is incorrect. If this experiment has proven anything, it has proven we are a couple of fools flying a kite in a lightning storm. If it does not happen soon, we may want to pick our equipment up and go home."

"Father, I am sorry. I know you wanted to..."

"Wait! William, look." Benjamin stares closely at the twine. "The strands of the twine, they are standing straight up, all evenly separated from each other. Could this be it?" Benjamin looks down at the Leyden jar, then back up at the key. "What if..."

Zach throws open the door and yells, "Get off my porch," scaring the living daylights out of both men. William bolts out into the rain. Benjamin scrambles backwards and trips, causing him to release his grip on the ribbon.

Zach spots the ribbon slipping away. He reaches out and grabs it just before it flies off with the wind. He quickly wraps the ribbon around the steel support, pulling the key tight up against the metal cleat of the support. He screams, "Now, Zane, now!" Not wanting to let go of the ribbon, he holds on tight and closes his eyes.

Zane presses enter. He hears the woman's voice on the computer say, "Password accepted. Time travel sequence initiated." Zane looks up to the acrylic tube; the colors start to spin, faster and faster. Again, the crackling static noise electrifies the air. The electrical arcs swarm EMITT, exactly as they did the first time. Zane screams, "Cover your eyes!"

Then, as expected, a loud bang and a brilliant flash of light knocks Zach to the floor of the porch.

TWELVE

SATURDAY, JUNE 8, 2019

A **FEW SECONDS** pass. Zach lies on the porch, his right shoulder against the side of EMITT. He moves his hand. It touches a foreign object, but he's unsure what it may be. He opens his eyes, and this time he's not blinded. "OH MY GOD!" he exclaims and scrambles his way inside EMITT with a frightened expression on his face. He stares at Zane and points outside.

"Zach, are you okay?" Zane questions. He stands up and steps to the door. "OH MY GOD!"

There lying on the front porch is Benjamin Franklin.

Benjamin sits up and immediately starts to scream, "Lord help me! I have been blinded. Lord, please let me see again." After several seconds, his vision's whiteout begins to fade. "Thank you, Lord. I can see. I can see. Thank you. Thank you. Thank you."

Benjamin does not yet realize it, but both boys stand in the doorway looking down at him, their eyes wide open and mouths agape. "Zane, what have we done?" Zach says.

As Benjamin attempts to stand up, he hears the voice. He looks up and sees two teenage boys staring at him and screams again. He stumbles backwards, this time off the front edge of the porch, and lands on his butt in a puddle on the sidewalk from the morning's rain.

"Who are you? Where did you come from?" Benjamin questions in an excited but demanding tone. "Why did you jump out and scare us like that? William? William? Where are you, William?" He looks around, not grasping his surroundings.

He looks back at the two boys as he again attempts to stand up. "Where is William? Where is William?" he demands. "What have you done with my William? I don't understand, what has happened? Please explain yourself."

"Mr. Franklin, are you okay," Zach says.

"How do you know my name? Do I know you?"

"No, you do not," Zach replies. "Uh…um." He stumbles for the right words. "My name is Zach Long, and this is my brother Zane. Something very weird has just happened to all three of us, but we can explain. But for us to do so you will need to calm down for a minute. You will need to trust us for a minute and we can explain. But we need the opportunity to do so. Can you do that?"

"Trust you! Why should I trust you? I don't even *know* you. You jump out and scare us half to death and now you want us to trust you?" Still looking around, he asks, "Where is my William? What have you done with him?"

"Please, Mr. Franklin, if you come inside, we will explain it to you. You're in a different time and we need a minute to explain it to you. Please come inside and sit down," Zane pleads.

With the sun peeking through a sliver of the clouds, Benjamin realizes he is standing on an unusual surface, which he has not seen before. Though confused, he recognizes the odd cabin but notices several large objects of various sizes lined in a row. A few more of these objects pass by in opposite directions of each other. He turns around and sees the Philadelphia skyline of high-rise buildings. With eyes spread wide, he gasps, "Oh Lord, where am I? The lightning must have killed me, though this is not what I expected of heaven."

"Mr. Franklin," Zane calls out, "please come inside. We must talk for a minute and explain what has happened. It's important."

Benjamin, still confused, picks up his hat that fell on the ground during the confusion. He cautiously steps inside. He steps in close to the two boys, his face only inches away from Zach's.

Zach leans back.

"Are you two angels?" Benjamin asks.

"No, sir, we are not, and you are very much alive."

"Is this the God you worship?" he says, pointing to the Spiderman image on Zach's shirt.

"No, he is a fictional superhero."

A scared, confused expression grows on Benjamin's face.

"Again, this is my brother Zane and I am Zach. Please, have a seat. You're in a bit of shock right now."

Benjamin sits in the chair. He notices the computer screens, the acrylic tube, and the other electronics. Confused and scared, he asks, "What is all of this?"

"Let us start from the beginning," Zach begins. "We accidentally traveled back in time from the year 2019."

"What?" Benjamin shouts. "You cannot travel through time. That is not possible," he declares.

"Well," Zane replies, "we can in the future. At least now we can," he says, glancing at Zach. "I know this will be hard to understand, but what we are about to tell you is true and we can prove it. First, you were not supposed to see us and you most definitely were not supposed to come back with us to 2019. That was an accident."

"2019!" Benjamin cries out. "You want me to believe that I have traveled into the future, accidentally, to the year 2019? Accidentally?"

"Yes, sir, that is correct," Zach replies.

"That's absurd." Benjamin sits with an exasperated expression, lips pinched and shaking his head. "This must be a nightmare," he mumbles.

"No, sir, it's not a nightmare," Zane replies in a reassuring tone.

"There is more. Our father built this time machine, "EMITT," but he has not been able to make it work. Apparently, he had a problem but is unsure how to fix it. We weren't even aware he was building a time machine. Anyway, we were asked to bring EMITT downtown, so our father could work with a couple of his colleagues to help him figure out the problem."

"EMITT?" Benjamin asks with another puzzled expression.

"Our father named this trailer EMITT," Zach replies. "We think EMITT stands for something, but we don't know what.

"Anyway, Zane and I decided to recreate your famous kite experiment, and somehow the lightning being drawn through the kite's twine activated the machine and it sent us into the past. We don't know exactly how it works; we just know that it does. We believe that the lightning is the missing link that our father has been looking for to make EMITT work."

Zach continues, but his explanation comes off as rambling. "We accidentally traveled back to 1752, but we were supposed to pick them up at the hotel. However, we fixed that problem, because we set our arrival time to be fifteen minutes earlier than when he would have called us to pick them up."

Benjamin is now more lost and confused than before Zach's explanation.

"Speaking of that," Zane says, "what time is it? Dad should be calling anytime now."

Zach pulls his phone out of his pocket. "Holy crap," Zach shouts. "It's ten minutes after three. You said we would be back before he would call. How did we miss the time?"

"I don't know. I entered the time and date so we would be on time. I don't know what happened."

"Dad must be furious with us right now. Zane, we're screwed."

Benjamin notices a man in his early forties, with shoulder-length, dirty blond hair and a brown scraggly beard, peek around the corner of the door. He recognizes the man. "Bernard? Bernard Ranter, is that you?"

The man takes off running. Both boys look at each other, then at

Benjamin. "Do you know him?" Zach shouts.

"Yes. We worked together for a few years, but recently I embarrassed him, though it was not intentional..."

But before he could continue, the boys bolt out of the trailer after the man. "Stop! Wait! Stop!"

Bernard, fit and faster than the boys, keeps running. He clinches his brown tricorn hat in his right hand and his long brown coat flaps behind him as he races away. After a couple of blocks, he rips off his coat, balls it up, and bolts into an alley between the buildings.

The boys realize his speed has created a separation between them, but they continue the chase. They bolt into the alley after him. A little more than halfway down they see Bernard on top of a chain-link fence that impedes their path. Bernard hops down on the other side and picks up his coat and hat that he threw over. He glances back at them, wearing knee-length brown breeches, a long-sleeve V-neck white shirt, white leggings, and short brown boots, then races away. By the time they reach the fence, Bernard has already reached the other end of the alley and turned out of sight.

Zach's hands clinch the chain-link fence, where he shouts in a deflated tone, "Come back…we can help." At that exact moment, a bus passes by the opposite end of the alley and Zach realizes that he probably can't hear him.

They look at each other.

Winded from the chase, Zach gasps for air with his hands on his hips and his back at a slight arch backwards. He says, "Now what? We can't let him run loose in the city."

"I agree, but we can't seem to catch him either," Zane replies, bent over with his hands on his knees, also panting from their chase. "We need to get back to Mr. Franklin. We can look for Bernard later."

"All right. But, Zane, we need to find him. Like Benjamin, I would imagine he has family and friends that would be curious to where he went or what happened to him. And, Benjamin and this Bernard guy, they don't belong here. William probably thinks his dad is dead. We have to send them back home."

"That's a good point. I didn't even think about their families. I agree, we have to send them back home."

"And Zane, our problems are multiplying by the minute. Not only have we missed Dad's call and embarrassed him in front of his colleagues, we travel in his time machine before he has the opportunity to try it out. We go to 1752, pick up Benjamin freaking Franklin of all people, and a possible enemy of his, and bring them both back to 2019. Then, we let the enemy run loose in Philadelphia, totally lost. Even with a plan, I don't think we could have screwed this day up any worse."

"I know it sounds really bad, Zach, but we need to focus on one problem at a time. We need to take care of Mr. Franklin first, then we can figure out how to find this Bernard guy."

The boys hustle back to EMITT.

They find Benjamin staring at the acrylic tube. Astonished by its beauty, he hears the boys and turns toward them. "Now that I have had a few minutes alone to gather my thoughts and process the events that have occurred, as farfetched as it may be," he says, scratching his head, "I have many questions."

"First, did you catch Bernard?"

"No," Zach replies. "Hopefully, he will come back, since this is the only familiar place to him. He will realize how lost he is, and if he heard any of our conversation, he may realize we can help him."

"I hope so, because that man cannot be trusted to run rampant in this era. He is not afraid of anything and that makes him dangerous. He is greedy but has nothing. He wants to be respected but never helps anyone. He is always after success even if he must cheat, instead of doing the hard work. He needs to be found as soon as possible. There is no telling what he will do in this era."

"We can wait around a little bit," Zach replies, "but we will need to go home soon so we can explain to our father what has happened. I'm sure he's upset with us right now. He was adamant that we not be late and now we have missed them altogether. He will be furious when he sees us."

"Where is William?" Benjamin asks again. "Is he okay?"

"Yes, he is fine and still in 1752," Zach replies. "I would imagine he is a bit confused at what has happened, but I can't imagine he would tell anybody. If he did, people in your era would say he's crazy. So, I believe he will keep it to himself."

"The Leyden jar!" Zane cries out. "Mr. Franklin's experiment to capture the lightning in the Leyden jar. We need to preserve history and find out if he captured it."

"Are you serious?" Benjamin asks rhetorically. "You just brought me and another man that does not like me into the future and you're worried about whether I captured lightning in a Leyden jar? I believe there are other important issues to deal with right now."

"No, Zane is right. Mr. Franklin, you need to check the Leyden jar to see if the jar has been charged by the lightning. It's very important that you verify this."

The two boys step outside; Benjamin follows behind them. "There's the Leyden jar, lying on its side," Zach says as he points to it. He reaches down to stand it back up, but pulls his hand back before he grabs the jar. "No, no, no, no, not this time. I'm not touching that thing."

"Oh, you finally learned from your previous mistakes," Zane says, poking fun at Zach. "Look, the wire on top of the jar is bent, almost as if it melted."

"That is the wire that attaches to the key," Benjamin determines.

"There's the kite." Zane points to the vacant lot. "Wait here." He marches inside EMITT and returns with their homemade discharge tool. "Mr. Franklin, here is the tool. Check the jar and see if you get a spark."

With the three of them bent down, Benjamin touches the two electrodes with the tool. *Zap*! A stout spark occurs. In a somewhat elated tone, Benjamin says, "Oh my goodness, it is true. Lightning is electricity. It is proven." Benjamin looks at the two boys with a smile on his face and again states, "Lightning is electricity. That is why I flew the kite. This means that sharp-pointed rods attached to the tops of buildings will be beneficial as I have hoped." But with the elation of his theory proved, his face droops with sadness.

"What's wrong?" Zach asks.

"I wish William were here to see this. He was so looking forward to this."

"Me too."

"Hey guys, we need to get ready to go home," Zane says. "We need to pick everything up and set it inside. We need to explain to Dad what has happened and if Bernard does not return soon, we will need Dad's help to find him. Zach, can you pick up the Leyden jar without getting shocked this time?"

"I think so. But I will discharge it one more time for safety's sake."

"Mr. Franklin and I will take care of the kite." Zane picks up the stick of twine and hands it to Benjamin. "Here, you wrap up the twine, and I will retrieve the kite."

With their items stored away, they sit on the porch, leaning up against the sidewall of EMITT, legs stretched straight out, to keep an eye out for Bernard. They talk with Benjamin for the next hour, answering his questions about the time travel. Eventually, the conversation gravitates toward today's society.

Zach explains, "Mr. Franklin, a 2019 society is far different from that of 1752. You may be overwhelmed with what you see. There are so many inventions that may shock you and possibly raise more questions than they answer. So, be patient and we will try to explain what we can."

"The surface that I fell onto earlier, what is it?" Benjamin asks.

"That is concrete. It is a hard surface made from a mix of sand, water, crushed rock, and some other chemical compounds. It's very solid and used to pave roads across the country for us to drive on. They also use it to build buildings, bridges, and so much more."

"I am a little familiar with the pavement of roads. I recently proposed to have the streets of Philadelphia paved to reduce the amount of mud and dust created from the dirt in the streets, but that has not yet been approved by the council members. But you said to pave roads to drive on. What do you mean by drive?" Benjamin asks.

"We have cars for transportation like you have horses, except our machines go much faster and never need a rest, but they require fuel to operate," Zane replies. "It's one of the great inventions of the nineteenth century."

"That is impressive, but what is a car?" he asks, with eyebrows raised.

"Wow, this will be harder than I thought to explain. It's so basic to us. The car is a vehicle with four wheels, an engine, seats, a steering wheel, and pedals for the gas and brakes. The engine is powered by gasoline. We press the gas pedal and the car goes. We press the brake pedal and the car stops, and the steering wheel controls its direction. It's much more complex than that, but it's an efficient method of transportation and it allows us to cover large distances in a short period of time. It's a necessity in our era, and for the most part we can go wherever we want. It's how our society gets around."

"That is amazing!" Benjamin remarks. "Is that those odd-looking buggies I have seen moving around?"

"That's them," Zane confirms. "Zach, maybe we should close up EMITT and take her home."

"I agree," Zach says as he looks back at Benjamin, "but before we do, I have a question. Would you prefer us to call you Benjamin or Mr. Franklin?"

"Benjamin, please."

"Benjamin it is," Zach replies.

"Benjamin," Zane says, "you will need a new set of clothes. Mom always has clothes for the center. She should be able to help. I don't know if you realize it or not, but you are a well-recognized person in Philadelphia, even today. The clothes you have on is the way you have been portrayed for many, many years. I believe the more you blend in the better off you will be. It will be temporary until we can take you back home."

"If you both believe that is best, then I too agree. Do you boys have a plan to take me home?" Benjamin asks, still trying to digest his situation.

"Not yet," Zane replies, "but we will. We need to take care of a few issues first, like find Bernard. We need to take both of you back home at the same time. Time travel is a little complicated and a little risky and we only want to do it once."

Zach stands up and steps off the porch. "It's been over an hour and there's no sign of Bernard. Let's get EMITT ready to go. Zane, while you take down the jacks, I will start the truck and start cooling it down."

Zach hops in the truck and starts it. Benjamin stands back and watches in awe, his eyes wide open and jaw agape as the truck rumbles to an idle.

"Amazing!" Benjamin exclaims. "I shall enjoy this ride." He then mumbles to himself, "This might turn out to be an interesting experience."

Zach returns to EMITT and lowers the support posts on each end of the porch, then presses the button under a protective cover at the front of the trailer. The upper canopy of the porch lowers down and closes tight to the side of the trailer, then the floor of the porch raises up to meet the upper door in the middle. With both doors closed, Benjamin sees the word "EMITT" written in white pointed letters against the dark space background of our solar system.

"Amazing!" Benjamin exclaims again. "The doors close by the press of a button. How? How does that work?"

"Electricity," Zane replies. "You should know. You discovered it."

"I discovered it?" Benjamin questions. "I did not discover electricity. I only intended to prove that lightning is electricity, and *that* you witnessed."

"Actually, you proved it 267 years ago," Zane says. "You just weren't expecting a time machine to whisk you away to the future to do so. But the lightning is what allowed us to travel back to your era, and back to

2019."

"Oh my goodness," Benjamin screams. "Bernard jumped into your car!"

THIRTEEN

SATURDAY, JUNE 8, 2019

THE ENGINE REVS high, then reduces.

"Hey, that's my truck," Zach hollers as he races toward it. "Get out of the truck!"

Right before he reaches the door, the truck slowly pulls away, then like a horse out of the starting gate it takes off, swerving erratically, speeding through the intersection's red light, narrowly missing two cars as they slam on their brakes, tires screeching as the drivers lay on their horns.

"You jackass!" screams one of the drivers while giving the middle finger.

Zach, Zane, and Benjamin run after him, but it's impossible to keep up. They watch the truck speed away as it swerves back and forth across the road. Zach screams at the top of his lungs, "Stop! Stop! You don't know how to drive!"

"Damn it!" Zach shouts. "Now my truck has been stolen by some guy from the 1700s who doesn't even know what a truck is, much less how to drive it. Damn it. This has been one hell of a day." Zach continues to shout as he now paces in circles, pulling at his hair.

"Son," Benjamin says with disgust, "that language is a bit vulgar and I do not approve. I would ask you to refrain from its use while in my presence."

"I'm sorry, Mr. Franklin. My apologies. That truck is my pride and it's very expensive. My father will have my head when he finds out today's events. This day has not gone the way it was supposed to. Again, please forgive me."

"Apology accepted."

"Wait, don't you have the keys?" Zane asks.

"No, I left them in the storage console of the truck."

"Brilliant," Zane replies with sarcasm, throwing his arms up in the air.

Benjamin speaks. "I assume the keys are critical to the car's functioning?"

"Kind of. Zach's truck has a fob. The fob is like an electronic key that allows you to start the truck from a distance, lock and unlock the doors, open the tailgate, and set off the panic alarm. Things like that. But the truck won't run if it does not detect the fob within close proximity of the truck. This prevents a thief from stealing the vehicle. But with the fob in the storage console…" Zane gives his brother an accusatory look. "…the truck will work as designed."

"I am confused," Benjamin says. "You said it was a car, but I have heard both of you call it a truck. Which is it?"

"I know, it's a little confusing," Zane replies, "but there are many different types of vehicles or automobiles. For example, that is a car." He points to a passing Toyota Corolla. "That one is a truck." He points to a pickup. "And that is a van." He points to a minivan. "They are all vehicles, or automobiles, but sometimes we incorrectly use the word 'car' as a generic term for a vehicle."

"Ah," Benjamin replies with a confused expression. "I think I understand. What do we do now?"

"We have to find Bernard," Zach replies. "We can't just let him run free. We have to find him before he hurts himself or someone else."

"Zane, we need your truck to pull EMITT home."

"I know," Zane replies, disappointed. "I need to flag down a cab."

"We could call Dad. He could pick us up and tow EMITT home," Zach says. "Although, that won't be a fun ride home."

"Wait," Zane blurts out. "My phone—it's in your truck."

"Good idea. Call Bernard?"

"No. We can track it on your phone. We can find Bernard by tracking my phone."

"Great idea!"

"Track your phone? What does that mean?" Benjamin asks.

"I'll explain it later," Zach says.

"Zach, let's not call Dad yet. We need to find Bernard and we need to do it as soon as possible. I will catch a cab home, sneak up to my truck. If I'm lucky, Mom or Dad won't see me and I will be back down here in an hour or two. You and Benjamin stay with EMITT. When I get back we will search for Bernard."

"Zane, how much battery life do you think is on your phone?"

"I'm not sure, but I did not charge it last night, so probably not a lot."

Zane looks for a cab and before long he flags one down, then hops in and provides the address to the driver. They drive away, leaving Zach and Benjamin with EMITT.

FOURTEEN

SATURDAY, JUNE 8, 2019

"**WHAT IN GOD'S** name is this thing?" Bernard mutters to himself as he erratically speeds away. "A buggy with power, incredible power...and fast. Never have I experienced such power. You control it with this round circle. This pedal makes it go. I wonder if this other pedal stops it." He jams the brake pedal hard and the truck comes to an abrupt stop. Bernard slams into the steering wheel, slipping off the seat.

"Whoa! Maybe a little less pressure on the pedal," he says as he pulls himself back into the seat.

"Unbelievable how it stops and goes with your feet. I am amazed." He presses the gas pedal. Again, he speeds off, extremely fast. He relaxes his pressure and learns how to adjust the speed with the pedal.

He realizes he is swerving all over the road, unlike the other vehicles. He tries to steady himself while at the same time figure out how the futuristic buggy works. "If I hold this round circle straight, the buggy stays straight. I need to stop and figure this buggy out—how others move about with theirs and what these buttons and levers do." He looks over his shoulder. "I think I am far enough away that Benjamin and those two boys can't catch me."

Bernard steers the truck to the side of the road and applies a little less pressure on the brake pedal. The truck slows down to a slow roll, then a quick jolt as it stops. "If I put the lever back where it was when I started, the buggy should stay stopped." He does so and takes his foot off the brake pedal, relieved that it does not move. "There you go, Bernard," he says, proud of himself. "You will have this futuristic buggy figured out in no time."

He starts to press buttons and turn knobs. Suddenly, the driver's side window rolls down. Though a little startled, he watches in amazement. He presses the button again but nothing happens. He pulls it in the opposite direction and the window starts back up. He presses another button and the window on the other side rolls down.

A man walks past on the sidewalk and nods to him. "Nice truck."

Bernard smiles back at him and, trying to blend in, says, "Thank you."

"So, they call this powered wagon a truck," he says to himself. "All right, what are the others doing?" He watches the other vehicles. "They stay in between the white dotted lines." He notices a light flash on one side of a car when it switches to another lane. "How do they make that flash?" He presses more buttons and moves levers to see what they do, learning the operation of each.

He quickly turns another knob and the truck's stereo volume raises fast and very loud. At that precise moment, the heavy metal guitar lick of the song "Eruption" by Van Halen screams in his ears. Bernard jumps back in his seat with a frightened expression. He scrambles to turn the knob back down. Startled from the loud noise, he sits for a moment. "I will not turn that knob again."

He looks at the dashboard in front of him and notices the gauges, but he does not understand their meaning. Again, he watches more vehicles and notices they stop at the intersection ahead of him. He notices the red light at the intersection, and when it turns green the vehicles move again.

He watches the others to see what else he can learn in his self-taught crash course of driving. After a few minutes, he believes he has enough information to continue. "I better leave before Benjamin and the two boys catch up to me," he mumbles. He pulls away, learning how to control the go pedal and the stop pedal with his feet. He follows the road to wherever it takes him.

He turns onto a major street that's wider and a much larger street than the others and hopes it will lead him away from town. He makes the turn and alarms sound inside the cabin, because he does not stay in his lane. He barely avoids an accident with another vehicle.

The other driver lays on his horn. "Stay in your lane, dumbass!" he blares out the window at Bernard.

"Sorry! Sorry!" He hollers, realizing his error. "I need to be more careful. I could not explain myself if I collided with another."

As he becomes more comfortable with the truck, he recounts the day's events. "Those two boys told Benjamin about traveling through time. I cannot believe I have traveled through time, although I cannot explain my situation. And, this is a futuristic place. Nothing appears as it does at home. But if I did travel through time, where am I and how do I find my way back home?"

Bernard has now traveled several miles. The more he replays the events, the more he realizes that time travel must be a possibility. It's the only explanation that makes any sense. Reality sets in. "I am hopelessly lost in time," he blurts out. "The only way back home is with the boy's time machine. I need to go back there and steal it, but I am not sure where 'there' is."

"If I do find it, I have no idea how to operate it." His mind contemplates a moment longer. "I figured out how to operate this truck; maybe I can figure out how to operate the time machine. Then I can travel home, without Benjamin."

"But first, I have to figure out where I was." He ponders for a moment. "The tall buildings. That's where I need to go." He exits the road, but it leads him in a different direction. He has no idea where he's going.

Several minutes later, the truck hesitates and sputters. It jerks again, then a couple more times. "What is happening?" The engine stops. He steers it off the road. He presses the button that says start, but to no avail.

"Now what?" Bernard shouts. "Now the truck is broken and I have no idea where I am much less where I have been. What a mess I am in. I should have stayed in bed." He sits for a moment and searches through the inside of the truck and notices an object in the seat next to him. "What is this?" He picks up Zane's cell phone and looks it over, but he has no idea what it is, much less how to operate it.

He presses a button. The screen turns on and displays an image of a night sky with thousands of stars. It startles him. He notices near the top of the screen the time, the day of the week, and the date displayed, but no year. At the bottom of the screen it says, "Press Home to Unlock." Not sure what it means by "Home," he presses the only button at the bottom. The screen changes to a set of numbers and says, "Touch ID or Enter Passcode." He tries a couple of numbers, but nothing happens. He mumbles to himself, "I have no idea what this thing does, but it may be helpful later." He stuffs it into his pocket.

After a while he realizes he is not making any progress and decides, "I guess I need to continue on foot."

He steps out of the truck and walks in the direction he was traveling.

FIFTEEN

SATURDAY, JUNE 8, 2019

"STOP HERE. I'LL walk the rest of the way," Zane informs the cabbie and pays his fare.

At the end of their street, Zane studies their house and finds his truck is the only vehicle in the driveway, but he has no way of determining if his parents' vehicles are in the garage.

Zane sneaks up to his truck, hops in, starts it, and speeds away. He arrives back downtown with Zach and Benjamin. He slips into the vacant space in front of EMITT, which Zach and Benjamin have held for his arrival.

He rolls down the passenger window to talk to Zach and Benjamin. "Mom and Dad were both gone. I assume they're out looking for us. Do not take any calls from them until we find Bernard, then we can explain."

"I agree," Zach says. "But I'm a little surprised they haven't called. Go ahead and back up to EMITT's hitch. I'll guide you, then we can track Bernard."

"All right."

Zach and Benjamin stand on the sidewalk while Zane backs his truck to EMITT.

Benjamin's curiosity level rises, triggering several questions in a row. "How does the trailer connect to the truck? What keeps the trailer from breaking away from the truck? What do the wires do? Is it difficult for the truck to pull the trailer?"

"Whoa! Slow down there, Benjamin. I'll explain it to you."

Zach hollers out to Zane, while motioning with one hand, "Come on back."

Zane eases the truck backwards with the use of the rearview camera to guide the truck's hitch and ball underneath the tongue of the trailer.

"That's good," Zach hollers.

The truck stops.

"Benjamin, come closer and watch," Zach says.

Benjamin steps closer.

Zach grabs the crank handle of the adjustable wheel and turns it. "I am lowering the trailer's tongue down onto the ball." The ball does not sit perfectly. He bumps the truck and the hitch slips over the ball. He finishes cranking the wheel up to secure it for traveling. "Then I slip the latch over, and now it is latched in place. But I need to insert the padlock, which will keep the latch from coming loose. Then, I plug in the trailer lights and we're ready to go."

"Trailer lights?" Benjamin asks, puzzled.

"The brake, turn signal, and taillights for driving. I guess I should explain their function too. When we press the brakes to stop the truck, the brake lights come on so the cars behind us know we're stopping. It's the same for the turn signals. When we turn on the blinker, the light on the side we want to turn toward will flash, telling others we are turning. The trailer's lights become an extension of the truck's and this cable is that extension."

"That is utterly amazing!" Benjamin gasps.

Wow, this is so basic, Zach thinks. *We learn this stuff when we are kids and don't even think about it. But explain it to a man like Benjamin Franklin and for him it's a new and astonishing concept.*

"Zach, you ready? C'mon, let's go. We need to find Bernard."

"Benjamin, you hop in the back," Zach says as he opens the door for Benjamin.

Benjamin notices an object deploy from underneath the truck. "Oh my goodness, what is that?" he asks while pointing.

"Running boards. They automatically extend out when the doors are opened. They make it easier to get in the truck."

Benjamin climbs in, astonished.

Zach climbs in the front passenger seat and turns around to look at Benjamin. "You need to put your seat belt on. Grab that strap," he points, "and latch it into the buckle there in the seat."

Benjamin follows his directions and latches himself in.

"This is a little scary," Benjamin speaks out, as if they could be hurt in the truck. "Is this dangerous?"

"Yes," Zane answers. "That's exactly why we have seatbelts. If we're involved in an accident, they will keep us in our seats and we won't fly around in the vehicle. They are a safety feature of the vehicle, and everyone's required to wear them while the car is in motion."

"You mean truck, don't you?" Benjamin says, correcting him.

"He is quick," Zach comments.

"This is incredible. The air is cool inside. It is not hot like outside. How does that work?"

"The truck has an air conditioner. It keeps the truck cool. Most everyone has air conditioners nowadays. They are a necessity on hot days like today. We also have heaters for the winter. We can adjust the temperature with this dial," Zane says as he points to the controls.

"Unbelievable!"

Zach pulls his phone from his pocket and presses a button. "The tracker opens." He selects Zane's phone. "Holy crap, he's over by..." He pauses for a second, zooming in on the screen. "He's near..." He pauses again.

"Well, where is he?" Zane asks.

"He's on Hog Island Road."

"Where's that?" Zane asks.

"It's down south at the edge of the Delaware. Go over the Platt Memorial Bridge and I will guide you from there."

Zane drives in the instructed direction.

"Benjamin," Zach says, "let me explain this phone and some of the technology that we have today. This is an iPhone, also called a smartphone. With smartphones, we can do a lot of things right from the palm of our hands. We can text, send emails, make phone calls, even do video chats, which allows us to communicate with another person anywhere in the world."

"I don't understand. Text, email, phone calls—what does that mean?"

"Oh boy," Zach says

Zane chuckles.

He looks at Zane. "You know he will need an explanation for everything we talk about or he sees."

"I see that now."

He turns back to Benjamin. "A phone call is where we can call another person's phone, regardless of their location, and have a conversation with them as if they were right next to us. A text is a simple message between mobile phones where we provide quick information or maybe a picture we want to share. An email is another method to send messages or large file attachments, like videos or letters, but usually they are sent between computers, but they can also be sent through phones. But there are many ways to send messages."

"What is a video?" Benjamin asks with a confused look on his face.

Zach gives a quick dumbfounded laugh. "Um, a video is where we can video something or somebody in action and then play it back and watch it over and over again. Say for example you were to do something silly and I happened to video you. I could replay the video and watch it as many times as I want. But then, Zane says he wants to see it. I could send the video to him, via text or email, and he would have it on his phone and he could watch it as well."

"I don't understand. How do you send it to him?"

"I type a text and attach the video to the text and press 'Send.' Then, it shows up on Zane's phone."

"No, you don't understand my question. How does it get out of your phone and into Zane's? It does not jump from one to the other."

"Yeah, it kind of does. It's complicated, but I'll try a simple explanation." Zach starts, but he lacks confidence in his knowledge of the complete process. "The information is transferred via satellite signals. A satellite is a device in the sky that receives and sends signals to phones and other electronic devices and routes the signal to the phone you have called." The more he talks the more he realizes how crazy his explanation must sound to Benjamin. "Okay, it's complicated, but it works quite well. Trust me."

"Ah. An Archibald Spence-like explanation."

"Hey, I learned about him too," Zach scowls playfully with pinched lips, nose, and eyes. "He could operate his electrical contraptions but didn't know how the electricity actually worked."

"Ah, very good. But how could you possibly know about him?"

"We learned about him when learning about you in school. Anyway," he continues, "we can take pictures…oh, and surf the internet."

"Take pictures and surf the what?"

Zach switches to camera mode and points the phone at Benjamin. *Click*.

"What was that?"

Zach pulls up the photo and shows Benjamin the picture of himself in the back seat.

He gasps at the image on the screen. "How did you do that?"

"With the camera."

"Unbelievable! And what was that other thing you said, something about surfing?"

"The internet," Zach repeats. "Wow, the internet, that could take a while," Zach mumbles to himself, wondering how he will explain it. "I will not explain how the internet works, but I'll tell you what we can do with it. You can search for whatever you want. Say you want a new hat. We could search the internet, find the one you like, and buy it. In a couple of days, it will arrive at our front door."

"Really," Benjamin pinches one eye closed and replies in a disbelieving tone.

Zach does a search for Colonial hats and finds several. He hands the phone to Benjamin to show him what he has found.

"That is unbelievable. Just amazing that you can see all of that on this little device." Benjamin studies the hats. "That is a mighty fine hat and they look a bit nicer than what we could purchase at Mr. Johnson's general store."

Zach takes the phone back and replies, "That is a nice hat."

"I admit, your phone is an interesting device. But you're telling me you can call anyone, anywhere in the world, even buy whatever you want anywhere in the world, all right from the palm of your hands, and it shows up at your door a couple of days later."

"Correct."

Benjamin chuckles and sits back in his seat. "That sounds a little farfetched and the two of you expect me to believe that. If you purchased the item in England, how would it arrive at your front door as you say?"

"Simple," Zane jumps in. "UPS ships it right to our house."

"You two are pulling my leg." Benjamin turns and glances out the window and realizes he is on a huge bridge, high in the air, and passing through the bridge's trusses at the top. "Oh, my," he gasps. "This is amazing. I have never had such an incredible view of Philadelphia. The bridges in the future are huge. And look at the size of those ships. They are massive. How do you build a ship of that size? And look at how many there are. This is amazing."

"Take Island Avenue," Zach says as he points to the road sign. "Don't turn onto I-95. When you get to the intersection, turn right."

Zach returns to his conversation with Benjamin. "The bridges are pretty amazing. Without them, it would take forever to get anywhere. But back to the phones and the internet. It really does work like I said. I can show you."

"Every phone has a unique phone number," Zach continues. "If there is a person we want to call, we pull up their contact in our address book, select the phone number, and press 'Send.' It rings on their phone and they answer the call. They could be in London and we could talk to them as if they were right next to us."

"Well, if that is true," Benjamin replies, "why don't you call Bernard? He has Zane's phone. Maybe he will answer it and we can find him, instead of this tracking thing."

Both boys look at each other. "Not a bad idea," Zane acknowledges.

"Turn left onto Bartram," Zach quickly blurts out.

Zane makes the quick turn, nearly missing it.

Zach holds the phone up for Benjamin to see. "Watch, Benjamin." He opens the address book and types in Zane's name. His contact shows up in the screen, including a picture of Zane. He selects the contact, and the pertinent information displays on the screen.

"I am astonished," Benjamin exclaims.

Zach selects Zane's mobile phone number and presses 'Send.' He puts it on speaker, so Benjamin can hear and talk if Bernard answers the phone.

The phone rings several times, then goes to voice mail.

They hear Zane's message. "This is Zane. I am busy right now. Please leave a message and I will call you back soon. *Beep*."

Zach speaks. "Bernard, this is Zach, Zane, and Benjamin. If you get this message call us back. Just press the words 'Call Back.' We can help you." Zach presses the "End" button and switches back to the tracker.

"Right after we pass under the freeway, turn right on Industrial Highway," Zach instructs again.

Zane turns as directed. "Where are we going?" Zane asks.

"We're getting close," Zach replies. "It appears he stopped or at least he has not gone very far for a while."

"Maybe we can catch up to him," Benjamin replies.

"Could we be so lucky?" Zane asks rhetorically.

"We're only a couple of minutes away," Zach says. "Turn left on Fourth Street. In a minute, we will turn left on Tinicum Island Road, then a quick right onto Hog Island Road."

"Zach, it says no right turns."

"We have to find Bernard. Do it anyway."

Zane makes the illegal turn onto Hog Island Road. The road is lined with tall brownish-green grass, cattails, and bushes on either side, blocking their view of everything, other than the road before them.

Seconds later, Zach hollers, "There's my truck!"

Zane pulls off to the side of the road behind it. They watch for a minute but see no activity inside the truck.

Zach hops out and approaches cautiously. The other two follow.

"Hello," Zach shouts as a car passes. "Bernard, are you in there?"

No response.

They approach a little closer and Benjamin shouts, "Bernard, it's Benjamin. Remember, I accidentally got mixed up in this too. These boys can help us get home."

Zach cautiously creeps up to the window on the passenger side and looks inside. "He's not here."

They look around but see only the tall grass, cattails, and bushes. A couple hundred feet further, the road turns, limiting their view. Bernard is nowhere in sight.

Zach looks back at the tracker. "He must have hitched a ride from someone because he's on the move again," Zach determines.

"I wonder why he left the truck here?" Zane asks.

Zach hops in the truck and tries to start it. "It's out of gas. I saw a gas station about a mile back."

"Zach, do you have a gas can in your truck?"

"No."

"Me either."

"Wait. I may have seen one in EMITT's outhouse," Zach recalls.

They march to the front area of EMITT. Zane opens the door that appears to be an outhouse, because of the half-moon cutout on the door, but instead it is the room that houses EMITT's generator. "Dad, you're awesome. I knew he would have one in here." He picks it up and shakes it. "Crap, it's empty." He scours around the closet and finds some tubing and a funnel. He pulls out the red plastic gas can and the tubing. "We could siphon a little gas from my truck. That would get us to the gas station."

"Okay, let's do it. It'll be quicker than driving to the gas station."

They step to the driver's side of Zane's truck, careful to stay close and avoid any passing traffic. They open the gas tank door and start to feed the hose into the tank.

Benjamin leans up against the backside of EMITT's outhouse and reflects on the day's events. He hears a faint whining sound, but pays it no attention. He mumbles to himself, "I wonder if William is okay. I wonder what he is doing." The whining sound intensifies, but he still pays it no attention. "I wonder if William is worried about me. He must be scared wondering if his father is dead. That whining noise, what is it?"

He steps away from EMITT to see what is causing the high-pitched noise. As he steps out, a huge passenger jet passes overhead, only fifty feet above them, its landing imminent beyond the cattails at the Philadelphia International Airport.

"Aaaaahhhhh!" Benjamin screams at the top of his lungs. He shoots across the road and dives into the tall-grass-covered ditch across the street, his hands cover his ears to protect them from the four screaming jet engines above him.

The boys hear Benjamin scream, stop, and watch as he dives into the ditch. Both boys burst into hysterical laughter while slapping their hands on their legs, laughing so hard that they both begin to cough.

Benjamin, lying in the ditch, raises his head and looks at the boys with a petrified look on his face, a bit wet as part of his left arm and leg landed in the water. He shouts a petrified question, "What in God's name was that?"

After the boys gain their composure, Zach answers, "That was a Boeing 747 jumbo jet. One of the largest passenger jet airplanes we have today. There is one other passenger jet that is larger, but the 747 is an aviation icon, because of its recognizable hump at the front of the plane."

"Passenger jet?" Benjamin questions as he stands up. "It carries people?" he asks as he brushes himself off, still trembling from the ordeal. "You mean people can fly in the future?"

"Fly? Not only can we fly, but we've sent men to the moon!" Zach says.

"Oh now, you two are pulling my leg again," Benjamin chuckles. "You can't fly to the moon."

"No, really," Zach responds. "NASA sent astronauts into outer space and to the moon. I believe the first one was in the late 1960s," he says as he looks to Zane for some confirmation.

"Yeah, Zach's correct." He nods in agreement. "And the International Space Station is circling Earth with people working up there right now."

Benjamin is dumbfounded. "Is that another jumbo jet?" He points to a plane on approach in the distant clearing sky.

"It's not a jumbo, but it is another jet arriving to land," Zach responds. "It looks like a smaller regional jet. We call them jets or airplanes, or planes for short. It's kind of like the car thing: cars, trucks, and vans."

The boys return to their efforts to siphon gas from Zane's tank, but they cannot get the tube to slide down the tank's neck.

"We will need to buy some gas and come back," Zane says. "We can continue to look for Bernard then. We have him tracked, so we should be able to find him."

SIXTEEN

SATURDAY, JUNE 8, 2019

ON THEIR WAY to the gas station, Zach notices the title of his favorite rap song displayed on the truck's stereo. "Check this out, Benjamin." Zach turns up the volume. About halfway through the song, the boys join in and rap along to the lyrics. Their hand gestures keep with the beat of the song. The lyrics flow from the short, fast rap beat into the song's popular rhythmic melody.

Benjamin's eyes widen, his teeth grit together, and his head and body push back into his seat as if he is cornered with no place to escape. To him, the music's jarring words and the boys' hand gestures resemble a demon's song and dance. For a moment he is truly scared, then realizes the boys have been so good to him the entire time. He is only experiencing the future's unusual style of music.

Soon the song ends, and Zach turns the volume back down. "Ah, man, I love that song. That dude can rap."

"What in the world was that?" Benjamin shouts.

"That's rap music. Pretty cool, huh?" Zach asks.

"Cool? What? I don't know what that was, but that was not music. At least not the way I know music."

"Benjamin," Zach says, "we have many different types of music in our era. That was rap, but we also have pop, rock, classic rock, country, jazz, soul, and rhythm and blues. In our era, there are many different genres of music."

"Benjamin would probably like classical," Zane adds. "You know, with those violins and cellos and soft crap. Blah, he can have it. I will take rap, pop, or classic rock any day."

They arrive at the gas station. "Zane, if you fill the gas can, I'll pay for it and buy us some snacks and drinks," Zach says.

"That sounds good, because I'm hungry."

"Me too," Benjamin states.

"C'mon, Benjamin, I'll show you a modern-day convenience store."

They enter the store.

Benjamin is flabbergasted by the sight inside. The store is nothing like what he expected.

"Benjamin, let's grab some snacks. You can experience some of the junk foods we have nowadays."

While Benjamin browses the racks of different types of snack foods, Zach grabs three sandwiches from a refrigerator.

He returns to Benjamin. "Find anything you like?"

"I have no idea what these foods are. I will go with what you pick."

Zach laughs. "Here, we'll get some corn nuts and...some peanut butter crackers and...three bags of Cool Ranch Doritos. That should satisfy our hunger for a while."

Zach steps over to a large icebox near the counter. Inside are several types of iced-down drinks. "Benjamin, what would you like to drink?" Zach asks as he pushes through the ice. There's water, Coke, Sprite, Dr Pepper, root beer…whatever you like. Oh, even Fanta Orange." He starts to sing the Fanta jingle. "Don't you want a, want a Fanta. Don't you want a, want a Fanta." He does a little dance.

Benjamin looks at him with a crazy look. "What are you doing?" he asks.

"Sorry, dancing to the Fanta jingle. It's a commercial on TV. You would have to see it to understand. Anyway, what would you like?"

"I don't even know what these drinks are."

"Hear, hold these." He hands the sandwiches and snacks to Benjamin. "We will buy a water and four soft drinks for you to try. If you don't like any of the soft drinks, you can have the water. But I'm pretty sure you will like them all."

"Okay," Benjamin says with a cautiously agreeable tone.

At the checkout counter, the clerk scans each of the items. Each time Benjamin hears a beep.

"And the gas," Zach adds, pointing to the truck.

Benjamin is confused, but decides to stay quiet until he can be alone with Zach to ask questions.

The clerk says in a monotone voice, "The total is $25.27."

Zach opens the wallet app on his cell phone and holds the screen near the contactless scanner.

Beep. The scanner displays on its screen, "Payment Accepted."

Zach grabs their bag of goodies and turns to leave when the clerk says, "Great Benjamin Franklin costume. You look a lot like him. Are you playing him in a play?"

Not being prepared, Benjamin is quick to think and replies, "Uh, I am auditioning."

"Good luck," the clerk replies.

Once outside the store, Zach says, "Great reply about the audition. That was quick."

"Thanks. But I am curious, do you not pay for the items?"

"I paid. I used my credit card on my cell phone."

"Is that why you placed your phone over that thing?"

"Exactly. They call it tap and pay. When the cell phone is about an inch from the scanner, the scanner detects the credit card and charges the bill."

"I have credit at Mr. Johnson's General Store and I return to pay him for my items a couple times a month, but I know Jim Johnson very well and he trusts me. I did not get the impression you knew that man. Is everybody that trusting in this era?"

"No, no. You don't understand," Zach says, reaching for his wallet. He takes out his credit card and shows it to Benjamin. "This is a credit card. I have entered the card's information into the wallet app on my cell phone. If the store has a contactless scanner, like the one they had, I present the phone to the scanner. When the scanner detects my credit card, via the internet, it immediately sends the credit card company an electronic verification request. If the request determines I am authorized to use the card and there is enough credit available, the charge is approved.

"Every month, through the internet, the credit card company sends us an email statement showing all of our charges. We pay the bill online through our bank, and the credit card company pays the store for the items bought. It's all electronic and very fast."

"What happens if they don't have a scanner?" he asks, still a little confused.

"No matter what, they will have some type of scanner where we can slide the card through and pay the bill. Almost every store has them."

"That is incredible and fast, and no money ever changed hands," Benjamin exclaims.

Zane hollers, "Let's go. We're burning daylight. It will be dark soon and we need to find Bernard before the sun goes down, if that's possible."

They climb into Zane's truck and Zach gives each a sandwich and a bag of Doritos. "Benjamin," Zach says, "try one of the Cool Ranch Doritos?"

Zane pulls away.

Benjamin opens the bag and eats a chip. "Wow, that is fantastic. Unique triangle design and crisp. The flavor is zesty. It's like nothing I have ever tasted."

"Here, try one of these corn nuts?" Zach pours a few into his hand.

"Crunchy. I like these."

"Here, try one of these peanut butter crackers?"

Benjamin tries one. "Mm, this is really good. I love the flavor of the cracker and the peanut butter together. Fascinating! Your foods are fantastic!"

"If you liked those, you will love these. We have five different soft drinks: Coke, Sprite, root beer, Dr Pepper, and a Fanta Orange. Let's see which one you like best."

"The first one is a root beer," Zach says, opening the plastic bottle's screw top.

"Is root beer an alcohol, because this is not the time to be drinking?"

"No, no," Zach says with a laugh. "It's a soft drink. It's good. Try it?"

Benjamin takes a sip.

"WOW, this is fabulous! It fizzles and tickles the roof of my mouth. I like this one."

Zach hands him the Sprite. "This one has a lemon-lime flavor."

"Yum, this one is really good too. I only wish we had these at home. I need to know how to make these."

"Try this one. It's Dr Pepper."

"Um, that's good. Real sweet flavor."

"This one is Fanta Orange." Zach hands him the bottle.

"Oh, I like that. Fantastic orange flavor that's different from orange juice."

"Okay, here is the last one. It's a Coke."

Benjamin tries it. "Oh my goodness, this is indelibly delicious. Adding flavors to drinks is a novel idea. I am impressed with the flavor of the future. I liked the Coke the best. If you don't mind, I would like to drink it while I eat my sandwich."

"It's all yours."

They arrive at Zach's truck. With the gas poured in the tank, it takes Zach a few tries before the truck starts. Zane follows Zach and Benjamin back to the gas station. Benjamin watches Zach insert his credit card into the pump. He fills the truck with gas. Benjamin sees the total of $76.70, and the machine prints a receipt.

"Zach," Benjamin comments, "the gas is expensive compared to the food and drinks you bought."

"Yes, it is."

Zane is parked beside Zach's truck, both with their windows down.

Zach opens the tracker. "That's crazy. Bernard is back downtown, but it appears he's not moving."

"How did he get there?" Zane asks.

"He must have hitched a ride with somebody."

"I guess we're going back downtown?" Benjamin asks.

"What is he doing?" Zane asks rhetorically. "I will follow you."

Zach pulls away and drives toward downtown. "Benjamin, you keep an eye on Bernard. If he moves, let me know."

After several minutes, Benjamin states, "It appears he may be moving, but it looks to be very slow."

"Keep an eye on him," Zach says.

"He disappeared from the screen," Benjamin says excitedly. "What happened?"

"What?" Zach glances at Benjamin. "The tracker's not showing him anymore?"

"No. What does that mean?" Benjamin asks.

"I'll bet Zane's cell phone ran out of battery power. We may have a hard time finding him now. Look at the screen. Can you pinpoint where he was last located on the screen's map?"

"Yes."

Zach pulls off to the side of the road to look at the screen to determine their destination.

Zane pulls in behind them and marches up to Zach's window. "Now what?"

"Bernard disappeared off the screen. The battery in your phone may have died. Benjamin showed me his last location, but I wanted to stop and take a closer look. He was moving when we lost him, but his movement was slow, so he may have been walking."

"Not good," Zane replies. "I will follow you. Stop once you get to the location where you last had him tracked and we will work out a plan there."

"Sounds good."

They arrive downtown.

"This is his last location," Zach says. "I have a plan. We have less than an hour before dark. It's eight o'clock now. Let's split up. Benjamin and I will search the streets that go this direction while you search the streets in that direction." He points each way. "If we're lucky we will spot him. If so, try to contact him and see if he will come back home with us. Whether we find him or not, we will meet back here at 8:30."

They agree.

After a half hour, they return to their rendezvous spot and are fortunate enough to park one behind the other. Zane and Zach hop out and meet between EMITT and Zach's truck.

"Any luck, Zane?"

"Not at all."

"Well, that's just great," Zach says. "Now the fun starts and we explain this to Mom and Dad."

Benjamin steps out of the truck, eyes wide open and staring.

"What is it, Benjamin? Do you see Bernard?" Zach asks.

Benjamin does not speak. Only a stare.

"Benjamin, what is it?" Zane asks.

"What a sight to behold." He chokes up a bit, one hand on his stomach and the other on his forehead. "I have never in my life witnessed such a beautiful sight."

Zach and Zane turn around to Benjamin's view of a futuristic Philadelphia skyline.

As nighttime nears, the darkening blue skies have replaced the storm clouds from earlier in the day. Only a few high cirrus clouds remain in the sky. Against the sky's deep blue background they glow radiant orange as the last glimmer of the sunlight reflects off them. The buildings before them glisten with the lights that illuminate the city's skyline. Benjamin is oblivious to the traffic sounds all around him.

He says, "That is the most wonderful, beautiful, and amazing sight I have ever seen in my life. From where I come from, the night's stars are the only place one can see as many lights as I see right now. I only wish William were here to witness it with me."

He continues to stare in silence at the scene. His thoughts turn to the day's events, then to William, and his emotions seep out of his eyes and onto his face.

He composes himself. "How do they work? How do you make so many lights work at the same time? I am astonished by the beauty I see."

"They all work because of electricity," Zach tells him. "Your electrical experiments and proving that lightning is electricity was the beginning to today's world with electricity. You made advancements that nobody else had. Your discoveries inspired many others interested in electricity to advance their research, and this is the result today. Most everything you see works because of electricity. Lights work because of electricity and they are everywhere—our homes, buildings, roads, our cars, planes, and gadgets. Electricity is the future, and without it, our society would not be possible."

SEVENTEEN

SATURDAY, JUNE 8, 2019

WITH THE FALL of darkness, Zach stops his truck short of their street. Zane pulls in behind him and walks to Zach's window. "Now what?" Zane asks.

"I have a plan to sneak Benjamin inside the house. If we go in through the garage, we can take him up the stairs to the media room. He can wait there until we have explained ourselves to Mom and Dad. Let's pull down the street with our lights off and park in the cul-de-sac."

"All right, I will follow you."

Benjamin interjects, "I believe you should introduce me to your parents and confront them with the problem and explain the truth. I will support you both and together they will understand. Once they hear what has occurred, they will be happy their two sons are home safe."

"No," Zach says adamantly. "We need to do this alone. We will introduce you at the right time."

"Then, I will do as you wish."

With headlights off, they park their vehicles in the cul-de-sac. They creep up to the porte-cochère and slip inside the garage. Slow and quiet, they climb the stairs to the media room. Before speaking, Zach gently closes the door to the rest of the upstairs.

"Benjamin," Zach whispers, "have a seat and please stay quiet. One of us will come and get you soon. There is a magazine you can read through until we come back."

They leave Benjamin and creep downstairs to face their parents.

Alone, Benjamin sits on one of the four dark-colored cushioned theater seats and picks up the magazine. Though reading is one of his favorite pastimes, the room's decor interests him more. He stands up and lays the magazine down on the table.

He mumbles to himself, "This room..." He gasps, because words to describe it escape him. "From what I have seen today, I can only imagine its possibilities."

Curious, he steps closer and examines a large, glossy, rectangular object on the wall. The object is framed by curtains, but he's unsure of its purpose. The room is silent except for a faint noise that emanates from a tiny closet in the corner. He opens the door; a slight wave of heat brushes his face. This warmth accentuates the coolness of the home. Again, he mumbles to himself. "Remarkable. The home is cooled like the truck." He peers into the closet. "More of those electronic gadgets." He closes the door.

"Their construction is so detailed." He slides his hand across the surface of the wall. "The wall's texture is fascinating. Their processes must be intricate and time-consuming. And the dark brown color makes the room look so rich." He scans the room. Another brown leather couch is situated perpendicular to the theater seats. "Why do they have two couches in this room?" he ponders. "With all this seating, they must use this room for some form of entertainment. But it seems odd there are no windows."

He examines a painting on the wall. "These paintings, they are so detailed." He moves in closer to examine the brush strokes. "These are not paintings. This is printing. Incredible! If only I could print this good. I see printing too has made significant advances. Impressive."

He steps back to observe the scene of the print. "What is this about?"

A man, "Rocky," with his arms raised high, fists clinched in triumph, stands before a statue of another man. Benjamin reads the caption to himself. "'His whole life was a million-to-one shot.' This must be a theatrical play about a guy named Rocky. It appears he has won or trying to win, but what? Maybe he has beaten a disease and he is winning his life back. Maybe it's a race. The day appears gloomy. It must be a good play, otherwise I do not believe they would put it in a frame to hang on the wall."

He turns to an adjacent wall with a long counter. "My goodness, they even have a machine that pops popcorn." He observes the yellow letters of "POPCORN," written against a red banner across the top of the machine. He peers into the clear glass to inspect the stainless metal bowl. "I guess you do not have to pop it in a kettle over an open fire anymore."

"What is this? It appears to be a modern-day wash bin with levers." He grabs one of the levers, but before he moves it he remembers he needs to stay quiet. Since he does not know what will happen, he pulls his hand away. He continues to explore the room.

In the darkness at the back door, Zane asks, "Are you ready?" He knows all too well that neither are, but they have no choice.

"As ready as I'll ever be."

Zach opens the back door and they enter the house.

"Zach, Zane," their father calls out in a strict tone, "is that you?"

"It is," both boys respond together as they walk through the unlit kitchen toward the living room, where they find both of their parents.

Mom sits in her dark-brown leather chair with her legs crossed. One hands rests on her knee while the other fidgets with her diamond pendant. The two lamps on the long console table behind her and Jeremy provide the room's glow. She is wearing blue jean capris, a light-yellow, button-down, short-sleeve, collared shirt, and a pair of black flats. She is not happy with the boys and her stern expression shows it, but she stays quiet for the moment to let Jeremy handle the conversation.

Jeremy stands in front of his chair in a pair of blue jeans, a brown belt, a tucked-in white polo shirt with the Philadelphia Eagles logo over his left pectoral, and a brown pair of lace-up Sketchers. His arms are crossed in a stance of displeasure. His stern, six-foot-three posture and the severely bent scowl on his face sets the room's mood.

"Sit down," he says in a harsh tone, before he himself sits at the edge of his chair.

The boys sit on the long brown leather couch that faces away from the kitchen, but directly at their parents.

Jeremy's lip twitches before he begins. "Do you have any idea how disappointed I am in the two of you? You have never let me down like you did today. I have never been so embarrassed in front of anybody as I was today in front of Mark and Sam. Your actions today delayed the resolve to some critical issues in my research.

"I need an explanation of your actions. I have never known you boys to lie to me or your mother and I don't expect it to start now. I want the truth. I also hope there is no damage to EMITT. That trailer represents several years of work and it is extremely important to me."

Sarah sits in her chair, without saying a word, and watches the boys' facial expressions and their body mannerisms. If they are lying, she will know.

Zach looks at Zane. "I'll take this," he says, then turns back to his father. "It was my idea and I should be the one to explain. First, I apologize that we missed you and your friends today."

Zane nods in agreement.

"It is important that you know it was not intentional. We also know their time was limited and that time was an issue for you to show them EMITT. But, we have a bit of a shocking story to tell you, no pun intended, but it is not a lie. So here it goes.

"To answer your question, EMITT is fine. But let me start at the beginning. Do you remember our class about Benjamin Franklin last month in school and you suggested that I read your books on him?"

"Yes, I remember," Dad replies.

"That lesson and his books gave me an idea." He pauses for a second. "I wanted to recreate Benjamin's kite experiment."

"Yeah, so," Dad responds in an irritated tone. He's so mad it does not sink in that his sons wanted to fly a kite in a lightning storm. "I don't care about last month. I am concerned with today."

"It's all part of today's events. You asked for the truth and it's important you hear it, all of it. There were no parking places near Independence Park for EMITT or the truck, so we had no choice but to look for another location. That's when we found the vacant lot right outside of downtown. We found a parking spot and set EMITT up for you, Sam, and Mark. Then, I sent you the text to call us so we could pick you up."

"Right," Dad interjects, "but you never answered any of my phone calls. They went straight to voice mail as if you had turned off your phones."

"I promise you they weren't off, but let me continue. With it raining, we didn't want to get wet, so we flew the kite from EMITT's front porch. We wanted to capture the lightning in a Leyden jar we made, and see if the lightning would charge the jar. Just like Benjamin Franklin did 267 years ago."

Mom interrupts with her eyebrows raised. "Wait a minute, are you saying you flew a kite in the lightning storm this morning? Have you lost your mind? The lightning could have killed you."

"We know, but it didn't," Zach continues. "After a while, with no lightning and Zane bored, he stepped inside EMITT to rummage around. He noticed the door to your lab was open and he entered. He saw your equipment, including the tube, which by the way is incredibly gorgeous."

"You know that room is off-limits," Dad shouts. "You should not have gone in there. The room is filled with highly sensitive equipment. Please tell me you did not touch anything. Please tell me you didn't."

Zane jumps in. "Wellllll…I accidentally bumped the desk and the computer came alive, and a timer started counting down. Which was right about the time Zach noticed the strands on the kite's twine start to stand up. He hollered at me to look and told me what was happening. When I looked outside, I told him to touch the key to see if he had caught any electricity. That's when it all started."

"WHAT?" Dad shouts at the top of his lungs, rising from his chair, eyes wide open, his hands grabbing his hair.

"Calm down, Jeremy," Sarah says. "Let them finish."

"We figured out later that the phrase 'Touch The Key' is the password," Zane continues. "So, with the password said, the computer started its time travel sequence and we traveled back in time."

"YOU DID WHAT?"

"To a time you had programmed into the computer," Zach adds.

"June 9, 1752," Dad says, shocked. "My God, it works. Are you two okay?"

"Yes, we're fine," Zach says as both boys display a bit of a smile, "but we have a problem that we need to show you."

"What happened?" Dad asks.

"Zane, will you do the honors?"

"Wait a minute. Wait a minute. Wait a minute," Sarah says waving both hands and sitting up on the edge of her seat, trying to wrap her head around what the boys have told them. "Are you saying you both traveled through time?"

Zach and Zane answer together, "Yes."

Sarah looks at Jeremy with a scowl. "It was supposed to be a monkey first."

Zane jumps from the couch and sprints upstairs.

"Where is he going?" Dad asks, confused.

"You will see," Zach says.

A moment later Zane returns down the stairs. Behind him is another man dressed in Colonial-day clothes. "Mom, Dad, I would like you to meet Benjamin Franklin."

Jeremy falls back into his chair in complete disbelief.

Sarah is confused and stands up. She knows he said Benjamin Franklin, but it does not register that they mean the real Benjamin Franklin.

Benjamin enters the room and greets them with his English accent. "Pleased to make your acquaintance, ma'am, sir." He nods to each as he extends a hand to Sarah. "My name is Benjamin Franklin. I know this must be somewhat of a shock to you—goodness, I know it was for me."

Stunned, Jeremy puts his thoughts together and stands from his chair. "Are you really the one and only Benjamin Franklin?" he asks as he extends his hand to shake Benjamin's.

"I am," Benjamin replies. "I have spent the better part of the day with your two sons, and may I say you both have raised a mighty fine set of boys. We have been..."

"Whoa, whoa, whoa," Zach interrupts before Benjamin can continue. "Let's all have a seat, because there's more to explain."

"There's more?" Dad exclaims. "What more could there possibly be?"

They all sit.

"So, we traveled to June 9, 1752," Zach continues, "which is the day before Benjamin conducts his kite experiment. Because we had to spend a night in 1752, we had plenty of time to retrace the day's events. That's how we figured out the password, and it allowed us to create a plan to travel home. We knew our only way home was to fly the kite again, in another lightning storm.

"When we woke up the next morning, the weather looked bad, but that was good. With the computer set up, we were about to fly the kite again, and guess who comes riding along in a horse and buggy." He points to Benjamin. "Yep, you guessed it, Benjamin and his son, William. Although at that time, we had no idea who they were.

"They approached EMITT and hollered, asking if anyone was home, but we stayed quiet, hoping they would leave. Of course, they didn't. We peeked through the curtains, and after a closer look we suspected that it may be Benjamin and his son, but we thought we were crazy. Then, we heard them talk about the kite experiment, and then we knew exactly who they were.

"Now, Dad, you can imagine our excitement when we realized we would be right there when Benjamin Franklin performed his famous kite experiment. Of course, history told us that he would catch the lightning and we realized this was our opportunity to go home. All we had to do was wait for him to catch the lightning, scare them off the porch, and, with the date and time programmed into the computer, we would be on our way back home, before we had to meet with you, Sam, and Mark, and nobody would be the wiser."

"Oh good," Sarah replies. "For a minute, I thought you were going to tell us William is here too."

"Wellllll…" Zane drags out the word again. "Not exactly. It's worse than that."

"What?" Dad blurts out. "What could be worse?"

"This man named Bernard..."

Benjamin jumps in on the explanation. "There is a gentleman that I know in my time named Bernard Ranter. Over the years, there have been issues between the two of us, mostly because of my success and his lack thereof. To make matters worse, I recently embarrassed him, though it was not intentional. But nonetheless, he was embarrassed.

"See, Bernard was trying his hand with the electric fire. He would perform his electric fire shows for anybody that would watch. While in town one day, I happened upon a simple gathering of people. Curious, I stopped and found Bernard performing one of his shows. But one of the experiments failed. I saw why and I explained it to him in front of the crowd. He made the correction and it worked. But, his embarrassment was noticeable because he quickly picked up his equipment and left.

"I thought he would have been happy with my help, since the experiment had already failed, but he saw it differently. It has been a few weeks since that day and I have not seen Bernard around. But, after today's events, it is obvious he has kept a close eye on me. He followed William and me into the pasture this morning, where we attempted to conduct my kite experiment in secret. He must have been spying on us, because he was close enough to EMITT that he also traveled forward in time with us. I can only assume he somehow wanted to make me look foolish."

"This is not good," Dad says. "Zane, go upstairs and bring him down. Maybe we can work it out."

"Welllll..." Zane drags out the word once again. "We lost him."

"You lost him?" Dad screeches. "How on earth did you lose him?"

Zach continues the explanation. "Right after we returned to 2019, we were trying to calm Benjamin down to explain the events that had occurred. During the explanation, Bernard peeked around the door to see inside EMITT. Benjamin saw him, called him by name, and he took off running. We chased after him, but he's much faster than us. We returned to Benjamin and waited for an hour or so, hoping he would return, because we were his only hope to get back home."

"Yeah, and..," Dad says, eager for the rest of the story.

"He did show up a little later. While we were preparing EMITT to be hitched to the truck, Bernard jumped into my truck and took off."

"He stole your truck?" Mom screeches.

"Sure did. Jumped in and took off like a maniac. Nearly had a wreck too."

"This is not good," Mom says.

"But we did have a little stroke of luck. Zane accidentally left his cell phone in my truck. That allowed us to track Bernard. So, Zane caught a cab home and returned with his truck. With EMITT connected, we tracked Bernard. We found my truck, but it had run out of gas and Bernard was gone. We assumed he hitched a ride, but another stroke of good luck: He took Zane's phone with him and somehow he ended up back downtown. We traveled back there to look for him, but we lost him on the tracker right before dark. We assume Zane's phone ran out of battery power.

"Tomorrow, we need to find Bernard and create a plan to send them both back to 1752. So, that was our day, how was yours?" Zach feigns a smile.

"Also, EMITT is outside if you want to see her."

EIGHTEEN

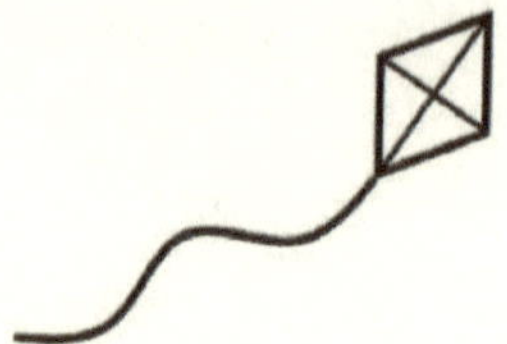

SATURDAY, JUNE 8, 2019

BENJAMIN STANDS AND walks to a nearby window, where he peers out into the darkness. He asks, "Where might I find the outhouse."

"Oh, Benjamin, it's this way," Sarah replies as she leads Benjamin to a door off the foyer's entrance. She opens the door and turns on the lights and the exhaust fan. "You may not have seen this before, but we no longer use outhouses. We have bathrooms inside the home. There's a silver button on the top of the tank. When you're finished, wave your hand near it and it will flush by itself."

Benjamin steps through the door and closes it behind him.

"We need to formulate a plan to find this Bernard guy," Dad says. "We need to return them both back to their time era. They cannot stay here. Benjamin Franklin has a lot of work to do that will shape the future of our country into what it is today."

"Zach and I talked about that earlier today."

"Yeah," Zach says, "and now that we know the lightning is what makes the time machine work, we need to figure out when the next lightning storm will occur and we can send them home."

"I agree, but first we need to find Bernard," Dad replies. "Then, we can worry about the next lightning storm. And when we're ready, we can fly the kite and send them home."

"We need to travel with them," Zach says. "We already know when the lightning will occur. If we can return them on June 10th in the afternoon, right after we plucked them away from their era, Benjamin can fly his kite to catch the lightning we need and send us back to 2019, without them. They can continue to live their lives, in their time era, and Benjamin will still create his inventions, perform his civic duties for our country, and sign the Declaration of Independence. We need history to remain unchanged, at least as much as possible. Although some details have already changed."

Sarah stands in front of the fireplace while the boys and Jeremy discuss the return plans. She becomes uncomfortable and interrupts the conversation. "Wait a minute, boys. I have listened to your plans of returning Benjamin and Bernard back home, which I agree they must be returned, but neither of you are going to be flying a kite to catch lightning again. You were lucky the first time, but I will not allow you to do it a second and especially not a third time."

She turns to Jeremy with a stern glare. "As you have told me many times, the time travel events could be dangerous. Our agreement for you to build the machine was a monkey would do the traveling and you would study the effects on the monkey before a person would travel. But never did we discuss risking your life or our boys' lives. That is where I draw the line."

"You're right, we did talk about that. I will promise they will not be involved in catching any lightning in the future. But it will be necessary that I travel with Benjamin and Bernard so EMITT can be returned safely."

Sarah starts to reply, but stops when Benjamin steps from the bathroom. He says with a laugh, "The 'outhouse' is now the 'inhouse.' But, where does the water come from? And where does the waste go? And now, a place to wash your hands. Cleanliness—brilliant idea."

"Let me explain," Jeremy says as Benjamin returns to the couch. "You may be aware that plumbing has been around for centuries, but modern-day plumbing was instituted around the turn of the twentieth century to help cities remove the waste and prevent epidemics. Over time, a huge network of pipes has been laid underground throughout the city. The water is pumped from the Delaware River to a water treatment plant, treated, then pumped to water towers around the city. Large pumps push water up into a large bowl at the top of the tower. Pipes leave the towers and feed the water to the homes in their districts. Gravity keeps the proper pressure in the water lines, and when someone turns on a faucet, the water flows out."

"That is incredible. I can only imagine the amount of work it took to build that system."

"It took many years and has evolved over time as technologies improve. And then there's the other side, waste. As water runs into our drains, either via the sinks, bathtubs, showers, or toilets, it goes into the sewer pipes and is pumped back to a sewer treatment plant. The water is cleaned and treated, then pumped back into the river."

"I am astonished by the advancements of today's society," Benjamin says. "This is an amazing era and so far ahead of ours. Now I don't want to go back home, but I know we need to find Bernard and send him and myself back to 1752. As amazing a place as the future is, we don't belong here."

"Unfortunately, we agree," Jeremy says. "The boys and I were just discussing that issue while you were in the restroom. Tomorrow, we will search for Bernard and attempt to coax him back home with us. We will keep an eye on the weather to determine our next chance for a thunderstorm. Then, we can plan our time travel back to 1752.?

"What do you mean, 'Keep an eye on the weather'?" Benjamin asks.

Jeremy speaks toward the corner of the room. "Alexa, please provide a three-day weather forecast?"

A woman's soft, somewhat robotic voice emanates from an area separating the kitchen and the family room: "Please wait a moment while I search for the three-day weather forecast."

Benjamin sits up, a bit dumbfounded at what he has heard, and turns around to see the woman. "Where is she?" he asks while looking around, then turning back to Jeremy.

Sarah and the boys snicker.

"Alexa is an internet tool, or gadget, if you wish. That's her," Jeremy says, pointing to the device on the counter, "the short black cylinder, the one with the blue lights. She's connected to the internet. We can ask her..."

Alexa speaks, "Sunday, June 10th, the weather will be warm with a possible chance of an afternoon shower. Temperatures in the morning will fall to a low of seventy degrees with an afternoon high of eighty-nine degrees. The humidity high will reach near fifty-eight percent. Wind will be out of the southeast at twelve miles per hour and change to a west-northwest wind up to twenty-four miles per hour."

Benjamin's eyes light up in awe.

"Monday, June 11th, the weather will be warm with a possible chance of an afternoon shower. Temperatures in the morning will fall to a low of sixty-one degrees with an afternoon high of seventy-seven degrees. The humidity high will reach near forty-seven percent. Wind will be out of the northwest and will vary between seven and twelve miles per hour."

"Tuesday, June 12th, the weather will be warm with a possible chance of an afternoon shower. Temperatures in the morning will fall to a low of sixty-two degrees with an afternoon high of seventy-nine degrees. The humidity high will reach near forty-seven percent. Wind will be out of the north and will vary from seven to twelve miles per hour. May I be of more assistance?"

"That will be all. Thank you," Jeremy responds.

"You're welcome."

"Unbelievable," Benjamin states. "I am astonished."

"The internet is a remarkable tool," Jeremy explains. "Present-day weathermen have the capability to predict the weather with some degree of accuracy. The information is uploaded to their computers and made available to the internet. The weather forecasters utilize satellites high in the sky to see weather patterns—for example, a "cold front" or "high pressure" system. This tells them, along with a lot of other information, whether thunderstorms or sunny days are on the way. With the other information, they can also predict the temperature, humidity, and the direction and velocity of the winds. This provides us the ability to see, with decent accuracy, three days ahead and even have a good idea up to ten days ahead."

"Alexa said the next few days will be hot with a slight chance of rain, but it does not appear we will see any thunderstorms or lightning," Jeremy says. "We'll keep watching."

Benjamin appears disappointed.

Sarah stands up. "You boys must be hungry. I say let's go out to dinner and Benjamin can try some of our fantastic modern-day foods. We'll let Benjamin decide the type of food he would like to eat."

"Oh, I don't know," Benjamin replies, "I do not believe I would be a good judge, since I do not know what's available."

"Well," Sarah asks, "what type of foods do you like that sound exotic? We have Chinese, Japanese, Italian, hamburgers, pizza, steaks, and barbeque, and we even have homestyle cooking if that suits your fancy. The choices are endless."

"I am not sure about Japanese or Chinese food. Several years ago, when I was in London, I had flat bread, which resembles pizza," Benjamin recalls. "We call it a poor man's food, but it was okay."

"Pizza nowadays," Sarah explains, "is like a round, flat bread, but its taste is zesty. It's made with tomato sauce, cheese, and many different types of toppings, like pepperoni, ham, bacon, green bell peppers, onions, pineapple, mushrooms, black olives, and many more. Pretty much however you want to make it. It's very tasty."

"What you described sounds different from what I ate. If it is okay with everybody, pizza sounds like a good choice."

"Pizza it is," Jeremy says.

"Mom," Zach asks, "do we have any clothes we could let Benjamin borrow? It may be best for him to change into some different clothes so he can blend in a little better. Not only that, his clothes got a little wet down by the airport when he dove into a ditch, because a 747 was coming in to land right above our heads. You should have seen it. It was hilarious."

"I can't believe you boys laughed at Benjamin like that," Mom scolds in a serious but playful manner, shaking her finger at them. "He had to be scared to death. You know he had no idea what that plane was. Shame on you."

"Thank you, Sarah. It's nice to know someone's on my side."

Chuckles by all.

"Come on, Benjamin, I have some clothes on the formal dining table that I have picked up for donation, but have yet to turn in to the community center. I believe I could have you looking pretty sharp with a few of the items."

"Sarah," Jeremy interjects, "if you will take care of Benjamin, the boys and I will put EMITT away."

Moments later, Benjamin returns to the kitchen in his new change of clothes. "How do I look?"

Sarah replies, "That brown collarless shirt goes well with the blue jeans and it looks like it fits pretty good."

"It does fit well. Thanks."

"Here, I found this brown blazer too. Try it on."

Sarah holds it out and Benjamin slips his arms inside.

"Now that looks nice," she says, straightening his collar and lapel. "And those brown leather shoes of Jeremy's, they're perfect with the outfit. It's a nice coincidence you two wear the same size shoe." She steps back and looks him over. "If I say so myself, you look pretty sharp."

"Thanks, Sarah. I feel a little out of place, but I do like the look."

With EMITT put away, Jeremy and the boys return to the house. "Whoa, look at Benjamin," Zane says with a bit of a swagger. "He looks snazzy."

"I agree," Zach says. "But I'm hungry. Let's go eat."

Benjamin rests comfortably in the rear seat of the truck between the two boys. "Sarah, tell me, how did you meet Jeremy?"

"We met in our senior year of college at the University of Pennsylvania," she recalls. "We were in a computer science class together. On the first day of class I arrived early. While seated, in walks this tall, handsome young man with short, dirty-blond hair and beautiful green eyes." She smiles. "To say the least, I was attracted. He strolled into the classroom, not late but not far from it either. By then, most of the seats were occupied, but as fate would have it, the one next to me was open. For the first few days, he didn't pay much attention to me, but he sure paid close attention to that professor."

"Isn't that the object of class?" Jeremy interjects, poking fun at her. "We were there to learn."

"Anyway, after a couple of weeks he loosened up a bit and his intelligent responses to the professor tilted toward witty and funny comments with me. Over the next few weeks his charm won me over, but he did not notice that aspect, because of his hunger for knowledge. He was ambitious and eager to succeed. He completed his bachelor's degree with a minor in computer science engineering, and the next year he started his masters in both electrical and mechanical engineering. He mentioned that he wanted to start his own engineering firm and have a family someday.

"We had a lot in common, and his outlook on life intrigued me. So, I found myself looking for reasons to run into him in the halls, between classes, at lunchtime, and even after school. The message finally became clear to him and he asked me out on a date, which of course I accepted. I mean who could turn down that charming smile?" She playfully grabs at his chin, which now has a beaming smile, because he's proud of their story.

"We dated for the next couple of years, and after Jeremy graduated with his masters we planned to marry the next spring. After my graduation, I applied for a job at the School District of Philadelphia and, being the fortunate recipient, I taught computer science for the next several years.

"For a couple of years, Jeremy worked at an engineering firm and gained some valuable experience. But his time there neared its end and we decided it was time for him to open his own firm. The company started to do well after the first couple of years, but about a year after he had opened for business, we found out I was pregnant...with twins. And with the business still young, we decided with the boys on the way and the high costs of daycare, it would be a better choice for me to stay home and raise the boys. It's been sixteen years now, and so far life has turned out pretty good."

"Interesting," Benjamin says. "I too believe in knowledge advancement. I have a vision of a public academy for higher education. In January of last year, I generated some creative fundraising and opened the academy. Let me correct myself; it was last year for me, but for you folks it was January 1751. But now, with it open and functioning, it promises to provide better education for reasons other than religion."

"Benjamin," Jeremy interjects, "the academy you refer to, we call it the University of Philadelphia. It has succeeded and today is a well-known major university."

"Fantastic! It is pleasing to know it has succeeded and provided education to so many people for all these years. I must say, this is a proud moment for me. I no longer have to just *assume* we did the right thing."

"That you did, my friend," Jeremy says. "That you did."

NINETEEN

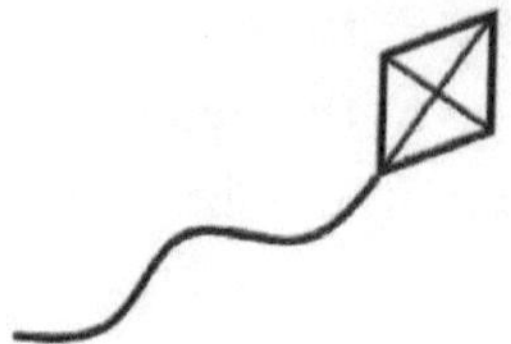

SATURDAY, JUNE 8, 2019

STANDING AWAY FROM the counter, Benjamin and Jeremy review a handheld, laminated version of the restaurant's menu. Jeremy is having a difficult time reading the menu's fine print. He reaches into his shirt pocket and pulls out a pair of bifocal readers. "That's better." As the words comes into focus, he says, "By the way, you did a great job with the invention of these bifocals."

"I did not invent bifocals as you call them," Benjamin replies.

"Uh-oh." Jeremy realizes he has made a mistake.

"But from that comment and expression, I assume that I do at some point in my lifetime."

"Yes, you do. But we will talk about it at the table, where we can have a little more privacy."

"I agree."

"Here's a list of the different ingredients," Jeremy says, pointing to a specific area on the menu. "Is there any ingredient that you don't like?"

"No, they all look good to me…well, except for the bell peppers. Jeremy, you choose. I will go with your recommendations."

Jeremy orders three different large pizzas. The cashier hands each of them a glass. "C'mon, Benjamin," Zach says and hurries to the soda machines. "They have Coke, but they have others as well. Here, you help yourself as often as you like."

Benjamin watches Zach operate the machine and mimics his actions. Zane stands right behind him.

A multitude of people and their chatter fill the establishment. Multiple televisions hang near the ceiling and display a variety of programs, mostly sports. One corner has several young kids surveying the video games. A few are being played.

After filling his glass, Benjamin follows Zach to a table. Mesmerized, he takes in the scene.

At the table, Sarah tears off several paper towels from the slimming roll, folding them in half. She reaches around the spiral pizza pan stands on the red and white checkered vinyl tablecloth to lay them out as napkins for everyone, no different than if she were at home.

With everyone seated at the table, Jeremy reveals his blunder. "Now that everyone is at the table, I have made a huge mistake that we need to talk about. I mentioned to Benjamin at the counter that he made a great invention with these bifocal glasses."

"Yeah. So?" Zach says. "He did invent them."

"Yes, but he does not do so for several more years."

"Oh, that is a problem."

"We need to realize, with Benjamin here, we do not need to be discussing inventions he has yet to invent. If a subject arises that we know Benjamin may have been involved with or possibly had some influence, then we need not talk about it. We do not want to prematurely influence his decision making. Benjamin has many accomplishments throughout his life. We need to ensure those accomplishments are not revealed. He will figure them out as his life unfolds. It will be our job to ensure history stays as natural as possible.

"I will send each of you a text with a link to a site that has a timeline of Benjamin's life. Save it as a favorite and learn it. Everything in Benjamin's life after June 10, 1752, we don't discuss.

"And Benjamin, you will see and experience many technological advancements while you are here. Many you will enjoy, but you won't understand the details of the technology, therefore preventing you from introducing them into your era. For example: the plumbing we talked about earlier, a water treatment plant would not be possible, because your era lacks the electrical power plants to generate the necessary power that will operate the equipment to pump the water into huge water towers. Not to mention pump technology or the process for treating the water. But nevertheless you will have learned that it is possible. It would probably be best that you not introduce the concepts to your society, because it could alter history."

"I believe that is a fair and wise decision," Benjamin replies. "I would imagine there are many aspects of the technology that would have to be developed before any of the amazing things I learn of would even be possible."

"I agree. Now, on to Bernard," Dad states. " Zach, where did you last see him?"

"We were a few minutes outside of downtown when we lost him on the tracker. We know he was near Rittenhouse Square. We searched the area until dark, but we could not locate him, so we decided to come home."

"Then, early tomorrow," Dad says, "we will arrive at Rittenhouse Square around 7 a.m. and search the area again. He will be on the streets somewhere and he will be hungry, so food and water will be our way to lure him."

"Zane," Zach says, "I guess we need to start another list. We need to know what Bernard may or may not have and what he may need to survive, like we did when we traveled back from 1752."

"We taught you boys right," Dad says. "You thought your problem through and when you found yourself in a dire situation, you figured out how to survive. I'm proud of you."

"Thanks," both reply.

"So, what are some things he may have?" Zach asks.

"He has the clothes on his back," Zane replies, "and from what I saw, he was wearing brown knee-length pants, a white long-sleeve shirt, white leggings, and brown boots. He was carrying his long Colonial coat and a hat. Oh, and he has my cell phone, which now appears to be dead."

"Zane," Benjamin interjects, "in case you wanted to know, the coat is a called a 'great' coat and the pants are called breeches."

"I did not know that. Thanks."

"Benjamin," Jeremy asks, "do you know if he carries a knife, a gun, or some type of a weapon?"

"I do not. Though many people of our time do carry a pocketknife."

"What about money?" Sarah asks. "Did he have any money on him?"

"I assume he has some, but I could not say for sure."

"I'm not sure what type of money is used in your day, but I am one hundred percent confident it's not what's used today." She reaches into her purse. "This is what our money looks like." She hands a bill to Benjamin with the back of the bill facing him. "Turn it over."

"Oh my goodness," Benjamin gasps. "That's me! Why is there a picture of me on your money?"

"Benjamin," Sarah says, "I'm not sure you're aware of the influence you have had on Philadelphia, America, and even the world. This is the reason we must be careful of what we say. Our situation here is vulnerable and I thought the money would be a good way for you to understand your stature and our vulnerability, without revealing anything specific. This may provide you a glimpse of your status and why it is so important to send you and Bernard back to your era."

Benjamin nods, understanding his accomplishments have made an impact on the future. A smile brightens his face before he hands the money back to Sarah.

"But, back to Bernard," Sarah continues. "If he had any money with him, I doubt any merchants would accept it, because they would not recognize it, but it would be extremely valuable to a coin collector, and through them he may be able to sell it for a substantial sum."

"Bernard is not a wealthy man of our time," Benjamin replies, "but he lives an average life. So, it would be safe to say he probably has some money on him. And, to answer your question, we use the English pound for our currency. I wonder what the value comparison between the English pound then and today's currency would be?"

"I too would be interested in that answer," Jeremy replies. "That is a tough question for us to answer here. Though, at home, I can figure it out with some online calculators."

"Okay." Zach jumps in to steer the conversation back on track. "So we have clothes for him to stay warm for the night. Maybe a knife for some protection, maybe some money, which is useless, unless he realizes that it may be valuable to a coin collector. And Zane's dead cell phone. He must be hungry, so he could use some food and water."

"He could probably use a friend right now," Benjamin replies. "With the confusion of what has happened, he could use some reassurance that it will be okay."

"We need to find him tomorrow," Jeremy says. "We don't want him to become desperate and get caught stealing. If that happens, it could be disastrous for him and us. We need to find him tomorrow."

"Well, the list is not long," Zach states, "but it's a start."

Items he has:	*Items he needs:*
Clothes	*Food*
Hat	*Water*
Coat	*Clean Clothes*
Money	*A Friend*
Knife	

"Our plan tomorrow," Jeremy says, "should be to locate him. Benjamin will need to talk to him to build some confidence. Then, we offer him food and water and let him know we are devising a plan to send them both back home. We will bring him back to the house and figure out a date to send them home. On that day, we will fly the kite, catch the lightning, send them home, catch more lightning, and come back to 2019, alone."

"Oh yeah. No problem. Sounds like a piece of cake," Zach says with loads of sarcasm.

"Somebody order some pizzas?" the server asks as he sets two of the pizzas onto the stands. "I have another one I'll bring out in a second." He scans the table. "I see you already have plates and parmesan cheese and crushed red pepper. The paper towels are a little low. I will bring another roll. Anything else you may need?"

"Nope, just the other pizza will take care of it," Jeremy replies.

"Parmesan cheese! I love Parmesan cheese," Benjamin states. The meal presented before him raises his eyebrows and bulges his eyes, while a huge smile accentuates the enthusiastic expression on full display. His taste buds jump up and down at the appetizing feast. "This looks delicious…and that aroma! Mmm…"

"Benjamin, grab you a piece," Zane says, handing him the pizza server.

Benjamin slips the triangular-shaped spatula under a piece and lifts it. The melted cheese stretches across the pan and the table toward his plate, creating a bit of a mess. "Brilliant, Benjamin," he says about himself. "You would think I were six years old with that mess."

"Not to worry, Benjamin," Sarah says.

He cuts at the cheese until it frees from the pizza pan and passes the spatula to Sarah. He picks up the shaker of Parmesan Cheese and sprinkles it heavily across the thin pizza slice. He picks it up and takes a bite and immediately spits it back out. "Good Lord, that's hot!" he exclaims, and takes a long drink of his Coke. "I burnt the roof of my mouth." He takes another drink.

Zach blurts out with a laugh. "He spit that pizza right out. I like it. Benjamin, you fit right in."

"Zach," Mom scolds.

"I'm sorry, Benjamin," Sarah says. "I should have warned you it would be hot. You should be careful. Our food comes out quite hot sometimes. Let it cool a minute."

After a couple of minutes, Benjamin tries the pizza, this time with a bit more caution. "Yum, this is fantastic. This is much better than the flat bread I talked about earlier. The taste, it's zesty. It's a lot better than the usual bread and hasty pudding we eat most of the time. And this Coke, I really like it. Any chance I could take some of this back home with me?"

"That's not a good idea," Jeremy responds adamantly. "If it were discovered, how would you explain it? Even if it were an empty bottle? It's not like you have plastic bottles back in your day."

"No, you're right, but my goodness the sweet taste with the fizziness. What an amazing creation."

On their return home, Zach says, "Benjamin, you have to watch a movie in the media room we left you in earlier. I thought maybe *Star Wars*."

"No, no, *Back to the Future*," Zane says excitedly. "How appropriate would that be?"

"No, *Star Wars*, the digitally remastered version, would be better, with the graphics, sound, and cinematography. Benjamin would get a cool theater experience and it's one of the best movies," Zach responds.

"You're right," Zane says, "at least for his first movie experience."

"Benjamin," Zane suggests with an excited laugh, "this movie will blow your mind."

"What?" Benjamin exclaims. "Jeremy, is this safe?"

"It's only an expression. You will be fine."

"Don't worry, Benjamin, once you see the Jedis fighting in space with their lasers, you'll love it. It is an amazing movie," Zach replies.

"Boys," Mom speaks up, "before you start the movie, I would like to go over a few details with Benjamin. I also need to show him to his room, so he will know where to sleep for the night."

Zach pulls his smartphone from his pocket and pushes a couple of buttons. He nods at Zane.

Zane says, "Benjamin, want to see something super cool?"

"Sure."

Dad turns onto their street.

"That's our house straight ahead. I will turn on the house lights from here. Watch."

"Now, you do not expect me to believe that? From here? That's not possible."

"Watch. Lights, turn on," he commands.

Zach's cell phone is down by his side, and out of Benjamin's sight, Zach presses a button.

After a short pause, the outside lights of the house turn on along with a few lights inside.

Benjamin's eyes open wide; his jaw drops. "How did you do that? That is not possible." He looks at Zane. "How...how did you do that?"

"We haven't told you yet, but we have magic in the future."

Sarah and Jeremy snicker. "That's enough, boys," Sarah says. "Benjamin, don't listen to them. They turned on the lights with their cell phone. It's an app on the phone that lets them control the lights at the house."

"Mom," Zach blurts out, "we would have told him later."

TWENTY

SATURDAY, JUNE 8, 2019

THE BOYS RACE upstairs to set up the movie, while Jeremy finds his way to the study.

"Benjamin," Sarah asks, "would you like a tour of the house before the movie?"

"That would be fantastic. I would love to see today's futuristic home."

"Follow me. We will start in the kitchen. It's the heart of the house and where many of our modern-day appliances reside."

Standing at the kitchen's island Benjamin remarks, "What a beautiful room. Spacious. And the work surfaces..." He gasps, sliding his hand across the island's smooth surface. "What type of material is this?"

"It's polished granite."

"Granite, like the rock from a quarry?"

"That's correct."

"I have never seen it look this beautiful. I love the gold swirls and how it flows throughout the white granite. The colors accent the cabinets. This kitchen is gorgeous. Ours is made of wooden walls, a stove, and a wooden table with rickety chairs. It is unheard of to see this type of detail. The king's palace is beautiful, but nothing like this. King George II would be in awe."

"Thank you for such a high compliment, Benjamin," Sarah replies with an appreciative tone. "But you have yet to see any of the appliances. This is our gas cooktop." She steps toward the cooktop on the island and turns one of its five knobs. A ticking sound occurs and then *poof*, blue flames.

Startled, Benjamin steps back and gasps.

"And turning the knob allows me to adjust the heat it produces," she says. Sarah adjusts the knob, causing the flames to rise and fall.

"Amazing! Deborah would love this. She has the stove I invented to cook over, but there are no controls, and starting the fire is time-consuming. Yours starts immediately with a turn of a knob. How does it work?"

"Most homes have natural gas piped in, which supplies the cooktop, the dryer, the heater for the house, the hot water heater, the gas lanterns on the front of the house, and the barbeque pit in the backyard. The natural gas is extracted out of the ground by the oil and gas companies and then sold to the public. It's a little more complicated than that, so you will need to ask Jeremy about it later."

"You said most homes. What about those homes that don't have the gas?"

"They have electric stoves that heat up an element to cook on."

"Fascinating! A controlled fire in the house for cooking that starts with the turn of a knob. I am impressed. I guess next you will show an appliance that freezes?" Benjamin says with a chuckle while stepping toward the cabinets on the other side of the island. "And these cabinets, the craftsmanship is incredible," Benjamin remarks, while opening a door and rubbing the outside surface to feel its texture. "Some have wood panels and others have glass panes with lights inside. The architecture is incredible and the attention to detail, unbelievable. We have a couple of shelves for the dishes and a basin to wash them. But first we have to heat the water from the fire."

"Life must be challenging in your era."

"It can be, but it is normal to us."

She continues, "This is the refrigerator." She opens the two top doors, which appear to be cabinet doors that match the kitchen cabinets.

"Clever design!" he gasps. "Built right into the cabinets. You cannot even tell it's there. And this appliance does what?"

"It keeps our food cold and preserves it until we're ready to cook it. We determine the temperature we want, set the dial for that temperature, typically about thirty-seven degrees, and it keeps the temperature constant. And yes, you guessed it." She pulls the bottom door open. "This is the freezer, where we keep frozen foods. We set the temperature to zero degrees and it keeps everything frozen. When we're ready, we pull the frozen item out, let it thaw, and we cook it that night."

"Remarkable!" Benjamin exclaims. "I am astonished with today's advancements. Our preservation is quite different. With our meats, we either dry them or salt them, but either way we extract the water from the meat, which prevents decay and bacteria. With drying, we typically smoke the meat in a smokehouse, though there are other ways.

"Salting is another common method to preserve our meats. The meat is covered in salt with a little saltpeter added, which draws the moisture out and keeps bacteria from growing. This process works best in colder weather.

"But either of the processes, if done properly, can preserve the meat for many years. Once the meat is ready, we seal it in a jar and store it for later."

"Now, *I'm* amazed!" Sarah remarks. "I did not know that. Really, I never thought much about how it was done before modern appliances."

"It helps to appreciate the past."

"Benjamin, you are correct."

"Then, what will you show me next, a machine that cooks it for you?" he asks.

"No, that would be me," Sarah says disappointingly with a giggle. "Here we have the oven to roast, broil, or cook large items or meats that take a constant heat for a longer period. We can adjust the temperature as needed and set a timer that tells us when it's ready."

She pulls a glass from one of the cabinets and fills it with water. "Take a sip of this water."

Benjamin takes it and sips from the glass.

Sarah takes the glass and says, "But the microwave…" She sets the glass inside, closes the door, and presses a few buttons. "…is possibly one of the most ingenious inventions the kitchen has seen. We place a glass of water or a small bowl of food, select thirty seconds, and, *voila*, it's ready. Literally takes seconds to a couple of minutes, depending on what you're cooking, and it's hot. It is excellent for warming last night's leftovers."

Ding.

She retrieves the glass. "Now taste the water."

Benjamin again takes a sip. "Oh my goodness. It's hot and it only took a few seconds. Amazing! How can that be possible? What an amazing cooking tool. For us, it takes longer than that just to bring in the wood for the fire. Modern technology has really come a long way. This definitely is a simpler way of life."

"Yes, but there is a cost associated with it. Homes these days are expensive. Once Jeremy figures out the conversion from the English pound to the US dollar, you will have an idea of the costs."

"And we have several small appliances as well," Sarah continues, pointing to each against the counter's cream and light caramel stone backsplash. "The blender, food processor, toaster, can opener, and even a wine bottle opener. They make the little details easier, like opening cans or bottles, chopping foods, or mixing drinks."

"Unbelievable! What will they think of next?"

"I'll show you. Let's step into the laundry room. This is the washer and the dryer." She points to each of the gray appliances. "We throw our dirty clothes in, add soap, set the cycle, and press start, and about forty-five minutes later they're clean. When it's finished, throw them in the dryer, and forty-five minutes to an hour later they are dry, ready to be folded and put away."

"The work table helps for treating and folding the clothes," she says, rubbing her hand across the wide cream-colored tabletop. "More storage," she says while opening a white cabinet door, "to store the laundry detergents, stain removers, fabric softeners, and other items. An additional refrigerator for more refrigerator and freezer space."

"Deborah would be in heaven. She works so hard, boiling the water, scrubbing the clothes on the washboard, hanging them to dry, and putting them away. It is a tedious and time-consuming process. It takes a long day for her to complete."

"It still takes time for us as well, but we have time to do other chores while the machine does the hard work. Let's go to the master bedroom."

They walk across the living room's hardwoods, past the sharp lines of the stacked stone fireplace and the two dachshunds. "Sarah, you have an incredible home. The tall ceilings make the rooms feel so much more spacious. And the lights throughout the home, very nice. Are all homes like this?"

"Oh no," Sarah snickers. "There are thousands of home styles. Each varies in size, from much larger too much smaller, and there are even more choices of amenities and finishes. Your home choice depends on what you like, how much room you need, how much you want to take care of, and how much you can afford."

"Wow, what a magnificent room," Benjamin gasps as they enter the master. "This is as large as the downstairs room to my own home. This is gorgeous." He gazes at the milk chocolate textures that accentuate the walls and the inset of the coffered ceiling, both separated by a beige-textured ceiling. "And these floors!"

"The floors are knotty bamboo. Jeremy and I really liked the knotty design in the wood. But with the dark stains of the high-arched headboard, the posts of the bed and the two matching nightstands the room was getting to dark. We thought the light stain of the floors would provide a distinct contrast to the room's rich colors. And it did, but it wasn't enough, so I threw a mix of white and brown linens and pillows to dress up the bed. Then I added the light gold colors of the distressed wood in the lamps and that helped bring the lighter color up from the floor."

"You did a magnificent job and it is beautiful. And the furniture, it is so meticulously crafted.... I did not know wood could be so beautiful." He moves closer toward the foot of the bed, rubbing his hands up and down the length of one of the bed's tall posts. He strolls over toward the two burgundy and blue paisley reading chairs in front of the bay windows. "This must be for the night's reading?" he asks, noticing a book on the table between the two chairs. He sits in one of the chairs, rubbing his hands along the armrest to feel the material's texture.

Sarah steps closer and flips a sidewall light switch. Two lights turn on, each spot a beam in the perfect reading position.

"Amazing. This would be perfect for my nighttime reading. My bare feet would love the throw rug." He stands and steps toward the shiny red vase to the side of the opposite chair and slides a few of the tall feathers through his fingers.

"When you buy the house, do they build the furniture too?"

"Oh no," Sarah replies. "When we built the house, we had to buy a lot to furnish it. We bought several new pieces of furniture along with some lamps to match. Some of the art and knickknacks we already had, but we did buy other pieces over the years. But that's the fun part of furnishing your own home. But the part I like the most is watching the boys grow up and the memories we—as a family—have created through the years. Those are irreplaceable."

"In here is the master bathroom..." She leads Benjamin along on the tour. "...with his and her sinks, a glass shower, a sunken jacuzzi tub, and the toilet. Of course, it would not be complete without his and her closets."

"Again, the finishes are beautiful in here as well, with the black granite counters. But, why two closets?"

"It provides more room for each of us. I have a lot of clothes and so does Jeremy, so the extra space is helpful."

"Sarah, I could not be more impressed. I am astonished by what I have seen in the few short hours I have been in the future. If Deborah saw this, she would never let us go home."

"Maybe," Sarah replies. "But I'm sure this would be a complete culture shock to the both of you. You have been in awe of everything you have seen, but this would only be the beginning."

"I cannot argue with you there."

Jeremy's voice emanates from the bedroom. "Everyone, I have the conversion worked out, if you would like to meet me in the study."

Benjamin looks around the door frame back into the bedroom, but does not see Jeremy. "I know I just heard Jeremy, but he is not here."

Sarah laughs. "He's in the study. You heard his voice on the Dot." She points to the small, round black device with the blue light ring that sits on the nearest nightstand. "It's connected to Alexa in the living room. The whole house is networked together. It makes it easier to talk to people in the other rooms. The boys upstairs heard it too. C'mon, let's see what Jeremy has figured out."

Sarah, Benjamin, and the two boys converge in the study.

TWENTY-ONE

SATURDAY, JUNE 8, 2019

"AFTER SOME RESEARCH and the help of an online calculator, I have determined that one pound in 1752…" Jeremy leans forward, putting his glasses on. "…would be worth about 133 pounds today. And at close of business yesterday, the British pound is valued at $1.48 US dollars. So, one pound in 1752 would be worth nearly $197 US dollars today."

"And ten pounds," Benjamin calculates, "would buy a decent workhorse. That means a horse today would cost about $1,970. Jeremy, how much would you pay for a horse?"

"I am not sure, because there is a wide range of pricing on horses due to their size and status nowadays. Let's look at something simpler."

"All right. Jeremy, may I use a piece of paper and a pencil?"

"Let's use the online calculator. It will be much easier than pencil and paper," Jeremy replies.

"All right then. Sarah, how much would flour cost today?"

"Funny you ask; I bought some yesterday. I paid $3.50 for a five-pound bag."

Jeremy enters the values into the calculator.

"$3.50 is equivalent to 2.36 pounds," Jeremy determines.

"Whoa!" Benjamin exclaims. "We can buy a hundredth weight, which is equal to 112 pounds, for a little over thirteen shillings, wholesale. Incredible how the prices have escalated since the 1750s."

Jeremy does the quick math on a calculator, mumbling to himself as he types in the numbers. "There are twenty shillings in a pound. That is just over thirty-four pounds for 112 pounds of flour."

"Wow!" Benjamin gasps.

"Boys," Dad says, "so you have an idea of Benjamin's price shock and what these costs really mean to you, a $2.00 bottle of Coke today, based on a two and a half percent annual inflation rate would cost approximately $1,460.00 in 267 years."

"Whoa," Zach says. "Now *that* is expensive."

"And you thought things were expensive today," Dad replies. "Imagine what those kids will think then?"

"No kidding," Zach says, but his real interest is showing Benjamin the movie. "C'mon, Benjamin, let's go watch *Star Wars*. This will blow your mind." The boys race upstairs to the media room.

"Benjamin," Sarah says, "let me show you to your room, then you can catch up with the boys." Sarah leads Benjamin up the stairs and introduces him to the guest room. "You should be comfortable here. There's a restroom down the hall on the way to the media room." As she turns to leave she says, "If you need anything, don't hesitate to ask."

"No, that is all. Thank you very much, Sarah."

"Goodnight, Benjamin." She steps into the media room. "Boys, your father and I are going to bed. We have an early start tomorrow. Don't stay up too late."

"We won't," Zach responds.

She leaves for downstairs.

Benjamin sheds his jacket and lays it on the brown and burgundy stripes of the queen-sized bedspread. He looks around the room and notices pictures of the family on top of the dresser. He picks up one of the pictures and looks it over, then sets it back down. He notices himself in the dresser's mirror. "What an interesting dilemma you have put yourself into, Benjamin." He stares for a moment longer, when he hears the familiar sound of popcorn popping. He leaves to join the boys.

Benjamin enters the room, where Zach and Zane await his arrival in large, dark-colored, cushioned theater seats. He smells a familiar aroma. "Popcorn. I love the smell of popcorn."

"Benjamin, you ready for this?" Zach asks. "Have a seat, take your shoes off, and kick back and relax. If you push back on your chair, the seat will recline and a footrest will come out. So, have a seat and make yourself comfortable, and I will get you some popcorn."

"Now that you mentioned it, I will take off my shoes." With his shoes off, he pushes back on the chair. The footrest raises under his feet. "Oh my! This is fantastic."

While Benjamin makes himself comfortable, Zach hops out of his chair, fills three bags with popcorn, and hands the two of them a bag. He reaches below one of the counters and, from a miniature fridge, he grabs a bottle of Coke for each. "Here, Benjamin, a little treat for your first movie experience."

"Coke and popcorn. This movie thing is starting out right," Benjamin says, gazing at the curtain-framed eighty-four-inch glass screen mounted on the wall.

"You can put your bottle in the drink holder here on the armrest," Zane says, pointing.

He sets his bottle in the drink holder. "I am not real sure what to do here. So, you boys will need to help me a little."

"All you have to do is sit and watch," Zane replies.

Zach presses a button on the console of the wide armrest. The lights in the room fade to that of a single candle.

Benjamin looks up at the ceiling. "What's happening to the lights? How did that happen? Is something wrong?"

"Relax, Benjamin," Zach says. "It's all part of the show."

He presses another button and the screen before them illuminates, but remains dark. The room is quiet. Suddenly, the screen comes to life with the 20th Century Fox intro. Its spotlights rotate across the screen as the strategically placed eight surround-sound speakers fill the room with the iconic sound rift.

Benjamin's eyes open wide. The deep sound from the bass speaker vibrates through his body. Not knowing what to expect, he presses back in his chair, both excited and a little frightened. The opening scene of the movie starts. The large and prominent words "STAR WARS," on a drifting horizontal plane, slowly fade into the distant background. A phrase displays on the screen: "A long time ago in a galaxy far, far away…" The iconic *Star Wars* theme starts to play. Benjamin relaxes in his chair. He now understands what is happening. "This is like a play, but on the wall. This is incredible!" Benjamin exclaims. "Absolutely amazing!"

Deep in the movie, Benjamin jumps in his seat, frightened from an incident on the screen and the thunderous roar of the surround-sound system that vibrates through the room. Benjamin pulls his chair's leg rest down and sits on the edge of his seat, elbows on his knees and his fingernail in his mouth, as a fight scene grows with intensity. Near the end, he cheers as an important scene occurs and Luke Skywalker defends the galaxy. He is elated at the end when Luke defeats the enemy and restores harmony to the galaxy, for now. The credits roll.

"What an amazing story," Benjamin exclaims. "That was incredible. I never in my wildest dreams imagined anything of the sort could exist. That was amazing. Thank you, boys, for bringing me to the future. This was worth it."

"I knew he would like it," Zach boasts. Both boys go on about the movie, discussing a few of its scenes, when they notice a frown creep onto Benjamin's face as he sits back in his chair.

"What's wrong?" Zane asks.

"My thoughts turned to William and what he might be doing right now. He would have enjoyed this. I am sad that he is not here with me to share this moment." Benjamin stands up. "Boys I really enjoyed the movie, but I must turn in. It is late and we shall be rising early to look for Bernard. We need to find Bernard. We need to go home."

"You will, I promise," Zach says.

TWENTY-TWO

SUNDAY, JUNE 9, 2019

AT 5 A.M. THE Spiderman alarm clock sounds. Zach wakes in a groggy state, sleepy from the late night introducing Benjamin to a new form of entertainment. "Benjamin Franklin!" he mumbles and sprouts up in bed. "Please let it be a dream. Please let it be a dream." He jolts out of bed and darts to the guest room to find the bed perfectly made, with no lingering clothes, hat, or shoes. No evidence the room has been disturbed. "Yes," he says with a fist pump, "Oh my God, what a dream. It was so realistic."

With déjà vu fresh in his mind, he slides into a pair of blue jeans, a black T-shirt with a white spiderweb across the front, and his orange, red, and yellow Nikes. He darts downstairs and into the kitchen to find only his mother, who is preparing breakfast in her gray and hot pink tennis shoes and blue jeans. Her bear apron covers her bright yellow, short-sleeve, shirt. He detects four plates at the table, which helps confirm his dream. He thinks to himself, *If Benjamin were here, there would be five plates.*

He sits. "I had the strangest dream last night."

"Really? What about?" Mom asks, glancing his way.

"I had this dream that Zane and I had traveled to the past and met Benjamin Franklin."

Mom turns away, trying to contain a growing smirk, but plays along. "Really!"

"And he came forward to the future with..." A toilet flushes and Benjamin steps from the entry hall bathroom wearing the same blue jeans and brown collarless shirt from last night.

"Good morning, Zach," Benjamin says cheerfully as he slips around to the back of the glass table in the breakfast nook. "I hope you slept well. I know I did. Those beds are outstanding. Like nothing I have ever slept on—so soft and comfortable. Today's technology has brought the slumbering experience a long, long way. I want to take that bed home with me."

"I'm sure," Zach says as he quickly turns his attention back to his mother. "And you didn't even bother to stop me."

Mom breaks out in laughter. "I couldn't help myself, but I knew it wouldn't last long. You, believing it, for a few minutes was sure to start my day with a good laugh. But really, why else would you be up at 5 a.m.?"

"Crap," Zach says disappointedly. "I mean, good morning, Benjamin. I'm glad you slept well."

"We have a busy day ahead of us," Benjamin says. "I look forward to finding Bernard. I believe one day in the future is plenty for me."

"Good morning." Zane greets everyone while taking a seat at the table wearing his blue jeans, white and blue Nikes, and a white T-shirt with a patchwork of black and white comic strips and red block opaque lettering that outlines the word "MARVEL," allowing the comic strips behind the word to transpose through. "Benjamin, no offense, but I really hoped yesterday was only a dream."

"Well, don't feel alone," Zach interjects. "Mom let me believe it was a dream."

"I couldn't help myself." Mom laughs.

Benjamin snickers.

Jeremy strolls into the kitchen wearing blue jeans, an untucked, pale-orange, short-sleeve, button-down shirt—with buttoned pockets on either side of his chest—and his brown Sketchers. "Good morning. Everyone ready to find Mr. Bernard Ranter?"

"After we eat some breakfast," Sarah says as she adds the finishing touches to the scrambled eggs. "I have biscuits in the oven that will be ready in a minute."

Mom asks, "Zane, will you put the orange juice on the table, please? And, Zach, can you set another place for Benjamin?"

"Yes."

"Sure."

Benjamin hears a beeping sound and looks around for its origin.

Sarah pulls the biscuits out of the oven and sets them on the cooktop, where she places them in a cloth-lined basket and covers them to stay warm. She sets the basket on the table next to the bowl of eggs.

"Benjamin," Sarah insists, "our guests go first, so please help yourself. We have plenty, so don't be bashful."

As everybody eats, Jeremy wants to go over their plan.

"We know Bernard will be near Rittenhouse Square. We'll take two separate vehicles to spread out our search. Zane, you'll ride with your mom and me. And Zach, you and Benjamin will ride together. Make sure you have your cell phones and take your chargers just in case. We need to check every store and business to see if anyone has seen him."

"Benjamin, I know you and the boys know what Bernard looks like, but can you describe him for Sarah and me?"

"I think the boys will be better at describing him. He only peeked inside the door, so I only saw his face."

"Dad," Zach says, "he was wearing a long brown coat with a length to his knee. He has one of those three-pointed brown hats."

"Zach, they are called tricorns," Benjamin interjects.

"Oh, yeah, those," he comments and then continues. "He also wore a long-sleeve V-neck white shirt and knee-length brown pants and white socks with brown boots."

"Again, Zach, to be correct, his pants are called breeches and his socks are called leggings."

"Uh, men wear leggings? Okay," Zach says, confused, with his left eye and eyebrow pinched. "And, he has a short, brown scraggly beard."

"How tall is he and how much do you think he weighs?" Jeremy asks.

Benjamin jumps in. "He is approximately five-foot-eight inches tall and weight I am not sure about. We do not have scales readily available to weigh ourselves. He is a medium-build man, and thinner than me, and he has shoulder-length dirty blond hair. Oh, and he is in his early forties. Also, remember, he may have removed his coat and hat, because that round thing on the counter said the temperature will be near ninety today. We may see him in only his brown breeches and white shirt."

"All right, good. Here is the plan. Sarah, Zane, and I will go up and down the streets that run east and west, while Zach and Benjamin will take the streets that run north and south. First, we will cover ten blocks. If no luck after that, then we will meet back at Rittenhouse Square and start covering the area on foot, checking with each store to see if anyone has seen him. Of course, if anybody has, call the others to tell them."

As they leave the house to perform their search, Benjamin stops under the porte-cochère and says, "I have one thing to say to everyone before we go: 'May the Force Be with You.'"

"Oh no," Zach cries out. "Benjamin's quoting *Star Wars*. Man, it is going to be a long day."

Everyone laughs.

TWENTY-THREE

SUNDAY, JUNE 9, 2019

UNDER THE OLD oak trees of Rittenhouse Square, Jeremy finalizes the last-minute details to make sure everyone's on the same page.

They drive down each street, slowly searching the alleyways and storefronts. An hour passes; neither has called the other.

Benjamin and Zach have covered most of their search area when Benjamin blurts out, "Zach, look." He points toward a shop. "That may be Bernard entering that shop."

Zach looks, but the man has already stepped through the door. He pulls over to the side of the street.

"Benjamin, wait here with the truck while I check him out. If it's him, I'll come back and call the others to figure out our plan."

"All right," Benjamin says.

Zach enters the shop.

In the truck's center console, Zach's cell phone rings. Benjamin turns it toward him and reads the screen: "Dad Calling."

Benjamin picks up the phone and mimics what he has seen Zach do with it. He presses the "Accept" button on the screen, but is unsure what to do next. He raises the phone to his ear. "Hello?"

"Zach," the female voice on the other end says. "Any luck?"

"No, this is Benjamin. I saw someone that looked like Bernard and he is checking it out now."

"Benjamin, this is Sarah. We are FaceTiming with you and all I see is the inside of your ear. Take the phone away from your ear and look at the screen and you will see me."

Benjamin pulls the phone away. "Hey, I can see you. How did you do that? This is incredible!" Benjamin shouts with excitement. "How is this possible? I would not believe it if I had not seen it with my own two eyes."

"How it works is for another time," Jeremy says, as Sarah turns the phone so that Benjamin can see him. "Did you find him?"

"Wait, Zach is leaving the shop. He is shaking his head *no*."

Zach climbs back into the truck.

"Here, they are facing us," Benjamin says, as if he has the lingo down, while handing the phone to Zach.

"What?" Zach says with a laugh as he looks at the phone. "You mean they are FaceTiming us?"

"Oh, FaceTiming. Yeah, that's it."

"Any luck?" Dad asks.

"No. Benjamin saw someone he thought may be him. But I checked it out and it was some old man in a long-sleeve white shirt. So, no luck here and we're about finished with our ten-block area. We will head back to the square and start searching on foot."

"Okay," Dad replies. "We too are finished. We will do the same. Let's meet before we start again. Park your…"

"Wait!" Zach interrupts Dad with a shout. "I see him. He just stepped out onto the corner at the next block." He points so Benjamin can spot him.

Benjamin nods. "Yes, I see him."

"Fantastic!" Dad exclaims. "Where are you?"

"We're at 18th street and Panama. We're going to get out and follow him on foot. We will stay back so he does not notice us. Call me when you get here."

"We will." Dad hangs up. "They found him." He shifts into gear and takes off.

Several minutes later, Zane, Jeremy, and Sarah have caught up with Zach and Benjamin.

"Where is he?" Dad asks.

Zach points across the street. "He is about a half a block up."

"Yeah, I see him."

"Me too," Sarah and Zane say at the same time.

"He is walking super slow. I mean, I have seen turtles walk faster than him."

"You would walk slow too, if you had no place to go," Mom comments.

"All right, here's the plan," Dad says. "Your mom and I will catch up and walk past him and then slow down. You boys close in behind him, and Benjamin, you approach him and let him know that we can help and he can have a hot meal if he will sit and talk. Let him know that he is safe with us and nobody will hurt him. Make sure he knows we can take him back home."

"I like the plan," Benjamin says.

The others agree as well. They cross the street and put their plan into action.

Bernard saunters along the sidewalk. This allows Sarah and Jeremy an opportunity to catch up to him. They follow close behind, with the others lagging behind them. Jeremy and Sarah pick up their tempo and walk past Bernard, then slow their pace again before they reach the next intersection. Zach and Zane trail Bernard. Benjamin paces past them and up to Bernard.

"Bernard," Benjamin says, "please don't run. We can help."

"Benjamin!" Bernard says in a startled tone. Nervous, he looks around and notices the two boys who chased him yesterday through the streets. He looks the other direction and notices a man and woman staring at him, realizing they too must be with Benjamin and the two boys. Scared and surrounded, and standing at a restaurant's doorway, he bolts inside.

Benjamin and Zach both take off after him, but bump into each other at the door.

Zane hollers to his father, "Go around that way and I will go this way. Hopefully, we can cut him off on either side." They both take off in their directions. Sarah follows Jeremy.

"Bernard, stop!" Benjamin hollers as they chase him through the restaurant. Bernard battles his way through the kitchen, knocking dishes to the floor. He pulls a pastries cart over as he passes to slow down his chasers. He knocks over a trash can while two frightened restaurant employee girls jump out of the men's way as they hurl through the kitchen. Bernard finds an open door and bursts into the back alleyway. He spots Jeremy enter the alleyway at one end and turns to run in the opposite direction.

Jeremy sees the events unfold from the end of the puddle-laden brick alley, when Zach and Benjamin explode out the restaurant's back door.

Bernard races as fast as he can through the musty, garbage-reeking alley. As he nears the end to turn onto the approaching side street, Zane appears around the corner and Bernard collides with him, knocking Zane to the ground where he scrapes his elbow. Bernard keeps his feet and stretches his distance.

Each of them yells, "Stop! Bernard, stop! We can help."

Bernard, races away and turns down another alley. Zane, back in pursuit, speeds ahead of Zach. Benjamin's lungs burn as he becomes winded and gives up the chase to catch his breath.

Bernard turns down another alley, trying to lose them, but this alley is a dead end. He stops and hears their calls and realizes they are not far behind. Zach and Zane round the corner and find he is trapped.

They stop several yards away. The three of them, winded, try to catch their breath. Jeremy catches up to them, and he too realizes Bernard is trapped.

"Please stop running," Zach pleads while he is bent over with his hands on his knees, breathing hard. "We will not harm you in any way. We want to help you."

"We need to explain what has happened," Zane says, gasping for air. "We want to sit and talk. If you stop running, we can explain."

"What kind of hell is this place?" Bernard shouts, trying to catch his breath, but manages to rattle off several questions in a row. "Where did you come from? What has happened? How did I get here? What was that bright flash of light and that loud explosion yesterday? Why did you take me from my home? What do you plan to do with me? This place is like nothing I have ever seen. I do not understand what has happened," he says with confusion on his face and anger in his voice.

"We can explain," Zach pleads, "but you have to quit running. We cannot explain unless we can sit and talk. I promise we will not harm you in any way."

Benjamin and Sarah come up on the alley and find the boys, Jeremy and Bernard. Benjamin races to them, Sarah following behind.

"Bernard, please let them explain," Benjamin pleads. "This is a difficult and confusing situation, but these people can help. I know this is nothing like what you and I have ever experienced, but they are good people. Please give them a chance to explain and you will understand. If you keep running, you never will."

Bernard, still winded, says, "But how do I trust them? I do not know what they plan to do with us, Benjamin. They may want to kill us or use us for some type of a sacrifice for their gods."

"Bernard," Benjamin replies, "they do not plan on any of that. I spent last night at their home. They were very accommodating to me. They took me out to dinner for pizza last night. We watched a movie for entertainment. They could have killed me anytime they wanted, but they did not. Once you hear their explanation, you will understand."

"I know I will not understand without an explanation. But they are the cause of this," Bernard says with anger still in his voice.

"Yes, and they realize that, but our only hope to go home is with them. They are the only ones that can provide the explanation, and they are the only ones that can take us home."

After a moment of hesitation, he says, "All right, I will listen, but I want to know what happened. I want to know what this place is. I want to know how to get back home. And I want the truth."

"They will explain everything," Benjamin says in a confident voice. "Remember, I am the only person you know and you are the only person I know. You did not plan this and neither did I, but we both are caught in this confusing situation. The Longs are our only hope to help ourselves."

"The Longs?" Bernard asks.

"Zach and Zane Long." Benjamin gestures toward the two boys. "As you may remember them chasing you yesterday."

"Hi, I'm Zach," he says, still breathing hard.

"And I'm Zane." He provides a simple wave of his hand.

Benjamin continues, "And this is Zach and Zane's mother and father, Jeremy and Sarah Long."

"Hello, I'm Sarah."

"And I'm Jeremy." He steps forward and extends his hand to greet Bernard.

Bernard is cautious, but he returns the greeting and shakes Jeremy's hand.

"I can only imagine the emotions you must be going through after yesterday's events. But we can explain what has happened—it may make some sense for you. Then, we can explain how we plan to correct it and send you and Benjamin home. Are you injured in any way?"

"No," Bernard replies. "But I do have many questions."

"Bernard," Benjamin says, "remember, I am in this as well and I too was very confused, scared, and angry all at the same time. But they have explained it to me and it does make sense, although farfetched."

"Bernard," Jeremy asks, "I would like to explain what has happened over lunch—our treat. Will you sit with us?"

"I am very hungry, so yes."

"There is a little café up the street," Jeremy recalls from their search. They all agree and walk toward the café.

TWENTY-FOUR

SUNDAY, JUNE 9, 2019

ONLY ONE OTHER couple sits in the café. This pleases Jeremy, because it provides them with a little more privacy for their conversation.

"Bernard," Jeremy says, "they have many different sandwiches here. They even have breakfast tacos if that interests you. Whatever you want, I will cover the bill."

Bernard is not accustomed to reading a menu on a board displayed with so many different options. In his era, a waitress would bring them the daily meal. Choices would be offered only in the wealthier establishments, which he could not afford. He browses the menu but is confused with the choices and does not understand many of the items' descriptions. This café, though normal to those of the current era, has him unsure of what to expect of the food.

"Jeremy," Bernard asks, "I do not know what to ask for. What would you recommend?"

"Do you like eggs?" Jeremy asks.

"They are good," Bernard replies, "but not what I want. What is a club sandwich? From the menu's description, it appears to be a little much on a sandwich."

"If you like cheese and meats, then you will be pleased. Club sandwiches are very tasty."

"Then I will have the club sandwich," Bernard decides.

With their food in hand, they sit in a corner of the café next to a window, away from the other couple.

"Mr. Bernard," Zach says, "I wish we could have caught up with you yesterday so we could explain, but you're a little faster than my brother and me. We could have saved you a night of sleeping outside. But now that you are with us, let me explain what has happened. First, you have traveled through time, to the year of 2019."

"2019?" Bernard replies loudly. "Like..."

"Shhh. Yes, like 267 years into the future," Benjamin interjects.

"My dad," Zach continues, "has built a time machine, which we knew nothing about. But he was having issues making it work. The night before this happened, he accidentally left EMITT in the time travel mode.

"The next day we were to bring EMITT to Dad, where he was meeting with a couple of colleagues. They planned to help Dad solve a math problem. But Zane and I wanted to recreate Benjamin's famous kite experiment and decided to leave early enough so we would have time to fly the kite before they arrived. But when we conducted the kite experiment, surprisingly we captured the lightning, and through a chain of events the time machine started and we traveled back to 1752.

"Believe me, we were pretty confused at what had happened as well. But once we figured it out, we planned to fly the kite again during the next thunderstorm to catch the lightning and travel back to 2019 before anyone had even noticed."

"And that's when our problems started," Zane interjects.

Zach continues, "Benjamin and William came upon us in their wagon, and to keep from being discovered we had to stay out of sight, but they decided to fly their kite from EMITT's porch. We knew from history that Benjamin would catch the lightning with his kite experiment. We decided to let him, and once he had, we would scare him and William off the porch, and with the electricity from the lightning, we could activate EMITT's computers and we would be on our way back to 2019, alone. No harm, no foul."

"What?" he says, confused at the explanation, with his head cocked a little to the side. "No harm, no foul? EMITT? Catch lightning? This makes no sense." Bernard remains puzzled, then takes a large bite out of his sandwich.

"Here, let me help," Jeremy jumps in. "'No harm, no foul.' It's an expression we use meaning nobody hurt, so no consequences. And my time machine's name is EMITT, which appears as a cabin, but in reality, it's my laboratory on a trailer. And Benjamin is a famous historical figure known for many accomplishments, including flying a kite in a thunderstorm, which proved lightning is electricity."

"That helps." He turns to Benjamin with an unexpected scowl. "So, now you're famous too. Seems like you win at everything."

Silence dominates their conversation.

The Longs understand there is a rift between the two, but it now appears it may be deeper than they understand. To avoid any confrontation, Benjamin says nothing.

To free the awkwardness, Zach continues, "The problem was we scared William off the porch, but not Benjamin, and apparently you were behind the trailer for some reason and the four of us traveled through time, back to 2019."

"Wow, this sandwich is really good," Bernard says. "So, you're saying Benjamin and I have traveled to the year 2019? That does explain a lot. I mean the buildings here are huge, larger than I have ever seen. The streets are so well defined. And the bridges—nothing like I have ever seen. And those powered wagons or trucks or whatever you call them. Incredible power, and fast. How do they work?"

"The one you stole yesterday is my brother's truck. Oh, by the way, do you have my phone?"

"Your phone?" Bernard asks. "What is a phone?"

Zach pulls his phone out of his pocket and shows it to Bernard. "This is what it looks like. We know you have it with you, because we have been tracking it. That's how we found you."

"Oh that." Bernard reaches into his pocket. "I did not know what it did and I could not make it work. Here, you can have it back." He slides it across the table.

Zane presses the "On" button but nothing happens. "The battery must be dead."

"To explain the truck," Zach continues, "there are many different types of vehicles, as I'm sure you have by now seen. They have a motor that runs on gas and they mostly operate the same way."

"Interesting. But I must apologize," Bernard says. "Somehow, I broke yours yesterday after I stole it from you. I hope you will forgive me."

"It's okay—you were scared and confused," Zach says. "And the truck's not broken. It ran out of gas. We found it yesterday, put gas in it, and it works fine. We took it home last night."

"So, when can we go home?" Bernard asks, again with a matter-of-fact tone. "I don't believe this is a place where I want to live. I would rather be back in 1752. That is home and I will be more comfortable there."

"Well," Jeremy replies, "that is our plan, to send you and Benjamin back to 1752. But to do so, we'll have to wait for the next lightning storm. If we're lucky, one may pop up tomorrow or the next day. But we will keep watching the weather and decide in the next couple of days. In the meantime, we will go back to our house where you and Benjamin will stay until we can make the time travel event occur. When that time arrives, we will send you and Benjamin home right about the same time you traveled forward. It will appear as if you had never left."

"If everyone's finished with their lunch," Jeremy says, "we can head home and let Bernard settle in."

TWENTY-FIVE

SUNDAY, JUNE 9, 2019

OUTSIDE THE CAFÉ, Mom suggests, "Maybe you boys would like to watch another movie with Benjamin and Bernard. Or maybe the two men would like to take a hot shower or bath and I can wash their clothes before they go home. This would provide them an opportunity to experience a modern-day shower."

"A nice hot bath would be wonderful," Benjamin replies. "From what I have seen at your home, it looks most intriguing. And if you don't mind, I would love to see the washing machine work."

"I had a bath last week at Connors Place in town," Bernard replies. "I am not ready for one yet. If you don't mind, I will wait."

"Bernard," Benjamin suggests, "you may want to reserve that comment until you have seen the home. You have never seen anything of the likes of this place. The bath would be a welcome treat. I have seen their shower and you will be impressed."

"Then I will decide later, but as you well know, baths are not a treat. They are time-consuming and a pain to deal with, and I don't want to take that kind of time here. But I will wait and make my decision then."

"Bernard, our baths, or showers, are very convenient," Sarah says. "It is commonplace for us to take a bath daily, because of its convenience and it makes us feel clean and refreshed. You may change your mind once you see what we have to offer."

"Benjamin, Bernard," Jeremy suggests, "why don't the two of you ride with Sarah and I back to the house? Zane and Zach can ride together."

The boys agree and leave in Zach's truck.

As they leave the downtown area, Benjamin notices a person at a construction site completely covered up and generating a bright bluish light.

"Jeremy," Benjamin asks, "what is that man doing to create that bright light?"

"That's arc welding."

"Can you explain it?"

"Sure. It's a process where two pieces of steel are joined together to form one. A welding machine creates the electric current, which passes through a welding rod. When the rod is held close, but not touching, it creates an arc. This arc melts the two pieces of steel and the rod and fuses them together. Now, the fused pieces of steel are as strong as the original. This is common practice for any construction site. Our buildings and bridges would not be possible without welding."

"That is truly amazing," Benjamin exclaims. "Do they still use timber to build the buildings?"

"We use wood to build homes and smaller structures, but once the project starts to reach a certain height, lumber can no longer support the weight of the structure. That's when concrete or steel or both are used."

"Jeremy," Bernard says, "I am still amazed at how you were able to travel through time. Can you explain how your time machine works?"

"That is a bit more complicated, and I would rather not divulge its mechanics. EMITT is an extremely complex machine, and if not operated with proper structure and guidance, it could completely change history, which could have dire consequences on all of society's future. So, I will not go into that one with anybody, at least not for a while."

"Then, maybe you could explain those flying machines I saw yesterday," Bernard asks.

"Yes," Benjamin agrees. "Please do. I had one scare the living daylights out of me yesterday. While the boys were trying to suck gas out of the truck, I stood alongside EMITT when I heard this high-pitched whining sound. I stepped away from EMITT to investigate the noise, when this huge flying machine soared right above us. I thought I was going to die. It scared me so bad that I ran across the street and dove into a crevasse and landed in the water. And of course, those two boys of yours laughed at me like I was a fool."

Sarah, Jeremy, and Bernard laugh at the image of Benjamin diving into the ditch.

"Benjamin, you have to admit, that is funny," Bernard says with a laugh. "I can see you diving for the dirt. I saw one yesterday as well, and the machine was enormous. I could not believe something that large could even be in the air. What is its purpose?"

"That was probably a passenger jet...," Jeremy says before Benjamin interrupts.

"The boys said it's a...uh...um...uh...a Bone 747," Benjamin recalls.

"You mean a Boeing 747," Jeremy replies.

"That's it," Benjamin answers.

"Ah yes, the airplane. One of the greatest inventions of mankind," Jeremy remarks. "The Boeing 747 is a large jumbo jet that carries a lot of passengers, somewhere between 450 to 600 passengers, depending on the configuration of the plane. But the large iconic hump on the front of the airplane is what makes it so distinctive and recognizable. That plane has the capability to fly across the Pacific Ocean or to any continent in the world without refueling."

"I don't believe that is possible," Bernard argues.

"No, it's true," Sarah reaffirms.

"So, you could fly from Philadelphia to London, England, without stopping?"

"Absolutely," Jeremy replies. "That flight takes a little under eight hours and they do it every day."

"Less than eight hours?" Benjamin exclaims. "Several years ago, in my time that is, my voyage across the Atlantic Ocean lasted eleven weeks. And now, you can fly there in less than eight hours. Incredible!"

"In addition," Jeremy continues, "there are over eighty-seven thousand flights that occur every day in the United States, and about thirty thousand of those carry paying passengers, like the 747 you saw yesterday. The remaining flights are private, cargo, and military aircraft."

"Eighty-seven thousand a day!" Benjamin questions. "That is an enormous number of airplanes. How can that be possible? How do they keep from colliding with each other?"

"With a remarkable tool called radar," Jeremy responds. "Without it, modern-day flying would not be possible, at least not safely."

"What is radar?" Bernard asks.

"Simply, radar is a radio signal that's transmitted out into the sky. If there's an object large enough to reflect the signal, then that reflected signal is detected at a receiving station and displays the information on a computer screen. The screen operator will see a blip indicating the airplane's location, sometimes out to a distance of a couple hundred miles."

"How does it know the distance?" Benjamin asks.

"The time it takes for the signal to return. The screen has a set of lines in a circle spaced equally apart. Each line represents a certain distance of miles away from the receiving station. Most airplanes come equipped with a transponder on board. The transponder transmits the plane's flight information next to its blip on the air traffic control tower's screen. The information usually includes an airline flight number, the direction of travel, the plane's altitude, and airspeed. The air traffic controllers provide the pilots directions and altitudes to avoid midair collisions. The pilots strictly follow their instructions and form a line to land at the airport."

He continues, "The governments, airplane manufacturers, and airline companies have created an intricate network for flying. The processes include procedures and many strict safety rules and regulations, by which all must follow. To create a safe flying environment, they created imaginary air highways where planes fly within predetermined altitudes. Are you familiar with a compass?"

"I am," Benjamin replies.

"Me too," Bernard says.

"Then, if you look at a compass, you will notice there are 360 degrees to determine a heading. A plane flying between a heading of zero up to 179 degrees will fly at odd altitudes; for example, thirty-three thousand or thirty-five thousand feet. Those flying between 180 and 359 degrees will fly at even altitudes, like thirty-two thousand or thirty-four thousand feet. This keeps planes from colliding in midair."

Once they approach their destination, the air traffic controller will guide each plane, via radio, into a line with other airplanes for their arrival. And because of the required safety measures put in place, the world's safest means of travel is flying."

"Bernard," Benjamin says, "if you tell anyone about any of this, I will surely deny it and you will surely be locked up as a crazy person. It's probably best we keep what we see to ourselves."

"You know, Benjamin, that is one of the few things we may agree upon. I promise you I will not tell a soul, and if you do I will surely deny it as well."

"I will say this," Benjamin says, "the future is an impressive place."

They arrive at the Longs' upper-middle-class suburban neighborhood, which Benjamin now sees in daylight for the first time.

"Look at the size of these homes," Bernard remarks. "We have nothing that resembles homes like this in our time."

"We built our home a little over thirteen years ago," Sarah comments.

"The subdivision was brand new at the time. Finally, the trees are starting to mature."

Jeremy turns onto their cul-de-sac street.

"That must be your home directly in front of us?" Benjamin asks.

"That's it," Sarah confirms.

"What a gorgeous home. Just as beautiful on the outside as it is on the inside. The large peaks with their windows," Benjamin ogles. "The white stone across the front of the home and the dark-colored exterior window shutters. The manicured grounds in front of the home are magnificent, with the bushes that line the forefront. Spiral trees on either end and white flowers down in front. Sarah, I know I said this before, but it's like a king's castle. Bernard is right, we have nothing like this in our time. The amount of time and money it must cost to support that type of a look.... It must be expensive."

"We do not have the money or resources for that type of a look in our time," Bernard remarks. "Your era is significantly different than ours."

"That, you are correct, Bernard," Benjamin replies. "That, you are correct."

Jeremy pulls into the two-car driveway and parks underneath the three-car porte cochère.

"Bernard, let me show you where you will sleep tonight," Sarah says. "I will put you in the media room and you will sleep on the sofa."

After getting Bernard settled into the room where he will reside during his stay, she shows Bernard the bathroom and shower area.

"You go to the restroom inside the house?" Bernard questions.

"Yes. That's what Benjamin said," Sarah replies as they make their way back downstairs.

"Sarah," Jeremy says, "I have some work to do with EMITT. I will need some quiet time to analyze the boys' time travel events."

"Okay," she replies. "But you need to figure out a way to send them back home without traveling yourself. The risk is just too great."

"I'll try." He says and turns to leave for EMITT, passing Zach and Zane as they make their way into the house.

"Benjamin, Bernard," Zach asks, "would you like to watch a movie? I thought we could watch *Back to the Future*. It's a time travel movie that you both will like, and it will be appropriate for the situation."

They agree and trot upstairs to the media room.

At the completion of the movie, Bernard responds, "They also needed the lightning for time travel. I thought you said you were the first persons to travel through time. It appears that Marty McFly and Doc were the first people to do so."

"No," Zane replies, "that's a make-believe movie. Those people are actors and play a role in the movie. The characters aren't real. The actors and actresses have gone on to make many more movies. It's all an act where a large production company takes a script and creates a movie, then they show the movie in theaters around the country—and many times, the world. Once the movie has been in the theaters for a while, its sales start to slow down as people go see the newest movies that arrive. After about six months they put the movie on a DVD and sell them in stores. That's what we watched—the DVD of the movie."

"That was all made up?" Bernard asks.

"Yep," Zach replies.

"It really did not happen?"

"Nope," Zane replies. "All an act to make money. It is what the entertainment business does. And they do it very well."

"Wow! So realistic."

"That was a fantastic movie," Benjamin says to Zach. "I am not sure which I liked best, that one or the *Star Wars* movie we watched last night. I do know one thing, though—that shower sounds intriguing. I must speak with Sarah about it."

"No need to talk to her," Zach says. "It's right here." He leads Benjamin to the bathroom. Bernard follows to watch. "I'll show you what you need to know." He opens the closet door and points. "These are the towels and wash cloths. Mom keeps a few disposal razors in here as well just in case we have company. She is always prepared."

"Disposal razors?" Benjamin questions with a confused look.

"Yeah, you know, to shave with," Zach says while contouring his face with one hand. It's not a problem Zane or I have to deal with, at least not yet, but they're here if you need them."

"Here's the shampoo for your hair and the soap for the wash cloth. This is the hot water side and this the cold side," Zach says, pointing to each. "Turn the hot water on first, then the cold and mix it to your liking. If you want to sit and soak, lift this lever and the tub will fill up; otherwise, lift this knob up and the showerhead will spray water on you. But, if you use the shower, pull the curtains closed first, so water does not spray outside the tub. Close and lock the door, hop in, and enjoy. When you're finished, the brush and combs will be in this drawer and a hair dryer will be below the sink." He opens the door below the sink.

"Hair dryer?"

"Yes, a hair dryer. We have that as well. If you can imagine it, we probably have it. Plug the hair dryer into the wall." Zach points to the plug on the wall. "But don't touch the metal prongs while doing it. If you do, those shocks you received during your electricity experiments will feel like a vacation compared to the shock you will receive from those prongs. Then, flip the switch on the hair dryer and blow your hair until it's dry."

"I remember the shocks from my electricity experiments. They hurt."

"Well, this can kill you," Zach informs them both.

"Hair dryers, razors. My goodness. These people do have everything," Benjamin mumbles to himself as he closes the door.

"I guess after he has finished, I too will take a shower," Bernard says to Zach before he leaves.

"Sounds good. I will let Mom know so she can get you some additional clothes to wear while she washes yours. Then you can change back into those if you want."

"I do appreciate it, Zach," Bernard praises. "You're a good kid. Thank you for the hospitality."

"No problem, Bernard. When Benjamin is finished, you can take yours."

TWENTY-SIX

SUNDAY, JUNE 9, 2019

JEREMY ENTERS THE house. "Zach, Zane, can you both come with me to EMITT?" Dad asks.

"Yes," both respond and follow their father outside.

Standing in front of the computers, the colors intermingle inside the acrylic tube as if they are slow dancing amongst each other.

"What you two have called 'the acrylic tube,' her name is Opal."

"You named the tube?" Zach asks sarcastically.

Dad mocks back with a whiny voice and his own sarcasm. "Yes, I named the tube."

"I like the name," Zane interjects. "I assume the name is because of the colors, or does it have another meaning?"

"No. The colors of the plasma reminded me of the colors in the opal stone. So, I named her Opal."

"What about EMITT? I'm sure it stands for something," Zane says. "We asked once before, but you gave us some bogus answer like 'to discharge or move forward' or something goofy like that."

"It is an acronym," Dad replies, "but divulging it then was not appropriate at that time. But, since you both have traveled through time with EMITT, I believe you have a right to know, but I want it to stay between us for now. It stands for Exotic Matter for Interstellar Time Travel. And it spells 'TIME' backwards, but with an extra T."

"Nice," Zane replies. "I like it."

"Me too. That's a pretty cool name for EMITT's purpose."

"I have a few questions," Dad says. "During either of the first two travel events, did some type of an electrical field or sparks occur when the event started?"

"Oh yeah," Zach and Zane both respond.

"That's what I figured. I would have expected something unusual to occur. Can you describe it?"

"Yes," Zach recalls. "There were these electrical arcs surrounding the trailer, and a loud static noise, which turned to crackling—then, a loud POW with a bright flash of light. It knocked both of us to the ground and temporarily blinded us the first time. The second time, we were prepared and protected our eyes."

"Smart. What about Opal? Did you notice anything with her?"

"Yeah," Zane recalls, "the colors started to spin very fast inside the tube, almost turning white."

"Perfect." Dad hesitates for a moment. "I want the two of you to be a part of everything that occurs with EMITT. She's a complicated machine and holds a large magnitude of responsibility. You both have demonstrated your readiness to handle that responsibility. If you boys wish, you may be partners in the EMITT project with your mother and me. We will share whatever information we have about EMITT. No more secrets between us, but you also must keep all information confidential. Any information divulged about EMITT, we decide as a group. Your mother has familiarity with most of EMITT's operations as well."

"So, Mom knows all about EMITT too?" Zane asks.

"She does. She knows the passwords, EMITT's capabilities, and how to operate her as well. Let's talk about what happened with the TTEs."

"TTEs?" Zach asks, puzzled.

"Time Travel Events," Dad explains. "I have reviewed the data and now have a detailed understanding of the events. The good news is we no longer need to fly a kite. EMITT's generator can provide the proper amount of current to open a wormhole and send her through."

"How does it work?" Zach asks.

"It has been the belief of many physicists that time travel could be possible through wormholes. The problem was, wormholes were only a hypothesis and had not been proven. To travel, a wormhole must be created, and the process to do so is with exotic matter. But wormholes are volatile and unstable, and as quickly as they open, they collapse. To travel through a wormhole, it needs to stay open long enough to reach the desired destination, meaning it will require a supporting framework to slow the collapse rate.

"That supporting framework is negative energy, which keeps the wormhole open long enough for EMITT to travel through. The more negative energy created, the longer the wormhole will stay open; thus, the further in time she can travel.

"The plasma that fills Opal has multiple purposes. It acts like a glue that keeps the particles in line for the collisions, and it holds the framework together to help slow down the collapsing process. And it provides her beauty. The spinning you witnessed are particles traveling at the speed of light and purposely colliding into each other. Those collisions create the exotic matter.

"After a review of the travel data from both TTEs, the lightning's current flowed through Opal and created enough negative energy that when combined with the exotic matter, the two created a wormhole that stayed open long enough for EMITT to slip through time.

"EMITT's computer tells Opal how long to generate the exotic matter, and EMITT's generator creates the current, which creates the negative energy. If those two are unlimited, EMITT could travel as far back as the Big Bang. But there is a limit. Opal can only generate a limited amount of exotic matter during a travel event. As the plasma heats up, it's structure breaks down and the particles miss each other; therefore, no more collisions and no more exotic matter. Because of this limitation, and a programmed safety precaution, she can only travel up to five hundred years in either direction. NO MORE! Beyond that, the potential for the wormhole collapsing is great."

"What happens if it collapses?" Zach asks.

"It's lights out. Everything traveling will be lost."

"That's a little scary," Zach replies.

"It's dangerous, and that's why your mother does not want any of us traveling. Which means, when it's time to take Benjamin and Bernard home, you two will have to stay behind and wait for my return."

"Dad, that's not fair. We are the ones who first traveled. We have experience with traveling, which could be very valuable to you during the TTE. Also, William will be there when we return. We need to apologize to him for scaring him to death."

"I understand, but I have to face your mother. Let's not decide anything right now and not a word of this to your mom."

"Okay," both boys respond.

"The night before you two traveled, I had tried to travel a few times, but to no avail. During my work, I had received a phone call from Mark and Sam to discuss our course of action after the lecture. We talked for several hours, which led me to the study. When we finished, I climbed in bed and forgot to close EMITT down. I had even left the travel parameters programmed to June 9, 1752. I chose that date because you two had recently learned about Benjamin Franklin and it sparked an interest in me as well. But my lack of focus allowed you two to travel to that time era.

"A couple of other details you both need to know. I have programmed some safeguards to help protect history, EMITT, and ourselves.

"First, I have programmed EMITT's computer so future TTEs will first send EMITT to our current time and date in 2019, which EMITT will send me an email packet containing that TTE's travel date, time, and some other system data, then continue on to the desired TTE. Again, because of this safeguard, no traveling over five hundred years from our date and time in 2019."

"Second, I have programmed EMITT's computer that after each time travel event, she will create an automatic return event to our current time and date in 2019. This automatic return event will occur upon the expiration of a thirty-minute timer. The timer can be bypassed with the correct password, 'Time For Benjamin.' If not, EMITT will automatically return to our current time and date, giving us an opportunity to find her on the tracker."

"And third, a few screen changes. I have added a button on the time travel screen to start the generator in case we need electricity when it's not readily available. I have eliminated the countdown timer as it no longer is necessary. It became a problem for me anyway. But this helps clean up the time travel screen."

"This will do a few things: 1) keep a thief from traveling far with EMITT, 2) keep an email log of what travel events have occurred in case we need to go back to a period to correct history or extract a thief, and 3) if EMITT were successfully stolen, there would at least be a log of EMITT's travel events and hopefully EMITT would be found at some point via the tracker in her computer."

"Wow," Zane remarks, "you've put a lot of thought into EMITT's protection. That's a great idea with the safeguards. But why don't you send Benjamin and Bernard back by themselves, and then because the password is not entered, EMITT will automatically return to us."

"No. When traveling, someone will always be with EMITT. What if Bernard, or Benjamin, decided to damage EMITT? We would never see her again. The safeguard is only if someone were to steal her from us."

"What about the original travel password, 'Touch The Key'?" Zane asks. "Has that been changed?"

"No, I will keep it the same," Dad replies. "Once we return Benjamin and Bernard back to 1752, there will be no need for it to change."

"I guess you have a point there," Zach agrees.

"One last thing: Any time we travel back to 2019, as a best-practice rule, we should always return five minutes after our last departure. We may be skipping ahead five minutes in time, but at least we won't be returning before we left in the first place, creating multiple versions of ourselves. Not to mention the possibility of landing on top of EMITT or possibly morphing into EMITT in some way. I have no idea what would occur in that scenario."

"That makes sense," Zane replies.

"I agree," Zach follows.

"I wanted to discuss this with you boys, so you can be a part of EMITT and share in her responsibility."

"Thanks, Dad," Zach says. "I will do everything in my power to make sure that EMITT stays safe."

"That goes for me too," Zane says.

"Then, I guess we are ready to send Benjamin and Bernard home," Dad determines.

The three of them leave EMITT and stroll back into the house.

As they walk around to the front of the garage, Bernard steps out from behind EMITT and thinks to himself, *Thanks for the passwords, boys. Now, to learn how to operate this machine, and that I will learn when you take us home.*

After the three of them return inside, Bernard sneaks into the garage and climbs the back stairs to the media room, unnoticed.

TWENTY-SEVEN

SUNDAY, JUNE 9, 2019

"DAD," ZACH ASKS as they enter the kitchen, "will we take EMITT back downtown to the same vacant lot to send them home?"

"That is a decision we need to determine," Dad says. "If we do, we run the risk of someone seeing EMITT vanish into thin air. I am curious if anybody noticed EMITT vanish when the two of you first traveled, then reappear later. I did not hear about it on the news or the internet."

"After yesterday's events," Zane recalls, "I don't remember watching any TV."

"There was nothing about it on the internet this morning," Zane interjects.

"Which means," Dad says, "we don't know if anybody saw anything or not. I don't believe this is something we can allow anyone to see, and I believe in the best interest of EMITT, and us, we should conduct the travel from the privacy of our own backyard."

"But there are issues with the backyard as well," Zach says. "We will return Benjamin and Bernard in a totally different place from where we originally took them. This would require them to walk twenty miles back to town, and they won't be happy about that. Remember, Philadelphia in

1752 was nowhere near the size it is today."

"Also, what time do we send them home?" Zane asks. "I thought we should return them right about the time we took them. At least William will still be there. He may be a little confused, but Benjamin could explain the events to him. Also, they would have their horse and buggy to ride back to town in, and Bernard would have his horse or whatever he used to follow them. At least everything would remain as close to the same as possible."

"Those too are good points," Dad says. "Let's talk with Benjamin and Bernard and see what they think. They should have some input here as well."

"I agree," Zach says.

"Me too," Zane agrees.

Jeremy sees Benjamin in the living room reading a book. He approaches. "What are you reading?"

"Oh, Sarah provided me with a fiction book by a man named Mark Twain. *The Adventures of Huckleberry Finn.* It is an interesting book with a unique style of writing."

"An interesting book!" Jeremy exclaims. "That's an understatement. That book is a masterpiece. As a man who loves to read, that one you will enjoy. Right now, though, we need yours and Bernard's attention for a moment to discuss your travel plans home. Do you know where Bernard is?"

"I believe he is upstairs."

Jeremy speaks. "Alexa, call media room."

A chime is heard. "Bernard, are you up there?"

There is a long pause. "Uh, yes," Bernard says with hesitancy, looking around the room. "Where are you?" he asks.

"I am on the speaker. Could you come downstairs to the kitchen for a minute?"

Another long pause before Bernard replies, "Uh, yes. I will be right down."

With the five of them around the breakfast table, Jeremy begins. "I have been working on EMITT and have made a few adjustments. After a review of EMITT's travel data from the two events, I am happy to say that we no longer need to fly a kite to travel through time. At least I'm about ninety-nine percent confident we will not. I have not yet tested it, but I am confident I'm right. The worst-case scenario, we just won't travel. The boys and I have discussed our plan to send you both home, and we believe you both should have an input. I planned on performing the TTE from our own backyard."

"TTE?" Benjamin asks.

"Time Travel Event," Zach answers.

"Ah."

Jeremy continues, "But, the boys brought up some good points. If we perform the TTE from the backyard, you will be about twenty miles or so from Philadelphia. That will make for a long walk back to town. The plan is to have you back a few minutes after the moment from which you originally traveled. It is necessary to send you back after the original TTE occurred; otherwise there will be two of each of you, and that's a bad idea.

"Traveling from the original location poses some problems as well. Somebody may see EMITT vanish, and that could raise some concerns for us upon our return. And, there is the issue of William seeing the trailer vanish right before his eyes, then moments later reappear. With us arriving immediately after the original TTE, Benjamin will be provided the opportunity to explain the events to William. His emotions will be all over the place. He will be frightened, elated, shocked, and confused all at the same time. He probably will not believe what he has seen."

Benjamin and Bernard sit and ponder their options for a moment.

"Jeremy, I agree with what you say," Benjamin states, "but Zach and Zane are correct; we should leave from the original travel location. If you leave us twenty miles from Philadelphia, I have no way to explain it to William before he leaves for home. He saw what he saw and he deserves an explanation. I will not lie to him and the explanation will be convincing.

When we reappear, he will again be traumatized. But upon him seeing my return, the explanation, and a quick tour of EMITT's equipment, and then watching the three of you and EMITT disappear again, he will believe. And, this will ensure he faces the same dilemma as Bernard and myself, by not discussing it with anyone. Otherwise, he too would risk being labeled a crazy person."

"I agree," Bernard chimes in. "We should go to the original location. My horse is there in the woods. If William asks, I will tell him I was spying on them and got caught in the time travel as well."

"Dad," Zach says, "it sounds like we should leave from the original travel location."

"I agree," Jeremy says, convinced. "It's settled. We shall travel from the original location."

"Now, what time do we leave?" Zach asks.

"I do not want anyone to see EMITT vanish into thin air. We shall leave early in the morning, around 3 a.m. The area should be vacant at that time of the morning."

"We will leave at 1 a.m. to provide enough time to drive downtown and set up," Jeremy decides. "But before we go, everyone should get some rest."

Jeremy slips off to bed. Benjamin, Zach, and Zane, not tired enough to go to sleep, sit down in the living room to watch some TV.

"I think I will take that shower now," Bernard says, then turns and walks away.

Zach turns on the TV. He searches for a program that will cause no harm for Benjamin to watch. "Benjamin, you'll like this. It's an old rerun of the *I Love Lucy* show. She is hilarious. This Lucy lady is crazy."

They sit back in the comfy couch and soon Benjamin is laughing at the scenes of Lucy's crazy ways. Before the second episode is halfway through, both Zach and Zane, having seen the shows so many times with their parents over the years, have become bored and doze off.

The Lucy show ends. Benjamin notices the two boys have fallen asleep. Benjamin's curiosity has gotten the best of him. He picks up the remote control and scans the control buttons. He presses the guide button, hoping to discover a program discussing today's current events. He stumbles through the buttons trying to understand how to operate the remote when he discovers an interesting show. "Top Ten Military Weapons," he mumbles to himself as he selects the channel and presses the volume-down button, hoping not to wake the boys. "This should be interesting. I can see how far their military has advanced."

As soon as the channel changes, a military jet lands on the deck of an aircraft carrier at sea, the plane comes to an abrupt stop, and a burst of steam rises from the deck. "My Lord," Benjamin whispers, in awe of the scene, and scooches to the edge of his seat. Another jet readies itself for takeoff. Suddenly, it catapults off the end of the ship. "Oh my!" he murmurs. "The power of this ship. The technology of the future is far beyond that of my wildest imaginations."

The scene switches to a distant profile view of the aircraft carrier as the narrator describes the events. Another jet lands on the deck before making a sudden stop. "Look at the size of that ship!" he remarks quietly. "It is so long that airplanes can take off and land on them, at sea. Those cables across the deck of the ship, they catch the planes when they land. The force must be incredible. How can that be possible?"

He continues to watch as the show progresses to other features of the ship, with its missile defense system and its rapid-fire guns, their accuracy, how its defense systems work together with the ship's radar. Mesmerized at the power and capabilities, he asks himself, "If the ship has that much power, what possibilities do the military jets possess?"

The show continues. He listens to the narrator explain how the fighter pilot paints its target with the use of satellites, then fires a laser-guided missile. "I thought Jeremy said those satellites were used for weather?" He watches the video of the missile until it explodes directly on top of its target. "The precision of today's warfare is incredible."

Benjamin is so entranced with the show, he does not hear Sarah enter the house. She walks into the living room. "Oh, Benjamin, I'm not sure you should be watching this type of a program," she says with concern while waking Zach and Zane from their snooze. "I know your curiosity is getting the best of you and you want to discover today's advancements. You will see many during your time here, but to search for them probably is not a good idea." She grabs the remote control from the coffee table and turns the TV off.

"You are right, Sarah. My apologies. When the boys fell asleep and the Lucy show ended, my curiosity was getting the best of me. After watching Zach operate the TV with that black thing, I tried operating it and when I came across this channel, I was very intrigued. I knew I should not have, but I could not help myself. I must say, your military today is incredibly powerful and precise. The future has come a long way."

"Yes, it has. And the black thing is called a remote control."

"That is an amazing device. You just point it at the TV, press a button, and it controls it. Just amazing! How does it work?"

"It's an infrared signal. Basically, it is an invisible light that works with the TV." She turns to Zach. "Where is your father?" Mom asks.

"He's asleep, resting for tonight," Zach answers. "We have a plan to take Benjamin and Bernard home tonight. We plan to leave at 1 a.m. and send them home around 3 a.m."

"That's good. But, as I have told your father, I do not want the two of you traveling on EMITT again until your father has done his studies on its effects."

"Mom, we've—"

"As I said, neither you or Zane will be traveling. Period! Also, I washed Benjamin's clothes. I will have them on his bed soon. Where is Bernard?"

"He said he was going upstairs to take his shower," Benjamin replies.

Ding-dong.

"I'll get it," Zach says, jumping up and strutting to the front door. He pulls the door open and recognizes the uniform's brown shirt and shorts.

The UPS delivery woman, holding a box in her hand, says, "I have an Amazon delivery." She hands the box to Zach. "Can you sign here?"

Zach signs for the package on the screen and closes the door.

"Benjamin, it appears a package has arrived for you."

"For me? Why would someone send me a package? Nobody even knows I am here." He opens the box, revealing a new brown tricorn hat. "This looks like the hat we saw on your phone in the truck yesterday."

"Yes, it is. I ordered it and had it shipped to the house overnight. This way you could see how the internet works and that we were not lying."

"That is incredible. The logistics of making that happen, in such a short amount of time, I cannot imagine. This society is incredible. I wish we did not have to go home." He puts the hat on his head and makes a minor fitting adjustment. "How does it look?"

"Fantastic," Sarah says.

"Yeah, looks great," Zach follows.

TWENTY-EIGHT

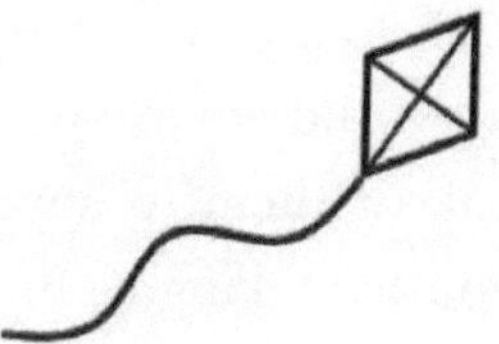

MONDAY, JUNE 10, 2019

IT'S 1 A.M., AND Jeremy, still in the same clothes from earlier—blue jeans and pale orange button-down shirt—has EMITT connected to his truck.

Benjamin, standing next to Jeremy and holding his long, brown great coat and his new tricorn hat that Zach bought him, is the only one to have changed clothes, wearing a loose-fitting, white button-down long-sleeve shirt, baggy brown breeches that gather just below the knee and over his white knit leggings, and his ankle-high brown boots.

As the men prepare to leave, Sarah steps out onto the driveway in her long pink robe and pink house slippers. "Benjamin, Bernard, I'm going to stay home while Jeremy and the boys take you back. I wanted to say it has been a great pleasure to meet both of you. I never in my wildest dreams..." She pauses for a moment, trying not to choke up, "Well, it has been an honor. I wish you both the very best. Benjamin, you are an incredible man. Please continue to do what is right. Our society today, as well as the past and the future, depend on you."

"Sarah," Bernard says, "thanks for the hospitality that you and your family provided to me, but I am ready to go back to my own era. This society is a bit more complicated than what I am accustomed to. Again, thank you."

Sarah reaches out and gives Bernard a hug.

"Sarah, you are a great lady and I only wish Deborah could have met you, but I am looking forward to seeing her, William, and of course my Sally. I would love to tell Deborah of the luxuries and gadgets you have in your home. I know she would love to have them for herself, but unfortunately, I cannot speak of them to anyone, so it shall remain our secret. I do want to thank you for taking us in. Again, thank you."

"You're so welcome," she says and gives him a heartfelt hug.

Benjamin and Bernard hop into the back seat of the truck.

They arrive downtown and find their original travel location. The area is dark other than a street light at each end of the block and on a few of the surrounding buildings. No cars are seen driving on the streets. The area is as deserted as they could have hoped for.

"Zach, Zane," Dad asks, "will you two walk the entire block to verify nobody's around that may be able to see us? Benjamin and Bernard can help me with EMITT."

After lowering the stabilizing jacks on the four corners, Jeremy asks, "Benjamin, would you like to operate EMITT's doors?"

"I would," Benjamin responds and follows Jeremy to the front of the trailer.

"Press the green button and hold it. That will lower the bottom door and then raise the top door. It will stop automatically when it's complete."

Benjamin presses the button and the doors open as Jeremy has described.

"Bernard," Jeremy asks, "can you raise the support on the far end and place it in the notch at the top? It will click in place."

"Yes," he says, mimicking Jeremy's actions from the other end of the porch.

Click.

With EMITT detached from the truck and the stabilizing jacks secured, Jeremy says, "Give me a couple of minutes while I program the computer for the correct date and time. When the boys return, we'll be ready."

Zach and Zane return from their scouting mission.

"Dad," Zach says, "we didn't see anybody. If you want, we could go now."

"I'm ready, but boys, I told your mother I would not let you travel. I am going to have to ask that you stay with the truck until I have returned."

"No way, Dad," Zach says adamantly. "We are not letting you go alone. We have traveled before and we know what to expect. If something goes wrong, we know how to get back with the lightning."

"Dad, I'm with Zach. Either we travel inside with the three of you or we travel outside like Benjamin and Bernard did originally."

Jeremy shakes his head with a new dilemma. He thinks for a moment. "I'm not letting you travel on the outside. Get in." He motions with his hands. "If you so much as tell your mother about this, I will have your heads before she gets to me."

"Let's go then," Zach responds.

"Benjamin, Bernard, are you ready?" Jeremy asks.

"I know I am," Benjamin responds.

"Me too," Bernard agrees.

"Great, let's go," Jeremy says, again motioning towards the door. "Everybody inside. I've already entered the time travel parameters, so if everyone can have a seat in the front room, we'll be on our way."

"Wait," Zane demands. "Dad, verify our arrival time. When we returned the first time, I programmed our destination time, but we arrived three hours later than planned. Which was the amount of time we waited for Benjamin to capture the lightning. I assume the timer continues to keep time after it has been entered."

"Yes, I discovered that as well and it's already been corrected. Once everyone's ready I will press the button. Please close your eyes before we go, so the flash of light will not blind you, if there is one."

"I'm ready," Jeremy states.

"Me too," Benjamin acknowledges.

"Let's go," Bernard says.

"I'm ready," Zane replies.

"Yep, let's do this," Zach confirms.

"Here we go. Everyone, close your eyes." Jeremy presses the button.

For the first time, Jeremy hears the computer's soft female voice say, "Password accepted. Time travel sequence initiated." Opal's multicolored plasma starts to spin, faster and faster. They hear a low vibrating hum, then two pops a couple of seconds apart, but that's it. No crackling static noise, no brilliant flash of light, no loud bang as before.

"What happened?" Benjamin asks. "It did not work. I do not want to be stuck here."

"Wait a minute," Jeremy says. "I made some changes to how EMITT starts the time travel event. Let me check, but I believe it did work."

Jeremy reviews the screen and reads the following data:

PREVIOUS TRAVEL DATE:	JUNE 10, 2019	TIME:	2:12	AM
CURRENT DATE:	JUNE 10, 1752	TIME:	2:00	PM
NEXT TRAVEL DATE:		TIME:		
PASSWORD:				
AUTOMATIC RETURN DATE:	JUNE 10, 2019	TIME:	2:12	AM
AUTOMATIC RETURN PASSWORD:		TIME REMAINING:	29:43	

NOTE: "AUTOMATIC RETURN DATE AND TIME" IS THE CURRENT DATE AND TIME IN 2019.

"According to EMITT's data, we made the trip to 1752. The current time is 2 p.m., which is about fifteen minutes after you originally left. But to confirm, let me look outside."

Everyone waits for an answer.

TWENTY-NINE

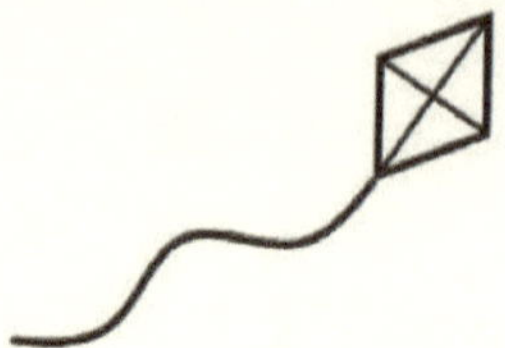

SATURDAY, JUNE 10, 1752

JEREMY STEPS TO the door and slowly pushes it open. He peeks out and sees tall grass, dark clouds, and a light rain falling. He opens the door further. A man in his early twenties stands in the rain.

"You must be William?" Jeremy asks.

"I...I...I am," he stutters, visibly shaken. "Who...who are you?"

"I am Jeremy. We have someone here you might like to see." Jeremy steps back to the computer to enter the Automatic Return password.

Benjamin bursts out the door and finds William standing in the rain, dripping wet. He bolts out and embraces William as if he has not seen him in thirty years. "Thank goodness you are okay."

"I am fine. It was you that disappeared. I have been concerned about you, Father," William cries in his English accent, his tears masked by his rain-soaked face. "One minute we are flying a kite and the next someone flings open a door, screams at us, which scares the living daylights out of me. When I turn around, poof; you, the boy, and the cabin disappear right before my eyes. I was frightened to death. I thought you died, were gone forever. Then, several minutes later, poof; you reappear again. Father, my eyes must be playing tricks on me. What has happened?"

"No, William, they are not," Benjamin says with excitement. "You and

I both are perfectly fine. But we have been caught up in an unusual set of circumstances. Please, please, come onto the porch, out of the rain, so we can talk. The strangest, wonderful, most amazing event has occurred and you have witnessed only a tiny fraction. But first, let me do some introductions."

William sees two men and two teenage boys step from inside the trailer.

"I know you," William says. "You are Bernard from town. But the others, I do not know."

"This is Jeremy Long and his two sons, Zach and Zane," Benjamin says. "You may remember Zach as he is the one who flung open the door to scare us. Zane was with him, but you could not see him because he was inside."

"Hello," William says with a nod and a wave.

"This is going to be a bit difficult to explain," Benjamin says, "but they have a time machine and have traveled from the future, 2019 specifically."

"What?" he says, looking back at his father as if he were speaking crazy talk.

"I know it is difficult to believe, but I have been gone for two days now and for you it has only been a few minutes. I too did not believe it when it happened, but then they proved it to me."

"Father," William asks as he peers into Benjamin's eyes with concern, "have you fallen ill? Do you hear what you say? A time machine? There is no such thing as a time machine."

"That's what I said, William. But we will prove it to you. First, look inside at the computers and the acrylic tube. Have you ever seen anything like it before? Have you?"

William steps inside and sees Opal, not even noticing the computers because his eyes immediately become fixated on the rolling and mixing of the tube's multiple colors.

"My goodness, what is that?" William gasps. "All of the colors in the tube, they are beautiful. I have never imagined such beauty."

"Look at the computers," Benjamin says. "Have you ever seen anything so advanced?"

He stares at the computer screens. The word "EMITT" slowly tumbles between the two screens.

"Father, what is this?" William asks.

"A time machine, William," Benjamin remarks. "I know it is hard to believe, but it really is. We traveled from the year 2019. My goodness, their world is so vastly different from ours. But, if the equipment and the beautiful tube does not convince you, there is one last thing that surely will. They must leave and go back to 2019, and doing so, they will once again vanish right before our eyes. Once they have gone, I will explain some of their amazing world that I have been fortunate enough to witnesses. But you can tell nobody of this. If you do, I will vehemently deny it. There is nobody that will ever believe you, so this is our secret. Telling others may cause them to have you condemned, and at a minimum, believe you are crazy. So, we cannot talk about any of the events witnessed today with anybody, including your mother and sister."

"William," Jeremy interjects, "it is true, we have traveled from the future. I have been working on EMITT for a few years, but my two sons were the ones to first make her work, although it was by accident. These events were not supposed to happen, but they did. I know we just arrived, and we would love to stay a while, but our sole purpose today was to ensure Benjamin and Bernard were returned to their rightful place in time. Now that we have completed our task, we need to leave as soon as possible. Being here could be detrimental to each of us and to history."

Jeremy turns and addresses Bernard and Benjamin as he extends his hand, shaking each. "It has been an honor meeting both of you. I hope you can return to your normal lives. I hope this little adventure, which you have accidently become a part of, does not provide you any ill will in the future. What you have seen in the future, I hope you will cherish for yourself and it provides you with some joy throughout your life. And

Benjamin, I hope it does not affect or influence your decisions toward your relentless desire for knowledge, your creative writing, your methodical research, and your quest to make the lives of every person better with your inventions and your participation in great civic duties. I wish you good luck, each of you."

"Thank you, Jeremy," Benjamin says, returning the gesture. "I too wish you good luck with your time machine. I hope this adventure has helped you in your knowledge of time travel and the responsibilities it holds. I hope you take extra precautions to prevent this machine from coming into the wrong hands. This machine holds great power and if not used with goodwill intentions, it could be devastating to all of mankind."

"I will," Jeremy replies, then turns back inside EMITT to program their return destination.

Zach and Zane both shake each of their hands.

"I am sorry we scared the three of you," Zane says, "but we surely did not plan this. I wish the three of you the best of luck."

"I too must apologize." Zach follows with the same gestures. "But, I will say, I would not have changed any of this. For me, this is possibly the greatest experience of my life. I had the privilege to watch Benjamin Franklin perform his famous kite experiment. What an amazing treat for me. I too hope this adventure does not affect your futures in any negative way. I wish each of you good luck."

Zach and Zane both return inside EMITT, while at the same time William, Bernard, and Benjamin step off the porch and into the light sprinkle.

"Zach, Zane," their father asks, "are you ready?"

"I am," Zane replies.

"Wait. The kite and the Leyden jar," Zach says, He picks up both and steps back outside. "Benjamin, here is your kite and Leyden jar. You may need them."

"Oh, thanks, Zach. I really do appreciate it." He sets them on the ground. As he rises he grabs at his elbow and realizes the weather has again inflicted its minor annoyance. He shakes Zach's hand one last time. "It was a pleasure."

"Trust me, the pleasure was all mine." Zach turns and steps back inside EMITT.

"You ready now?"

"Yes. Let's go home."

Zane and Zach give a final wave goodbye, close the door, and sit down in the front room.

William and Benjamin stand watching from about twenty-five feet away. Bernard stands directly behind them. After a couple of seconds, Bernard bursts through the middle of both William and Benjamin, knocking both to the ground, and jumps onto EMITT's porch, while Benjamin and William both holler at him. Benjamin jumps to his feet and bolts after him, but EMITT vanishes into thin air before he can reach her.

"No, no, no, no!" Benjamin screams. "I knew he could not be trusted." He is angry at himself, for he was not prepared for a Bernard trick. "This will be bad. I only hope they realize what he has done."

THIRTY

MONDAY, JUNE 10, 2019

JEREMY AND THE boys arrive in the early hours a few minutes after their original departure time. Bernard, standing on the front porch, sees the city's lights and knows they have arrived back in 2019. He quietly flees the porch, darts behind EMITT, and flits down a side street into the darkness.

The boys break down EMITT, while Jeremy prepares the trailer for connection to his truck. With EMITT connected, they leave for home. Jeremy and the boys have no idea Bernard has traveled with them.

Bernard wants to make 2019 his new home. He slips into a dark alley, where he sits on the ground, resting up against the building. *Whew, what is that smell?* he thinks. Because he has no place to go, he decides he can live with the smell for the night. At least for now he is out of sight. He reminisces about the events of the past couple of days. Before long, his reminiscing turns to dreaming and he falls asleep.

7 a.m. *Beep! Beep! Beep!* A large delivery truck backs up at the end of the short alleyway and stops, the front of the truck visible to Bernard. Its diesel engine rumbles and knocks as it idles.

Bernard yawns, then stretches his arms. He sits for a moment longer, pondering if he had made the right decision. “No looking back,” he mumbles to himself. “My decision has been made and now it’s time to figure it out.”

A door opens near him. An elderly Asian man steps from the back door of his restaurant carrying a couple boxes to the trash dumpster. Upon seeing Bernard, he sternly states in his Vietnamese accent, “No, no, you no sleep here. You leave now.” He shoos him away with his free hand.

Bernard stands up, removes his coat and throws it over his shoulder, and settles his hat on his head. “I am leaving, old man.” Soon, thirst and hunger tug at his stomach. He remembers from the day before, when he tried to buy water from a store clerk, he was told his money was no good there. “If my money is no good here, how do I earn their money to buy food and water or, more importantly, a place to sleep?” he mutters to himself. “I have no skills to work in this new era, so, Bernard, life may be tough for a while.”

He ambles about the streets with no place to go, cars buzzing around in the morning’s rush hour traffic. He discovers a circular newsstand on the sidewalk near the front door of a local coffee shop. He takes one of the papers and continues along. He flips through the pages of the circular and scans through a couple of the articles. Disinterested, he closes the paper and prepares to throw it into a trash can when he notices advertisements on the back page. He scans the ads: “Sudsy Cleaners…The Hole Donut Shop.” *That’s odd. They must have shops that sell only half a donut?* He keeps reading. “Philly’s Coin Dealer—We Buy Old and Rare Coins.”

“In 2019, my coins would be old,” he murmurs. “I wonder if they will buy mine. I need to find this place.” He continues to read the ad. “1731 Spruce Street. This must be a marking of some kind for the business. And it must be located on Spruce Street. But what are these numbers in front of the street name, and how can I find Spruce Street?” He picks up his pace. He notices the business in front of him has a set of numbers above the door. He pays attention to the numbers as he walks and realizes a pattern. "The numbers count down the further I walk. This must be what those numbers represent. I need to find Spruce Street."

He approaches a man walking in his direction. "Sir, can you..."

"I don't have anything," he says, cutting Bernard off and walking away.

What happened to the friendly people in 2019?

Bernard approaches several people standing around as if they were waiting for something. He asks a lady, "Can you tell me where I can find Spruce Street?"

"I'm not sure," she responds.

But another man hears the question. "Hey, buddy. Spruce Street is about ten blocks that way." He points in the direction he was traveling. "It's near Rittenhouse Square."

"Thank you." Bernard remembers Rittenhouse Square.

After walking several blocks, he locates Spruce Street. He again pays attention to the numbers above the doors and determines he is walking in the right direction. "I am impressed with myself. I have figured out their numbering system. That numbering system is an ingenious idea. It sure makes it easy to find a place." He continues. "1691, 1693. Not too much farther."

"1731, and there's the sign: Philly's Coin Dealer. I am impressed with myself." He enters the shop.

A husky Greek man behind the counter, wearing a light blue long-sleeve shirt and an odd contraption on his head, greets him. "Good morning, sir. How can I help you today?"

"The sign outside says you buy old coins."

"I do," he says, tugging at one corner of his thick, dark mustache. "I buy gold, silver, rare coins, old money, and many types of old and rare valuables."

"I have some old coins I would like to sell. Would you be interested?"

"Sure," he says with perfect English. "May I see them?"

Bernard pulls a handful of coins out of his pocket and lays them on the counter.

"Whoa," the man gasps, "these are some old coins you have here." He examines a couple of them. "How did you come about these?" he asks.

Not prepared, the simple question takes him off guard. He stumbles over his words for a split second, but quick with his thoughts, he provides a convincing lie. "Uh, um, my father recently died, and while going through his things I found a can and this is what was inside." He ad-libs his lie as he continues. "Many years ago, he told me about some old coins that had been handed down to him from his father, which came from several generations back. He never showed them to me, but now that they are mine, I would like to sell them."

"Do you want to sell them today?"

"I do, but I want the best price. I have had two others look at them and you are the third. The best price is where I will sell them."

Bernard watches the man pull the odd contraption on his head down over his eyes and peer through the thick glasses. He gleams with an intent study of each coin. The man reaches for a book and reviews some of its pages, frequently looking at the coins and then back at the book. He continues this process for several minutes with each coin. Each time he makes a note on a piece of paper.

"Nice," he murmurs to himself as he continues to study each with great detail.

An hour passes and Bernard is becoming anxious.

"These are in excellent condition," the collector states. "How have these coins been kept in such excellent condition for so many years when they have not been kept sealed?"

"I am not sure. I found them in the can. That's all I know."

The collector knows his customer has not shown these coins to any other person, because there is no way they would let him walk away without buying them. "These coins are in pristine condition and very rare," he states. He estimates the coins are worth approximately $4,700. But he knows Bernard has lied to him. He offers him a number below market price. "I'm willing to buy the whole package for $3,500 if you're interested. That's a significant sum for these coins. I'm not sure what the others have offered you, but I would expect my price will be in line with their offers."

"Okay, I accept," Bernard agrees. The dealer pays him for the coins and soon Bernard is out the door with money he can use. After eating some breakfast at a nearby restaurant, he continues to walk the streets. Several hours pass when he comes across Franklin Court. Many people have gathered in the area and some have formed a line. He is curious about what's occurring for people to be standing in line. He asks a lady, "Excuse me, ma'am, what is the line for?"

"Oh, my son and I want to see Benjamin Franklin's Ghost House and the Franklin Museum."

"I see," he replies and steps back. "That Benjamin Franklin will be a thorn in my side forever," he murmurs to himself. "I so despise that man. What makes him so great hundreds of years later?"

He overhears a young boy, ten or eleven years old, in the same line, enthusiastically asking his father questions. "Dad, at the library with Mom the other day, I looked up Benjamin Franklin. Did you know he flew a kite in a lightning storm and discovered that lightning was electricity?"

"I did," his father replies. "Did you know he signed the Declaration of Independence?"

"Yeah, I read about that too," he answers.

The boy poses another question. "Did you know he invented swim fins?"

"Really, I did not know that. Now you're teaching me."

"Yeah, and he invented those bifocal glasses that Grandpa wears."

"Now that I did know. Did you know that he invented a stove?"

"Yeah, I read that too. But I'm not sure what's so great about a stove. I thought everybody had stoves. How else would they cook dinner?"

"Back in those days most people had fireplaces to keep their homes warm and their stoves were for cooking. But having both meant they needed more firewood. And how did they get firewood?" he asked his son.

"Um, they bought it?"

"No, they had to chop down a tree, then chop the tree into logs short enough to fit in the fireplace or the stove. Then, each log had to be split so it would burn easier. And that was a lot of hard work. Imagine if you had to chop the firewood as one of your chores."

"No way," the boy responds while shaking his head.

The father continues, "And fireplaces were dangerous too because you would have to keep them burning at night to keep the house warm. Sometimes, a log would roll out and catch the house on fire. But fireplaces were necessary, because the stoves could not heat the house very well. Their heat would escape through the chimney, which meant they had to burn a lot of firewood.

"Benjamin Franklin's stove was much more efficient and safer. His stove had plates on the top that could be opened. This would allow the heat to warm the house instead of escaping through the chimney, and you could cook on them. And because you kept the heat inside the house, you did not need to burn as much wood, and the logs could not roll out of the stove to catch the house on fire."

"That meant less wood and they were safer."

"Oh yeah. I guess that would be a great invention."

Hearing this conversation incites Bernard, but it also provides him with a farfetched idea. "If I could learn a little more about Benjamin, maybe going back home would not be a bad idea. If Jeremy found out I was here, he would have no issues sending me back home."

He buys a ticket for the tour. He listens to the narrator on a headset. Astonished, he thinks, *The people of this museum have gone to great lengths to write about Benjamin's accomplishments. I could learn about his inventions and maybe even steal a few. I could make a great deal of money by patenting them. I could be rich in our era, and no one would have any idea I stole from Benjamin. A Bernard Ranter Museum has a nice ring to it. People should be lining up to learn about me.*

That afternoon, on his walk back toward Rittenhouse Square, he notices a sign that says, "Hotel."

"Maybe I have enough money to splurge on a room for a couple of nights. I do not want to sleep in the park again—or worse, where it smells." He enters the hotel.

He pulls the golden-framed glass doors open and steps inside. He is impressed with the magnificence of the hotel's lobby. His eyes indulge upon the pointed, parquet-wood slatted floors that lead his eyes across the room and up the tall, dark, walnut walls dotted with large gaudy paintings of old people he does not recognize. The red and white paisley ceiling is something he has never seen before, but he likes its unusual style. Gold chains suspend the three oversized decorative candelabra light fixtures. Each light bulb is dressed in its own small, ornate fabric shade with dangling crystal pendants. The area rugs blend a mix of colors with the ceiling, and the fading red fabric of the wingback, English-style chairs set into groups of four surround wooden coffee tables.

At the check-in desk he tells the cute lady with dark, shoulder-length hair, wearing a white long-sleeve shirt and a gold and green uniform vest, "I would like a room for a couple of nights."

"Yes, sir. Give me a moment." After completing the check-in process, she says, "Here's your key, Mr. Ranter."

"I do have a question. I am here to learn about Benjamin Franklin. Can you tell me of some places that will be helpful?"

"Well, you came to the right city for that," she says as she pulls out a tourist map of downtown Philadelphia. "You will find several artifact locations and a few Benjamin Franklin museums highlighted on this map. Don't forget about the library; it holds a wealth of information. It is..." she pauses to scan the map, "...right here." She circles the location.

"Thank you. You have been most helpful."

"If you need any assistance, please dial "0" on your room phone and someone here at the front desk can help."

"Thank you." He turns to walk away. He looks at the card but has no idea what to do with it. He assumes he will figure it out when he reaches the room. He stops and turns around to ask, "Which way to the room?"

"Take the elevator," she points, "and you're on the tenth floor, room 1006."

"Thank you." He walks away.

THIRTY-ONE

TUESDAY, JUNE 11, 2019

BERNARD FOLLOWS HIS map to the library. He climbs the few steps to reach the large iron-framed glass doors. He pulls on one and enters. His eyes feast upon the vast size of the grand room. The white marble floors are inlayed with dark marble veins that create intricate square designs, which mimic the high ceilings supported under the oval marble columns. Recessed lighting details the ceilings while the side alcoves accentuate the room with soft hidden light. *As magnificent as a king's castle,* he thinks.

He approaches the guest counter and inquires, "Can you tell me where I may find some books on Benjamin Franklin?"

"Yes, sir. We have an extensive section on Benjamin Franklin. Most of those books will be located on the second floor," she says, pointing toward a network of polished stairs at the far end of the room. "There will be someone upstairs that can help you to the right area."

Bernard learned to read as a child, but through many of the past years reading has not found its way into his life. His thoughts wander with concern. *If writing has advanced like today's technology, I only hope I can read their books.*

Another clerk guides him to a section of interest. He peruses the selection and chooses a few books that may help his newfound purpose. He sits alone at a nearby table of six chairs and reads through the material of Benjamin's achievements. After each achievement, he becomes more annoyed, yet excited. Several hours pass, and his eyes become tired and his stomach growls. He decides he has had enough of his nemesis for one day. He will return tomorrow and develop a plan.

WEDNESDAY, JUNE 12, 2019

After a late breakfast, Bernard arrives at the same table he became familiar with the day before. With a paper pad and a pen from the hotel, he takes notes for his devious plan. "I only need to know how he designed his inventions, then the idea will be mine." He grins. By the afternoon, he has a detailed list of Benjamin's inventions created after 1752. He has spent several hours detailing the information and copying sketches, but more work remains.

A clean-cut, rugged man near his same age, height, and build sits down with a couple of books. He's wearing blue jeans and an untucked gray, short-sleeve, button-down shirt. His hair is short, dark brown, and parted on the right side. His thick mustache is neatly trimmed and slides down just past the corners of his mouth. He reads quietly. An hour passes when the man, flipping through the pages, stops and starts to laugh under his breath, shaking his head. The gesture captures Bernard's attention, but he ignores him.

A few minutes later the man again chuckles under his breath.

Bernard looks up at him.

The man apologizes. A few more minutes pass and the man laughs again. Bernard looks up again. "What's so funny?"

The man looks at Bernard and responds, "Sorry, man. Stupid crap they put in these history books. What are you reading?"

"Benjamin Franklin."

"I don't know about you, but my opinion on Franklin is the historians made that man out to be much more than he really was."

This sparks Bernard's interest. "What do you mean?"

"Doesn't it seem a little farfetched that one man has achieved such great recognition in his lifetime? Historians tell us that he was a printer, successful businessman, inventor, experimentalist, civic leader, postmaster, and a diplomat, yet he barely completed two years of education. I mean really, that's a lot of different trades for one person to master, when experience tells us it takes many years to master one. Most people go through life mastering one trade, sometimes two and rarely three. It seems a little odd to me."

"I agree. I despise the man. He always wins, like he has no faults."

"Exactly."

"You appear to know a lot about Benjamin. If you despise him so, how did you come about so much knowledge of him?"

"College. My English lit professor required everyone to write a detailed paper on a famous figure in American history. I chose Benjamin Franklin. After completing the paper, I began to question his achievements. There were a lot of achievements for one person. I became skeptical and chose not to believe in all things Benjamin Franklin."

"Well then," Bernard says, "you and I should be friends, because I too do not believe in all things Benjamin Franklin. My name is Bernard."

"I'm Jack."

They talk for a while and each likes the other's views. Over the next few hours Bernard bashes Benjamin while Jack bashes politicians and government. Eventually, the conversation slows and Jack says, "Well, it's time for me to leave. I have a cat waiting for me. Maybe I will see you around here again soon."

Bernard replies, "Probably. This is the only place I have to go right now."

"You homeless?" Jack asks.

"Kind of, but I will be on my feet soon."

"Me too. Well, not homeless, unemployed. At least for now. I lost my job last week, but another will come around soon. That's why I am downtown. I had a job interview. C'mon, you can stay at my house for a few days. I could use the company anyway."

"Are you sure?" Bernard asks. "I am not one to impose."

"Not a problem."

Bernard gathers his hat and coat and his notes and the two men leave the library.

That night, well north of Philadelphia's city center, Bernard and Jack relax in a couple of comfortable outdoor chairs on the back porch. After quite a few beers, the subject of Benjamin Franklin again arises. This time the two are not feeling much pain and the Benjamin bashing becomes more intense. Then Jack makes a comment in his somewhat slurred voice. "Wouldn't it be cool if we could go back in time and kick his ass? Teach the old boy a lesson."

Both laugh.

Bernard too slurs his words. "We could do that."

Jack laughs harder.

"No really, we could do that."

"Now, how do you suppose we could go back in time? You have a time machine lying around somewhere, do you?" Jack says, still laughing.

"I do," Bernard says, then sits up in his chair, trying to gain his composure.

"Yeah right. Where in the world did you find a time machine?" Jack asks, knowing Bernard's full of crap. "Because, if you really had one, we could make a quick fortune. But since time machines don't exist, we can only daydream about it. But it would be cool."

"All right," Bernard says with a bit of a smartass tone, "if I told you a story, and then I were to prove it, would you help me destroy Benjamin Franklin?"

"If you could prove you had a time machine, you would be my hero, but you can't, homeless boy. They don't exist."

"Not only can I, but I will. You lie back in your chair and let Bernard tell you a story. Then, I will show you the time machine."

"Okay, I'm in for a good story, so get to storytelling, homeless boy." Realizing this could be entertaining, Jack lays back in his chair.

"A few days ago, I accidentally traveled to 2019 from 1752."

Jack busts out in hysterical laughter.

Bernard stares at him until he has finished. "Are you done?"

"I'm sorry, go on."

"Anyway, I followed Benjamin and his son, William, out to a field when it started to rain. They rented a horse and wagon from Mr. Stevens' stables."

"Oh, this is going to be good," Jack says with a chuckle.

"Benjamin and William come upon a cabin in this field. I knew Benjamin was up to something, but *what* I had no idea. I just wanted to catch him doing something stupid. Then, he starts to fly a kite, in the rain."

"A kite?" Jack screeches, then laughs hysterically again. "You're not going to tell me you watched Benjamin Franklin perform the lightning experiment, with a kite and a key." He laughs harder, slapping his leg multiple times.

"Do you want to hear the story or not?"

"I'm sorry, keep going."

"Let me start over at the beginning. To earn money, I performed electrical demonstrations in town. In my time, the electric fire is exciting and people are intrigued with it. People pay to watch a show. A few weeks back, in one of my street demonstrations, Benjamin stumbled upon my act. He is a prominent man in town, and with him there it made me nervous, and of course my experiment failed. To make matters worse, he corrected my mistake in front of the crowd and it worked. I looked like a fool and he looked like a genius. Infuriated and embarrassed by the incident, I picked up my equipment and left. How many people will pay to watch my shows now? He destroyed me.

"So, I vowed my revenge. Somehow, Benjamin would have to pay with his own failure and everyone must know. He needed to be shown as a fool. I thought if I could somehow sabotage his equipment or maybe catch him in a ridiculous act, I could print it in the circular of his competitor and have a little revenge."

"Over the next couple of weeks, I watched Benjamin's home and I kept track of his every move. Then, on a recent sunny day, I watched Benjamin walk to Mr. Stevens' stables, where he rented a horse and buggy.

"As Benjamin left town, I followed him from a distance. His actions were odd for him. He took a ride around the countryside. Every so often he would stop, dismount the wagon, walk around, return to the buggy, and ride off. This occurred several times throughout the day in many different areas. But at this one pasture, he spent a considerable amount of time at a dilapidated old cabin. For the next several days, I watched him from a distance. I knew he was up to something, but *what* I did not know."

"I will say, you have a vivid imagination," Jack interrupts. "But keep on, this is good." He takes another swig of his beer.

"Then, early Saturday morning, you know, one of those dreary, drizzly rainy mornings, I wanted to stay in bed. But I thought if Benjamin were going to do something crazy, today could be the day. So, I drug myself out of bed and slipped on my clothes and..."

"You must have really wanted to make him pay. Because I would have given up a long time ago. This is intriguing. Continue."

"I pulled on my boots, grabbed my coat and hat, and stepped out into the rain. I mounted Red and rode into town to my usual place, where I silently watched his place. I looked around the corner and I saw Benjamin and his son, William, loading their wagon."

"In the rain?" Jack clarifies.

"It was only a light sprinkle at that time. But I thought, 'Where are they going in this weather?'

"Then it occurred to me that maybe the rain is what Benjamin has been waiting for and is the reason he went about the countryside a few days earlier. He was searching for a place to conduct one of his crazy experiments.

"I watched as they left and followed way behind, but at that point I was pretty sure I knew where they were going. I went to another area through the trees where I could spy on them without notice. Then, the rain began to come down harder. I covered up tighter with my coat to stay dry and pulled my hat down. When I spotted them, they were stopped at an odd-looking cabin, which I was sure was not there a few days earlier. The dilapidated cabin was there, but it lay further across the field."

"Where did the cabin come from if it wasn't there the first time you followed him?" Jack asks.

"You will understand in a minute. As I watched, I saw them both scurry around the front porch of this cabin. I wondered what they were up to."

"Then, William runs out into the rain with a kite and I thought, surely, they did not come all the way out here to fly a kite in the rain? But sure as Red was a horse, Benjamin tugs on the twine and lifts the kite into the air—higher and higher it goes. I thought, 'This is perfect.' Everybody will think he has lost his mind. Nobody in their right mind would fly a kite in the rain, much less a thunderstorm. Benjamin is acting like a complete fool. And I thought to myself, 'I need to be closer.' This is what I have been waiting for. Once people hear about this, Benjamin and his son will be complete fools and I will get my revenge."

"I tie Red to a tree. I hike further down the tree line where I can come out of the woods from behind the cabin and they cannot see me. I sneak my way through the tall grass toward them. Once there, I can hear most of what they say. I only hoped they would not walk around to the back side of the cabin."

"After a couple of hours, I hear Benjamin scream, 'William, come look. The strands are standing up. I think it's working.' Then, a second later, I hear another voice yelling at them. Benjamin and William both scream. Then, I see these electrical arcs surround the cabin. Arcs everywhere. I jumped up against the cabin, hoping not to be hit by any of them. There is this loud noise that crackles, then a loud *POW* and a bright flash of light. When I woke up, I was lying in a street, trucks zooming past me real fast—although, at that moment, I had no idea what they were. I had no idea what had happened."

"Bravo," Jack says as he starts to clap. "That is a great story. You, my man, are a storyteller. But, you don't really expect me to believe you're from 1752."

"There's more, a lot more."

"Oh really."

Bernard continues describing the chase through the city streets, stealing Zach's truck, them finding him the next day, the movie at their house, EMITT and the computers, Opal, taking Benjamin and himself back to 1752, then him jumping back on EMITT just before they traveled back to 2019.

"Really. Then, why did you come back to 2019 if your home is in 1752?"

"I was intrigued with the advancements the future holds and I wanted to be a part of it. I have nothing in that era to keep me there."

"That was an impressive story, but I don't believe it."

"I knew you wouldn't, but now, I will prove it to you. But before I do, I need to know, will you help me destroy Benjamin Franklin?"

"What's in it for me?" Jack asks.

"You said we could make a fortune if you had a time machine. I know where a time machine is and I know the passwords to make it work. But, we will need to steal it and destroy Benjamin with my plan. Then, we can make the fortunes you talk about."

"Wait a minute. Why do we have to wait to make the fortunes? Let's do that first."

"No. We destroy Benjamin first, then we make the fortunes. This will give you the opportunity to see the time machine work. It's my way or it does not happen."

"All right, I will play along," Jack says, knowing Bernard's story is crap anyway.

"So how do we make a fortune with the time machine?" Bernard asks.

"The lottery."

"What is the lottery?" Bernard asks.

"Really, you don't know what the lottery is?"

"Never heard of it."

"A couple times a week people around the country can buy a lottery ticket. You pick a set of numbers and if your numbers match exactly with the drawing's numbers, you win millions. We will research and find the largest winning lottery drawings. Then, we'll determine the lottery numbers from the previous drawing, which did not win, and those will be our lottery numbers. We will travel back to the day of the drawing, buy the lottery ticket, and claim our millions. And nobody will ever know, and you and I, my friend, will be super-rich millionaires."

"Interesting concept. I like the idea. My original plan was to steal Benjamin's inventions and make them my own, but I have since had a change of heart. I want to be known as the person who performed the famous kite experiment, which discovered lightning was electricity. I will steal Benjamin's fifth letter he wrote to Peter Collinson in London. I will copy it with my name, describe the kite experiment, and be remembered in history. I want that fame, and the key to that happening is Peter Collinson receiving my letter instead of Benjamin's."

"I like your demented ways. Deal. But you, my friend, have to produce a time machine."

"I can do that, but we will need to steal EMITT. Do you have a way of pulling a trailer with your truck?" Bernard asks.

"I do, but why do we need to steal the trailer? If it's a time machine, let's travel off in time. Nobody will ever find us."

It does not work like that. EMITT can travel in time, but it never moves. It just travels in time. So, we need to steal it, bring it back here, then we can do what we want."

"How do I know this is not a scam?"

"What is a scam?"

"A scam. Oh my God. Do you know anything?"

"There is a lot I do not know about your society and how it works, because it is so different from ours. So, you must excuse my ignorance."

"A scam is where you say you will do something for me, usually for money, but once it's done, you will be stiffed and get nothing."

"So, it's a trick. I will not trick you if that's what you mean. You will see. Once we steal EMITT, we can steal Benjamin's letter, then we will go after the lottery winnings. EMITT looks like an old cabin, but she is really a trailer—an impressive trailer. But it's what's inside that makes her so impressive. It is sure to amaze you, with those computers and that astonishingly beautiful tube. Jeremy built an awesome machine."

"Okay, I got it. It's beautiful, blah, blah, blah. We need to scope out the area. Where do we go?"

Bernard stares at Jack with a blank look. "Uh, um, I am not sure. Jeremy drove the truck, but I have no idea where we went."

"What the hell do you mean you don't know?" Jack raises his voice. "I knew this was a bunch of crap."

"No, Jack, there really is a time machine," Bernard argues. "It's just…I am not sure where they live."

"All right, do you know their last name?"

His eyes widen and his eyebrows raise. "Yes, I do," he blurts out with confidence. "Jeremy, Sarah, Zach, and Zane Long."

"Easy there, buddy. Just the father will be fine."

"Jeremy Long."

"Wait here a minute." Jack gets up and steps inside the house, then returns a moment later with his laptop. He sits back down in his chair and opens Google. "Let's see what we can find on the internet; maybe we can find their address." He does a search for "Jeremy Long." Several hits are returned. He opens Google Street View and one by one, he copies each street address into the search bar. A picture of a home pops up on the computer screen. He turns the screen toward Bernard. “Is that their house?”

“No.”

He tries another. “This it?”

“No.”

“How about this one?”

“No.”

Jack tries a few more; each produces the same result. Discouraged, he tries one more. “This one?”

“No.” A split-second pause. “Wait, maybe. Yeah, that might be it. Can your computer see into the backyard? This might be the one. I remember those spiral trees on each side of a white stone house.”

Jack zooms out to an aerial view.

“There’s the trailer. Like I said, chimney and all,” Bernard says while pointing at the screen.

“Okay, maybe you’re on to something.”

“These computers are amazing. How did you find them so easily?” Bernard questions in awe.

“The power of the internet, my friend. The power of the internet.”

“Unbelievable.” Bernard points to the computer. “Technology, that is why I decided to make 2019 my new home. The future is utterly amazing.”

“Bernard, tomorrow we will take a drive and check out the place.”

THIRTY-TWO

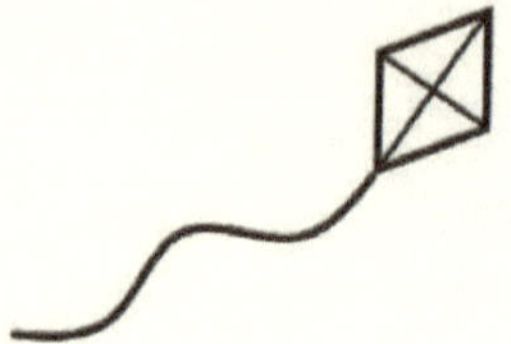

THURSDAY, JUNE 13, 2019

AT MIDMORNING, THE two men hop into Jack's truck. Bernard is in his same old clothes. Jack wears a pair of blue jeans, a camo T-shirt, and his favorite pair of brown Timberland boots. He programs the address into the truck's GPS.

Bernard watches the screen on the truck as it tracks their location. "You're telling me that this screen will take us to their home," Bernard says.

"Absolutely, right to their driveway. And it's about a twenty-five-minute drive."

"Wow!" Bernard's eyebrows raise and his mouth is ajar. His face dances with excitement. "This technology is impressive."

Jack realizes a time machine is a farfetched idea, but there is something about Bernard's story, his clothes, the way he talks, and his limited knowledge of today's society that allows him to continue with this little charade. If it does turn out to be true, the risk is worth the huge payday. But the possibility of time travel has also grabbed his excitement.

Soon they arrive in the Longs' neighborhood.

"Bernard, keep your eyes open in case they drive by. They won't recognize me, but you they will. So be prepared."

They approach the Longs' street. Bernard says, "Don't go down their street. They could easily spot us, because they live on the end of a circle."

Jack stops and stares at Bernard. "Are you leading me on here?" Jack says, raising his voice. "This isn't some hokey-pokey dream of yours, is it?"

"No. I swear."

"Good, because I'm driving down the street. You duck down in the seat and I will take a couple of pictures as we pass."

Jack continues and turns onto the street.

Nervous, Bernard says, pointing, "It's that house straight ahead. Oh Lord, please do not let them see me." He slouches down in his seat below the window's edge.

"There's nobody outside," Jack says as they slowly approach the cul-de-sac. He takes a couple pictures as they approach the house, then a few more as they turn in the circle. They leave the street and Bernard rises back up in his seat.

Back at the house, Jack downloads the pictures to his laptop to study them closer. Again, Jack opens Google Earth to look at the house from a satellite view to see the home's surroundings. "There's EMITT, behind the garage, but how do you get it out to the street?" Jack asks, puzzled. "There's no way to pull the trailer around the garage."

"Oh, both the front and back of the garage open up and they pull EMITT straight through."

"Interesting. Garage doors on both sides. I like it."

Jack's excitement has risen. "Maybe you're not full of it after all, but it better be a time machine. Otherwise, we are stealing a stupid trailer. I don't want the risk of going to jail over a freaking trailer."

"I swear, Jack, it is a time machine. You will see."

They plan their heist. Jack starts to rattle off several questions.

"Do you know any of their patterns? What time do they go to work?

Are the two boys at home throughout the day? Do any of them have an activity they attend at a certain time every day or week? Do they eat dinner out every night or maybe on a specific night? Anything, Bernard. We need to steal the trailer when they're not home."

"I really don't know. Those things did not come up when I was there."

For nearly the next two weeks, they make several trips to the Longs' neighborhood and scope the area to watch for patterns. They watch at different times of the day and in the early morning hours in case the heist needs to be performed under the cover of darkness. They time each drive, so they know how long it takes from Jack's house to the Longs'. They also time entering and leaving the neighborhood. They time separate exit routes in case an issue arises. They watch for obstacles they may encounter on their route back home. Jack even checks websites for street closures.

Jack trains Bernard how to connect a trailer to the ball on the truck and connect the lights. They practice with one of Jack's trailers. They go over every detail: wood blocks in front of the wheels, the support jacks on the corners, and the trailer avoiding the garage on the way out. They discuss filling the gas tank before they leave. They even bring bolt cutters and their own lock for the hitch.

"We have one glaring obstacle," Jack says. "The Longs have no set patterns except sleep. We will perform the heist at night, while they're asleep."

"Jack, isn't that a little risky?"

"Yes, it is, but we have no other choice. But I'm telling you right now, Bernard, it better be a time machine."

"It is. I promise."

"Bernard, we have rehearsed our plan as much as we possibly can. I think we are ready. Tonight's the night. We will do it tonight at 3 a.m."

"I am nervous, but I believe I am ready," Bernard replies.

They arrive at the Longs' street at their designated time. Bernard dons his usual attire and his tricorn hat, but Jack has suggested he also wear his long brown coat to cover up the white from his shirt and leggings. Jack also dressed to be inconspicuous and planned to perform the heist in a black T-shirt and blue jeans. "Apparently, luck is on our side tonight," Jack comments as he slowly drives toward their home. "The cul-de-sac is dark, because the street light burned out." Jack parks in the center of the cul-de-sac with the truck facing the direction of their exit, just in case there is a problem and they need a quick escape.

"Jack, look." Bernard points. "Neither of the trucks are blocking EMITT's side of the garage."

They sneak up to the garage. Jack mulls his options.

"Bernard, I will probably have to pry the door open, but once it is open, you watch the house. If any lights come on, or if you hear any alarms or beeps, we leave immediately."

"All right."

Jack tries the doorknob on the garage door first and surprisingly it's not locked. He opens the door slightly. He pauses for a second, but they hear no alarm sounds. Jack slips inside and turns on the flashlight app on his phone. He passes behind a truck and an SUV to reach the far-side garage door. He releases the door from the automatic opener as quietly as he possibly can. He slowly raises the door, trying not to make any noise. Once opened, he raises the backside garage door.

"It all looks good—no lights have turned on," Bernard whispers.

They both look over EMITT with Jack's flashlight. Jack sees the word "EMITT" on the side of the trailer with the space background, and for the first time he has a reason to believe Bernard, although he is not yet completely convinced.

Bernard whispers to Jack, "They did not put the support jacks down."

"Remind me to thank Jeremy later," Jack whispers back with a little sarcasm. He quickly checks out the trailer hitch and mumbles his observations to himself. "Perfect. They left it open as well. And it appears to be up high enough that my hitch should slip right underneath. It's as if they just dropped it off and left. The cable for the trailer lights is ready as well."

"Bernard," Jack whispers, "go back and watch the house for lights or any movement. If you see or hear anything, let me know."

"All right," Bernard whispers and darts back through the garage.

Jack looks around the backyard with what available light he has from the full moon and his flashlight app, then disappears around the side of the garage for a moment. He returns to Bernard and whispers, "The trailer's ready. I'm going to back the truck up. Are you sure this trailer will come right out of the garage without any obstacles?"

"Yes."

"Okay, you hook the trailer onto the hitch and raise the front wheel support. Once it's out of the garage, hop in the truck and we will get the hell out of here."

"All right," Bernard says, scared but excited.

Jack backs his truck into the garage and up to EMITT. Bernard lowers the trailer hitch onto the ball, plugs in the trailer lights, attaches the lock to the trailer hitch, and cranks up the wheel. Bernard jumps into the bed of the truck and whispers a yell at Jack, "Go." Jack pulls forward, and as he is pulling out of the garage, they notice a light turn on inside the house. Jack quickly pulls out of the driveway. EMITT bounces a bit, but they speed away.

There is a stir in the house. More lights come on; the back door opens. Zach and Zane emerge barefooted and in their Marvel pajama boxers. Jeremy follows behind a few seconds later. He too wears his long Philadelphia Eagles pajama pants. Sarah scampers out as well in her pink robe and pink fuzzy house slippers.

"The garage door is opened," Zach states and rushes to the open door.

"Oh no, this can't be happening." Jeremy hustles over and peers into the opened garage door. He shouts in a panic-stricken tone, "Oh my God,

EMITT is gone! Zach, Zane, get in your truck and chase after them. They are probably headed for the freeway. I will track EMITT on the computer."

Zach zips back inside, where he grabs his keys and both of their cell phones.

Sarah looks around in the darkness and notices an object lying in the grass. She picks it up. "Does anybody recognize this hat? It looks pretty familiar to me," she says sarcastically, knowing exactly who it belongs to.

"That can't be," Zane cries out.

"No way," Zach screeches with astonishment. "How did he get back here?"

"He must have jumped onto EMITT right before we slipped back through time," Jeremy says. "What is he up to? You boys go look for him, but stay way back. I will track EMITT on the computer and let you know where they're located. We have to find EMITT tonight."

"Neither of these two boys are going after him," Sarah barks. "You can track EMITT and when they arrive at wherever they take EMITT, you can figure out what to do then. But the boys will not be chasing after him."

"No, you're right. I don't know what I was thinking." Jeremy turns and sprints inside to the study. The boys and Sarah follow him. Jeremy sits at the computer and opens the tracker, but the program is void of any information. He opens Internet Explorer and discovers there is no internet connection. He tries some troubleshooting, but it doesn't work. He barges his way outside behind the garage where the internet cable enters the house. The boys follow him.

"He has help," Dad determines, while grabbing the cut cable line. "The internet's coaxial line has been cut and there's no way Bernard would have known to do that."

They return inside.

"Sarah, Bernard has help. The internet line has been cut and Bernard could not have known to do that."

"Jeremy, we could be dealing with a professional, which means Bernard too faces potential danger. We should have installed the security system on the garage doors as well."

"I know, but that is hindsight now."

"Dad, can't you track EMITT from your cell phone?" Zane suggests.

"Unfortunately not. I haven't written a mobile version for the tracker. For now, we must wait until we restore the internet. Also, I believe it's best we create a plan."

A few blocks away, Jack stops the truck. Bernard jumps out of the bed and into the cab. "Wahoo! We did it, buddy!" Jack screams excitedly as he speeds away. "We did it." Jack holds his fist out for a fist bump.

Bernard looks at his fist. "What?" he asks with a confused expression, not understanding the gesture.

"Fist bump, my man," he instructs Bernard.

Still confused, Bernard says, "I don't understand what you want me to do."

"You don't know about fist bumps either?"

"Fist bumps?"

"Man, maybe you *are* from the 1700s. A fist bump is where I hold my fist out and you bump it with your fist. It means we are celebrating a win." Jack holds his hand up again. "Bump it."

Bernard makes a fist and bumps Jack's.

"There you go, buddy. Now you understand. So, if somebody sticks their fist out like that, you bump it. It's a common courtesy in our time. Man, you have a lot to learn."

They arrive at Jack's house. Jack backs EMITT alongside the house.

"All right, Bernard, the moment of truth has arrived. Let's see this time machine you have been talking about," Jack says as he walks around the outside of the trailer with a puzzled expression. "Where's the door?"

"We have to unhitch the truck before we can put the support jacks down, then we can open the doors."

"All right," Jack says while hopping back into the truck.

Bernard disconnects the trailer lights, lowers the front wheel support, and unhitches the trailer from the truck, then hollers at Jack, "You're disconnected."

Jack pulls his truck off to the side of EMITT, while Bernard lowers each of the four jacks.

Bernard steps to the front of the trailer. "Step away, Jack."

Jack takes a couple of steps backwards toward the house.

Bernard presses a button. The bottom door lowers down, then the top door raises up.

"Holy crap," Jack shouts. "It looks like a cabin, like you said. This is freaking awesome."

"Jack, raise the support on that end," he says as he reaches for the support on his end.

Jack follows his instructions.

"Wait until you see the inside," Bernard teases Jack while opening the door. He steps inside. Jack follows behind him.

Jack's eyes widen and his jaw drops. He's speechless. Then, he musters up a couple of his masterful words. "Holy crap, dude. This is un-freaking believable. What is that?" He points toward the tube.

"Jeremy calls it Opal."

Astounded by its beauty, he emits only one word. "Mesmerizing!"

In an excited and somewhat stunned state, Jack stares for a moment longer, then turns and bear hugs Bernard. "If this works like you say it does, we will be so rich. I mean, beyond-your-wildest-dreams rich."

"Are you ready to travel through time, my friend?" Bernard asks.

"Hell yeah. Let's go."

"Take a seat in the front room and we will be on our way."

THIRTY-THREE

WEDNESDAY, JULY 29, 1750

BERNARD ENTERS THEIR travel data.

PREVIOUS TRAVEL DATE:	JUNE 10, 2019	TIME:	2:17	AM
CURRENT DATE:	JUNE 26, 2019	TIME:	4:40	AM
NEXT TRAVEL DATE:	JULY 29, 1750	TIME:	5:30	AM
PASSWORD:	TOUCH THE KEY			

AUTOMATIC RETURN DATE:	TIME:
AUTOMATIC RETURN PASSWORD:	TIME REMAINING:

NOTE: "AUTOMATIC RETURN DATE AND TIME" IS THE CURRENT DATE AND TIME IN 2019.

Jack can see into the other room but cannot see the information Bernard is entering on the computer.

Bernard presses enter on the keyboard and dashes to sit in the front room with Jack.

Jack hears a woman's voice on the computer: "Password accepted.

Time travel sequence initiated." Jack can partially see the plasma inside Opal start to spin. They hear a low, vibrating hum, then hear two pops a couple of seconds apart from each other.

"Wait here," he tells Jack. He reviews the computer screen and enters another password, "Time For Benjamin," to stop the Automatic Return Event. He presses enter. The woman's voice on the computer says, "Password accepted."

Bernard steps back into the front room. "Welcome to 1750. Today is July 29 and it is 5:30 a.m. Let's get to work."

Jack is quiet for a moment, staring at the wall. His lips grab at the hairs of his dark mustache, pulling them in for his teeth to bite at, as if he is giving himself a little trim. He pushes his thin, fit physique from his chair. He stares at Bernard. "You better not be messing with me."

"You will see, my friend. Be my guest." He gestures toward the door.

Jack pauses at the door, glances at Bernard, then pushes it open. With daylight breaking, Jack screeches, "Oh my God!" He stares in disbelief; the limited light confirms it. "My house..."

He steps out onto the porch, dumbfounded. A field of tall, straw-like grass now occupies the patch of land where his house once stood. A light breeze pushes the field's tall fibers back and forth. He listens: no city sounds; only a rustle of leaves from a nearby mature oak tree. Birds chirp while others fly in search of their morning meal. He steps off the porch into the vast field. Behind EMITT he recognizes a slight rise in the land that has always afforded a scenic view from his kitchen window. As the early morning light grows brighter, the familiar ridge bestows an unfamiliar but distinct tree line in the distance that blocks his view of the sunrise. Other than a few puffs of white cotton, the clear blue skies beckon to provide them a perfect day.

"Oh, my freaking God. Bernard, it works. This is freaking amazing. You weren't kidding. It's early morning like you said. The air is still a little cool, just like our mornings. But...where's the town? Are you sure we're in Philadelphia?"

"We are, but you must realize, a 1750 Philadelphia is much smaller than the futuristic Philadelphia you live in. Do you know the direction toward town from here? I am not familiar with this area."

"Yes, it's south. If we drive that way," he says, pointing toward the south, "we will find it."

"Jack, we don't have trucks, here," Bernard replies. "We have to walk to town."

"Walk to town?" Jack shouts. "That's twenty-five miles or so. You must be crazy? I'm not walking to town."

"Then stay here. I will be back in a week or so."

"Stay here, for a week! Have you lost your mind? What do I do for food? Where do I find water? Where do I sleep?"

"Then come with me. I have a cabin on the outskirts of town. We can stay there and you can experience life in 1750. I spent my time in 2019; now it's your turn. It will be a little different for you, but you should enjoy the experience. After a week here, I imagine you will appreciate your life a little more."

"Don't have much of a choice, do I? What the hell, let's go to Philadelphia."

They begin their journey toward town. "How far away is your cabin?" Jack asks.

"If it's twenty-five miles and we keep up a good pace," Bernard calculates, "we should arrive sometime tonight."

"Tonight?"

"Jack, if you wish to be a rich man, you will have to work for it."

A full day's trek through the fields as well as the sun and lack of water have taken their toll on the two men. The sun falls toward the horizon and daylight fades to darkness, and the night's cooler air replaces the sun's heat. With a full moon rising, the limited glow provides just enough light for Bernard to recognize the area's landmarks. Soon, he spots an odd cluster of trees that signals him to turn and send him in the direction of his cabin.

"Thank goodness for the moonlight," Bernard says. "Otherwise we may have had a difficult time locating the cabin."

"I'm glad you know where you're going, because I have no idea where we are."

"We have arrived on the outskirts of town." He points in one direction. "Philadelphia is that way, but we need to go this direction to my cabin. It should not be much longer now. We will come across a path soon, where I ride into town." Exhausted from their long hike, they push on.

Jack peers at the moon as it rises further into the night's sky. "Other than the stars and the moon there's not a single light, anywhere. I don't remember the last time I have seen it this dark, if ever. And look at all the stars."

"There it is," Bernard shouts.

They enter the tiny one-room cabin. Bernard pulls a match from a tin mounted on the wall near the door, strikes it, and lights a candle, then a lantern.

With the room dimly lit, Jack scans the dusty old wooden cabin. "Not exactly the Marriott," he mumbles to himself.

A wood-burning stove sits in the corner for cooking and to provide heat on those cold winter days. Ironically, it's a Franklin design. A wooden table with two benches are positioned near the stove. The front and two side walls each have a simple window, each adequate to provide natural light. Two wooden chairs sit near a window with a rickety wooden table between them. In the corner opposite the stove lies Bernard's log bed, draped with several blankets.

"I am really out of my element here," Jack mumbles to himself as he sits down in one of the wood chairs. The chair wobbles. "I hope it doesn't give out on me."

"That chair is solid. It may make a little noise, but it will hold you."

"I don't suppose you have any food and water?"

"I too am hungry. Give me a moment and I will pull out some jarred meat. It looks like the water pail is empty. Come on, you can help."

"Where are we going?"

"Outside, to the well. We need to fill the pail."

Bernard grabs the lantern and the wooden pail and walks out the door. Jack follows behind. After a fifty-yard walk, they approach the well. Bernard sets the lantern down on the ground. "Here, you hold the pail while I pump."

Jack starts to laugh. "You have got to be kidding me. We pump the water from a well? I guess next, you will have me searching for firewood, building the fire, then cooking the meat. Hell, we could be here all night."

"Welcome to 1750."

Bernard pumps the well while Jack collects the water. They return to the cabin.

"I have a little good news for you," Bernard states. "You do not need to build a fire. The meat is already cooked, salted, and ready to eat."

"Great, let's eat."

Jack sits in the same chair. Bernard hands him a jar of salted meat, a large piece of bread, and a tin cup filled with water. He joins him, with his own jar of meat.

"Bon appétit," Jack says, as he holds his jar of meat up at Bernard. He pulls out a piece of meat and takes a bite, then immediately spits it back into the jar. "Blah, puhey! Oh my God, what is this crap? That's salty as hell," Jack exclaims as he wipes his mouth.

"It is salted beef. From a cow I slaughtered last October."

"Last October! Are you freaking kidding me?" he says as he stands up. "Are you trying to give me food poisoning?"

"Ah, Jack, sit down. The meat has been preserved and is perfectly fine. I eat it every day." He pulls a piece from his jar, bites it, and tears off a chunk. He chews while he talks, his voice a little muffled with food in his mouth. "After slaughter, I cut the meat into strips, then cure it with salt and saltpeter for a couple of months in a barrel. When it is ready, I store it in jars for the next several months. The salting preserves the meat for a couple of years, and the saltpeter helps remove the moisture from the meat, so it won't spoil. Don't worry, you will get used to it. I enjoy it, but most definitely, it is different from the food of your era."

"I'll say," Jack says. He tears his bread open to place some of the meat inside for a makeshift sandwich. "I guess if you can get past the salt, then it's okay."

"You must have had some leftover salt on that one piece. Usually, the salt is not a problem. Maybe it's a little more salt than what you are used to, but I like the taste."

"I guess," Jack comments. "It's kind of like eating beef jerky." Jack takes a drink of the water from his tin. He immediately spits the water back into his cup. "Oh my God! Is this water safe to drink?"

"Yes. It is fine, Jack. I drink it every day. It does taste different from your water, probably because it is from the well."

After Jack's complaining and after they have finished their meal, Bernard says, "It has been a long day and I am tired. We probably should get some shuteye." He reaches under the bed and pulls out several blankets and hands them to Jack. "You can make a pallet on the floor."

"Why do I have to sleep on the floor?"

"Because that's my bed," Bernard states in a stern tone. "And you're not sleeping with me."

Jack is not happy about it, but he makes his pallet and slips in for the night. Bernard blows out the candle and lantern. It's not long before both are asleep.

Sometime after midnight, Bernard awakes. Somebody has crawled in bed with him. "Jack, get out of my bed. Get back on the floor."

"Who the hell are you?" a voice of slurred words resonates in the darkness.

It's not Jack. A scuffle occurs between the two men. They start to fight and holler at each other in the darkness.

"Who the hell are you?" the man shouts.

From the smell of liquor on his breath, he's obviously drunk.

"Who the hell are *you*?" Bernard shouts back.

"What are you doing in my bed?" the man shouts as he scrambles to get away.

The commotion has woken Jack from his sleep. Realizing there is an intruder in the cabin, he jumps to his feet and scrambles his way to the door to light the candle. Once it's lit, everyone can see each other in the dim light. They stop and stare. Bernard and the man stare at each other for a moment with astonishment.

Jack himself is awestruck and says, "You didn't tell me you had a twin brother."

"I do not have a brother!" Bernard hollers back with confusion in his voice.

"Then, who in the hell is this?" Jack asks. "There are two of you, staring at each other. If you don't have a twin, why does he look exactly like you?"

"Why are you in my house and in my bed?" the man barks at Bernard again. "And who are you?" The man points to Jack.

"Bernard, who is this guy?" Jack asks again.

Both men reply at the same time, "I don't know."

The intruder asks, "How do you know my name? Do I know you?"

"Holy crap, Batman!" Jack screeches. Y'all are the same freaking person. Holy crap! This time travel stuff just got really weird." Jack starts to laugh hysterically. "This is freaking awesome."

Both men look at Jack. "What is so funny? What are you talking about?" Bernard asks.

"You don't get it, do you? What year was it when you traveled to

2019?" Jack asks.

"1752."

"Exactly. Now, you and I traveled back to 1750, two years before you originally traveled to 2019. And you have run into yourself."

"My God, you are right. I see it now."

"What a mess," Jack says. "This should be fun. First, we need a way to distinguish the two of you apart. I will call you Bernard and you Drunk Bernard." He points to each as he laughs.

"What in the world are you two talking about?" Drunk Bernard asks, with a puzzled expression planted on his drunken face.

"Drunk Bernard, you better sit down," Jack tells him. "Listen, we have come from the future."

Bernard steps back and stays quiet knowing Jack will stumble trying to explain time travel to a drunk man.

"This man is you, two years later," Jack says, pointing at Bernard. Jack now hears the words spilling out of his mouth and realizes how crazy he sounds, especially to a drunk man, but he continues. "In 1752, you will travel to the future, then return back to 1750. Which is where we are right now. And now, you have run into yourself."

"Wow." Jack stands up straight and mumbles to himself, "This is one screwed-up conversation. I sound like an idiot. Bernard, you need to explain it to him."

Bernard laughs. "No, no, you go ahead. You're doing a fine job."

"I think the two of you are drunker than I am," Drunk Bernard slurs.

Bernard decides to help Jack out. "I am you, from a couple of years in the future. This man's name is Jack. I met him in the year 2019. We are on a mission and have traveled back to 1750."

"Jack, show him your cell phone. This should convince him."

"Great idea." Jack picks his cell phone up from the floor near his sleeping pallet and bends down to show it to Drunk Bernard. He opens an app of a card game.

Drunk Bernard stares at the object, trying to focus, and he slurs out a question. “How does that light up like that?”

“By tapping on the screen...uh, electricity,” Jack says.

“Okay, I believe you. You’re from the future, now get out of my way.” He quickly stands and pushes Jack aside. “Time to flash the hash.”

“What?” Jack asks, confused, with the corner of his lip cocked up. He jumps out of the way.

“You’ll see,” Bernard remarks.

He stumbles out the door.

They both hear Drunk Bernard throw up.

“Flash the hash. I like it,” Jack chuckles.

The sounds of puking turn to dry heaves.

Several minutes later, he stumbles back inside the cabin. Bernard hands him a cup of water. He sips it, rinses his mouth, and spits it back outside and closes the door.

“You need to lie down and sleep it off,” Bernard says.

Drunk Bernard drops the cup on the floor. “Out of my way.” Pushing past Bernard, he crawls into bed, rolls over to one side, and immediately falls asleep.

Jack glances back at Bernard. “I guess this conversation is over.”

“I guess so.”

Jack wiggles back into his pallet.

Bernard makes another pallet on the floor for himself and blows out the candle.

THIRTY-FOUR

THURSDAY, JULY 30, 1750

BERNARD AWAKES BEFORE the sun peaks over the horizon. He rises from his uncomfortable sleeping arrangement, grabs a piece of bread and a glass jar from a shelf, and slips outside. "Love that brisk fresh air," he says quietly under his breath. He rests his sore back in a porch chair and enjoys his usual fare. He watches the sun peak above the horizon. Its rays illuminate the few high clouds to a reddish orange against a brightening blue sky. He opens the glass jar and pulls out some money he has stashed away and stuffs it in his pocket.

Jack too wakes with a bit of a stiff back and notices Bernard missing. He stands, stretches, and steps outside, where he finds Bernard kicked back in a chair. "Getting comfortable in your own surroundings, I see."

"Yes, I am," Bernard says. "It is good to be home again. I will miss this place."

For the first time, daylight allows Jack to gaze across Bernard's land. The golden fields of dry grass sprawl out before the scattered trees in the distance. He watches the sun climb over the horizon. He could not ask for a better day to visit an old historic Philadelphia. "What a beautiful morning," Jack comments.

"Yes, it is. I love the view here."

A horse *neighs.*

Jack notices a wooden shed to his right. The weathered wood—deteriorating from years of exposure to the summer heat, the spring rains, and the harsh winter snows—provides protection on three sides. A wooden gate allows him a view inside to two horses, who munch on dry hay.

"Now that I know this time travel stuff really works, I'm ready to win a lottery. What's your plan, and how do you intend to find this letter?" Jack asks.

"I have been bouncing ideas around in my head and believe I have one that will work, but it will require your participation."

"Great. Now, add *accessory* to my growing list of crimes," Jack says sarcastically.

Bernard ignores him. "My plan is to find a job at the ship docks, hopefully working with the mail. Before I relocated to Philadelphia, I worked in Savannah loading ships for a little over a year. I worked there long enough that I should be able to muddle myself into a job. When I relocated here I had no interest in ship work. The work is hard and I have no interest in working that hard again. Though many people in town know me, those around the docks likely will not. If someone will hire me, I will keep a watchful eye out for any letters concerning Benjamin or Peter Collinson.

"You will work it from a different perspective. You introduce yourself to a few merchants near Benjamin's shop; inform them you are new in town with hopes of a new life. You have started a new business, which offers services to run errands or make deliveries. Your business will provide a benefit to both the merchant and yourself. The first week you will perform these services for free, to allow the merchant to experience your dependability. You tell them that after the first week you will charge a small fee for the services. This will be a great opportunity for the merchant, because he can determine if this is a viable service to his business. You will go to a few businesses first, then to Benjamin's print shop. If we are lucky, word will spread and you will have some opportunities with Benjamin. I know this type of business would never work, but for free it may provide an opportunity to steal the letter."

"Oh really." Jacks says, with his arms crossed. "I'll bet if you asked UPS, FedEx, or DHL, they would disagree with you."

"What?" Bernard asks, confused.

"Never mind. And what's this crap about working for free? You must be crazy. Jack doesn't work for free."

"Look at the big picture, Jack. This lottery thing you keep talking about is your payday. And the money you make here cannot be spent in 2019. Trust me, I know. Even if it could, it sounds like small potatoes compared to this lottery thing you talk about."

"Good point. All right, let's do this."

"Here is some money. It will help you while in town. It's not a lot, but it should suffice for a couple of days." Bernard gives Jack a couple of sixpence coins, a couple of pennies, and a few farthings.

Jack stares at the money with confusion. He does not understand its value or how to apply it to purchases.

"Before we go into town, you need to put on some different clothes," Bernard says. "You need to blend into our era. Fortunately, you and I are nearly the same size. You can wear some of my clothes." The two men step back inside the cabin, where Drunk Bernard snores excessively. "Here, put these on," Bernard says, as he hands him a long pair of pants, a brown V-neck, a short-sleeve shirt, a hat, and a pair of short brown boots. "While you dress, I will saddle up the horses."

Bernard leaves for the shed, allowing Jack to dress.

Moments later, Jack walks out to the shed. "You're kidding me, right? I look silly in this getup. Brown pants, brown shirt, brown boots, a brown hat. Don't you people believe in a color other than brown? I mean really." He points with his finger. "Brown grass, brown barn, and a brown cabin. For God sakes, even the horses are brown." He throws both hands up in the air.

Bernard laughs as he continues to saddle the two horses. "Again, welcome to 1750. You ever ride a horse, City Boy?"

"A couple of times many years ago, and don't call me City Boy. But you may need to remind me."

"All right," Bernard replies while he leads both horses out of the shed. "You will ride Red today," Bernard says while mounting his horse. "So, saddle up and let's go."

"Finally, a different color," Jack states. "Although the horse you call Red is freaking brown."

Bernard laughs.

Jack tries to insert a foot in the stirrup, but Red bobs his head, knickers with small grunts, and moves to the side with a nervous step.

"Easy, Red," Bernard says to calm the horse, which appears to work enough for Jack to get a foot in the stirrup and pull himself up and into the saddle. Bernard grabs Red's bridle and pulls her along.

"All right, Jack, listen up. To stop her, pull back on the reins, but not too hard. Pull and lean to the right to turn right or pull and lean to the left to turn left. A light kick in the flanks with a *click, click* should send her into a trot. A hard kick to the flanks and a loud 'Yah' will send her running, but you better hold on. Got it? Good. Let's go."

Bernard lets go of Red's reins. He gives a quick *click, click* and a light kick. "C'mon, Betsy." They trot off toward town. Jack provides the same and follows behind him.

"I wonder what Drunk Bernard will remember from last night?" Jack questions.

"I doubt he will remember much, but he will be madder than hell when he finds both his horses missing."

Both laugh as they continue toward town.

Bernard realizes Jack needs a cover story. They make up a believable story that Jack has recently arrived from Savannah, Georgia. He has started a new life here and needs work.

They arrive on the outskirts of town. They slow the horses to a casual walk and make their way through town. Jack chokes up for a second while seeing old Philadelphia for the first time. Awestruck, he surveys the street's dusty scene. Horses are tied to the hitching posts outside many of the wooden buildings. They ride their horses with a casual gait through town. Some of the buildings have boardwalks for people to move about; others do not. Many people bustle about, wearing Colonial-day clothing. Horse-drawn wagons carry people down the streets to conduct their errands. "My God, it's like a scene right out of *Little House on the Prairie*," Jack murmurs to himself.

As they pass through, Bernard points out a few of the establishments. "Jack, there is one of many taverns throughout town. And that is Jim Johnson's General Store. Many of the merchants at the far end of this street conduct business with the shipping and trade partners."

"This is so bizarre. I don't even know what to say."

"Now you know what I felt like in your day." Bernard leads them down another street, pointing out other familiar businesses as they ride through. He turns on yet another street. "Benjamin's home and print shop are up ahead."

A minute later, Bernard points. "There's Benjamin's place."

"Wow!" Jack says, a little awestruck. "Benjamin Franklin's house. I'll bet they don't have this on the Hollywood celebrity house tour."

"Jack, I will leave you on this street. There are many merchants who you could possibly make some deals with for your newfound business." Bernard reaches into his pocket and pulls out a pocket watch. "It's now 8:30 a.m. Let's meet around 1:30 this afternoon at Bernie's Tavern down the street," Bernard says as he points toward the tavern. "That should give you some time to meet with several merchants, while I try to find a job at the docks."

Bernard leaves Jack and mumbles to himself, "I hope he does nothing stupid."

On the way to the river he approaches the post office and decides to stop inside and ask a few questions.

"Good morning, sir," the clerk says to Bernard as he enters. "How can I help you?"

Bernard walks to the counter. "I have a friend looking to send a letter to London. Would he bring the letter here or take it to a trades shipper at the docks?"

"Either through us or directly with them. If he sends it through the postmaster, we will ensure it arrives on the ship before she sets sail."

"Thank you. I will let him know. Also, are you hiring? I have mail experience."

"I am sorry, not at the present. But if you stop by a couple of days each week, I will let you know if I hear of any opportunities."

"I will. Thank you," Bernard says and turns to leave for the docks.

At the river's edge, Bernard's senses awaken. People bustle around like ants. Shipmate chatter resonates through the wharf. The scent of the river is drowned out by the dust of the streets, but somehow a whiff of fresh-baked bread sneaks its way to his nostrils. Wagons and their metal rings clink against each other. The *clip-clops* of nearby horses pound the dry dirt road. The aroma and the sounds of the picturesque port remind him of commerce in action from his days on the Savannah docks.

Bernard notices two smaller vessels moored nearby, but it is the magnificent three-mast ship moored before him that captures his full attention. She stands strong with three huge timbers rising high above the deck, garnished with a network of ropes to govern her sails while underway. Her main mast supports four large square-rigged sails to be set at sea, while her fore and mizzen masts support three large sails of their own. When she churns her way on the open seas, three forward jib sails will rise from the bowsprit that points toward the ship's heading.

He catches the name "Patience" prominently written across her stern, something he is not sure he has enough of at the moment. However, it pleases him to see the flag of England flicker in the light breeze high above her deck.

He dismounts Betsy and wraps her reins around a post. A warm, light breeze brushes the side of his face, though the river remains calm with only a slight ripple. Three more ships rest anchored near the river's center. Each waits their turn to be moored and unloaded, though the passengers have already disembarked via shore tenders. A nearby church bell rings nine times, signaling the morning is progressing and he has work to do.

Surely, one of these ships will embark on a voyage to London, but which one and when? he thinks. *I must find out.*

He surveys the docks, the river, and the area nearby. He raises his nose. This time the fresh-baked scent of bread is profound. "Oh, that smells good."

When ships tender their passengers to shore, the local bakers are prepared, knowing passengers will be eager for something sweet. After an oceanic journey of more than eight weeks, they crave anything not resembling fish and scarf up the bakers' tasty offerings.

Bernard enters the shipping office at Penn's Landing. The large windows on either side of the entrance let in ample light, affording the office personnel a view of the wharf it controls. A thin, scraggly gentleman in his early thirties, donning typical Colonial dress, sits behind one of the two wooden desks. "May I help you, sir?" he asks.

"Yes, I am looking for work, hopefully on the ships. I have experience with break-bulk shipping, balance, mail, and package storage to ensure a ship's safe voyage," Bernard says with confidence.

"We do not have any openings today, but tell me about your experience. It may be helpful," the man says in a way that leads Bernard to believe there may be an opportunity.

"I worked at the docks in Savannah, Georgia, for several years. I am familiar with the process of loading barrels, hogsheads, and other goods on and off the ships as well as use of ballasts for storage and balance. As you are aware, balance is critical for the ship's voyage."

"I am. But what brings you to Philadelphia?" the man inquires.

I have heard many good prosperity stories of Philadelphia, and I have longed to see my family in Thornbury. I decided to sell my land in Savannah and relocate here. As you know, Thornbury is not too far away, and being here would put me much closer to my mother. But, before I departed on my journey to Philadelphia, I received word of my father's passing. I felt it best to stay with Mother for a few weeks before I traveled on to Philadelphia. But now the time has come that I must return to work and start a new life. I believe my skills would be useful here at the docks. I believe I would be a benefit to your operation," Bernard says convincingly.

"Interesting," the man replies while scratching his head. "As I said earlier, I do not have any openings today, but if you return tomorrow, there may be a possibility. What is your name, sir?" the man asks.

"Bernard. Bernard Shoemaker," he replies, not wanting to provide his real surname. He wants to make sure his name is not recognized, in case something goes wrong. He does not want the law chasing after Drunk Bernard and creating a problem for him later.

"Great. Mr. Shoemaker, please check back with me tomorrow and I will let you know if anything becomes available."

"I thank you, sir," Bernard replies and leaves the office.

A large, tall, burly man, with a thick, dark beard and mustache, wearing a long-sleeve white shirt, a brown vest, brown breeches to his knees, and tall black boots, steps through an open door that leads to the back corridor and other offices. He runs one hand through his receded hairline, while his index and middle fingers of the other hand pinch the large, unlit cigar he has been chewing and pulls it away. He asks with a deep voice, "John, who was that man?"

A grin jumps on Johns face. "Michael," he says, rising from his chair, "his name is Bernard Shoemaker. He is from Savannah and looking for work. He is experienced in break-bulk shipping, load balance, and mail handling. I told him to check back tomorrow and I would let him know if anything became available."

Realizing this is his opportunity to sell Michael on replacing old man Olson, he says, "You know, everyone has been unhappy with old man Olson, yourself included. The man is an absolute tyrant and he treats everyone with disrespect. He has a demoralizing attitude and his work ethic is not very good. This is your opportunity to replace him. The timing couldn't be any better, since the *Patience* is near loaded and ready to go. It would provide Mr. Shoemaker a chance to become acquainted with our processes and take care of some final details. And, this would give Tom an opportunity to check his skills. He appears courteous, which would be a great benefit to the other workers, and it could bring up morale just having Olson gone. This could be a good change, Michael."

"You are right. Neal has been a thorn in our sides for a long time. I agree. See that Mr. Shoemaker starts immediately. Give Olson the next couple of days off with pay. If Shoemaker lives up to his skills, you can fire Neal next week."

"Yes, sir. It would be my pleasure," John replies, elated.

Bernard watches the people bustle about the ship, preparing her for the next voyage. The conversation felt good. His hopes rise at the possibility of completing his devious goal. He realizes, even though the ship is English, it does not mean she is destined for London. It occurs to him that he never inquired about the ship's destination or her departure date. Curious, he steps back inside.

"Forgive me, sir. I meant to ask..."

"Oh good, you came back," the man interrupts. "I have good news. I spoke with Michael, our shipping manager. He would like you to start work tomorrow at 7 a.m., if that is possible."

"Absolutely. Thank you, sir." Bernard is elated and shakes the man's hand, then turns to leave.

As he opens the door the man says, "Wait, you had a question?"

"Oh, yes, thank you. With the excitement, I forgot to ask. The ship, *Patience*, where is she sailing and when does she leave?"

"She is due to leave for London on Saturday, weather permitting. Why do you ask?" John questions.

"No particular reason. I have always been interested in ships and their journeys and I was curious."

It seemed an odd question to the man, but he paid it no attention.

Back outside, Bernard mumbles under his breath, "Today is Thursday. That does not leave us much time. We need to act fast. I need to find Jack and see how his part of the plan is coming along. He needs to understand our time restraints." He mounts Betsy and with a loud "Yah," Betsy races down the dirt street.

Upon his arrival, he finds Red tied up outside Mrs. Virginia's bakery. Jack steps out.

"Jack?" Bernard calls out as he rides up and dismounts Betsy.

"Back so soon?" Jack asks. "Any luck?"

"Let's sit down and talk a bit. I have some good news and some bad news."

THIRTY-FIVE

THURSDAY, JULY 30, 1750

THEY ENTER BERNIE'S tavern. The two-story grand entrance dominates the room. A wooden staircase to the left leads to the second-floor balcony and wraps to both sides of the room. Jack's nose quivers from the lingering tobacco smoke, while his eyes gaze with astonishment at what he considers an outdated style of Colonial decor. Beneath the rustic wooden balcony before them, two patrons drink alone, each occupying a stool at separate ends of the polished wood bar. The bearded bartender, wearing a white long-sleeve shirt and a green vest, wipes out a glass with a white cloth. They can see themselves in the mirror, which is lined with liquor bottles and glasses. They find a dining table in the room to their right, where the lower ceiling provides a slightly quieter space for their conversation.

They sit at a table near a window facing the street. A beautiful, busty woman in her early thirties with long, blond hair pulled back in a ponytail approaches the table. She bends over and rests both elbows on the table. With her low-cut white blouse, she allows both men a close but concealed view of her ample bosom. "Would you two boys be interested in something to nibble on?" she asks with her seductive English accent.

"No, ma'am," Bernard answers quickly, knowing she wants to share more than her friendly smile. "We would like something to eat, along with a pint of ale."

She rises. "I guess I can help you boys out."

Her seductive tone excites Jack.

"I will bring out today's special and a couple of pints. But if there is anything, and I mean anything, you boys would like, you just let me know. Shirley can surely satisfy your pallet, if you know what I mean." She winks.

"Yes, ma'am, we do. But the food and ale will be enough for now," Bernard replies, avoiding the situation. Although intrigued, for now he has other issues that require his attention.

While she walks away. Her long, light blue gown conceals the beauty Jack imagines. Jack gasps. "WOW! She's hot. She can have some of my money any day. What was her name?"

"Keep you sugar stick in your pants, Jack. You don't have the time or the money to play with a Bushell Bubby like her. We need to focus on the task at hand."

"Sugar Stick? Bushell Bubby? Okay, Sugar Stick I understand, but what in the world is a Bushell Bubby?"

Bernard leans toward the table and whispers, "You know, a woman with large breasts." He gestures with his hands, cupping at his chest. "A Bushell Bubby."

"I guess that's Colonial slang. Kind of like Drunk Bernard's 'Flash the Hash' comment last night."

"Listen, I have great news and some not so great news. They hired me at the Penn's Landing. I start tomorrow morning. The good news: the ship moored at the dock is going to London. The bad news: it leaves Saturday. We need to find the letter tomorrow, to give me time to copy it in my hand and store it on the ship with the other mail."

"That's not much time. But, I too have some good news," Jack counters. "I talked to three different merchants and each said they would be interested in my free services. If they like it, they will continue to use the services. But I have not yet talked to Benjamin. I would like to do that today before we ride back to your cabin."

"Jack, that is fantastic, but with our time limited, you need not worry too much about the others and focus strictly on Benjamin. After lunch, you talk to Benjamin and sell him on your new venture. If the other three agreed, Benjamin will do the same, but be sure to mention their names. It will help."

For a moment, they stare out the window. Bernard says, "We will stay here at the tavern tonight and tomorrow night. We cannot waste time traveling back and forth to the cabin."

"Only if you're paying for the rooms," Jack replies.

Shirley returns, with two specials and two pints of ale and sets them down on the table. "If you need anything else, please let Shirley know. I aim to please."

"No. But thank you," Bernard replies.

She turns around to walk away but stops to give a quick look over her shoulder and a wink to the boys, then continues with a slower, seductive walk.

Bernard digs in.

It takes Jack a moment to turn his eyes away from Shirley. When he glances down at his plate he is not impressed with what he sees. "What in hell is this?"

Each plate contains a small portion of dried meat, a bowl of Hasty pudding, a couple of dumplings, and half of a potato.

"Complaining again, Jack? This is a hell of a lot better than what you had last night. Try it. It's good."

Jack picks up his spoon and dips into the bowl of pudding, a porridge-like staple with milk added. He lets it spill off the spoon splashing back into the bowl. "The food in 1750 sucks. I don't know if I can eat this crap."

"Try it. It's good. You will need your energy, so eat up," Bernard says as a smirk slithers across his face. He enjoys Jack's displeasure, knowing the food is nothing like he expects back home.

"Fine, I'll try it," he says with reluctant discontent.

"I can say one thing; this food does not have near the appeal the waitress has. I mean, she is some kind of hot," Jack remarks again, glancing back toward the bar. "You know, the girls of the 1750s are sexier than I expected."

"Eat up, Jack," Bernard barks. "You need to focus on the task at hand. Our time here is limited."

They finish their meal, pay the bill, and leave the tavern.

Jack is anxious to meet Benjamin Franklin and sell him on his plan, but he mostly wants to wrap up this little charade and return to 2019, where he can eat real food and collect his lottery winnings.

Jack starts into the street but slows for a passing horse and buggy. He enters Benjamin's print shop. The Colonial-style printing equipment sparks nostalgia. He observes two men at work with their respective presses. One man presses two black padded, flat, ball-like devices against each other in rapid succession, creating a sound as if two sticky pads were being pulled apart continuously. Unbeknownst to Jack, the man is spreading ink over their surfaces in preparation to apply it to his print stencils, which are already set in the press. The other man fills his press plate with letters before placing them in their frame. A third man approaches Bernard at the counter, wearing a black vest over his long-sleeve, white shirt. "Can I help you, sir?"

"Yes, sir. My name is Jack and I would like to speak with Benjamin."

"He is not here right now. My name is David Hall. Benjamin and I are partners, but I run the print shop while he pursues his experiments and other endeavors. How can I help you?"

"I'm from Savannah and new to Philadelphia. I hope to make a new life here and I have started a new business. I will provide delivery services or run errands for local businesses. Since people in town do not know me, I hope to build a little confidence and trust by providing my services for free for the first week. I have talked to a few other businesses and they have agreed to provide me with an opportunity. I was hoping Benjamin and yourself may also be interested. I will be prompt and efficient, and if you use my services, it will free your time up for other details."

"If you are new to town, how do you know Benjamin?" David questions.

"I do not know him. Mrs. Virginia across the street told me I should talk to Benjamin and that I may find an opportunity here as well."

"I see. Your services do sound intriguing. How would we contact you?"

"I will stop by a couple of times a day to check with you."

"All right then, since your services will be free for the first week, I will give you an opportunity as well. I believe everybody deserves a chance to prove themselves. If you will come by a couple of times a day, I will provide you with some errands. Benjamin will agree with my decision."

"Thank you, Mr. Hall. I will not let you down," Jack says excitedly, then turns to leave. Although Jack knows he is running a scam, he still enjoys the euphoria he receives after closing a sell.

Jack sits at their usual table and orders an ale from Shirley while he waits for Bernard. Half an hour pass before Bernard enters the tavern and joins him.

Bernard sits at the table and asks, "Did you meet with Benjamin?"

"Not with Benjamin. But I did speak with a man named David Hall, Benjamin's partner. He liked the idea and agreed. He said he would inform Benjamin about it but knew it would be fine. He said they both believe a new man in town should be afforded some opportunities. I told him I would come by a couple of times a day to see if he had any deliveries. Now, I just need to keep working him and hopefully we will find the letter."

"Fantastic," Bernard states. "I paid for a couple of rooms for the next two nights. I picked up some writing paper, a pen, and some ink, so if we find the letter, I will be prepared. There is not much we can do until the morning. Let's celebrate with a pint of ale."

"I have a better idea. Why don't you show me around town? I am here; at least show me a little Colonial charm."

"That's a great idea. You will enjoy a tour of our Philadelphia. We can celebrate when we return."

They have one day to find the letter.

THIRTY-SIX

FRIDAY, JULY 31, 1750

BERNARD, WHO'S UP early, knocks on Jack's door to make sure he is up and moving.

"Yeah, I will be out in a minute," Jack replies through the door. "Meet me downstairs."

A few minutes pass before Jack steps from his room.

Bernard sees him exit the room and turns to wait for him outside, where the sun has not yet broken over the horizon but casts its light on the morning sky.

They meet at the horses.

"Jack, I will be at the dock throughout the day. I hope to have an opportunity to go through the mail already on the ship. I will work as long as they let me. But, if you find the letter, come find me. Otherwise, I will see you back here this evening. Then we can discuss our day's progress."

"All right."

Bernard mounts Betsy and trots toward to the waterfront.

Jack strolls to Benjamin's print shop. Still early, he enters the shop, where business has already started for the day. The same two men from the day before are engrossed in their print run. David approaches the counter.

"Good morning, David. I wanted to drop in and see if you had any errands to be done."

"Nice to see you here so early. I like promptness. I do not have anything yet but check back around nine this morning. I should have some prints ready to be delivered."

"Yes, sir."

Bernard enters the Penn's Landing office. "Good morning, sir. I am here as you have requested and anxious to get started," he says, extending a hand.

"Ah, an early riser. I like that." He shakes Bernard's hand. "We too are excited to have you aboard," John replies with energy. "Please have a seat. Tom will be here in a few minutes to show you around the ship."

Bernard sits down with his hat in his hand.

Several minutes pass when a large man steps from his office wearing black breeches to his knees, tall black boots, and a red vest covering his long-sleeve white shirt. "Good morning. My name is Michael," he says while chewing his cigar. "I am the shipping manager here at Penn's Landing. I understand you have some skills working around the ships."

"I do." Bernard stretches the truth a little.

"Great. Come into my office. We can talk for a moment before Tom arrives. He will show you around."

Bernard rises and offers an energetic handshake.

"Have a seat." Michael gestures to a chair in his office, then relaxes in his desk chair. Tell me a little about your last job. I believe John said you worked at the docks in Savannah."

"That is correct, sir," Bernard begins. "I would ensure the ships..."

"Hello, Michael." A tall, broad-shouldered man interrupts as he enters the office. He wears a dark brown, long-sleeve white shirt, light brown breeches to his knees, and tall brown boots. "I understand you have a new man to replace Olson."

"That was fast. Yes, I do," Michael says, as he stands to provide the introductions, "Tom, Bernard. Bernard, Tom."

The two men shake hands.

"Pleased to meet you," Tom says.

"Likewise," Bernard replies.

"Tom is our dockmaster and responsible for the ship until it leaves the dock. He will show you the ship. Go with him and we can catch up later."

"Michael, I would like to thank you for this opportunity. I will not let you down. I will work hard and make sure the work is complete before I leave at the end of the day, even if it is on my own time. I want to make a good showing."

"Well, we appreciate your enthusiasm. If you need anything, talk with Tom."

After boarding, Tom says, "Let's take a tour of the ship." He picks up a candle lantern. They descend a wooden ladder into a light-starved corridor. A lantern at each end provides them with enough light to find their way down the corridor. Tom lights his lantern before he begins the tour. "This is the kitchen," he points out before passing a few storage areas, which encompass the food storage, goods storage, postal storage, and the ship's vault, which is chain-locked. Tom points each out as they approach.

They descend a ladder to a lower deck, where the crew and passengers sleep on their long voyage across the Atlantic. Several hammocks hang in a room stacked two high. He stops at another set of stairs leading further down. "I assume you are familiar with the bottom deck and its contents?"

"Yes, I am," Bernard says. "Usually the heaviest commodities—sugar, tobacco, spices, and coffee—are stored in barrels, hogsheads, or tons on this deck. They provide weight to help stabilize the ship. Many days in Savannah, we would use barrels full of water if we were not shipping rum or other liquids to use as ballasts to help stabilize the ship."

"You sound as if you know ship storage and balance. That is good to hear. As you can see, the *Patience* is loaded and ready to go. Only minor details remain. Once she sails tomorrow, we will bring in the *Bombay Castle*, which is anchored midriver. She too is a large ship, and that's when the hard work will start. We will need to do some warping to get her dockside."

"She does look ready for her next voyage. As far as the hard work, I look forward to it. Makes the day go by faster."

Through their conversations, Tom is convinced that Bernard's days in Savannah have provided job experience, although it may be a little less than what he had hoped. However, he believes the tradeoff for replacing Neal Olson will be worthy of any efforts he must provide to help Bernard reach the skills necessary for his liking.

Bernard knows each ship carries a log, detailing her cargo. "May I review the ship's Cargo Manifest?" he asks Tom. "It would be good to see the methods here at Penn's." Bernard hopes to find anything that may indicate Benjamin has letters aboard the ship.

"Yes, you can review those in a bit."

"That would be great," Bernard comments as they both climb back to the ship's main deck. "She does appear ready."

"She is. The heavy items have been aboard for days now, and only a few small packages and postal items remain. I understand you have experience with handling mail as well."

"I do."

"Great. Could you make sure those last few details are in order and properly stowed?"

"I will get right on it. Where does the mail arrive before it is brought aboard the ship? I would like to check that area as well."

"Good question," he replies, pointing toward the dock office. "See the door on the side?"

"Yes."

"We store the mail there before bringing it down to the ship. You will find a wheelbarrow in the room to carry the mailbags down to the ship."

"Great. Is the door locked?"

"Yes, but you can obtain the key from John in the front office."

"Then, I shall talk with John."

"Let me show you to those logs, then you can deal with the mail," Tom says, and he escorts Bernard to a room located on the main deck. "The logs always remain in the first mate's quarters. Beyond that door," he points, "lies the captain's quarters."

"I do appreciate your help."

Tom leaves Bernard to his job. Bernard eagerly reviews the Cargo Manifest first. He finds no mention of Benjamin Franklin or Peter Collinson's name. *No packages,* he thinks. *That means it could only be a letter, which means an hour or more in the mail storage sifting through the sacks of letters.*

He descends the same ladder to the lower deck and enters the light-starved corridor. His eyes adjust to the limited light, and he approaches the mail storage closet. With the trivial loading that remains for the ship, the area has been vacated. He slips into the mail closet unnoticed and closes the door. Void of any light, he slides his hand along the wall on either side of the door. He finds a tin with several matches. He strikes one and finds a lantern mounted on the side wall. With the area now lit, he discovers his task at hand. Five large mailbags lie on the floor. Each bag is bulging at the top, stuffed full of letters.

Bernard's eyes widen and rage pries its way onto his face, but he composes himself. "Unbelievable. This will take a week to go through." He finds a fraction of luck with an empty bag lying on the floor. He picks it up and hangs it on a nail. He opens the first bag and reviews the name of each letter, one by one. He tosses each into the empty bag until it is complete.

He leaves the room after each bag, blows out the candle, and moves about the ship, making himself appear busy, hoping not to call any attention to himself.

After several hours, he finishes his search through each of the bags. He mumbles to himself. "Unbelievable. Not a single letter to or from Collinson or Benjamin. Has the letter already departed on another ship? Maybe it will be sent on one of the ships anchored in the river waiting their turn at the docks. I still need to check the letters from the mail storage at the dock office. Maybe it's there." He climbs the ladder to the deck of the ship and marches off to the mail storage at the dock office. As he steps onto the gangway, Tom catches him.

"Bernard, we need some help down below. We had a couple of barrels that were damaged and have since burst open. There's molasses everywhere that needs to be cleaned up. Can you lend us a hand?"

Bernard, a bit disgusted, puts on a cheerful face. "Sure."

After a couple of hours, and the mess cleaned up, he states, "Gentlemen, I must leave the rest with you. I need to make a run to the dock office before John leaves for the day." He turns and walks away.

Bernard enters the dock office. "Hi, John. I wanted to thank you again for this opportunity."

"Trust me, the pleasure is everyone's here. Old man Olson has been a tyrant for years. Replacing him will be a welcoming change that has been needed around here for a long time. So, welcome aboard." John provides a quick laugh. "Figuratively speaking of course."

"Ah yes, good one," Bernard responds with a quick laugh of his own. "I am making some headway down on the ship, and Tom told me I could obtain the key from you for the mail storage. I need to store the mail onto the ship."

"Oh, yes." He reaches into a desk drawer. "If I have left by the time you have finished, put the key in the top drawer."

"I will. Thanks."

"Do you know the room's location?"

"Yes, I do." Bernard turns and leaves the office.

Bernard unlocks the door and enters the tiny room. Two bags of mail hang from a frame below two wall slots, where the mail is deposited from inside the main office, but neither bag is half full. He wants to close the door but finds there is no candle mounted in this room. The door must remain cracked open to allow in some light. It's a risk he does not want, but he has no choice. He empties one of the bags onto the floor and starts a new search. Nothing. He dumps the second bag onto the floor and continues his search. Again, no letter.

"Where is that letter?" he mumbles under his breath.

Bernard takes the bags with him to the ship. He leaves them in the mail storage closet. He scrounges around a few of the other storage areas to verify no mailbags have been accidently placed in the wrong room. Still no luck. Discouraged, he climbs up to the ship's deck and realizes the letter will not be found today. He peers out at the other anchored ships. "It must be leaving on one of those."

He feels defeated, but he has stayed longer than most of the other workers. He sees Tom. "I guess this day is finished," he says.

Tom too prepares to leave and says, "Bernard, I appreciate your hard work today. I will see you early tomorrow?" he asks.

"Yes, sir, I will be here."

"Great. See you then." Both men part ways.

Bernard mounts Betsy and takes her on a steady gait to Bernie's. He sits at their usual table and orders an ale while he waits for Jack.

Halfway through his second ale, Jack walks through the door.

"Jack," he calls out.

Jack nods at Bernard and joins him at the table. "Any luck on the ship?"

"No," Bernard says in a depressed tone. "Tom acquainted me with the ship, but I spent a lot of time helping clean up molasses from a couple of damaged barrels. I did go through the mailbags, but no letter existed. I hope you had better luck than me."

"I will say this, she's a large and beautiful ship that you...."

"What were you doing at the ship?" Bernard sharply interrupts. "You should have been working David or Benjamin for errands. Jack, we don't have time to waste. The ship leaves tomorrow and we are nowhere closer than we were two days ago," Bernard says in an upset and disappointed tone.

"Don't worry, Bernard, you'll get the letter."

"I'm glad you're confident."

"If I may continue.... I left the print shop this afternoon. David had me deliver some printing to a couple of the businesses down by the river, and that's when I saw the ship. But then, an interesting occurrence. On my ride back to the print shop, guess who I ran into."

"No idea."

"Benjamin. He was in his buggy passing by in the opposite direction when a lady ran out of her store screaming. Something about her husband. Benjamin stopped, and I decided to as well. I thought this may be a great opportunity to meet him. We both entered, where we found her husband lying on the floor. He had fallen and cut his head and hurt his arm, probably broken. Benjamin and I helped him up and Benjamin made a tourniquet for his arm. This is the interesting part. He said he must leave because he had a letter that must be at the docks before they closed for the day."

Bernard's head rises with an intrigued look upon his face. "Yeah? What happened?"

"I introduced myself as the man providing the errand services for David at his print shop and I could deliver the letter if he would like. I was not much help there and he could help the man with his injuries. He agreed and said I would find the letter in his buggy outside.

"And there in the buggy lay the letter. I returned and asked if I had the correct letter, and he agreed."

"Where's the letter?" Bernard asks excitedly.

He reaches behind his back and says, "This letter?"

Bernard snatches the letter from Jack's hands. "Wasting my time with that story." He opens the letter. "This is it. This is the fifth letter. You do whatever you wish for the rest of the night. It is time for Bernard to enter the history books. I will be in my room the rest of the night if you need me."

Early the next morning, with the letter rewritten, Bernard arrives at the ship. "Good morning, Tom," he says, boarding the ship in a cheerful mood.

"Morning."

Bernard stops and gazes back toward the dock office. "I see passengers gathering. They must be anxious to board the *Patience* for their voyage to London?"

"Yes, they are. The weather appears right for her departure this morning. The loading is complete and boarding will start soon. The winds are favorable today, and she should have no problem reaching the ocean. Once boarded and we have her kedged to the open river, we will start the warping with the next ship."

Bernard looks up to the ship's flag and finds it standing in a stern, easterly wind. "That is a good sign. Tom, I will catch up with you in a bit. I have another piece of mail that needs to be placed below."

"All right."

Bernard descends to the mail storage closet, where he drops his letter in one of the mailbags. "Perfect. Four more letters to go."

Back on the ship's main deck, Bernard mentions to one of the crew, "I see they have started to board. Looks like you will depart soon."

"In a couple of hours," the man replies.

"Good luck on your voyage," Bernard says, then turns to disembark the ship. He marches back to the shipping office, but instead of entering he continues around back. He mounts Betsy and trots back to the tavern.

Upon his arrival, he finds Jack sitting at their usual table staring at a bowl of porridge.

"It's not going to jump into your mouth. Maybe a dish in 2019 would satisfy your pallet?" he says with a jubilant tone.

"Did you get the letter on the ship?"

"I did. Let's go home."

"Hell, yeah. That's the best news I've heard in days." Jack stands up to leave the porridge.

"No, no. Sit back down and finish your breakfast. We will not leave until the morning. I need to rent a horse from Mr. Stevens' stables to take with us. We will leave in the morning at daybreak, and we will take Drunk Bernard along. He can bring the horses back."

"I would rather leave today, but you're right, we need the entire day to reach EMITT. We would never find her at night."

That evening, while eating in the cabin, Drunk Bernard enters. "There he is," Bernard says. "We have been waiting for you."

"Hell's bells and a bucket of blood. You two really do exist. I thought I had dreamed of you and your crazy story. But when I found both of my horses missing, I knew it must not have been a dream. So, where are they?"

"In the barn, with a third one," Bernard replies.

"A third one. Whose horse is that?"

I rented her for the next couple of days. I will explain later."

"Okay, second question. Was it a dream, or did you say you are me from the future?"

"That is correct," Bernard replies.

"That is absurd. Not possible."

"That's what you said the other night, but we proved it to you then and we can prove it to you again. Jack, do you have your phone?"

"Sure do." He reaches into his pocket and pulls it out. "Do you remember this?" Jack activates the screen. With it lit, he hands it to Drunk Bernard.

"I remember this." He presses a button on the screen and an application opens. He is amazed with the phone. "Where can I get one of these?"

"You can't," Jack answers. "They will not work here in 1750. You have to be in the future for them to work."

"I cannot explain this phone thing, but I still do not believe you are from the future. If you say you are me, then you should know about my childhood. Tell me something only I would know."

Bernard thinks for a minute, then says, you should remember this, "You and your brother, Gerald, took one of Daddy's rabbits down by the river. You accidently dropped the rabbit and she fell in the water. You tried to save her, but the river swept her away before you could reach her. She died. When Daddy asked about the rabbit, you told him you had not seen her."

"I never told anybody about that. Gerald must have told you that story."

"Nope. Gerald has been dead for several years. He could not have told me."

"I am not convinced. But if you did arrive from the future, why are you here?"

"We have come here to complete a mission," Bernard explains. "A mission that in a couple of years will make you a well-known man. We cannot tell you about the mission, but I can tell you it has been completed. But there is one thing left to do and we need your help."

"My help. What do I have to I do?"

"It's simple," Bernard explains. "We want you to ride with us tomorrow morning to our time machine. We will travel to the future and you will watch us vanish right before your eyes. Once we have gone, you will take the horses back to the cabin and return the rented horse back to Mr. Stevens."

"Where is this time machine you talk about?"

"It's north, a little more than a half day's ride."

"If you two disappear right before my eyes, that will make me a believer. When do we leave?"

"Daybreak," Jack answers. "It's time to go home."

"I agree," Bernard says.

That night, after the other two have drifted off to sleep, Bernard quietly slips out of his pallet and sneaks out of the cabin with his clothes. He dresses outside, saddles up on Betsy, and rides off into the darkness.

Jack awakes at dawn and notices Bernard is missing. He rises, expecting to find Bernard in a porch chair. He opens the door, but Bernard is not there. He hears one of the horses make a noise, and that's when he notices a horse missing.

"Son of a bitch! If Bernard left me here, I'll kill him." He storms back into the cabin. "Wake up, Drunk Bernard!" he shouts. "Your twin left me here. He traveled back to the future without me. I will kill him if I ever get my hands on him," he says, madder than a hornet.

He hears the gallops of a horse. He storms outside to find Bernard, riding up on Betsy.

"Where the hell have you been? I thought you left me here. I am pretty pissed off right now, Bernard. You better not be screwing with me."

"Calm down, Jack. I did not leave you. Listen, I had an idea and I reacted and I came back for you. I knew you would not agree to my plan, so I did this on my own. I rode to EMITT and traveled to the dates of each of the first four letters. I stole each, copied them, and sent them to

Peter Collinson. Now, my plan is complete. It will be Bernard Ranter who is known as the genius of the electrical experiments and the famous kite experiment. And Benjamin Franklin is nothing more than your average Benjamin. Let's go home."

"How long have you gone?" Jack says with a raised tone, still fuming over the incident.

"About four and a half months."

"Drunk Bernard," Jack hollers, "time to saddle up. Bernard and I are going home."

THIRTY-SEVEN

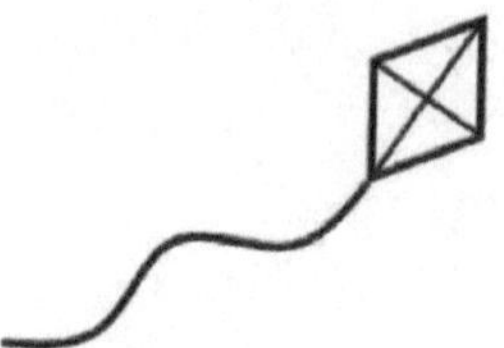

WEDNESDAY, JUNE 26, 2019

AFTER A COUPLE of hours they have repaired the cut internet line. The boys stand in the study beside their father while he attempts to track EMITT's location.

Dad and the boys each wear blue jeans. Dad has on a green polo shirt with a white stripe on each sleeve. Zach has slipped on a red T-shirt with the word "SPIDERMAN" written across the front in bold black letters with tiny webs in the lettering, and Zane wears his favorite Incredible Hulk T-shirt.

"She's not showing up," Dad says.

"What does that mean?" Zach asks.

"Probably that she's traveling."

"Traveling?" Zane shouts. "How can that be possible? Bernard doesn't have the passwords."

"Let me check my email. If EMITT has traveled, there will be an email indicating so." Jeremy opens his email. "That's not good. Not only has Bernard traveled, but he has done so in five separate events."

"How did he steal the passwords?" Zach asks. "I didn't tell him."

"Me either," Zane replies.

"It doesn't matter. He has them and he is traveling. We need to figure out if he has a plan or just joyriding."

Jeremy reads the travel dates aloud. "His first travel event took them to July 29, 1750, and it appears he was there for five days. Then, to October 1, 1749, where it looks like he stayed for about three months. He then traveled to April 22, 1749, and stayed for a week, and then to July 22, 1747, where he stayed for six weeks. The last TTE takes him to August 2, 1750. With this many travel events, it appears he has a plan."

"What's significant about these dates? And why did he travel to 1750 twice?" Zach asks.

"I am not sure, but I believe Dad is right. Bernard is up to no good."

"The dates must have some meaning. I wonder what occurred on them?" Jeremy asks.

"I have an idea," Zach states. "Those dates may be associated with Benjamin's letters." Zach turns to the bookshelf and pulls down the *Experiments and Observations on Electricity* book he had read before he came up with the crazy idea to fly a kite. "I'll bet we can find the answer here."

Zach starts to flip through the pages. "The first letter is dated July 28, 1747."

"That's close to Bernard's second to last travel event," Dad confirms, "which is exactly one week after Bernard arrives."

Zach flips the pages to the second letter. "The date is September 1, 1747."

"That date is not listed," Dad states. "Wait, Bernard stayed for six weeks after traveling to the date of the first letter and that would encompass the date of the second letter."

Zach continues through the pages. "The third letter is dated April 29, 1749."

"His travel date is April 22, 1749. Those dates are exactly seven days apart."

Zach flips through more pages. "The fourth letter does not have a date." He flips through more pages and finds the end of the fourth letter. "Nope, still no date."

"The next date going backwards would be October 1, 1749," Dad adds. "If these are about the letters, I don't understand this date. If there is no date, how would he know what date to travel to?"

"What is the date of the fifth letter?" Zane asks.

Zach flips through the pages and stops. "July 29, 1750."

"Bingo. That is the date of his first travel event," Dad responds. "It appears that at least four of these travel events may be associated with Benjamin's letters. But what does the August 2, 1750 date have to do with anything?"

They think in silence for a minute when Jeremy says, "Ah, the two dates in 1750—August 2 and July 29—they are five days apart. Something is going on with this date, but I'm not sure what. It's like he forgot something and went back to get it."

"I have an idea," Zach states.

"What is it?" Zane questions.

"Benjamin's fifth letter to Peter Collinson is dated July 29, 1750—his first travel event. In that letter, Benjamin discusses his theories about lightning being electricity and the experiments that lead him to believe his theories may be true. The fifth letter is what leads Benjamin to the kite experiment to prove lightning is electricity."

"Right," Dad says. "Continue."

"Benjamin told us that Bernard did not like him. He was jealous of Benjamin's success and Benjamin had unintentionally embarrassed him in front of several people during one of Bernard's electrical demonstrations. He also said Bernard always looked for anything that would benefit Bernard, even if it were at somebody else's expense. Benjamin's explanation paints Bernard as a jealous and selfish person. Let's assume for the moment that is true. If he did not like Benjamin and they had other fallouts, would it make sense that Bernard would want to beat Benjamin somehow?"

"It does have merit," Dad agrees.

"But what is he winning?" Zane asks.

"Success, notoriety, and fame. If his success were equal to or better than Benjamin's..." He pauses for a second. "...or worse, he stole Benjamin's success, he would be famous. Oh my God! Could Bernard be attempting to steal Benjamin's letters and take credit for Benjamin's successes in electricity and conducting the kite experiment?"

"A time machine would make it possible," Dad replies.

"And he would surely be recognized for it in the history books," Zane interjects.

"That's an interesting view, Zach. But there is no mention of the kite experiment in Benjamin's *Experiments and Observations* letters," Dad counters.

"Correct. But Bernard was there for the kite experiment, and through our conversations Bernard knows about the fame it brought Benjamin. If he stole Benjamin's letter before it sailed to London and replaced it with his own letter and added the details of the experiment, we might be looking at Benjamin Franklin in a completely different manner."

"Worse," Zane remarks, "we might be looking at Bernard Ranter in a completely different manner. He may be the one on the hundred-dollar bill."

"Or neither of them. It may be John Adams for all we know," Dad interjects. "The theory has merit, especially since the dates he traveled to correlate with Benjamin's letters. You may be on to something."

"We have to find EMITT before history changes because of a crazy lunatic," Zach states adamantly.

Jeremy's cell phone dings.

"It's another email. He's back." Dad opens the tracker on the computer. "It looks like EMITT is located about thirty miles away on the outskirts of town." He prints the map. "Let's go."

On their drive to find EMITT, Jeremy's phone rings. "Hello, Sarah."

"Where are you?"

"The boys and I have tracked EMITT and we are going to steal her back."

"Jeremy, that's crazy. You have no idea who or how many people Bernard is working with. We must consider them dangerous. We need to call the police."

"You know we can't do that. We will handle this on our own. Nobody can know about EMITT. And I'll need the boys' help to steal her back. We'll call you later to let you know our status."

"Jeremy, I do not want the boys involved in stealing EMITT back. We need to figure another way."

"Sarah, there is no other way. We have to steal EMITT back and I need the boys help to do so. We have a plan and we will be careful. Also, check my email periodically. You can track EMITT's travel events. If she travels, call me."

"I don't like this, but I will call you if she travels."

Jeremy presses "END."

They close in on EMITT's tracked location and approach the area carefully.

"The homes here are sparse and spread out," Jeremy states. "It looks like each home has a few acres of land. Keep your eyes open; she could be inside a barn."

They stop the truck as they near the location on the map.

"Do you see anything?" Dad asks.

"I don't," Zane replies.

"Me eith..." Zach stops midsentence. "Wait, look at that house." He points across the road and down a couple of houses. "It appears the tongue of a trailer is sticking out from the other side of that house. That may be EMITT. Do you see it?" he asks.

Both Zane and Dad stare closely.

"I see what you're talking about," Dad says.

"Me too," Zane agrees, "but I can't tell if it's EMITT. Maybe?"

Dad reviews the truck's GPS to see a map of the area's street. "It looks as if this street goes straight through." He gestures at the screen. "We could drive down the street a little fast and see if it's her as we pass by."

"We need to know, so let's do it," Zach agrees.

"Bad idea," Zane comments. "Let's take the truck back the way we came and go down the next street over. I will bet we can see it from there and we will be much more inconspicuous."

"That's a good idea," Dad says.

He turns the truck around. On the next street, they have a clear view.

"Look, there's EMITT!" Dad shouts.

"And there's Bernard and another man. They're entering EMITT," Zach says as he takes a picture with his cell phone.

"Let's stay put for a bit," Dad decides.

They watch for a couple of minutes.

EMITT disappears.

"Holy crap!" Zach shouts. "They're traveling again."

"Oh, this is bad," Dad says. "This has been my worst fear. There's no limit to what they could do. Creating EMITT may have turned out to be a terrible idea. This could be disastrous."

"Dad, EMITT is an awesome invention," Zane says. "This is a situation of bad people using her in the wrong way. Could better security have prevented this? Maybe. But for now, with them gone, this can work in our favor."

"How do you figure?" Dad asks in a raised tone as if Zane were crazy.

"They're gone, aren't they? Now we can drive over there, and when they come back we can surprise them and steal EMITT back."

"You're on a roll today. Great thinking," Dad says proudly.

"We know, when EMITT returns, she will arrive in her same location," Zach comments. "Let's back the truck up to where she was and we may be able to catch them off guard."

"But first, we will need to deal with Bernard and this other guy," Dad reminds them.

They pull the truck around to the house, back it up to EMITT's approximate location, and wait at the back of the truck. Zach takes a couple of quick pictures of the area and Jack's house, in case he needs them later.

"What are you taking pictures of?" Dad asks.

"You can never have too much information. Isn't that what you always say?"

"Yes, it is. I'm glad you listen. All right, here's the plan," Dad says. "When they arrive, as soon as they open the door, I will point the stun gun at them and you two will tie them up with the cable ties. We will take Bernard home and leave his accomplice with him. Then, we will travel back to today and take EMITT home."

Several minutes pass when suddenly EMITT appears out of nowhere, startling Jeremy and the boys. They rush into place, and as EMITT's door opens, Jeremy has the stun gun pointed directly at Jack.

"Get back inside," Jeremy says with force.

Both boys follow their father inside EMITT. Zane shuts the door behind him.

Bernard and Jack are taken off guard and not prepared for their situation. Jeremy points the stun gun at Bernard, switching between the two men. "Both of you, up against the wall."

They both back up to the wall.

"Now, down on your knees."

They both comply.

"Tie them up, boys."

"Hands behind your back, Bernard," Zach tells him as he pulls out a large cable tie they have brought along and binds Bernard's hands behind his back.

"You too, mister. Hands behind your back," Zane dictates.

The man puts his hands behind his back, and as Zane gets close, the man grabs Zane around the neck with one arm and the other produces a gun that he points against Zane's head.

"Back off, you son of a bitches, before I kill this little punk! Drop that stun gun and step back. NOW!" he screams at Jeremy. "NOW!"

Jeremy realizes the deep trouble he has placed him and his two sons in. "All right, take it easy," he says, complying with the man's demand. He lays the stun gun on the floor and pushes it toward the man. He protects Zach by pulling him backwards and steps in front of him. "Mister, we weren't going to hurt anyone. We only want EMITT back and to take Bernard back to 1752, where he belongs. We don't care about anything else."

"Yeah, well, shut the hell up," Jack shouts. "This time machine you call EMITT is now mine. And everybody does what I say now."

"Boy," Jack gestures to Zach with a head nod, "untie my friend."

"Jack, what are you doing?" Bernard asks. "Where did you get a gun?"

"Don't worry about it, Bernard. I have this under control. Once we drop them off in 1750, you and I can finish our plans."

"Mister," Zach says, "I have to cut it with a knife, which I have in my pocket. I need to pull it out, so don't do anything crazy."

"Fine. Pull it out and cut him loose," the man sternly instructs Zach. "But you do anything stupid and your friend gets it."

"Yes, sir." Zach slowly pulls a knife from his pocket and cuts the cable tie that binds Bernard's hands.

"Close the knife and slide it to me across the floor," Jack demands.

"What's your name, boy?" Again he gestures with a nod.

"It's Zach, sir. That is my brother, Zane, and this is my father, Jeremy."

"All right, Zane, you and I, we're going to stand up slowly. Try any funny business and it will be lights out for you. Understand?"

"Yes, sir," Zane replies, trembling, eyes welling up with tears.

They both stand together, the gun still firmly against Zane's temple. Jack pushes Zane off him and toward his father.

"Bernard, tie them up," Jack demands. "If one of you blink wrong, I will put a bullet right through your daddy's eyes. So, nice and slow. Down on your knees and put your hands behind your back, so Bernard can cinch you up nice and tight."

Bernard binds their hands behind their backs, then cinches their feet together.

"That should keep you still for a while," Jack says of Bernard's binding of the three.

"Bernard," Jack says as he continues to point the gun at the three of them, "let's take them back to 1750 and drop them off. I would like to win our lottery. Dial us up a time—would you, my friend?"

"Dialing it up now," Bernard says. But now that Jack has produced a gun, he is concerned that he may be in some trouble as well. He knows that Jack will not hurt him, because he knows EMITT's passwords, but to be cautious he decides to send them back to June 10, 1752, at 2:10 p.m., minutes after they originally returned him and Benjamin. He understands they are nowhere near the same location of Benjamin's kite-flying experiment, but at least Jeremy and the boys could make their way to Benjamin and have an ally.

"Here we go," Bernard says. He presses enter. They hear the low vibration noise, then two pops.

THIRTY-EIGHT

SATURDAY, JUNE 10, 1752

JACK RAISES HIS voice with a condescending demeanor. "Thank you for traveling on EMITT Time Travel Adventures. Now get the hell off my machine. If you try to come close to EMITT before we leave, I will put a hole in one of you."

"Bernard, cut the cable tie from their feet first," Jack orders while handing him Zach's knife.

Bernard follows his instructions.

"Zane, you stand first. When Bernard cuts your hands free, you keep walking straight ahead. Do you understand, boy?"

"Do what he says, Zane," Dad tells him.

"Yes, sir. No funny business. I will leave," Zane says.

Bernard cuts his hands free. Zane steps out the door and continues to walk away.

"Zach, you're next. Bernard, cut him loose. But Zach, I want you to walk about twenty feet out, stop, and turn around. If you don't, I'll kill your father. Do you understand?"

"Yes, sir." His voice quivers.

"Do what he tells you," Dad says.

Bernard cuts him loose as well.

Zach walks out, stops as instructed, and turns around.

"All right, Jeremy. On your feet," Jack demands as he steps out onto the porch and steps to the far end. "Any funny stuff and I will kill Zach." He takes dead aim at Zach's head. "Cut him loose, Bernard."

Bernard cuts the cable tie.

"You can go now," Jack says.

Jeremy catches up with Zach, grabs him by the arm, and says, "Just keep walking. We need to be as far away as possible. Let them go."

Zach turns around to look back at EMITT and sees Jack standing in the doorway, waving his gun as if pushing them away. He hollers at Bernard, "Let's get back home. I'm ready to win the lottery." A moment later, there is a quick flash and they are gone.

"Boys, your mother is not going to be happy with me. I only hope she has an opportunity to let me have it." He gives a quick chuckle. "Probably the first time I have ever wanted to be yelled at. I guess my plan didn't work out the way I expected. We have nobody we can even turn to. Since we're in 1750, Benjamin won't even know who we are, because he didn't meet us until 1752."

"That's not correct," Zach replies.

"What do you mean?" Dad asks.

We're in 1752, not 1750 like Jack said. I saw Bernard enter June 10, 1752, at 2:10 p.m. on the computer. That's right after we took them back. So, Benjamin and William will know us."

"If he entered that date, then Bernard realizes he too is in trouble. I'll bet this guy, Jack, plans on doing the same with Bernard and keeps EMITT for himself," Zane says.

"You're probably right," Dad replies. "But not until he steals EMITT's passwords from Bernard. That is the only reason to keep Bernard around, at least for now."

"We need a plan," Zach says.

"I agree," Zane says.

Suddenly, Zach takes off running back to the spot where EMITT sat a few minutes earlier.

"Where's he going?" Dad asks.

"C'mon," Zach waves as he races away. He stops in the vicinity where EMITT sat a few moments earlier.

Dad and Zane catch up to him. "What was that about?" Zane asks.

"I want to mark off the area where EMITT sat. If they return, I don't want the trailer landing on top of one of us. And if they do return, hopefully we will be on the back side and can stow away on her without being seen. I was afraid her impression in the grass would go away and I wouldn't remember her exact location."

"Ah. That's smart thinking," Dad replies.

The three of them mark off the area with some sticks. Afterwards, they sit on the ground and formulate a plan.

"Most importantly, somebody must stay at this location at all times," Dad says.

"I'll stay here," Zach blurts out. "After all, I am the one that created this mess."

"All right, but if Jack and Bernard return, you need to be ready," Dad says. "The only reason Bernard would return is if Jack were stealing EMITT for himself, and at that, I'm not sure he would even come back to this time, but we need to be prepared. You will need to jump onto the tongue of the trailer and travel to the next TTE. Then, you can steal EMITT and come back to pick us up."

"Zane and I will go into town to find Benjamin and solicit his help. We will have a day or two's walk to town. So, if you do steal EMITT, remember to take that into account for your return or you may be sitting here for a couple of days."

"I will."

"And don't leave EMITT alone."

"I won't."

Zane and Dad start for town.

THIRTY-NINE

WEDNESDAY, JUNE 26, 2019

BERNARD AND JACK return to Jack's at 10:45 a.m.

"Bernard, before we travel again, I want to get EMITT inside the barn. I do not want anyone to see EMITT disappear. With her in the barn, we can close the doors and travel as often as we would like, without any suspicion."

"Good idea."

After a little tussling with the trailer and Jeremy's truck, they have EMITT inside the barn. Jack closes the barn doors. "Now we can travel at our own free will," Jack states.

With EMITT opened back up and the stabilizer jacks back in place, Jack says adamantly as he rubs his hands together, "Bernard, let's find us a date to win our lottery. Does EMITT have internet access?"

"I have no idea."

"Forget it. We'll use my computer inside the house. I know I have internet and I need to use the restroom."

Moments later, both men sit in front of Jack's living room computer. After a few searches, Jack blurts out, "Oh, I remember this one. I left for

New York the Saturday before the drawing. I remember, because I was at the airport and on one of the TVs they were talking about the lottery's huge jackpot. I bought several tickets there at the airport. Of course, I didn't win. But the following Wednesday, three people won and shared a $1.4 billion jackpot. If we travel to the Saturday prior to the winning drawing, we can win it. It will only be worth $900 million, but that should sustain us for our first lottery jackpot, don't you think?"

"To be honest, I have no idea how much money that is."

"Don't worry, Bernard, even with only half of the lottery winnings, you could not spend it all in your lifetime." Jack writes down the date and the winning numbers. "C'mon, let's go. We can search other dates later."

Both men dart back out to EMITT.

"Bernard, dial up our lottery date. It's time for us to become millionaires."

"What is the date?"

"Take us to 8 p.m., January 9, 2019. That will give us time to buy the lottery ticket and return to the house to watch the drawing on the internet. And since I will be out of town, I won't..."

"Wait, what?" Bernard interrupts. "What do you mean you will be out of town?"

"I guess I need to clarify. In January, I traveled to New York. I guess I should refer to myself in January as January Jack. Since January Jack will be in New York, we don't have to worry about running into him, like you did with Drunk Bernard."

"Ah, that makes sense. I will admit, seeing myself two years in the past was awkward."

"After we watch the drawing, and we know we have won, we will travel back to June 29 to claim the prize. We don't want any issues with January Jack. If he found such a large amount of money in his bank account, he would freak out."

"Good point," Bernard replies.

"And since we have an entire year to claim the winnings, we will be good."

Bernard enters their date. "Ready?"

"Hell yeah. Let's go."

Bernard presses enter. Again, they hear the low vibrating noise and two pops.

"8 p.m., January 9. We have arrived."

"Great. It's time to win us a lottery. There's a convenience store a few blocks away."

They burst out the door. "Holy crap, it's freaking cold outside. It didn't even occur to me. I know it's January, but with the excitement, I didn't even consider the cold," Jack remarks. "Oh crap. We have another problem. Because January Jack took the truck to the airport, we have to walk to the store."

"Walk. You must be joking? It's freezing outside." Then Bernard remembers his coat and steps back inside the trailer and grabs it from the front room, where he had thrown it on one of the chairs after heisting EMITT. "This should help keep me somewhat warm, but if you have something else it may help to keep me warmer."

"I have several coats inside. With January Jack gone, he won't miss them."

They step outside the barn and run to the house, trouncing through six inches of snow on the ground.

"Good Lord. It must be twenty degrees out here—maybe even in the teens with the wind chill," Jack says while trying to shake off the cold.

A few minutes later, they both exit the house dressed in warmer clothes and start their walk to the store.

"We should have come during the day," Bernard snarls. "It is dark and cold, and the wind is not helping. How far is that store?"

"It's only a few blocks away. It's not too far."

After forty-five minutes in the freezing, blowing wind, they arrive at Jack's with their lottery ticket.

"Pull up a chair while I load the website."

Bernard finds a chair and sits in front of the computer with Jack. The two men sit and wait for ten o'clock. Soon the video feed launches.

A pretty brunette in a short blue dress starts her upbeat spiel. "Welcome to Powerball. This week's Powerball drawing has reached an unprecedented high of $900 million. Let's get started and good luck."

The lottery balls bounce around in two separate chambers. The machine sucks one of the white balls up into the chamber. "The first number…thirty-two." Another ball lunges into the chamber. "The second number…sixteen." Another ball. "And the third number…nineteen."

Both men scooch to the edge of their seat. Though they know they will win, the intensity of the drama unfolding has them excited. "The fourth number…fifty-four. And the fifth number is…thirty-four."

"My God, Bernard, this is it! We're fixing to be rich." The chamber for the red Powerball opens; a ball is sucked in. Both men lean forward for a closer view of the screen and try to read the number on the ball as it rolls down the chute.

The lady says, "And the Powerball number…thirteen. Good luck to everyone."

"Were rich!" Jack jumps up, screaming at the top of his lungs. "Holy crap, Bernard, it worked! It freaking worked! We're rich—richer than rich!"

Both men jump around, screaming, hollering, and laughing.

"You are the man, Bernard. You are the man. It was worth the wait. This is incredible."

Bernard, jumping up and down and beaming, asks, "Jack, how do we get the money?"

"We present our winning ticket to the Lottery Commission and they will tell us when we should receive it. It may take a few days, but it will be ours very soon."

Bernard's excitement suddenly stops. A somber look slides onto his face.

Jack notices the change in demeanor. "What's wrong, buddy? We just won $900 million. What could possibly be wrong?"

"It just occurred to me. After all my efforts to steal the letters, I have no idea if it worked. I have no idea if I, Bernard Ranter, has become the man synonymous with Benjamin's electrical experiments and the famous kite experiment. You got yours, but I may still be plain ole Bernard. Jack, can you check the internet to see if it is him, or me, that is known for the kite experiment?"

Jack settles down from the excitement. "That's a good question. I guess, after our hard work and your efforts to chase down the letter, we should at least confirm it worked."

Jack searches for "Famous Kite Experiment," and consistent results appear: "Ranter's Kite Experiment—US history.org," "Bernard Ranter's Daring Kite Experiment in Lightning Storm," and "Why did Bernard Ranter fly a kite in a Lightning Storm?"

"Fantastic," Bernard says. "Do another search, this time for 'Bernard Ranter.'"

Jack performs the search. The results come up: "Bernard Ranter—Father of Electricity" and "Bernard Ranter—Daring Kite Experiment in Lightning Storm, Proves Lightning is Electricity." Many more appear on the page as well. Although he has not yet read what they have written about him, the results are enough to satisfy Bernard of his efforts to steal Benjamin's letters.

"Bernard, you are now known as the 'Father of Electricity.' That's a pretty high honor."

The designation makes Bernard happier than winning the lottery. "Now, I can celebrate." He stands up straight, with a distinguished pose, his right foot propped on top of Jack's coffee table while his right hand grabs at the breast fold of his imaginary vest. He says in a deep, sophisticated voice, as he looks upward, "Bernard Ranter—The Father of Electricity." He and Jack again jump around the room to celebrate their successes.

After an extended period of celebration, Jack says, "Bernard, we need to travel back to June 27th and claim our winnings."

"I agree."

FORTY

WEDNESDAY, JUNE 26, 2019

BACK INSIDE EMITT, Jack says, "Bernard, dial up our date, my friend. Let's go claim us a lottery."

Bernard enters their date: June 26, 2019, 9:45 a.m. "Ready?"

"Hell yeah. Let's go."

Upon arrival, they leave for the Pennsylvania Lottery Headquarters in Middleton, about an hour and a half away to present their winning ticket. They enter the reception lobby and check in with the receptionist behind the glass window. Jack's excitement has him a bit jittery, knowing his part of the deal is about to come true.

They sit in the reception area and wait for the lottery officials. Bernard leans toward Jack and whispers, "You said it would be more money than I could spend in my lifetime. If that is so, what do I do with all of this money? How will I carry such a large amount of cash? It's too much to bury in the ground and I do not have a bank to use, so what do I do with it?"

"That's not a problem. We have plenty of banks. We will go to my bank and open you an account. The Lottery Commission will wire the money directly to your account. Then, you can spend as much money as you want. Even buy yourself a house and a car."

They sit for a moment longer.

Jack leans toward Bernard and whispers, "Do you have a Social Security number?"

"What is a Social Security number?"

"Oh, you're screwed." Jack smirks. "In today's time, you're required to have a Social Security number. Without it, nobody will work with you, whether it's with a bank, the lottery, or anybody else. And filing for a Social Security number will take a little time. Let's do this: I will claim the ticket and have it wired to my account. Then, we can travel back to the '80s to file for a Social Security number. Once you receive it, we will return and you can open a bank account. Then we can win more lotteries to fill your bank account."

"I don't like this idea. You win all the money and I get nothing."

"Look, Bernard, we're here and they know we have the winning ticket. We cannot leave now. We have no choice but to claim the winnings now. When we arrive home, we will work on setting you up in our era. You are the only one that knows EMITT's passwords to make her work, so you still control how things are done."

"All right, you claim the money, but at least give me some money for now."

"Deal," Jack agrees. "Then, we set you up."

The door in front of them opens. A slightly overweight woman in her mid-sixties and a slender middle-aged man step into the lobby, both with smiles on their faces. "Hello. My name is Maggie Reynolds. I am the Pennsylvania Lottery commissioner. This is James McKenzie, director of Lottery Financial Management. We understand you have the winning Powerball ticket from January 9th?" she asks enthusiastically.

"I do," Jack says as he stands up with a smile from ear to ear. "I'm Jack Carlson and this is my friend Bernard. I have the winning ticket and you can imagine my excitement."

"Fantastic. Please come in. It is a pleasure to meet the both of you. Please, follow us to the conference room, where our Lottery team will confirm the ticket. Once we have verified the ticket, we will present you with your ceremonial check and set up payment for the winnings."

"Awesome!" Jack says and follows the officials down a hallway to a conference room.

"Now, did both of you win?" Maggie asks.

"No, ma'am. Just me. Bernard is along for support."

"Well then, Mr. Carlson you are a lucky man. Can we see the ticket?"

"Yes, ma'am." Jack pulls the ticket from his pocket and shows it to Maggie without letting it leave his hands.

"Have you signed the back of the ticket yet?" Mr. McKenzie asks as several others from the lottery commission enter the room to witness the largest-ever Powerball winnings awarded.

"I have not. With all the excitement, the thought didn't even cross my mind."

"If you will sign the back, we will run the verification," he says, handing Jack a pen.

Jack signs the ticket and hands it to Mr. McKenzie.

"I see you have selected the "Cash Payout" option."

"Oh, yes I did. I wanted the cash up front instead of over many years."

"I understand." He pulls out his calculator and pushes a few buttons. "The 'Cash Payout' option will work out to be around $540 million." The director inserts the ticket inside the machine, and the computer screen displays the words "Winning Ticket Verified."

"Jack Carlson, congratulations. The ticket has been verified and you are the sole winner of the January 9th historic Powerball Lottery. Again, congratulations, and we would like to present this ceremonial check to you as the winner of the largest-ever Powerball drawing." He hands the large ceremonial check to Jack. A lottery employee takes several pictures to capture the moment.

"Wow, this is amazing. Thank you very much. When will I receive the real check?" he asks.

"The money will be wired to your bank account and it should be available in a few weeks, possibly up to six weeks, but I doubt it will take that long," Mr. McKenzie indicates. "But first, we will need to gather some information from you to move your payment through the system."

"Absolutely!" Jack complies.

Once the paperwork is complete, Maggie asks, "Mr. Carlson, it took you over five months to claim your prize. What happened that you did not come forward sooner?"

"I had lost the ticket but found it under my couch yesterday. I didn't even know if the ticket was any good or not. Shoot, I didn't even know it was for this drawing. But you can imagine my surprise when I checked the numbers on the website. I about freaked out. Could not believe my eyes. I had to check it several times. To say the least, my excitement went through the roof when I realized it was a winner." Knowing his entire conversation is a complete lie, he smiles for a picture.

After the ceremonial hoopla and the paperwork complete, Jack and Bernard leave for home a little richer and very excited.

"Jack, that was pretty exciting to watch, but now I want to win. How do I sign up for this Social Security number you talked about?"

"Once were home, I'll look on the internet and figure out how to apply. It shouldn't be too difficult, but it's been a long time since I had to apply. I'm not sure of the exact procedures, but I'll figure it out. Once I understand what to do, you can file for the number. Then, you can set up a bank account and fill it full of cash with a lottery win. You will be a rich man, Bernard. You will be a rich, rich man."

"Great. Let's take care of that right away."

After some research on the internet, Jack says, "Bernard, I understand the procedures, but we need to travel back to the '80s when the process is easier for you to get your Social Security card. Today, you will have to prove your age, identity, and your US citizenship, and you can't do that. So, we need to travel again."

"Great. Let's go," Bernard says and turns toward EMITT.

Upon entering, Jack asks, "Bernard, show me how EMITT works."

"I can't do that, Jack. That must remain my secret. Otherwise you could steal EMITT and I would be lost."

"No, I understand. You're right. I only wanted to see how it works. Can you show me without showing me the password? I'm curious what the screen looks like, and I would love to see the tube in action when we travel."

"I guess there would be no harm in letting you see it." As they stand in front of the computer screen, Bernard points to each as he explains, "This is the 'Previous Travel from Date & Time,' which is the last time we traveled. This is the 'Current Date & Time,' which is the current time and date of our present location in time. This one is obvious: 'Next Travel Date & Time.' I enter the time and date I wish to travel to, enter the password here, and press the enter button and it starts."

"That is way too cool," Jack remarks. "What is this? 'Automatic Return Date & Time'?"

"The computer automatically sets that one to keep someone from stealing EMITT. If you don't enter the correct password after you have traveled, the computer automatically sends EMITT back to the current date and time in your era."

"Ah, ole Jeremy trying to be slick when he programmed the computer. How did you steal the passwords?"

"I overheard Jeremy explaining to the boys the changes he had made to EMITT. He told them the passwords and I memorized them immediately. If you will sit down, we will be off."

"I'm ready. But I want to watch the tube when it starts. If you don't mind, I will turn around while you enter the password. You tell me when it's safe to turn around."

"All right, Jack, but you stand over there." He points to the wall. "I want you to be far enough away that you cannot read the screen."

"Fine. Will this be sufficient for you?" He stands with his face against the wall. "I will stand with my back turned and arms crossed. You can watch my every move."

"I can live with that, but no looking."

Jack complies.

"How far back do we need to go?"

"Several years." Jack says as he pulls his phone out. He presses a couple of buttons and says, "Try June 1, 1988."

Bernard enters their date, time, and the password and presses enter.

"You can turn around."

The lady's voice in the computer again says her familiar phrase: "Password accepted. Time travel sequence initiated." The colors in the tube start to spin.

Jack turns around, and for the first time he sees an unobstructed view of the tube and its spinning colors. "Amazing! Ole Jeremy created one fine machine."

They hear the low, vibrating, humming noise and again, the two pops.

"Welcome to June 1st, 1988. Jack, you need to turn around again. I need to enter the password for the automatic return date and time."

Again, Jack complies.

Bernard enters the password and presses enter. "You can turn around now."

"In 1988, this area had not yet been developed. I will bet you'll find nothing but grass outside."

Bernard opens the door and finds a grass field where Jack's house would be built in the coming years. "You are correct. Give me a minute before we head in to town. I need to pee," Bernard says and steps outside to relieve himself.

"No problem. I will be right here."

Jack uncrosses his arms, revealing his cell phone. He clicks on the screen and views it for a moment. He pinches at the screen to zoom in for a closer view.

Bernard returns and opens the door. "Hey, Jack, we don't have a..." He stops midsentence when he sees Jack has a gun pointed at his head. "What the hell, Jack? Put that gun down. Let's go."

"End of the road for you, buddy."

"What are you talking about?" Bernard asks, now a little nervous, because Jack has not lowered the gun.

"I'm stealing EMITT from you. Enter a date and time that you want to live out the rest of your life, because 1988 is a little too close for my comfort. Once you're out of the picture, EMITT will be mine."

"Jack, I don't know how you're going to operate EMITT, because I definitely will not give you the passwords. You will need to kill me first, and then you will be stuck in 1988 with no access to your money. C'mon, let's find the Social Security office."

"I have both passwords. 'Touch The Key' and 'Time For Benjamin.' Rather ironic for EMITT, aren't they?"

"How, Jack? How did you steal them?" Bernard shouts, realizing he has been betrayed. "I knew I could not trust you."

"Bernard, you forget, in 2019 we live in a technological world. These cell phones have video cameras. I held the phone under my arm when they were crossed and videoed you typing the passwords. While you were outside, I reviewed the video and it clearly shows the passwords."

"You double-crosser."

"You catch on quick. Dial up your date and let's go," Jack says as he gestures to the computer with the gun. "I will be the richest, most powerful man in the world, but I have a lot of work to do. So, start typing. I need to get started."

"How do you plan on being the richest man in the world, Jack?"

Bernard asks.

"The stock market, my friend, the stock market. Which is something you know nothing about."

FORTY-ONE

SUNDAY, JUNE 10, 1752

BERNARD REALIZES HIS only hope to stop Jack is to travel back to the date they dropped off Jeremy and the two boys, but a couple of hours later. He enters the date—June 10, 1752, at 4:10 p.m.—and within a flash they have arrived.

"Now get out before I put a bullet in you."

"No need to be hostile, Jack. I will leave," Bernard says, cracking the door open before he takes a quick stare at Jack. "You won't get away with this."

"My gun says I will. Go on, it's time for you to leave," he says again, gesturing with the gun.

As Bernard turns to step outside, he sees Zach running for EMITT and it startles him, but he stays calm, realizing Zach probably has a plan. He stalls for a couple of seconds to give Zach a little time. "Jack, have you thought this through? I can help you with more lottery winnings. We could make a good team together."

"Get out," Jack shouts. "I'm serious, Bernard. Get the hell off this machine before I shoot you and drag you off myself."

"All right, I will leave. I had to ask one more time." He steps outside.

Jack peers out the door to verify nobody is around. "Keep walking, Bernard," he shouts from the doorway.

Shaking, Zach stands behind EMITT, waiting for Jack to close the door.

"Go on. Keep walking, Bernard. You need to be a good distance away before I leave," Zach hears Jack shout.

Moments later, Zach hears the door close and believes Jack must be entering the date for his next travel. He sits on the tongue of the trailer and closes his eyes. Even though his feet dangle in the air, he believes he will be safe, since that's how Benjamin and Bernard traveled the first time.

The low, vibrating, humming noise starts. Zach becomes startled when he realizes it has been the generator making the noise. Then, the two pops.

FORTY-TWO

WEDNESDAY, JUNE 26, 2019

ZACH OPENS HIS eyes to his new surroundings. *Where am I?* he thinks. *I expected to see Dad's truck and Jack's house.* He scans the room. *We must be in Jack's barn.* He hides behind EMITT again, hoping Jack will not discover him.

Zach hears the door open. Jack grumbles under his breath, but not loud enough for Zach to understand. A few steps occur on the porch's wood planks, then his feet land on the dirt and he walks away. He hears a door open at the other end of the barn, then it slams closed, as if it were on a spring. He stands still for a moment to ensure Jack has left.

Through the frosted-covered panels over each end of the barn, the natural light is muffled, but it allows Zach plenty to see with. He bends over and peeks under the trailer to confirm Jack's exit. *Good, he's gone. But for how long?* he wonders.

Unsure of his surroundings, he steps out from behind the trailer and notices another door on the back end of the barn, which he makes his way toward. He opens the door and slips out, closing it so not to make any noise. He sees a few sparse houses in the area and assumes he's at Jack's house.

Jack must have pulled EMITT inside the barn, allowing him to travel unseen.

He peeks around a corner. "Definitely Jack's house." He sees his father's truck out front, but he cannot run to it without Jack easily spotting him.

He reaches into his pocket, pulls out his cell phone, and dials. The other end answers. "Mom," he whispers, "we're in deep trouble and we need your help."

"Where are you?" she asks.

"Listen, I may not be able to talk long so I can explain later, but everybody's okay. I'm at Jack's and he's a bad dude."

"Who is Jack?"

"He's the guy that helped Bernard. I'm trapped behind his barn, but he doesn't know I'm here. He believes Dad, Zane, and I are trapped in 1752. I need your help. We tracked EMITT to Jack's address. You can find it on Dad's computer. Text me when you're close and I will call you if I can. Then, we can figure out how to get me out of here."

"All right, I will leave right now."

"I'll be waiting," Zach says and hangs up. He flips the side switch to turn his phone on silent.

Fifteen minutes pass.

Zach calls her back, believing he has a little time to explain their events, including Jack holding them at gunpoint, Jack's plan to steal a lottery, and leaving them in 1752.

This does not sit well with his mother, but she holds her tongue.

Jack exits the house and bolts for the barn. Zach tenses up and whispers, "Mom, Jack's coming. I'll call you back." He presses the end button.

If he catches me, I'm dead, he thinks.

FORTY-THREE

WEDNESDAY, JUNE 26, 2019

ZACH FINDS A hole in the barn's wall and peeks through to spy on Jack's whereabouts. He faintly hears the barn door open at the opposite end, then it slams shut. Jack steps inside EMITT, and in an instant she disappears. "No, this cannot be good. What's he up to now?"

Zach calls his mother again. "Are you close?"

"Yes. I'll be there soon."

"Hurry. Jack traveled off with EMITT to who knows where. We can discuss my plan when you arrive. By the way, what is the date?" Zach asks, running toward his dad's truck.

"June 26, 2019."

"Oh good. I'm back in the present."

"I will be there in a few minutes. If he comes back, let me know."

"I will," Zach says, then hangs up.

He spots his mom and gives a vigorous wave. She parks across the street.

"Come on," he dictates as he waves his hand for her to follow. "We need to be at the back of the barn before Jack returns."

Wearing light yellow capris, a bright orange, yellow, and green flowered top with and a pair of yellow flats, she grabs her white purse and shouts, "Zach, I know my timing is terrible, but I have to use the restroom, like right now. I ran out of the house as soon as you called and now Mother Nature has dialed my number."

"Uh…uh…," Zach stutters, searching for an idea, "Jack's gone. Maybe you can use his bathroom."

They approach the front door but it's locked. They try the back door. Luckily, Jack left it unlocked. Zach cracks open the door and whistles to see if a dog appears. He hears no barking. They enter the house, checking the surroundings. They find a Calico cat, but it's no bother.

"I will keep an eye out from behind the barn," Zach says. "Meet me there. If he returns, I will call you, but you should be okay for a few minutes at least."

"I will hurry."

Mom rushes through the house in search of a restroom. She accidentally bumps the computer desk in the living room as she passes. She finds the restroom and does her business. As she departs, she cannot help herself from scrutinizing the surroundings of the home.

She mumbles to herself, "A maid wouldn't hurt, that's for sure." She notices clothes strewn about the floor in one of the bedrooms. The living room is in disarray as well; newspapers lay across the sofa, and a wooden coffee table is cluttered with an array of dirty dishes. She trips but catches herself and realizes her shoe caught a hole in the carpet.

She notices the computer and that his bank account login page is displayed on the screen. She remembers Zach mentioning the lottery.

Mom sits down at the computer but knows nothing about Jack. The username is already entered. She tries his address for the password. "Invalid Password." She tries his name backwards. Again, "Invalid Password." She scans the room and notices a picture frame on the wall. It's a scene of a man with a woman holding a Siamese cat with the following caption inscribed below: "Denise, James and Breeze, my family, my lost world." She pulls the picture frame from the wall and flips it over. There is another inscription: "Mom, Dad and Breeze—1983." She enters each of their names. They do not work. She tries the three names together; still nothing. She tries each of them backwards; again it does not work. She tries a couple of more times, but she is not having any luck.

"I need to leave before he returns," she mumbles, but then tries one other idea. The hourglass spins on the computer display. The program opens and his bank account information displays on the screen. "Oh my gosh. It worked." But to her surprise, the account shows only a few hundred dollars, not the millions she expected. She writes down the pertinent login information, logs out, and stashes the piece of paper in her purse.

She peeks out the back door. "Good, nobody around." She sprints to the back side of the barn, where she finds Zach.

"Good Lord, where have you been? You were making me nervous," Zach screeches.

"Sorry," Mom says. "Sometimes things don't work out like you expect. What can I say."

"I have a plan. We..."

"Stop," Mom interrupts. "You, your brother, and your father had a plan, and that did not work so well. We'll do it my way. Step inside the barn."

Inside, Mom says, "You locate some rope."

"What for?"

"Do as I say. I will explain in a minute."

Zach searches the barn. "Can you believe it. This entire barn and not a single piece of rope. I did find a spool of electrical wire." He approaches his mother to discuss her plan further when EMITT appears out of nowhere. Zack is startled and freezes directly in front of the door, where

Jack should emerge. Mom steps to the side, just out of sight.

The door opens. Jack is startled to see Zach standing before him with a spool of wire in his hands.

"Well, well. What do you plan on doing with the wire there, chump?" Jack says as he casually reaches for his gun, stuck in the back of his pants.

With her stun gun ready, Mom steps out and pulls the trigger saying, "To tie you up with, chump." One electrode digs in just above his heart while the other buries itself deep into his lower stomach.

Jack collapses to the floor in violent convulsions, screaming in pain as his body absorbs fifty thousand volts of electricity. While writhing on the ground, his muscles rapidly contract and release. Every five seconds he receives another jolt of high voltage.

While he convulses on EMITT's floor, Mom says, "Zach, tie him up. You can touch him, but don't touch the electrodes. If you do, you will flop around like him."

Zach grabs Jack's gun and slides it across the floor into the other room. He grabs the wire and binds Jack's hands behind his back, but he struggles with the wire's stiffness.

"Zach," Mom says in an excited tone, "use the duct tape on the shelf. It will work better."

Zach grabs the duct tape and secures Jack's hands behind his back.

Mom flips on the gun's safety lock, which stops the voltage. "If you stay still, Jack, you will be okay. If you fight it, I will hit you again."

Jack starts to resist Zach's actions to secure him. She hits him again with another fifty thousand volts. His body again trembles violently with the convulsions. Zach finishes with his hands and continues down to his legs.

"That should do it," Zach says and stands up.

"That's not good enough for me," Mom says. "Hold the stun gun. If he struggles, pull the trigger and hit him again." She snatches a pair of wire cutters from the shelf and drags the roll of wire next to her as she squats down behind Jack. She takes one end of the wire and ties it to his feet. She does a quick measurement and cuts the wire to length. With his legs bent at the knees, she wraps the other end around his neck and ties a knot. "Now, Zach, that is how you hogtie a man. He will not move. If he does, he will choke himself," she explains as she picks up Jack's gun.

"Whoa, Mom, what a badass," Zach howls. "Note to self: Don't piss off Mom."

"Jack," Sarah says as she kneels down while tearing off a four-inch strip of tape, her eyes to his, "you need to open both ears and close your mouth and listen real close. I'll even help you close your mouth." She presses the strip of duct tape over his lips. "You have met your worst nightmare. A mother with her family in despair is not someone you want to tangle with. You will do as I say and lay there and be quiet, while we fix yours and Bernard's shenanigans. Do you understand?"

Jack, his eyes wide open with fear, nods his head a tiny bit in acknowledgement. Sweat rolls down his face, and his body still twitches from the effects of the stun gun.

Sarah removes the cartridge from the gun, winds up the electrode wires, and rips the probes from Jack's chest and stomach. Jack screams under the tape. She tosses the used cartridge into a trashcan below the computer desk. She reloads another cartridge.

"Let's go find your brother and your father," she says in a tone that indicates she is in complete control and confident of her actions. "But first, I need to grab my purse." A moment later she returns. "I'm ready."

Zach closes the door and dials up their date, when Mom says, "Wait. Enter the date July 24, 1600. That should be a good era for Jack to live out his life."

"Mom, we can't leave him there."

"The way I see it, we can't kill him, we can't call the police, and he cannot stay in our era. So, he has bought a trip to the 1600s. If he remains in 2019, we will look over our shoulder for the rest of our lives. And my family will not live in fear like that."

Jack starts to scream underneath the tape.

"Oh, shut up, Jack," she scolds him.

"July 24, 1600, here we come," Zach says and dials up his mother's requested date. He sets their arrival for noon.

FORTY-FOUR

MONDAY, JULY 24, 1600

ZACH OPENS THE door. The field of tall brown grass is comparable to the scene in 1752, except this time the grass is droopy and wet from a recent rain. Multiple shades of gray clouds continue to share a light drizzle of moisture.

"Zach, grab him under the arms. I will carry his feet and we can lay him down outside."

"Mom, we can't leave him in the rain."

"We can and we will. Trust me, he won't melt. He stole from us, he helped Bernard change history, and he kidnapped my family at gunpoint. In my opinion and the law's, that is a punishable offense. He made his bed and now we will put him in it."

"Yes, ma'am," he says, not willing to argue.

Jack squirms and yells under the tape across his mouth as they struggle to carry him through the tall grass. "There is a tree we can leave him under." Mom nods toward it.

They lay him in the wet grass.

"Mom, we can't leave him here like this."

"Oh, I won't leave him like this. He will have the opportunity to free himself, but he'll have to work for it." She undoes the hog tie from around his neck and ties it to his hands.

"Zach, program EMITT for our next travel date and let me know when you're ready."

"Yes ma'am." His slow stride carries him toward EMITT, but after a few steps he stops and turns around. "You know, Jack, Mom's right. You deserve this place. You don't care about anybody. You only care about yourself. I hope you enjoy the 1600s. You may learn to appreciate things, because you won't have much, at least not like in our era." He turns and marches inside EMITT. He programs their new travel date to June 12, 1752, 12:00 p.m. "We're ready," he hollers to his mother, who is still standing over Jack.

Sarah kneels to Jack one last time. She takes his wallet and cell phone. "You won't be needing these anymore, but if you do, they will be sitting on your computer desk in your living room. Right on top of the picture of your mother, father, and cat." Jack's eyes open wide. "You know, your cat, Breeze3."

Rage permeates his eyes as he yells underneath the tape, his face turning red. His body starts to thrash around as he tries to free himself.

Sarah stands up. "I know you and Bernard were attempting to steal a lottery win. Jeremy has EMITT tracked and we know of every travel event you made. Earlier, I hacked your bank account, but it only had a couple hundred dollars. I know the lottery money will hit your account in the next few days. When it does you will be making large charitable donations to many deserving organizations. For once, you will do something good for this world." She flashes a devious smile. "And Jack, that's 'your worst nightmare' I talked about." She turns and struts back to EMITT.

Jack squirms and screams underneath the tape on his mouth while she walks away.

Upon reaching the porch, she turns around and looks at Jack, her hand dangling Zach's knife. She tosses it high over the top of EMITT. "If you can find it, you can set yourself free." She steps inside EMITT and looks out the window to watch him squirm toward the knife. "Let's go."

Zach presses enter and EMITT vanishes.

FORTY-FIVE

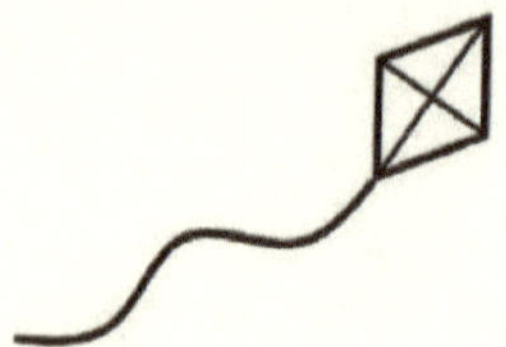

MONDAY, JUNE 12, 1752

ZACH AND MOM step outside.

"They're not here," Mom says. "Are you sure we are at the correct date?"

"They should be back soon. I figure Dad and Zane had about a day's walk to Philadelphia. Then, they had to find Benjamin. Then another day back. That's two days. I took that into account and we've arrived at noon. I would imagine they will arrive in a few hours."

While they wait, Zach explains more in-depth details of the previous events. This conversation goes on for a couple of hours.

Zach looks at his mother. "Did you hear that?" He stands up and looks around, but sees nothing.

"I didn't hear anything," Mom replies.

"Listen."

This time they both hear the noise as if someone is shouting in the distance. Then, the heads of three men in a horse and buggy appear at the top of the ridge.

"They made it!" Zach shouts as he points.

He hollers back, "Zane, Dad!"

"I see them. Is that Benjamin with them?"

"I believe it is."

The three men pull up in their horse and buggy.

"Hello, Mrs. Sarah Long. Welcome to 1752."

"Hi, Benjamin. Never thought I would see you here in your era."

Jeremy jumps off the buggy and embraces Sarah. "Am I glad to see you."

She hugs Jeremy and gives him a quick kiss. "These are the consequences I talked about during your development. We were not prepared for any of this. But I'm glad you and Zane are okay." She reaches for Zane and hugs him tight.

"How did you know we were here?" Zach asks Zane.

"When we approached the top of that ridge," Zane says, pointing toward the ridge, "we could see the top of EMITT. And if EMITT were here, I knew you had to have tricked Jack and stole her back. How'd you do it?"

"Like Dad said, if they returned, it was probably because Jack was stealing EMITT from Bernard and that's exactly what happened. And out of nowhere, EMITT appears," Zach explains. "Of course, it scared the you know what out of me, but I happened to be standing in front of the door about fifty yards away. I raced straight toward the generator when the door opened and I saw Bernard. He saw me too, but instead of ratting me out, he stalled for a second, which gave me time to reach the front of EMITT before Jack could see me. His stalling told me that Jack was stealing EMITT. I could hear Jack hollering at Bernard, telling him "to get lost" or he would shoot him. While Bernard walked away, I heard Jack close the door. I sat on EMITT's trailer tongue and *poof*, we were back in 2019. That's when I called Mom."

"Jack didn't expect a thing, did he?"

"Not at all. You didn't happen to pass Bernard on the ride back?"

"No. We never saw him," Zane answers.

"Zane, I wish you could have seen Mom. What a badass. I mean, don't piss her off. She put a hurting on ole Jack. Stunned him in the stomach with the stun gun, then hogtied him. What a sight to watch."

"Where is Jack?" Jeremy asks.

"Let's just say he's resting under a tree," Sarah answers.

Jeremy, Benjamin, and Zane have a confused expression on their face, but before either of them can ask a question Mom continues. "All right, we have a real problem that needs to be corrected. Bernard has changed history. He stole Benjamin's five electricity letters, copied them, and sent them to Peter Collinson. In the fifth letter, he even added details of the kite experiment. The internet now reflects those changes, and Bernard is now known as the Father of Electricity."

"The Father of Electricity?" Zane cries out. "No way. That has to be corrected."

"Yes, it does," Mom expounds. "We have an obligation to correct history and restore Benjamin's name to its rightful place."

"I most certainly agree," Benjamin interjects while shaking his head. "I will not stand for Bernard taking credit for my hard work. Like I have said before, *he wants to be respected, but never helps anyone.*"

"And you shouldn't," Sarah responds.

"What do you propose, Sarah?" Jeremy asks.

"It will be a challenge, but I have a plan. First, we travel to 1750 and capture Bernard, then we leave him with Jack. They belong together. There is one certainty: If they live in ours or Benjamin's era, they will retaliate. With them no longer a threat to any of us, life will go on as it did before any of this time travel stuff ever occurred.

"Second, if we can capture Bernard before he steals Benjamin's fifth letter, we will preserve it as well as the first four letters, because he will no longer be able to travel to those dates to steal them."

"Mom, that's a great idea," Zane exclaims.

"Third, we will return to 2019 to verify history has been restored. If so, we can return Benjamin home, then we will go back to our era and we can return to our normal lives."

"For this to work," Sarah continues, "we need to capture both Bernard and Jack in 1750 and stop them from stealing that letter."

"How do you suppose we capture them?" Jeremy asks.

"That's where Benjamin can help. Benjamin, you know the town and the people. We do not. You know where you delivered your letter when you sent it to Peter Collinson. And, I would bet that's where you will find Bernard and Jack. I assume they will be working together. You need to let them know we have returned to steal EMITT, and being she is their lifeline to the other letters and the future, they will come racing back. When they return, we will capture them and send them to July 24, 1600, with the other Jack. Once there, they cannot travel to the first four letters and those will remain unchanged."

"Sarah, I believe you have missed an important element in your plan," Benjamin counters. "On our ride, I spent a good deal of time reflecting on the time travel scenarios. They are complicated. I believe no matter what has happened or will happen, each of the five letters has already been stolen. Let me explain. If we travel to 1750 and capture Bernard and Jack and send them to 1600, the premise is they can no longer travel to steal the other letters. Correct?"

"Right."

"If that were true, that means we would stop Bernard and Jack in 1750 from stealing that letter, but we would also stop them from stealing the other four letters and their return to 2019. Which means Jeremy and the boys would not be afforded the opportunity to confront them. Therefore, Jack and Bernard would not be able to foil Jeremy and the boys' attempt to steal EMITT from them. And, that means Jeremy and the boys were never dropped off in 1752, where they proceeded to locate me. And Zach could not have stowed away on EMITT when Jack stole her from Bernard. Therefore, you and Zach could not have stolen EMITT from Jack and leave him in 1600, then travel back here to 1752 to find Jeremy, Zach, Zane, and myself, who could not possibly be standing right here, right now, having this discussion. But clearly, we are here. That means, the letters have already been stolen and history has already been changed."

They each stare at Benjamin with stunned looks on their faces while they try to absorb the complexity of the actions that have occurred with the time travel.

Benjamin continues, "To correct history, we must travel to the date of each letter to stop Bernard before his letters can replace mine. If we can succeed at stopping Bernard, then I believe the history of each letter will be reversed, because my letter will continue onto Mr. Collinson as it originally occurred."

"I hope my explanation has made sense?" Benjamin asks.

Jeremy stumbles over his own tongue and tries to find the right words. "Uh, well, um...Benjamin, you have explained a disturbing side of time travel, to which I have not given much thought. As you have stated, we are here, history has been changed, and lives have been affected. Now, I see time travel's greater complexities. It can be a vicious circle that will only disrupt the direction of the past, present, and the future with a high chance of destruction to each. At a minimum, it creates the opportunity to cheat humanity and even the possibility to destroy it. As much as I love EMITT, she must be destroyed."

"But not until we have corrected history and we get back home, right?" Zach asks.

"Yeah," Zane agrees ecstatically.

"Absolutely," Sarah states.

"I too agree," Benjamin concurs. "This will not be easy, but history must be corrected. Before we are through, we may have several Bernards and several Jacks to send to the 1600s."

"We need to work on the plan," Zane determines.

"Maybe we need to think like Bernard," Zach ponders. "We know he steals the letters, but what would be the easiest way for him to do that?"

Mom speaks up. "The most likely place to mail a letter would be the post office. Maybe he finds a job there."

"Penn's Landing," Benjamin spouts.

"What's that?" Zach asks.

"The ship docks. That is where I delivered my letters. And any item that crosses the pond starts at Penn's Landing. Bernard knows that as well."

"What pond?" Zach questions.

"The ocean. In our time, we refer to the ocean as the pond. Now, you have a sampling of what I experienced," Benjamin says with a chuckle.

"Okay. We possibly know the *where*," Jeremy declares. "Now, the question is *how* do we stop them from stealing the letters?"

"I have an idea," Benjamin contemplates. "If I were to use a little of my prominent influence, I could impress upon the right people of Bernard's plans. Then, let Bernard prove me right. Jack should be nearby. Somehow, I will chase him back here too."

"You cannot let Bernard steal the letter," Zane expresses.

"Don't worry, that will not happen. In fact, if I do encounter Bernard, I can assure you, he will not yet have the letter. Remember, when Bernard or Jack returns, you need to be prepared. There is no telling what either will do if they find the four of you here."

"We will set a trap for them," Jeremy contemplates. "Once we have both of them captured, we can leave them with the other Jack. And we can travel on to the next letter. Benjamin, you send them here and we will take care of the rest. We will be ready."

Benjamin turns and starts toward Myrtle. He grabs her bridle and leads her underneath a nearby tree. "Jeremy," he says, "I will need to bring Myrtle along. Can we bring her inside EMITT? Otherwise it will be a long walk to town."

"Of course, Benjamin. But the buggy must stay."

"Dad," Zane butts in, "we can take Myrtle and the buggy. We can bring Myrtle inside and push the tail end of the buggy up onto the porch. If the buggy touches EMITT when we travel, it will travel with us. We saw it occur with Benjamin's Leyden jar and Bernard."

"That would be fantastic," Benjamin replies.

"Benjamin, turn Myrtle around and back her up to EMITT," Jeremy says.

"C'mon, Myrtle," Benjamin says while leading her around. "Once lined up, the four of you will need to lift the back end of the buggy onto the porch," Benjamin instructs. He pushes her backwards while talking to her. "Back, Myrtle, back."

The wheels touch the porch. With Jeremy and Sarah on one side, and Zach and Zane on the other, they lift the back end. "It's on," Jeremy hollers.

Benjamin and the boys detach Myrtle from the buggy. She neighs and bobs her head a couple of times while she whips here tail to knock off a few nagging flies. Once Myrtle is detached, Sarah opens EMITT's forward door and Benjamin leads Myrtle inside.

Jeremy shouts, "Everyone inside?"

Jeremy follows behind and closes the door.

"Zach, dial up our date," Dad orders. "And put us there at 7:00 a.m. Benjamin will need the daylight for his ride back to town."

"I will be happy to," Zach replies excitedly. "July 29, 1750, here we come. Everybody ready?"

"Zach," Benjamin says with a change of plans, "take us to July 30th. I don't believe Bernard will find a job the first day back, being they have a full day's walk to town. It will be a minimum of at least a day before he could possibly find work. I remember, the ship leaves on a Saturday. I did not take the letter until the evening before the ship departed. That means they cannot steal it before then. Zach, what day of the week is the 29th?"

Zach opens a calendar on the computer and searches for the date. "It's a Wednesday."

"That gives them Thursday and Friday to find work at the docks and only Friday night or Saturday morning to steal the letter. I believe July 30th will be a perfect day for me to arrive."

Zach changes the date as indicated. "Everybody ready?"

A clutter of voices affirms they are.

"Here we go." Zach presses enter. "We have arrived."

Jeremy opens the door and their scene appears to be the same except for one detail. The EMITT Bernard and Jack stole from their home lies about fifty yards away, in line with theirs, except it has been turned around—evidence that Jack pulled EMITT into his barn.

Benjamin and the boys lead Myrtle outside and hitch her up to the buggy.

With Benjamin in his seat, Sarah asks, "Benjamin, before you go, let's go over the plan..."

"No more need for talking, Sarah. It is time for action. I know exactly what to do. Getting them here is the easy part. The four of you and EMITT must be prepared. I will not confront them until tomorrow. So, I would expect Bernard will not be here until sometime tomorrow afternoon. After I have assured myself that Jack is on his way back, I too will return."

"Benjamin, we will be ready," Sarah agrees.

"I will see you soon." Benjamin gives a couple of quick clicks and snaps the reins. "Let's go, Myrtle."

Before dusk, Benjamin arrives in Philadelphia. He is hungry, thirsty, and tired from the long ride. He realizes he will not be able to see his family or sleep in his own bed, as he might encounter himself creating an awkward and unexplainable scene. He turns Myrtle down the dusty dirt road toward the docks.

Benjamin arrives at The Danish Inn, known as an upscale facility that provides luxurious accommodations for the wealthier seagoing travelers. Benjamin enters the inn and saunters across the meticulously crafted rich, dark cherry wood floor. Every step emits a soft drum tone, different from the loud, sharp sounds of the typical wood plank floors. Benjamin approaches the walnut desk and admires the detailed carving of a Danish tall ship on its face. He greets the innkeeper. "Good evening, sir. I need a room for the night."

"Yes, sir," the clerk replies in his Danish accent. He knows of Benjamin because of his status in town, but is confused why he needs a room for the evening when it is only a few blocks from his home. He does not ask any questions. The innkeeper retrieves a key from one of the room slots on the dark walnut wall behind him. He lays the key on the desk. "The night's stay will be twelve shillings, Mr. Franklin."

Benjamin lays the coins on the desk and takes the key. He asks, "I am quite hungry after traveling the entire day. Is there a possibility to eat a meal before I retire?"

"I am sorry, sir, but our cook has left for the evening. Though, if you wish to sit in the parlor, I could put something together for you."

"That would be most kind of you. Whatever you have would be appreciated."

After finishing his meal, Benjamin retires to his room.

FORTY-SIX

FRIDAY, JULY 31, 1750

AFTER A STOP at a local bakery near the docks, Benjamin enters the dock office at Penn's Landing. A thin, scraggly man wearing a long-sleeve, white V-neck shirt sits behind one of the two desks. "Good morning, sir." Benjamin greets the man.

"Hello," the man says, excited and awestruck by Benjamin's status. "How may I help you?"

"My name is Benjamin Franklin. Are you the shipping manager?"

"No, sir, Mr. Franklin, I am not. That would be Michael. May I be of some assistance?"

"No, sir, I must speak with him privately. It is of great importance. Is he in?"

"He is, but..."

"Hello," a large man says as he steps from his back office wearing his traditional white shirt and red vest with his trademark cigar standing from the bite of his teeth.

"Michael, he wants to speak with you in private."

"I heard, John. Mr. Franklin, what do I owe the pleasure?"

"If we could speak in private?" Benjamin asks. "I have a matter of great importance and I need a few minutes to explain."

"This way, please. My name is Michael. Come in and have a seat." He gestures to a chair in his office and closes the door behind them. "What is on your mind, sir?" He takes a seat.

"This conversation needs to remain confidential."

"You have my word."

"My request may involve others of your staff, but when it does, I would ask for your discretion in the matter."

"That will not be a problem, sir."

"Thank you. As you may know, I have been experimenting with the electric fire and I have made a few discoveries, which have been detailed in a letter to a Mr. Peter Collinson in London."

"Ah, electricity. Yes, I have heard. But how does that concern us?"

"I know on good authority that a man, Bernard Ranter, will try to steal my letter, copy it, then send the copy as his own to Mr. Collinson. I believe that this Bernard fellow may actually work for you or may be sneaking onto your ship in some capacity to search for my letter, but his process is unclear."

"Why do you believe he works for us?"

"I only assume he does, because any letters I send to London have only been sent through your establishment. If the letter is stolen, then it could only be through Penn's Landing and I am the only one to deliver the letter. Working for you would be the most logical method to have free access to the mail aboard your ships."

"I see. We hired a fellow that started this morning. What's odd, his name too is Bernard, although his surname is Shoemaker."

"He could be providing you with an alias. Could we meet with him? I will be able to confirm one way or the other. If it is true, I would suspect he would leave not wanting to be caught."

"If it is true, then I lose a hired hand," Michael responds.

"A thief is what you lose, sir. I don't believe you would tolerate a known thief working for you. How could you trust him?"

"You are correct. I will bring him in. How will you handle this meeting?"

"First, if it is not him, I will say so up front. But if it is, I will confront him with the issue. If I am right, we will know right away. If he declares the letter his, I will challenge him to perform one or more of the electrical experiments, but I do not believe it will come to that. He would not be able to successfully perform any of the experiments. Most likely, he will leave."

"Okay." He stands up and opens the door. "John, can you come in here, please?"

"I will be right there, Michael."

He enters. "Yes, sir."

"John, I need you to find Tom and have Bernard come up here to the office. Tell him I have a couple of ideas that I want to discuss about our next ship and need his input."

"Yes, sir. I will find him right away." He leaves the office.

Benjamin leaves the room to wait for Bernard.

Several minutes later, Bernard arrives in the dock office. "Michael, you wanted to see me—something about some ideas?" Bernard asks.

"Have a seat," Michael says as he stands briefly, then sits back down. "I have a gentleman that would like to ask some questions."

"Sure," he responds.

Benjamin enters the room. "Hello, Bernard. How have you been?"

"What is he doing here?" Bernard questions in a raised, disturbed tone. "What is this about?"

"You two know each other?" Michael asks.

Benjamin looks at Michael. "He is Bernard Ranter, not Shoemaker as he has lied to you."

"I do not know what you are talking about. My middle name is Shoemaker and sometimes I prefer to use it instead of Ranter. Michael, why is Benjamin here? He has hated me for years and is always looking to make my life a living nightmare."

"I thought you said you were from Savannah?" Michael questions.

Benjamin confronts him. "Bernard, I know you are here to steal my letter."

"What letter? What are you talking about? I am not stealing any letter. I am not stealing anything. I am only trying to make an honest living."

"Then, if an honest living is your only interest, you won't be too discouraged to hear that Jeremy and the boys are riding out to EMITT to take her home."

"What?" Bernard shouts. "No, no, no, no, no!" He jumps up, pushes Benjamin into the hallway, knocking him to the floor. He frantically sprints outside.

"Bernard," Michael screams.

Michael helps Benjamin to his feet. They chase after him outside. Out of their view, they hear a loud "Yah," as Bernard has mounted his horse and races away.

"I guess that answers the question," Benjamin declares.

"I guess it does. Thanks, Benjamin, for giving me help I didn't even know I needed. If you ever need anything, please let me know."

"I will. Again, thanks for your help."

"Anytime."

FORTY-SEVEN

FRIDAY, JULY 31, 1750

BENJAMIN LEAVES AND mumbles to himself, "Now to find Jack. He must be in town somewhere, and it's obvious they are working separately." He climbs into his buggy. "Let's go, Myrtle," he says as he snaps the reins.

He guides Myrtle to a steady trot in the direction of his print shop. He sifts several scenarios through his mind, but one stands out the most. *If Bernard has worked the docks, Jack must be working the print shop. That is the only other place that makes sense. But finding him will be difficult, because I do not know what he looks like.* As he nears the shop, he slows Myrtle's pace when he notices a slightly younger version of himself leave the print shop, climb into a buggy, and ride off in the opposite direction with another version of Myrtle.

This gives me an idea. He waits for the younger Benjamin to turn out of sight. He steers Myrtle to the print shop.

He hopes David does not pick up on the subtle differences of his clothes between him and the younger Benjamin that left only moments before.

"David?" he calls out.

"Back so soon? I thought you had left."

"I did. I mean, I am. But I had a question I meant to ask. I had spoken with a gentleman about some work. Has he come by?"

"Oh yes, Jack. I mentioned him to you earlier. He said he is new in town and has started a delivery business. He would deliver packages or run errands for us at no cost for a week. After that, he would charge a minimal fee for his services. I am not sure how it will work, but for free, what could it hurt? But he did not mention you two had talked. I told him I would let you know about it and if he would stop by each day, I would try to help."

"Great. Did he mention where he may be staying?"

"No. But I did see him leaving Bernie's Tavern earlier today."

"Thanks."

Benjamin makes his way to his desk, where he sits to jot down a note for Jack.

"Jeremy and the boys are taking EMITT home. Bernard is leaving with them."

Benjamin

He pours a dab of wax onto the edge of the note. He folds the note in half and seals it closed. He blows on the seal to help it dry, then stands from his desk and stuffs the letter in his breast pocket. "David, I am leaving now." He turns to leave, then stops and walks back to David and whispers in his ear, "Let's not mention this conversation or that I have returned to anyone. Don't even bring it up with me. I have my reasons."

"Uh, okay." A confused expression grows on David's face as Benjamin walks away. "That is an odd request." He shakes his head and returns to what he was doing.

Benjamin enters Bernie's Tavern. He approaches the bar and asks the burly bartender, "There was a gentleman in here earlier named Jack. Is he around?"

He responds in his deep, rugged voice as he tugs on one side of his thick, dark mustache, “Yes, he was here earlier, but I have not seen him for a few hours. He and another fellow, I believe his name was, uh...Bernard. Yeah, I believe that’s right. They have rooms here again tonight. I would expect them back sometime today.”

“Great. I would like to leave a note for Jack. Could you see that he gets it when he arrives?”

“Sure.”

Benjamin hands the note to the bartender. “It is of most importance.”

“Consider it done, Mr. Franklin.”

Atop Betsy, while holding his hat and the reins in one hand and slapping at her hindquarters with the remaining length of the reins in the other, Bernard pushes Betsy as fast as she will run, slowing her for short periods, hoping she won’t collapse on him. He mumbles to himself, “I must reach EMITT before they do or I will be stuck here and my name will be mud…no place in history…no 2019. Yah, come on, Betsy.”

Several hours later, he arrives at the top of the ridge. He finds two EMITTs, although they sit apart from each other with not a person in sight. “Where are they?” he questions.

He can see the porch the nearest EMITT and the back side of the other. He again murmurs, “I have to move closer. If I approach from the side, it will be easier to see the front of both.”

He dismounts Betsy. “Shoo, go on.” His hands gesture at the horse. She quickly turns and trots off, then slows a short distance away and ambles about the pasture.

Slow and quiet, he makes his way near the two EMITTs. He crouches down to observe the area. A light breeze rustles the leaves in a nearby tree, while the tall grass sways. He believes he hears voices in the far EMITT, but the distance is too great to be sure. He stays low several yards away, observing for any activity. The door to the front room of the farthest EMITT stands wide open. Both doors at the EMITT nearest him are closed. He makes his move and sneaks up to the nearest EMITT, but remains low in the grass.

He creeps up to EMITT's door, opens it, and slips inside. After a quick check to ensure he is alone, he sits at the computer. "Let's get out of here," he utters, then enters a date, a time, and the password. He presses enter. The woman's soft voice speaks an unfamiliar phrase. "Password invalid. Please re-enter the password."

"What happened?" He re-enters the password.

Again, he hears the same unfamiliar phrase. "Password invalid. Please re-enter the password."

He frantically tries a third time. Still the same result.

He grunts, but not loud enough for anyone to hear him. "Someone changed the passwords." He paces around the trailer. Then, in the other room he notices something on the floor—a gun. "I don't know how this got here, but this is exactly what I need." He flips open the cylinder. "Perfect—fully loaded." He closes it. "Someone will give me the passwords or someone may die."

He barges out toward the other EMITT with a vengeance. As he approaches, he hears voices inside. He bursts up to the open door, gun drawn.

"Well, well. What do we have here?" Jeremy, Zach, and Zane are sitting in the chairs. "You changed the passwords, did you? That will not work for me. Tell me the new passwords now or I kill one of your boys. You have ten seconds. One, two, three..."

"Four, five...." Sarah counts with him as she appears from the side of EMITT with a stun gun pointed in his direction.

He quickly turns, pointing the gun at her, and notices an unfamiliar and strange-looking gun. "Drop it or I will kill one of your boys," he demands.

"No, you won't," she says in a calm tone, then pulls the trigger.

Bernard flails in convulsions. He pulls the trigger of his gun, but no shots fire. He screams in pain as fifty thousand volts electrify his body. He collapses to his knees, then falls to the ground, shaking violently.

"Tape him up, Zach." With the tape in his hand, he binds Bernard's hands behind his back. She turns on the safety switch to stop the flow of electricity.

"Bernard," Sarah says, "if you stay still I will not hit you with another jolt of electricity, but if you try to resist, it's going to hurt again."

"Okay, okay," he cries out while writhing in pain. "Don't hit me."

Zach continues to bind his legs together. Then he secures his hands to his legs, somewhat like the hog tie his mother showed him with Jack.

"That's not exactly how I showed you, but it will suffice."

"Yeah, but it's a little more humane. I didn't want it around his neck."

"Well then, good job," Mom says, while Jeremy and Zane stand watching in awe of their actions. "Now, we wait for Jack. He will be here soon."

"Wow, you weren't kidding," Zane bellows. "Mom *is* a badass. She taught you well. With your newfound skill, maybe you have a future in the Mafia."

"Yeah, I don't think so."

Sarah kneels down to look him in the eye, "Bernard, you actually thought you could get away with this? Change history by stealing Benjamin's letters and his electrical notoriety, so you could be famous. Then, you and Jack could travel through time to steal a lottery jackpot. I assume you planned on living your life in our era. But that cannot happen. You do not belong there."

Bernard lies quietly, not responding to her comments.

"I have to admit, the idea to steal Benjamin's letters was clever, although the idea must have been Jack's. I'm not so sure you're smart enough to pull off this type of a scam."

"I did not steal Benjamin's letters. I have only stolen EMITT."

"Really. Then, why am I here, Bernard? Did you not notice there were two EMITTs? Let me explain. You have already stolen each of the five letters and changed history. You are now known as the Father of Electricity. Fortunately for us, after you completed your little scheme with the letters, Jack stole EMITT from you after winning the lottery, then he left you in 1752. But we were lucky and had the opportunity to steal EMITT away from Jack. And now that we have EMITT, our plan is to return to each of the five dates and destroy your plan. That's why you see the second EMITT, because we have returned to the date of the fifth letter. And since you just admitted to only stealing EMITT, I can safely say we have foiled your plan.

"See, this is only the first letter we have stopped you from stealing. That's why you are confused, because you believe you have not yet traveled to the dates of the other letters, but you have. I know it's confusing, but don't worry—you will have plenty of time to discuss it with the other Bernards and Jacks. See, at each of the letter dates we will capture you and Jack before you steal the letters. And once we have completed our task, your history of stealing the letters will vanish and Benjamin's history will be restored."

Mom stands and turns toward Zach and says, "Zach, cover his mouth. I don't want him to make a lot of noise when Jack arrives."

Zach tears off a piece of tape and covers Bernard's mouth. "That should keep you quiet for a while."

"Zane, grab the gun," Dad says. "Your mother and Zach have Bernard secured. You and I need to place it in the other EMITT before Jack arrives."

FORTY-EIGHT

FRIDAY, JULY 31, 1750

THE INTERMITTENT RAYS of the sun gleam between the patches of clouds that hang near the horizon. Jack knows his destination lies a short distance away. Though he is the only one who can hear his voice, he speaks. "I recognize the lean of that odd tree from when we left. EMITT should appear beyond that tree line." He rides on and soon spots a saddled horse grazing in the pasture. "There's Betsy."

Short of the ridge, he pulls back on the reins. "Whoa." He dismounts and yields a cautious approach to the ridge. "Two EMITTs? How is that possible?" he quietly questions. Puzzled, he contemplates the possibilities but does not understand. He realizes he has a goal—get back to 2019. "I can only assume the boys and Jeremy have returned as Benjamin said in his note. But why would they not have already taken both EMITTs home? And where is Bernard? Why would he not have already left with EMITT?"

He ponders for a moment to dissect the situation. "They must have set a trap for Bernard and have him captured. That's why Benjamin left the letter for me. They plan to catch me as well. Not today, boys, not today."

Jack waits for darkness to own the night's sky. A light turns on inside the furthest of the two EMITTs. "There they are. But somebody could be waiting in the first one as well," he whispers to himself. He approaches the EMITT nearest him. He pushes his ear to the side wall to listen. If movement or voices occur inside, he will detect them. Several minutes pass and he has heard nothing. He takes a chance and slips inside.

He reaches for his cell phone and turns on the flashlight to check his surroundings. "Good, nobody here. They must be waiting for me in the other EMITT." He notices the shelf is void of the tools that were there before. He glances toward the computer when he notices a gun near the computer's mouse. "This is my gun. How in the world did they get my gun?" He reaches to the small of his back and removes the same gun. With two guns in hand he returns his to the small of his back and flips open the chamber of the gun they left near the mouse. "It's loaded!" He flips it back closed.

He cannot believe they would leave a fully loaded gun out in plain sight. Suspicious, he reopens the cylinder and inspects the bullets closer. "These casings have been fired." He removes a bullet from the chamber and finds only an empty shell casing. He says with a devious smile, "Think you're clever, don't you? No doubt, they have a trap set for me, but I'll show them who's smart."

He slips outside, crouches down, and slithers his way toward the other EMITT. Beyond EMITT, he notices a slight movement in the darkness. "Ah, there's the trap. She must be the mother. What is she up to?" He watches for a few minutes. "I guess I'm not supposed to know about her. When I surprise those inside EMITT, she will surprise me. Got it. I will take her as a hostage, but it will have to be fast, because she thinks my gun is not loaded."

Jack slips further out and around toward the front of EMITT. The breeze has picked up as night has fallen, rustling the grass and the leaves in the tree, providing enough cover for him to sneak up from behind.

He surprises Sarah with a vicious attack, tackling her to the ground. She loses control of the stun gun she planned to subdue him with.

With her arms flailing, Sarah screams. "Let go of me! Jeremy, help!"

Jack wraps his arm around her neck and with a squeeze, his chokehold has her secured. With the other hand, he points his gun to her head. "Surprise! You can't outsmart ole Jack." Jack discovers the stun gun lying near him, but just out of his reach. "Now, I know you think I have a gun that's not loaded, but you had better think again. My gun is loaded." He fires a shot into the ground and places it back at her head.

Sarah jumps, but the warmth of the gun barrel only solidifies her predicament.

"Don't make me kill you."

"Okay, okay. I won't do anything stupid," she says trembling.

"Good. You are going to lay face down in the grass for a minute while I grab that stun gun. Then, we will stand up and take care of some business."

Jack releases his grip and allows Sarah to roll over in the grass. He gets on his knees and reaches for the stun gun. He secures it under the front of his belt.

Upon hearing Sarah's call for help, Jeremy and the boys rush out.

Jack points his gun at Jeremy.

"Jeremy, he has a loaded gun."

"I figured out your trap," Jack yells at Jeremy. "I assume you have Bernard tied up inside, but you can keep him. I have your little lady and she is my ticket out of here. You will give me the passwords to operate EMITT or I will shoot her."

"Don't hurt her. I'll give you what you want."

"All right, little lady, you are going to stand up. Nice and slow, understand? Try anything and you will wish you hadn't." He grabs her by the hair.

"I will do as you ask. Please don't hurt me."

She rises slowly. Jack's tension on her hair has her head pulled back.

"Jeremy, I know you took the tools out of the other EMITT. There was duct tape in there, so I know you have it. Get it, but be very, very careful. I will not hesitate to kill her."

"I won't try anything. It's right inside the door." Jeremy slowly steps into EMITT, then emerges with the roll of tape. "I'm coming out with my hands in the air. Don't do anything crazy."

"Come on out. Now, tape the boys' hands behind their back. Then, tape them to the front porch post."

Jeremy and the boys comply. Soon both boys have been secured to each post.

"Now, sit down and tape your ankles together."

Jeremy complies with his instructions.

Tears start down Sarah's cheeks. She realizes their plan has taken a detour, placing her and her family in grave danger.

"Wrap the tape around one of your hands and lay face down on the ground," Jack shouts, "and place your hands behind your back."

Jeremy again complies.

"All right, pretty lady. Your turn to finish the job." Jack walks toward Jeremy, pushing Sarah along, while keeping a firm grip of her hair. He stops a few feet from Jeremy. "On your knees. You will crawl the rest of the way. If you try anything, I will shoot you in the back. If I miss, you can bet I will not miss Jeremy and then I will go after one of the boys."

"I will do as you say," she says, sniffling.

Jack holds her hair tight as she kneels, then releases her and stands a few feet away. She crawls her way to Jeremy. She tapes Jeremy's hands together behind his back.

"Excellent. Now, wrap the tape around one of your hands and lay face down with your hands behind your back."

She complies.

Jack kneels over her, placing one knee on her back, and lies the gun on the ground near her leg, freeing both hands to finish securing both of her hands together.

Jack grabs the gun and stands up. "Good job, everybody," he says sarcastically. "Nobody dead. That's good. Now, I want the passwords for EMITT."

Jeremy rolls over to look at Jack. "The password is 'July-Twenty-Fourth,' which is Sarah's birthday. The first letter of each word is capitalized. There is a hyphen between each word, and 'Twenty-Fourth' is spelled out."

"For your sake, you better hope that's correct. But first I need to destroy this EMITT. Can't have y'all come chasing after me."

"Jack, no, you can't do that," Jeremy shouts with confidence and conviction. "If you do, you too will be stuck here in the past. Time travel is complicated. You will destroy the chain of events: Any EMITT that is destroyed means any duplicate EMITTs will also be destroyed. That means you too will be trapped here. It's complicated, but you don't have a choice other than to trust me here. You will be stuck in the past with us if you destroy her."

Jack stares back at Jeremy, not sure if he is lying to save themselves or if he is telling the truth. He studies his face but is unsure. He looks at Sarah. She nods in agreement with Jeremy. He turns to the boys. They both nod in agreement with fear in their eyes. He decides it's not worth the risk.

Jack marches back to Sarah. He grabs her by the arm to lift her up and starts toward the distant EMITT. "Come on."

"No, no, no. Jack, go by yourself," Sarah pleads. "Nobody will ever find you. You have won."

"Don't flatter yourself. I need you to show me how to operate EMITT. Trust me, you will not be traveling with me."

Jack pushes her toward EMITT. Inside, he sits in front of the computer. "How do you operate it?"

"Shake the mouse to exit screen saver mode."

Jack shakes the mouse and the travel screen appears.

Still scared he might be lying, she tells him how to operate the computer. "If you enter the date and time you wish to travel to, and then press 'Enter,' you will be on your way."

"What's this other field? 'Automatic Return Date'?"

"Jeremy put that in, so if someone did steal EMITT, they would have to enter another password or EMITT would return to 2019 automatically."

"And what's that password?"

"'Time For Benjamin.' You have to enter it before the timer expires. You have thirty minutes."

"What else do I need to know?"

"That's it. If you don't mind, I will step outside and you can be on your way."

"Good deal. Get out."

Sarah hurries outside. Standing a good distance away, she watches the EMITT before her disappear.

"Good riddance—idiot," she says, happy to see him go. She races back to Jeremy and the boys, but passes them by and darts inside EMITT. She searches for something to cut the tape from her hands, but finds nothing. She steps outside and finds the corner edge of the outhouse and rubs the tape against it multiple times. Eventually, it cuts through, freeing her to cut the others loose.

Once Jeremy has verified Sarah is okay, the family has a comforting celebration hug. Sarah says, "Now, we need to send Bernard to July 24, 1600, before Jack arrives. He will be so mad when he figures out you reprogrammed EMITT. He will be furious. Jeremy, what time will he arrive?"

"Four o'clock. That should give us plenty of time to drop off the others before he arrives. I hope we don't have any other issues like that. That plan did not work as expected, but at least it worked."

"Yeah, but a little too close for my comfort," Sarah responds.

"Dad, is that true what you told Jack about destroying EMITT?" Zach asks.

"No. But I had to do something. Otherwise, we would never get home. I am glad y'all helped convince him, or at least create some doubt. At least it worked."

"Wow. That was close," Zane remarks. "We could have been stuck here forever."

"Yes, but we're not," Dad replies.

They climb aboard EMITT. Jeremy sits down at the computer and reviews the previous travel records to determine the exact time Sarah and Zach left the first Jack in 1600. "It looks like you left Jack at 12:07 p.m. We shall arrive at 12:15 p.m." Jeremy sets the parameters and presses enter.

FORTY-NINE

MONDAY, JULY 24, 1600

SARAH LOOKS OUT the window and spots Jack squirming his way toward the knife, but he stops when EMITT reappears. She opens the door and steps onto the porch. "Jack, you haven't found that knife yet?" she says sarcastically. "I thought you would have mastered squirming by now. Anyway, we found a friend of yours and thought you might like some company. You two may have some issues to talk about."

Jack squirms and screams unrecognizable words from his taped mouth.

Zach and Zane emerge carrying a tied-up Bernard, who struggles in their arms.

They lie Bernard down next to Jack and return to the porch with their father.

Sarah kneels before them.

"Now Bernard, you make sure you fill Jack in on our conversation about correcting the letters. Oh, and don't forget to ask him why he stole EMITT from you and left you in 1752, without any money from the lottery winnings."

Jack squirms and hollers. His face turns red with rage, but his struggling does not free him from his bindings.

"I want to fill you both in as to what will occur over the next few hours. Right now, we have only traveled to the date of the fifth letter, where we captured Bernard and Jack. This is the Bernard we captured, but more on Jack in a minute. We were successful in forcing you both to return to EMITT before you could replace Benjamin's letter with your own. Therefore, Benjamin's fifth letter will continue onto Peter Collinson and the history of the letter will be restored. Now, we will travel to the first four letters and again capture you both before you succeed."

And with a cheerful smile, she adds, "Before we go, you should know, there will be several more Bernards and Jacks arriving over the next few hours. But, let me warn you..." She lets out a deep sigh. "...the last Jack will arrive at 4:00 p.m. But be aware, he will be furious.

"See, he thought he was stealing EMITT from us and whisking himself back to 2019, alone. But, he will learn EMITT was reprogrammed to send him here, with all of you, regardless of any date he entered. Here's the best part: EMITT's computers are programmed to self-destruct once he arrives. A set of relays has been programmed to reroute a large amount of high voltage back into EMITT's computers, which will destroy her circuitry. There will be no possible way for EMITT to ever travel again. With him seeing all of you, the realization of our trap will suddenly become very clear to him and he may take his frustrations out on somebody.

"Once everyone has arrived, you may want to take a little time and start working on some of your trust issues, because you're not going back home. Your new home is here, July 24, 1600." Sarah stands and turns toward EMITT. Jack and Bernard start to squirm and holler under the tape across their mouths.

She turns and ushers her family inside EMITT.

"Jeremy, take us back to 1750 right after we've left to bring Bernard here. It will be dark when we arrive. I would imagine Benjamin will not show up until tomorrow and we can get a little sleep. Then tomorrow we can work on the other letters."

"Sleep," Zane exclaims. "That's the best idea I've heard in over four hundred years."

"Not yet," Zach says. "All of this time traveling has given me an idea of how we can capture Bernard and Jack very easily, at each of the other letters, and we can be finished in a few hours. *Then* we can sleep."

FIFTY

SATURDAY, AUGUST 1, 1750

SHORTLY AFTER NOON, Benjamin arrives at the ridge. Out in the distance he observes Jeremy stirring outside of EMITT. "C'mon, Myrtle," he says, snapping the reins.

"Hello," Benjamin hollers as he nears EMITT.

Jeremy hollers toward EMITT. "Benjamin's back."

Sarah, Zach, and Zane emerge.

"Hello, Benjamin," Sarah says.

"Hi, Benjamin," Zach and Zane say in unison.

"I see the other EMITT no longer exists. Can I assume that your plan worked and Bernard and Jack will no longer be a threat?"

"Yes, you can. We had a bit of a terrifying situation, but we achieved the plan's result," Jeremy replies.

"A *bit* terrifying?" Sarah questions, raising an eyebrow. "I would characterize it more like a *lot* terrifying, at least for me. Jack tackled me, held a gun to my head, threatening me with my life."

"Correction," Jeremy says. "The experience was extremely terrifying, especially for Sarah. We captured Bernard exactly as we planned, but Jack was a little more complicated. He was supposed to come to the EMITT we were in, but somehow he spotted Sarah, and that's when the plan turned terrifying. After he had us all tied up, he fell right into our plan. He took the other EMITT, expecting to travel back to 2019, but I made a couple of programming changes and regardless of the date he entered, the computer automatically sent him to July 24, 1600, with the others, but he doesn't arrive until late in the afternoon. That gave us some time to drop off the other Bernards before he arrived."

"Great idea, Jeremy. But what will keep him from traveling off again?"

"I programmed the computers to self-destruct upon their arrival, destroying the computer's internal components. There is no possible way for his EMITT to ever travel again. They will live their lives in the 1600s."

"Great job," Benjamin cries out. "What about Bernard, Jack, and the EMITT at the dates of the other four letters?"

"After we deposited Bernard and Jack yesterday in 1600, Zach came up with a great plan.

"It turned out that only Bernard went to steal the first four letters. We traveled back to each of the dates, but we arrived a couple hours before Bernard. Zach and Zane hiked their way toward town, so they could be well ahead of him. With Bernard on his horse racing toward town, he encountered the boys, and they informed him that I was on my way to steal EMITT. Of course, each time he bolted back to EMITT. When he arrived, I had already loaded the new program into the computer. Sarah took our EMITT a few hours into the future. I hid off in the distance, and when Bernard returned I chased after him. Of course, he hurriedly entered in some dates to travel off with EMITT, only to find out he arrived..."

"On July 24, 1600," Benjamin exclaims.

"You guessed it. And each time, he bought it."

"Brilliant plan!"

"We should have thought of that plan before I ever traveled to town."

"That's what I said," Zane recalls.

"By the way, Benjamin," Sarah says, "great job getting Bernard and Jack to return. It appears your plan worked out as well."

"Yes, it did."

"So, are you ready?" Sarah asks.

"Ready for what?" he asks with a puzzled look.

"To travel to 2019 and verify our plan has worked and that history has been restored. You should be there with us. After all, it is your history and a significant part of your life. If we confirm history has been restored, we will return you back to June 12, 1752. Then, we will return home and we can return to our normal lives."

"Why not? One last TTE for old times," he says, holding one finger up in the air, craving to use the acronym one more time.

They push the buggy onto EMITT's porch, detach Myrtle, and lead her inside. The others follow behind.

"Zach, take us to 2019, my good man," Benjamin commands.

"Yes, sir," Zach says with a smile as he dials up their date.

"Everyone ready?"

Again, they each agree.

Zach presses enter. The lady's voice on the computer speaks. "Password accepted. Time travel sequence initiated." Again, they hear the low vibrating hum and the two familiar pops. Zach glances to the computer screen. "We have arrived. The current date is June 27, 2019."

Mom looks out the window to confirm, "Yep, Jack's barn. We have arrived."

"Zach, open Google and search for 'Bernard Ranter' and 'Father of Electricity.' Let's see what the internet says," Mom says as they crowd around behind Zach.

Zach starts typing on the keyboard when Jeremy cries out, "Wait! Benjamin, I hate to do this, but you really should not see these results. There is no telling what may show up on the screen. You should stand away for now."

"Unfortunately, I agree with you. I would love to see the internet again, but you are right." He backs away to the other side of the room. "All right, Zach, you may continue."

Zach finishes the search phrase "Father of Electricity" and presses enter. "'Michael Faraday,' it says. But it goes further and indicates that William Gilbert is credited as the Father of Electricity, but Michael Faraday is one of the great contributors in the field of electricity."

"That's a good sign," Mom determines.

Zach types Bernard Ranter. "The only thing for Bernard Ranter is an advertisement for ancestry, but I don't see anything in regard to the Bernard Ranter we know."

"Try 'Benjamin Franklin,'" Mom asks.

Zach types 'Benjamin Franklin.' "Well yeah. There's a lot of hits for Benjamin. Scientist, inventor..."

"Stop," Mom interrupts. "Read to yourself. Benjamin cannot hear these results. We still need to preserve history."

"Sorry. You're right. I got a little carried away," Zach says.

"Try a search for 'Benjamin and the kite experiment,'" Zane says.

Zach complies and an image of Benjamin Franklin displays. They turn around and stare at Benjamin with dazzling smiles on their faces.

"From the looks of your faces, I can safely assume good news?"

"Oh yeah," Zach exclaims.

"All right, one last search," Dad determines. "We need to know if Benjamin's five letters are safe and secure in history. Search for '*Experiments and Observations on Electricity*.'"

Zach again complies.

The page loads. "There it is," Zach states. "Benjamin's picture and it says he is the author of the famous papers."

"That's it," Jeremy says as he walks toward Benjamin, extending his hand for a handshake. "Benjamin, you have your name back and your place in history has been restored. You shall remain the man who will forever be known for your groundbreaking experiments in electricity and, most importantly, for flying a kite in a lightning storm to prove lightning is electricity."

"That is very nice to hear. With that, my good people, it is time to take me home." Benjamin beams a huge smile, ecstatic that his name and history have been restored.

"Zach, dial up 1:00 p.m., June 12, 1752. Let's take Benjamin home."

"Dialing it up now," he replies. "Everybody ready?"

Each agrees.

Zach presses enter. The lady's voice once again says, "Password accepted. Time travel sequence initiated." The associated low humming noise and the two pops occur.

FIFTY-ONE

MONDAY, JUNE 12, 1752

"BENJAMIN, WE HAVE arrived," Zach says.

They exit EMITT and again attach Myrtle to the buggy. It's time to say their goodbyes.

"Benjamin, it has been a pleasure…correction…an *honor* to meet you," Sarah says. Her eyes well up and tears trickle down her cheeks. "I have learned so much in the short time I have known you. I will miss you very much. I would so much love to give you something as a memento, but you know that's not possible."

"Sarah, it too has been a pleasure. The hospitality you showed me in your home…your initiative to take control when tough times arose…. I have never met a stronger woman, and I will always remember you."

Benjamin turns to Jeremy. "You, my friend, have been an inspiration to me. Your knowledge of electricity, computers, and beyond…. Your invention of EMITT…what an incredible machine! Through this entire adventure, we have learned a few lessons that we probably never envisioned or even thought about, until now. If you harness the machine right, I can see good. But in the wrong hands, I can see malicious intent and rampant greed. Protect her with everything you have, but if you feel that is not possible, then destroy her for the sake of humanity."

"I will," he says with sadness, because their time has come to an end. "Outside of my family, you have been the single most prominent person I have ever met. You will continue to do great deeds in your life. Please, do not ever underestimate your ability and always believe in yourself. I too will miss you."

Benjamin looks at Zach and Zane. "I was so scared from the events that had occurred when I first met the two of you. I had so many different emotions occurring all at once that I was unsure how to deal with them. I did not know what you planned to do with me. But soon, I began to realize that a strange phenomenon had occurred, which neither of us understood. You two did not know how to react with me being here, as I did not know how to react to you. But, I can say, your accidental time travel has been one of the most exciting, scary, and truly eye-opening adventures I have ever experienced. I do not believe anything I ever do in the future could surpass my experiences with the two of you. Probably the hardest part of this whole adventure is I will not be able to reminisce with anybody about it. So, from the bottom of my heart, I want to thank you for letting me have a glimpse into the future and all the incredible technological advances your society has achieved. Everyone in the future should be grateful for what they have. It is truly remarkable."

"I will miss having you around," Zane says. "I have learned a lot from you during the past couple of weeks. Although I have many experiences to come in my life, I do not know how another could ever top this one. I believe my future will be in computers, electricity, and maybe even something to further the name of Benjamin Franklin." He pauses for a moment. "It will be weird without you around, but you will always be in my heart. But like Dad said, you have a lot of great successes to come, so don't screw it up. The future depends on you." Zane gives Benjamin a huge hug. "We'll miss you."

"Wow, I don't know where to start," Zach says. "I will never forget you. You have been an inspiration to me. The one moment that stands out for me is when my brother and I, together, were fortunate enough to witness you and William conduct the famous kite experiment. That is a moment that I will remember for the rest of my life. I too will do whatever I can to ensure Benjamin Franklin's name is remembered in our society, and not only as a name, but as a person. You have been a truly inspirational figure in history, and I'm so happy I was able to meet you." Zach too gives Benjamin a huge hug. Zane and his parents join in for a group hug.

They break apart. "I guess it's time for us to leave," Dad says when he notices Benjamin has a tear in the corner of his eye. "Me too, big fella."

They step away and onto EMITT's porch. Benjamin steps back as well. They provide their final waves and say goodbye. They step inside EMITT and close the door.

Dad sits down at the computer and enters their date and time. "I would like to take us home. Everyone ready?"

They each nod, as the mood turns somber from the goodbyes to such a prominent historical person.

Dad presses enter and the lady's voice on the computer says her familiar phrase. "Password accepted. Time travel sequence initiated." But the low, vibrating, humming noise with which they have become accustomed is now silent. The two pops do not occur. Opal does not spin as usual.

FIFTY-TWO

MONDAY, JUNE 12, 1752

"WHAT HAPPENED?" **JEREMY** asks with a puzzled look on his face. "I'm not sure we traveled."

Grumblings occur inside EMITT.

"What's going on?" Zach asks.

"Something is wrong," Zane snarls.

"This is not good," Sarah moans.

Zach opens the door and steps onto the porch. "We didn't travel. Benjamin is still here."

"Is there a problem?" Benjamin asks.

"Yeah, EMITT didn't travel. We're not sure what the problem is just yet."

Jeremy, still at the computer, performs a diagnostic test on EMITT. "The diagnostics show all systems are normal," Jeremy says, scratching his head.

Zach returns inside EMITT.

Benjamin follows, standing in the doorway.

Zach says with a nervous look on his face, "I have a suspicion."

"What?" Mom asks.

"When I stowed away on EMITT to steal her back from Jack, being at the tongue of the trailer, I realized the generator is what produced the low, vibrating, humming noise. I'll bet the generator ran out of gas."

"That would keep EMITT from traveling," Dad comments.

They open the outhouse door to access the generator. Jeremy climbs up into the closet and opens the fuel tank. "Yep, that's the problem," he says. "With the numerous travels, I never thought to refill the fuel tank. Not a problem. We can add some gas and be on our way." Jeremy climbs down and looks on the floor around the generator. "Where's the gas can? I had a full gas can in here." He steps back and looks at the two boys. "Did either of you remove the gas can?"

A blank look comes across Zane's face as he reluctantly replies, "Uh...yeah. When Bernard stole Zach's truck, it ran out of gas. There wasn't any gas in the can, though. But we used it to put gas in Zach's tank and I remember leaving it in the back of my truck."

Suddenly, the grim reality of their issue strikes each of them.

"This is not good." Jeremy's voice cracks. "Without fuel, EMITT cannot travel."

Distraught, Sarah asks, "What do we do?"

"I don't know, but we have a problem that needs to be solved," Dad says.

"Oh God, here we go again," Zane says. "Time for another list."

Zane enters EMITT and returns with paper and a pencil. "Well, let's hear the ideas."

"Let's start with our options," Dad declares.

They each spit out ideas.

"We could fly the kite again and capture the lightning like we did the first time," Zach says.

Everybody looks up to the blue sky.

"That's not an option today," Dad replies. "Not to mention, it's extremely dangerous, and it would not work without some work. The structural changes I made to isolate Opal, which allows her to travel via the generator, eliminated that option for traveling."

"There's bio fuel, but we don't have access to the internet to figure out how to make it. So, that won't work," Dad determines.

"Benjamin, I don't suppose kerosene has been invented yet?" Jeremy asks.

"I do not know what kerosene is. But I am positive we do not have any fuels that would be useful for your machine."

"What about EMITT's batteries? Could they produce enough power to send us home?" Zane asks.

"I could run some voltage calculations, but I believe we will be well short of the required power for EMITT to travel," Dad contemplates.

"We're striking out here," Zach realizes. "It sounds like the only choice is to run the battery calculations."

"I agree. It might take a while, because I'll need to do it on paper. I'm going to shut down EMITT to conserve her power," Jeremy says while returning inside.

After a little more than an hour, Jeremy emerges, but the look on his face tells the story.

"That's not the look we wanted to see," Sarah states.

"It's not good. We may be here for a while. The batteries are at about ninety percent of their charge. And no matter which way I run the calculations, we need the batteries to be at one hundred percent power, and even then we would cut it close. If the batteries were fully charged, we would have a chance. But we have no way to charge the batteries. We either need to charge the batteries to one hundred percent or we need an external source of power to make up the additional ten percent."

"Is there anything inside EMITT that draws power unnecessarily that could possibly free up part of the ten percent?" Zane asks.

"The only components that draw power are EMITT's computer, its associated electrical equipment, Opal, and the room's light. The light we can turn off, but the others are required for her to travel."

"Jeremy," Benjamin asks, "can you explain a little of how EMITT works? Maybe if I understood her operation, I could be of some help."

"I can explain, but you cannot use any of this information. It will be many years after your death before most of what you have seen electrically will be discovered. Can you keep this information out of your electrical experiments and not discuss them with anyone?"

"Jeremy, you have my word—it will not be used or discussed. Sending you and your family home is the most important task at hand."

"I agree. EMITT and Opal are complicated machines that work together. EMITT is the computer that delivers the commands and regulates the voltage and current to Opal. Opal creates the wormhole for EMITT to travel through time. Opal requires ten thousand volts to operate, but it must be a constant for the duration of the travel," Jeremy explains.

"Oh, I know, the stun gun produces fifty thousand volts," Sarah blurts out. "That should help."

"That would be helpful, but unfortunately, Jack has the stun gun," Jeremy replies.

"Oh yeah. How could I forget?"

He continues to explain EMITT's operation. "The generator itself cannot generate ten thousand volts, although I solved that problem with a phenomenon called "fly-back voltage," which are very high voltage spikes produced the moment a relay releases and stops the flow of electricity. The voltage spike is back-fed into the capacitors for storage, then released to Opal in a continuous, steady flow of electricity at the precise voltage. But the capacitors cannot produce the required voltage unless there is a continuous flow of high-voltage spikes. That means, many spikes need to occur in succession. I programmed EMITT to control the timing activation of the relays, each releasing in a precise timing pattern to keep the capacitors properly charged. Without it, or with a misstep in the relay timing, the time travel event could be in peril—meaning the wormhole would collapse during our travel. I think everyone understands what that would mean.

"This is our problem: Because EMITT is short the ten percent in battery power, there is a good chance some of the spikes will be too low. Therefore, the capacitors cannot provide the steady flow of voltage."

"I understood most of that, but I have one question. What is a wormhole?" Benjamin asks.

"The simple answer: It is a hole in space that allows an object to travel great distances of time in less than a millisecond," Jeremy explains.

"Too complicated for me. But I have another question. Since I do not know how you measure the electricity, do you have any idea how much electricity the Leyden jar generates when it throws out the electric fire?"

"Benjamin, you may be on to something," Jeremy says, raising an eyebrow. "The spark from static electricity is usually low, but in certain situations it can be extremely high. A few rubs to Benjamin's Leyden jar will not generate enough for what we need. But several rubs to a much larger jar could produce more electricity that could generate upwards of twenty or even fifty thousand volts. But we would still need to generate multiple voltage spikes in short duration for it to be helpful. The Leyden jar would only provide one large voltage spike."

"Then, that brings me to another idea," Benjamin says, recalling a previous experiment from his letters. "I built an electric wheel. Two Leyden jars were placed on opposite sides of the wheel. One provided a positive charge while the other provided a negative charge. The wheel consisted of glass rods with thimbles attached to the ends."

"Benjamin, that's it! I remember your electric wheel. That could work." He dashes inside EMITT to perform more calculations. He returns a while later.

"The math indicates it will work, but it will need to be bigger, much bigger. Here is a list of supplies we will need. Zach will go to town with you and help bring back the items we need. Any tools you have would be helpful, including a saw or two. You may even need an additional wagon."

"Jeremy, don't worry. We will find the supplies."

"I don't know how I can repay you for these supplies, but I will find a way."

"Jeremy, whatever you need. Money is not the issue," Benjamin declares. He studies the list. "That is a lot of material. I only hope the amount of glass you have requested is available."

"Whatever glass you can find, bring it. There is always a possibility some could break on the ride back out."

Benjamin and Zach climb aboard the buggy. "We should be back sometime tomorrow evening," Benjamin says as he turns the buggy around. He snaps the reins and ushers instructions to his horse. "Click, click! Let's go Myrtle."

FIFTY-THREE

MONDAY, JUNE 12, 1752

"ZANE," **DAD SAYS**, "we have a lot of work to do before they return. We need to perform some rewiring to redistribute some power for this to work. I don't know how that roll of wire ended up inside EMITT, but I'm sure glad it did. And, I will need to write some new programming for the infusion of voltage from the wheel."

After an hour of rewiring, it occurs to Jeremy he did not put a metal rod on the list for Benjamin, which will be needed for the center axis of the wheel. With Zach and Benjamin too far gone, they must make do with what they have. "Sarah," he asks, "I need a strong metal rod. Could you see if you could locate anything that may be useful?"

"Of course, but I don't know where I can find any metal out here."

"Look inside EMITT to see if there's anything we can use. The ceiling, the floor, the walls, the doors...anything."

"I'll see what I can find."

A couple hours later: "Zane, that completes the rewiring," Dad says as he wipes the sweat from his brow. Why don't you help your mother with the metal rod? I need to work on the programming."

"Yes, sir."

Zane hears his mother in the front room. He steps in to see her progress. "Mom, what in the world are you doing?"

She has one of the chairs flipped upside down and the bottom torn wide open.

"Your father said he needed a piece of metal wire and to do whatever it takes to find one. I've had no luck. But while sitting in the chair, it occurred to me. Typically, chairs have a metal wire brace across the bottom. I decided to rip the chair apart to find out, and guess what? They do. This one has a thick metal brace across the bottom, but it won't come out. Can you give me a hand?"

"I would've never thought to look there," he says, observing the installation of the brace. "It looks like a bunch of *S*es put together, end on end. It will take a lot of work to bend it straight for us to be able to use it."

"Let's pull it out first, then we can figure out how to straighten it," Mom replies.

"Let me find the hammer and a screwdriver. That should help." He leaves only to return a several seconds later. With a little muscle, they have the brace out.

"It may work," Zane contemplates. "I know it has a lot of bends in it, but we could build a fire outside and heat the rod, then pound it with the hammer to straighten it out. Let's show it to Dad for his opinion."

"Dad, can you take a minute to look at this?"

He holds a finger up, signaling he needs a second. A moment later he turns around and sees the curvy metal piece. "Unless you can straighten it out, it probably won't work. Because it will be the center piece of the wheel, it must be perfectly straight; otherwise, the wheel will wobble while it spins. If it wobbles, chances are the sparks from the voltage spikes will be missed or not generated at all."

Mom adds, "This is the only metal piece we have, but Zane has a plan to straighten it out."

"Great. I will let you two work on it. I need to work on this programming."

Zane and his mother step outside.

"It will be dark in a few hours," Zane comments. "We will need a lot of firewood to straighten out the metal rod, and we will need some wood for this evening. We had better work on building us a nice stockpile of wood first."

"I agree," Mom says. After a few hours, they have piled up enough firewood for their work and still have plenty to last through the night. They clear out an area and start their fire.

"Mom, I believe we will need daylight to straighten the rod, and with darkness falling, we should wait until the morning before I try my hand at blacksmithing."

"I agree. And since it will be near the end of the day before Benjamin and Zach return, we should have plenty of time to work on it."

They both sit on the ground in front of the fire.

Daylight succumbs to darkness, where a dull orange half-moon levitates low on the horizon. The stars shine bright in the Philadelphia night sky. Mom and Zane gaze at their fire. The fire heats up the tiny pockets of oxygen trapped inside the wood, each exploding to the crackling noises of the fire. The background of the night's cooling air has erupted into the familiar sound of crickets.

"I know we're stuck here in 1752, but this feels peaceful," Mom says. "Our world is constantly busy and sometimes so complicated that our lives interrupt us and we miss the opportunity to spend quality time together."

"It is nice," Zane agrees, "but definitely different from home. It would be pretty cool if we had some marshmallows right about now."

"Yes, it would."

"I wish we could do this more often, you know, as a family. It would be nice if Zach were here too. Maybe Dad can join us soon. I know he has to finish the programming, but it would be nice if he were out here with us," Zane says, as he glances at EMITT's open door, where a faint glow of light can be seen from his father's cell phone flashlight.

"It would," Mom says, staring at the fire.

An hour passes.

"Enjoying the fire?" Jeremy says as he steps onto EMITTs porch.

"Did you finish?" Sarah asks.

"Yeah. I had to turn EMITT's computer on to do the programming, and that burned up another four percent of power that we will need to make up. Once we build the wheel, I can determine how much voltage we will harvest from the wheel and add that to the programming, but that is minimal work. Other than that, she's ready."

"Great! Have a seat." She pats the ground next to her. "We were talking about how little time we actually spend together as a family, while we watched the fire. When this is over, we need to plan a vacation and do some camping with the boys. We need some family time together."

"I like that idea," Dad says and sits next to Sarah.

"Zane will try his hand at blacksmithing in the morning."

"Blacksmithing?"

"Zane believes he can heat the metal up in the fire, then beat it into shape with a hammer to straighten it for the wheel."

Zane smiles, as his father nods his head with approval. "That's a great idea."

The three of them reminisce for a while longer while enjoying the fire.

"We should catch some shuteye," Dad says. "It is going to be a long day tomorrow."

"I'm not tired," Zane says. "I might stay up for a while longer. I've enjoyed sitting around the fire."

"All right," Dad says.

Mom and Dad retire inside EMITT for the night.

Zane watches for a couple more hours before he doses off near the fire.

FIFTY-FOUR

TUESDAY, JUNE 13, 1752

THE MORNING'S SUBMERGED sun rises toward a fast-sinking horizon. The day awakens to share a scattering of cirrus clouds, resting high in the deep blue sky, glowing brilliant orange, yellow, and white from the strokes of Mother Nature's windswept paintbrush. Another sunny day will grace the fields with the growing day's heat. Zane's fire has been reduced to a flameless, smoldering pile of coals; a light gray haze of smoke rises from its clumps of ashes. Zane awakes to birds chirping nearby when the door opens behind him.

"You still out here?" Dad asks, stretching his arms to grasp the top of EMITT's porch to help him bow outwards for a good morning stretch.

"Yeah. I guess I fell asleep," Zane says, standing up to stretch.

Jeremy sits on the porch's edge, where Zane joins him.

"I wonder what time Zach and Benjamin will get back?" Zane asks.

"I would not expect them before midafternoon. They have a long ride. I assume they will go into town this morning in search of our supplies. As you remember, the ride lasted about eight hours. And with all the supplies and the glass, they will need to be cautious, which means it could be later in the afternoon."

"That should give me plenty of time to work on straightening the rod."

"I agree. You should have it ready before they arrive."

"How long will it take to build the wheel?"

"I don't know. Things tend to move a little slower in this era, because we don't have any power tools. Maybe a full day?"

Zane adds a few logs and dry grass to stoke the fire, and with a little poking, prodding, and fanning, he has flames surrounding the new logs.

Mom opens the door. "Good morning."

Zane and Dad both reply the same.

Zane steps inside EMITT and finds the hammer and a pair of pliers. Back outside, he shoves one end of the metal rod in the hot coals, checking it occasionally to determine its readiness for a beating. Soon, he pulls the glowing orange rod from the fire. He lays it on the tongue of the trailer and starts to hammer it straight. Soon he has part of it resembling a straight piece of a metal rod.

"Not bad," Dad comments on his handiwork.

"Thanks."

"Zane, put these on." Dad hands him a pair of gloves he had inside the generator closet.

"Thanks. I didn't know we had these."

"While you work on the rod, your mother and I will clear an area for us to build the wheel."

After a while, Jeremy and Sarah have an area cleared. Dad checks on Zane's progress. "How's the rod coming?"

"I have it straightened, but it's not perfect."

"Not bad. It can use some fine-tuning, but not bad."

Zane and Dad continue to work together to refine the rod. Soon they have it about as straight as possible. "Now, if we can make one end into a point to allow it to spin on the contraption, then it will be perfect."

Finished, Zane marvels over his handiwork. He holds the rod up and out using his eye to confirm how straight he has it. "Not bad, if I say so myself," he says while rolling it between his fingers.

"I agree," Dad says.

Looks pretty good to me too," Mom comments.

They let the remaining end cool.

They spend some time gathering more firewood. A possibility of another night's stay exists and they need to be prepared. By early afternoon they have enough wood collected to last through the night.

Near two o'clock, the sun bears down on them from high in the sky. They hear a familiar voice shout in the distance. They each stand up to discover Zach, Benjamin, and a third man arriving in two separate wagons.

"Hey!" Sarah waves vigorously, excited they have made it back. "Jeremy, who is the other man?" she asks.

"That looks like William, Benjamin's son. I'm glad he came along. We could use the extra help."

As they approach, Jeremy says, "You're back sooner than I expected. That's fantastic. It will give us a little more daylight to work on the wheel. And, I see you brought reinforcements."

"I did. I thought an extra hand would be beneficial," Benjamin replies as they climb down from the wagons.

"Hello, William. It's good to see you again," Jeremy says, reaching his hand out to shake William's. "This is my wife, Sarah."

"Very nice to meet you, ma'am."

"It's nice to meet you as well."

"I brought some meat, bread, and water," Benjamin says. "I figured everyone may be hungry. There should be enough to suffice for today."

"Benjamin, you are a lifesaver," Sarah says. "If my stomach has been growling, I'm sure Jeremy and Zane's have been as well."

Benjamin hands a loaf of bread to each and says, "There is water in the pail if you wish."

"How were you able to arrive so soon?" Jeremy asks while tearing off a piece of bread. "There was a lot of material on that list."

"I have learned when a challenge arises, you meet it head-on. I called upon a few friends who owed me a favor. I explained I had a situation that needed their attention right away. They each obliged and worked late through the night to ensure we had what we needed. The glass strips were the biggest of concerns, but fortunately we have two glassmakers in town. Between the two of them, they pulled together the glass we needed as well as the two large glass jars, which I filled with water. Stocking favors can help when you need it most. We were ready to go late last night, but figured it best to have a good night's sleep and leave early this morning. We even brought several tools and a few saws."

"Benjamin, thank you very much for all of your help," Jeremy effuses. "You are an inspiration, and again I thank you."

"Thank you for the kind words, but this is my pleasure."

"I created a sketch of the wheel when I originally built it. I brought it along as it may help us build the contraption," Benjamin says as he hands the sketch to Jeremy.

"I took a few pictures of the wheel in his workshop, in case you need a visual," Zach says. "Dad, you would love his workshop—and the contraptions he has set up for his experiments. Super cool."

"I saw it with Zane after Bernard and Jack left us here. He does have a nice setup, but we are burning daylight and we need to get these materials unloaded. Boys, if you could start by laying the materials out over there," he says, pointing to the area he and Sarah cleared earlier. "Benjamin and I will go over the process to build the wheel."

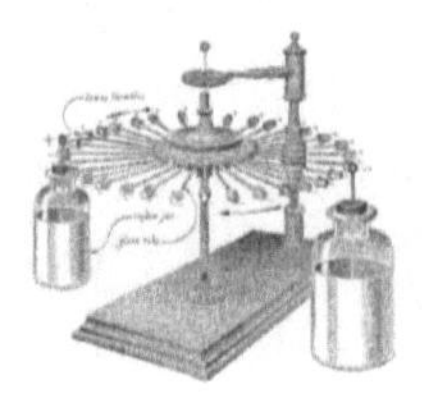

"Benjamin, because the wheel will need to travel with us through the entire trip, we should build the wheel where it protrudes out from the center of EMITT's porch." Jeremy describes the vision of the project with his hands. "When it's complete, it will be large enough to produce the voltage spikes that EMITT will require."

"I agree with the location, and it should not be too difficult to build," Benjamin says.

Sarah listens to the two men as they discuss the wheel's dimensions and the metal rod that Zane straightened.

"I noticed that you had left the rod off the list. So, I brought a wooden rod along, but I was concerned that it would not be strong enough to support the wheel. I believe your metal rod will be more than sufficient," Benjamin remarks.

"There will be an addition to the wheel to make this work," Jeremy says. "We need to harvest the voltage spikes from the nails. We will build a brace to hold the wire, so it will contact the nail and transfer the voltage spike to EMITT. This will occur at both jars."

"I can see this working," Benjamin replies, nodding his head.

They begin to build their wheel.

Benjamin and Jeremy instruct the others of their roles in the project before they begin to build the wood plank base to be connected to EMITT's porch. Sarah wraps the bottom half of the two large glass bottles with aluminum foil. Zach and Zane work on the thirty-nine wood strips. They cut each into one-foot long strips, each being a half inch wide and a quarter inch thick. They will have one extra wood strip and glass plate for testing.

William works on the thirty-nine glass plates, cutting each of the one-inch-wide strips into twelve-inch lengths. As soon as a wood strip and a glass plate has been completed, Sarah glues the glass to the wood. On the end of the glass plate she glues a nail to create a fat, blunt surface to attract a spark from each of the jars' electrodes.

After several hours of work, their electric wheel takes shape. Many of the wood and glass plates have been completed. Jeremy and Benjamin have secured the two glass jars on their separate supports on either side of the wheel. Each of the jar supports can be pushed in and out and both include a stop, so the jar will be in the correct position to receive the spark.

Jeremy and Benjamin install the center wooden wheel onto the metal rod, where the wood strips with the glass plates will attach. The metal rod attaches to supports that extend out from the bottom and the top of EMITT's porch. These supports will allow the metal rod and its attached wheel to spin with little effort. They install a cross bracket on the top bracket that will allow the wires to make contact with the nails as the wheel spins, where they will harvest their voltage.

"Zane," Zach says as he peers out at the horizon, "we may want to revive that fire. The sun is going down and Dad and Benjamin will need light to complete the wheel."

Zane turns to look at the dipping sun and says, "You're right. Let's throw a few logs on it and get it rolling again."

Both boys add several more logs to the smoldering coals. After stirring and adding more dry grass, the fire is roaring again.

"Good idea, boys. We will need the light soon," Jeremy says before turning his attention back to Benjamin. "Let's attach the glass plates to the center piece. Once that is done, I believe the wheel will be ready for testing."

While the men work, darkness has brought about the nightlife. A few lightning bugs glow nearby, something that was missing from the previous night. The crickets stroke their legs to sing their magical tune, and the fire crackles. Zach, Zane, Sarah, and William stand away from the fire and watch Benjamin and Jeremy finish attaching the last of the wood and glass strips.

"That should do it," Jeremy states while stepping back for a better view.

"I agree, Jeremy," echoes Benjamin. "It's time for some testing."

Jeremy steps back to the wheel and gives it a little push. "It spins surprisingly better than I expected, but still a little off balance. We need to add some weight to a couple of areas on the wheel to provide some balance. I need everyone to look around and see if you can find anything with a little weight."

With everyone looking, Jeremy finds a few small rocks, then sets them in specific positions on the wheel and gives it a careful spin. "Still needs a little more on this side," he says as he watches the wheel closely as it rotates around. After a few more adjustments, he believes he has it right.

"Let's glue these in place."

"Here's the glue," Sarah says, handing the can to Jeremy.

Jeremy glues each of the rocks. And gives it another spin. "That looks pretty good," he says while they watch the wheel spin around. "No wobble. Perfect!"

"Now, to test the jars for spark," Jeremy informs Benjamin.

Benjamin prepares the jar. With it secure, he takes his cloth and wraps it around the top section of the jar, above the aluminum foil.

"Stop," Jeremy says. "This will create a much larger spark. You cannot be that close to the jar. We need to make it longer for you and William to be further away. I don't want you two electrocuted."

Sarah says, "I have an idea. The blankets they protected the glass with on their ride here, we can tear them into strips and tie them onto the silk cloth. That will allow them to be at a safer distance. Benjamin can wrap the cloth around the jar and pull each end rapidly to charge it."

"Excellent idea, Sarah," Jeremy exclaims.

With only the light from their fire, they move closer to the fire to see while they work on the cloth. After a little effort, they have the cloth ready.

Benjamin wraps his long piece of cloth around the jar. "Is everybody ready?" he asks.

Everybody acknowledges.

He vigorously pulls the cloth in opposite directions about forty times to charge the jar.

Jeremy holds the extra wood strip and glass plate and slowly brings it near the electrode. At about two inches away, a large spark jumps to the end of the nail—*POW*—knocking Jeremy back a little and disfiguring the nail head.

Everybody gasps in their own way.

"Whoa!"

"Oh, my!"

"Wow!"

"Holy crap!"

And Sarah jumps with a slight scream.

"What a spark," Benjamin gasps.

"A little too much spark," Jeremy shouts.

"Probably near ten thousand volts," Zach claims. "But it looked really cool in the dark."

"Wow," Benjamin exclaims, "that could be dangerous."

"Very dangerous," Jeremy says, in awe of the power. "I would say, more like fifty thousand volts. It could easily kill a person. That's why I wanted you back. Let's try the other jar, to make sure we have no issues, but this time a little less rubbing."

"Wait," Benjamin says, "Zach, would you find the tool in the wagon?"

"Oh yeah. Can't believe I have forgotten again." Zach springs to the wagon and returns with the tool.

"What is that?" Sarah asks.

"A discharge tool," Zach replies. "Once we charge the jar, we need to discharge the lingering charge that remains. If we touch it, we may have a real problem. I know from past experiences."

"Yes, you do," Zane states with a laugh. "It almost killed you."

Zach takes the tool, which is a four-foot metal rod passing through a long wooden handle of about three feet, and touches the top of the electrode and the ground at the same time. A discharge spark occurs, removing any remaining static charges. "This jar is discharged."

Benjamin prepares the other jar. "William, you rub this one. You need to practice too."

William wraps his cloth around the jar, steps back, and asks, "Are you ready?"

"Yes, but this time rub the jar fifteen times and let's see how it responds," Jeremy states.

"Okay." William rubs the jar, stopping after fifteen rubs.

Jeremy brings the nail on the glass plate closer to the electrode of the jar. This time, the nail receives the spark a little closer, but the power lacks the punch Jeremy wants.

"We will need a little more than that. Let's do it again, but this time rub it twenty-five times."

Zach uses the discharge tool to discharge the jar. Another light spark occurs.

William rubs again, stopping after twenty-five strokes.

Jeremy brings the nail to within about an inch and a half of the electrode and the electric fire jumps from the electrode to the nail. This time the spark has power, but not enough to knock Jeremy away. "That will be perfect. It should be sufficient for what we need—probably fifteen to twenty thousand volts."

Zach again discharges the jar.

"All right, it's time to test it through EMITT to see if she receives enough voltage," Jeremy says, rubbing both sides of his face. "The moment of truth is upon us. If this works as planned, the only remaining item will be to program EMITT. The programming will allow EMITT to distribute the voltage as needed. Then, we will be ready to go home."

"Great. Then it is time to test the wheel with the jars," Benjamin states.

"Benjamin, can you and William electrify the jars? Don't start until I'm ready," Jeremy instructs them.

"Yes," both agree at the same time as they go to their respective jar and pick up the cloth. "We are ready, Jeremy," Benjamin declares.

"I want to explain what will happen so everyone understands. After my explanation, if there is any one person that does not want to go through this, then we will stop and rethink our plan."

"The electrode on this jar," Jeremy says, pointing to Benjamin's, "is rising from the center of the jar. When Benjamin rubs his jar, the electrode will become positively charged. The electrode on William's jar is attached to the outside of the jar. When William rubs his jar, the electrode will become negatively charged. We know the saying 'opposites attract'—that also means 'likes repel.' When we push in the charged jars, the positive electrode on Benjamin's jar will attract the closest nail. As the nail approaches the electrode, we will see a spark. The spark passes positive electrons to the nail; therefore, the nail will also become charged positive. Because it is charged positive, the electrode pushes it away, because they are now the same charge, and, as I said, 'like charges repel.' As it is pushed away, the next nail becomes attracted to the positive electrode, because again 'opposites attract.' As this continues, the wheel is placed in motion, and when the first positively charged nail approaches William's electrode, which has a negative charge, what happens?"

"The nail will be attracted to it because 'opposites attract,'" Zane answers.

"Correct, and what else happens?" Dad asks.

"The spark will occur, changing the nail to a negative charge, and because like charges repel, it too will be pushed away," Zane answers.

"Exactly."

"Thus, the wheel will keep spinning," Sarah comments.

"Precisely," Benjamin chimes in. "It will eventually stop, but because there is a large enough charge within the jar it may spin for thirty minutes or more, creating hundreds of sparks. And that should be plenty of voltage for you to make your trip through time."

"You got it," Jeremy says. "And my plan is to harvest this spark, or the voltage spike, and send it to EMITT, which will in turn send it to Opal. If Opal receives the required voltage, we will not have any problems traveling. If she does not receive the necessary voltage, we will not travel."

"Of course, there has to be a 'but.'" Jeremy raises both hands and double clicks the first two fingers on each hand, signaling quotations. "If for some reason the wheel stops producing the voltage after the travel has started, we could be in peril. But only if the batteries cannot complete our journey. I really don't expect that to be a problem, but that's why I want everyone to understand exactly how the wheel will work. Does anybody have any questions?"

Nobody says a word.

"Let's do some testing," Jeremy says. "Benjamin, William, charge your jars."

They both muscle out twenty-five vigorous rubs.

Jeremy pushes William's jar near the nails. Nothing happens. He pushes Benjamin's jar near the nails and the wheel draws forward. The first nail is attracted to Benjamin's jar. A flash occurs with a loud pop from the spark, then the nail repels away. The second nail approaches. Another flash and a loud spark; the wheel continues. When the first nail approaches William's jar, two flashes and two loud pops occur. The wheel picks up speed. Sparks continue with each nail that passes.

Jeremy times each spark, while the others stare with amazement as the wheel spins, close to fifteen rounds a minute. It continues to spin for several minutes before Jeremy pulls Benjamin's jar away from the wheel. After another half spin, the sparks stop and wheel slows before Jeremy can pull William's jar away.

Zach discharges both jars.

"It works as I expected," Jeremy says. "Now to make some last-minute programming changes and we should be ready. Then, we can test and verify that EMITT receives enough voltage. If so, we will be ready to go home."

"One last detail, though," Jeremy says. "I need to connect the wires to the brackets above the nails to harvest the voltage spikes." He adjusts the placement of each wire, so it will contact each nail as they pass by. He gives the wheel a slow spin to verify he has both wires in the correct place. "Benjamin, I must say goodbye once again. Please stay true to your path. It has been a great pleasure meeting you, and an incredible experience. Thank you for your help building this wheel. The opportunity to build it and watch it operate is an eye-opening experience. None of us can possibly forget this. We will miss you, my friend."

"Jeremy, I too will miss you, but we have said enough goodbyes. We need to send you good people home," he says, patting Jeremy on the shoulder.

"William," Jeremy says, "thank you for your help. It means a lot to us. I wish you the best of luck."

"Mr. Long, I hope you arrive home safe. It was a real pleasure meeting each of you. Good luck."

"Sarah," Jeremy continues, "you and the boys say your goodbyes as well. I need to power up EMITT, and once I have completed the programming, we will perform one more test. If it is good, we will leave immediately. The longer we stay the more power we take away from EMITT."

Jeremy enters EMITT to power her up and make the programming changes, while Sarah and the boys again say their goodbyes.

Several minutes later, Jeremy emerges. "The programming is complete. Benjamin, can you and William charge the jars? Let's test this once more and see if EMITT is receiving enough voltage."

"All right, Jeremy. The jars have been charged. When you are ready, we will push the jars in to make contact."

"Push them in."

William and Benjamin push in the jars. Benjamin's side pops first, releasing a large spark. The wheel starts in motion. Another spark, then another. Then, two sparks.

"It's working. I see great voltage readings on the computer." Jeremy continues to monitor EMITT's screen and watches as the voltage spikes hit perfectly. "Over twelve thousand volts each. This is perfect. You can pull them away."

Jeremy steps back outside. "It's time to go home."

Zach discharges the jars one last time.

Another quick handshake and several hugs by everybody.

"We need to go," Jeremy says. He steps inside and programs their destination date: June 27, 2019, 5:00 PM.

Sarah, Zach, and Zane follow behind.

"Benjamin, charge the jars. The TTE is programmed. We are going home."

Benjamin and William charge their jars. “Jeremy, they are ready. On your instruction, we will push the jars into position.”

Sarah, Zach, and Zane provide a final wave goodbye.

“Benjamin, we are ready. Push in the jars. Goodbye.”

Benjamin and William push the jars into place. “Good luck to each of you,” Benjamin hollers. The wheel begins to spin. Suddenly, there is a spark accompanied by a loud pop. Then another and another. Quickly, the first nail reaches the second jar, producing two sparks and two loud pops. The wheel picks up speed. “Good luck, my friends!” Benjamin hollers.

“Good luck!” William shouts.

A quick flash and they vanish into thin air.

Benjamin and William stand there, awestruck at the engineering they have witnessed using one of Benjamin’s experiments. “William, you and I have witnessed the most incredible feat of engineering we will ever see. Cherish it forever.”

“I will, Father. I will.”

FIFTY-FIVE

THURSDAY, JUNE 27, 2019

"IT APPEARS TO have worked," Jeremy exclaims. "The computer indicates June 27, 2019, 5:00 PM."

Zach pushes the window curtains aside. "We're in Jack's barn." He turns to his father with a gigantic smile. "Great job, Dad—you did it!"

"No, we all did it."

They hug each other and exit EMITT happy and proud, but at the same time, a little sad.

"Let's go home," Sarah says, putting her arms around the two boys. Jeremy joins them, wrapping an arm around Zach. Jeremy and Zane push open the barn doors and the four of them leave Jack's barn in stride.

Four weeks later, Mom is preparing a homecooked meal for the family. Dad glances up at the television mounted on the breakfast nook's wall. The screen fades into a closeup of the well-dressed, clean-cut TV news anchor.

"Headlining the news tonight, we have an unusual but heartwarming story that began to develop earlier today and has gone viral with public school systems across the nation. Many have posted on their Twitter or

Facebook accounts that a mysterious donor has pledged to provide $540 million in donations to high school science departments around the country. Over fifty schools have reported they have received a $1 million pledge from the mysterious donor.

"In addition, our own Benjamin Franklin Museum has received a charitable pledge in the amount of $30 million. The anonymous donor requires that $15 million of the pledge shall be provided for upgrades to the museum and the remaining $15 million is to be pledged for electricity scholarships to local Philadelphia schools. The University of Pennsylvania has reported they have received a pledge of $10 million.

"But every recipient has two requirements: The appropriations of funds for each purpose, project, or scholarship shall incorporate the title "Benjamin Franklin's Electric Fire Fund," and all the funds shall be used to further the education of Benjamin Franklin or his electricity experiments. Though the donor is still a mystery, it's clear there is an admiration for Benjamin Franklin and his work with electricity.

"Even though the mysterious donor has yet to reveal their identity, the recipients have said they would love to thank the donor in person. We will keep you up to date once we learn more about this developing story, it's numerous donations, and the criteria to receive donations."

"What a wonderful story, Dan," his attractive co-anchor comments. "There will be some happy science teachers around the country."

"Yes, there will, and a lot of students will benefit from this as well."

Zach glares at his mother. "You're the mysterious donor. That's what took you so long in Jack's house. He won the lottery and you hacked his account and provided the money to the schools. One last little jab to Jack. If only he knew."

"Don't worry, he knows. I made sure of it."

Zane and Jeremy stare at Mom in disbelief, when Jeremy remarks, "I knew I married the best woman in the world."

"You mean the best mom in the world," Zane replies.

"Dad," Zach says, "you know Benjamin never wrote about his kite experiment in his five letters to Peter Collinson. But did you know he only wrote about the experiment once? He wrote one brief statement and had it printed in the *Pennsylvania Gazette*, a little more than four months after the experiment. His statement explained the experiment, but he never said he was the one who flew the kite. And it's not described in his autobiography other than he wrote about his pleasure from the success of a kite experiment conducted in Philadelphia. Then, fifteen years later, he explained the experiment to a friend, Joseph Priestley, who detailed the event, which helped make Benjamin's great achievement notable."

"I knew the experiment had not been included in his five letters, but are you sure it's not in his autobiography?"

"Nope, there is no description of the experiment. It makes me wonder: Did Benjamin limit his writing about the kite experiment…because of us? If you remember, you did ask him not to use anything he had learned from our era and that we did not want to influence him in any way, and if he did he could alter history."

"I hope you're right and our presence did not restrain him from writing about the experiment. Surely, he did not misinterpret what I meant by my statement and avoided credit to one of his greatest achievements. I hope we didn't change history!"

FIFTY-SIX

MONDAY, JUNE 14, 1752

"DEBORAH," BENJAMIN CALLS out. "I will be at my desk reading. Please don't let anyone disturb me for a while."

"Yes, Benjamin. I will see to it."

Benjamin enters their upstairs bedroom and closes the wooden door behind him. He pushes the bolt in to lock it. He approaches his desk, which is situated along the wall, but perpendicular to one of the room's two windows. For a moment, he stares out the window, then sits at the desk. He leans over to raise a loose picket from the floor. He removes a medium-sized object wrapped in a cloth and lays it on the desk. He unwraps the cloth, exposing a book. He reaches down again and retrieves another cloth-wrapped object. He unwraps it, revealing a plastic bottle of Coke. He leans back in his chair and takes a sip. He opens the book, *The Adventures of Huckleberry Finn*, and continues where he last left off. He stops once again to peer out the window and says to himself, "Wow, the future will be an incredible place!"

THE END

AUTHOR'S NOTE

I had always been intrigued with the idea of Benjamin Franklin somehow traveling forward to the future and discovering how electricity has progressed in our modern-day society. Upon my beginnings for the novel's research, I stumbled upon a very informative website, "Project Gutenberg," and found Benjamin Franklin's experiment letters that were sent to Peter Collinson in London, which Collinson later compiled into a pamphlet titled "Experiments and Observations on Electricity, Made at Philadelphia in America," printed as the first edition in 1751.

As an elementary school student many (many, many) years ago, I remember learning about Benjamin Franklin and his famous kite experiment, but never about any of his other experiments, the processes of those experiments, or what led him to fly the kite. After reading the five letters detailed in the first edition, which spanned almost four years, I was amazed by Franklin's thoroughness with his experiments and his documenting of each. This led me down an exciting and fantastic journey to share his experiences in an intriguing and fun time travel adventure.

But, there were complications. In the first edition, letters one, two, and five were clearly dated, but the start of the third letter had a limited date of 1748, but also a date of April 29, 1749, at the end of that letter. And the fourth letter had no date at all. Time travel dates were important to make the story work. I thought to myself, *How will I make this work?* So, I researched it further and my head just about exploded. There were many varying dates that started to come forward. This occurred through different editions.

There are six editions of Franklin's manuscript: editions one, two, and three (editions two and three added additional pages), the fourth and fifth editions, and the Bowdoin manuscript, which is only a copy (never published) of all his letters that Franklin supervised, corrected, and sent to a young James Bowdoin. But Franklin certified that these letters were correct. The separate editions brought into question the dates documented in the letters. Francis Philbrick's research suggested the first two letters were printed in the wrong order and with differing dates.

In the Bowdoin manuscript, Franklin noted dates earlier than those published in the first edition of his letters. I. Bernard Cohen picked up on this, questioning Philbrick's research, and raised questions that there may be letters that existed before those chronicled in the first edition. But no letter has ever been found to support this claim. My head was spinning.

Below is a synopsis of the editions of the manuscript.

Edition	Part	Publish Date	Summary
First	1	1751	Benjamin's original five letters (86 pages)
First	2	1753	Supplemental experiments (added 20 pages)
First	3	1754	New experiments and observations (added 44 pages)
Second	1 and 2	1754	Reprint of parts one and two; similar to the first edition
Third	1, 2, & 3	1760, 1762, & 1764	All three parts continuously paged; similar to the first edition
Fourth	1	1769	Significant differences between editions one, two & three. Franklin supervised and annotated the original parts of the first three editions with many corrections and additions and added a number of scientific letters on other subjects.
Fifth	1	1774	Few variations from the fourth edition
Bowdoin MS Copy			The Bowdoin manuscript was a copy of Franklin's letters. Most importantly, he supervised and corrected this copy, which antedates the first printed edition of *Experiments and Observations on Electricity*. This document also contains additional details not seen in any other printed edition.

Benjamin Franklin wrote many letters discussing his electrical experiments with many different people (Peter Collinson, James Bowdoin, John Mitchel, Cadwallader Colden, and many others), although Peter Collinson is the main character referenced in this book. Franklin's practice was to keep drafts of his letters to Collinson, from which he made other copies for friends in America. Franklin hired transcribers to rewrite several copies of his letters. These letters may have been dated with their current writing dates instead of the actual dates written by Franklin himself. This possibly created the confusion with the dates of his letters. It is possible his earliest electrical letter may have been written on March 28, 1747, discussing his earliest experiments. However, no version of that letter has ever been located.

This research was a rabbit hole I needed to go down and I am glad I did, because I learned a great deal about Benjamin Franklin and his letters. But in the end, I decided that the best course of action for the book was to allow the basis of the book to be founded on the writings of Benjamin Franklin's first Edition of *Experiments and Observations on Electricity, made at Philadelphia in America by Mr. Benjamin Franklin, and communicated in several letters to Mr. Peter Collinson, of London F.R.S.*, as found on the website "Project Gutenberg" and documented as "Printed and sold by E. CAVE, at St. John's Gate. 1751."

The research for this story was fascinating and enlightening. It gave me a glimpse into the past and a sense of the hardships of living in that era. While they washed clothes by hand, we have machines to do the grunt work. They chopped wood for cooking or to heat the home, and all we do is push a button. They killed an animal for food, salted its meat, and preserved it in jars for consumption over the next year or two, while we just go to the grocery store, buy it, and store the foods in the refrigerator, freezer, or pantry. We don't have to hitch the horse to the buggy to make our way to the grocery store. Life was complicated then, and no matter what our everyday difficulties are today, we have a much easier life. The future we live in has created so many luxuries and great technologies that our lives are easy compared to the olden days. I am happy for it. Franklin himself would have been astonished and in shock trying to understand it.

I very much enjoyed the past three years working on this project, but now I am a bit sad it has reached its end. I look forward to the next adventure the future holds.

Glenn Christmas

ACKNOWLEDGEMENTS

To Jo, for taking care of everything that makes our family and home run like clockwork. Thank you so much.

A special thanks to my super fantastic grandkids, Allie Hicks, Dylan Seaman and Jocelyn Williams, who have endured Pawpaw's many stories and facts about Benjamin Franklin during these last three years. And yes, you still have to read the book.

To my beta readers, Jo Christmas, Donna Bradwell, Bob Kaczmarek and Tana Schot for taking time out of your busy schedules to read my story and answering my endless questions about it's logistics. Thank you very much. Your help was invaluable.

To everyone at Airline Graphics, Kathleen Warren, Jason Wallace, Brian Wallace, Alan Wallace, Marcus Wallace and all of the fine people there for printing the first couple of drafts, so I could see the project on paper and move forward with the editing phase of the project.

To Sam Messina for reading a sample and providing encouraging words. And thank you for putting me in touch with Ed Lippman.

To Ed Lippman for reading a sample of the book and steering me in the right direction to develop the story's world.

To all of my family members, "Thank You" for your support and encouragement and listening to the story description on countless occasions: Jo Christmas, Robert and Lola Christmas, Joanna Seaman, Randy Hicks, Donna Bradwell, Merry Christmas-Cox, Stan Cox, Lauren Cox, Sheila and Joel Graham, Stephanie Christmas, Charles Hall, Sam Messina Sr., Sam Messina Jr., Ross Messina and Pam Messina, Stacy and

Joe Summers, Krystal and Andrew Smith, Kathleen and Marc Warren, Jason and Adriana Wallace, Brian and Hannah Wallace, Alan and Tiffany Wallace, Marcus and Valencia Wallace, and all of their extended families.

And to all of my many friends—the list is long, but you know who you are—I thank you for your support and encouragement.

I would like to thank Project Gutenberg for their extensive collection of electronic books, specifically Benjamin Franklin's "*Experiments and Observations on Electricity*" and making them available on their website at no cost. Project Gutenberg was instrumental to the research for this story and without them, this story probably would have never happened.

Thank you to the fine folks at the National Archives and The Library of Congress. They provided many electronic documents that aided in the research of the story.

A special thank you to Christopher Schaffer, Michelle Armstrong, Bob Kingston and the School District of Philadelphia for their help with the Career Technology Education courses and aiding me with local information that was to far away for me to access.

Thank you to Coin Database for providing todays monetary value of the 1750 coins Bernard sold in the story.

Thank you to John Nicks, a commercial airline pilot, with his knowledge of air highways that helped with the explanation in the story.

Thank you to David Aretha for your expertise in editing and help me make the story stand out.

Thank you to Dane Low and the team at Ebook Launch for being patient with me in the cover design phase. You did a fantastic job.

www.ingramcontent.com/pod-product-compliance
Lightning Source LLC
Chambersburg PA
CBHW030549310726
48979CB00010B/2085/J

* 9 7 8 1 7 3 2 4 0 4 5 1 9 *